Disclosures

I Found My Heart in San Francisco
Book Four

Susan X Meagher

Susan X Meagher

DISCLOSURES
I FOUND MY HEART IN SAN FRANCISCO: BOOK FOUR

ISBN 0-977088-54-5

THIS TRADE PAPERBACK ORIGINAL IS PUBLISHED BY BRISK PRESS, NEW YORK, NY 10011

FIRST PRINTING: FEBRUARY 2006

Acknowledgements

Thanks to the following people who helped proof this book. It took a lot of time and effort on everyone's part: Stefanie, Edye, Judy, Karen, Laura, Lori, and Elaine.

As always, to Carrie.

By Susan X Meagher

Novels
Cherry Grove
All That Matters
Arbor Vitae

Serial Novels
I Found My Heart in San Francisco:
Awakenings
Beginnings
Coalescence
Disclosures
Entwined
Fidelity
Getaway

Anthologies
Girl Meets Girl
Tales of Travelrotica for Lesbians: Vol 2
Undercover Tales
Telltale Kisses
The Milk of Human Kindness
Infinite Pleasures

To purchase these books go to
www.briskpress.com

Chapter One

Glittering blue eyes sparkled with mirth as an impossibly long, leather-covered leg gracefully swept over the bulk of an aqua and cream-colored Harley-Davidson. Muscular legs wrestled the silent beast into position as a pair of shorter but similarly muscular thighs slid into place.

The driver turned and caught the gaze of her passenger. Stunningly white teeth were revealed behind luscious, full, rose-tinted lips. "Ready?" the deep alto voice rumbled.

"Let's go," the confident voice of her passenger agreed.

The right leg of the driver sprang into action, giving the lever under her boot a hearty kick, causing the machine to roar to life. Her passenger was, as usual, slightly stunned by the crescendo of sound and sensation that flooded her body as the bike thrummed under her. She spread her fingers apart to gain additional purchase on the waist of the driver, smiling slyly as she reveled in the feel of the supple leather that covered her lover's torso.

This is so trippy, the blonde ruminated. *A year ago I was having my new engagement ring fitted. I was twenty years old, and I thought that I'd already made most of the important decisions in my life.* She laughed softly, shaking her head at her callowness. *I knew who I would marry, I knew where my husband would work and what kind of life we'd lead. I knew we'd have children, join a country club, and participate in the social scene of San Francisco. I'd never been on a motorcycle. I'd never given conscious thought to even kissing a woman. And I'd certainly never even heard of such a thing as a Dyke March!*

The motorcycle turned onto the quiet street and was immediately guided up a steep hill. Jamie tightened her hold, slipping her right arm snugly around her lover and smiling to herself, as she considered the woman she clung to.

When Ryan got home this afternoon and told me that she was going to teach me the secret handshake, I almost lost it! she mused as they rolled through the streets of the Noe Valley. *I mean, she'd been teasing me about that for months, but I certainly never expected her to make good on the offer!*

The trip was a short one, lasting only until they reached Dolores—just six blocks from Ryan's home. As the bike was maneuvered into a semi-legal parking space near Dolores Park, Jamie looked up to witness one of the most amazing sights she'd ever seen.

Women … lots of women … lots and lots of women. Women of every size, shape, color, and age. Women in wheelchairs, with walkers, with guide dogs. Women alone, with partners, with groups of friends. Women with children, women and their dogs, and even a woman with a loquacious parrot balanced upon her shoulder.

All of them were converging on the park, filling the flat expanse of ground that made up most of the land, and even now beginning to dot the rather abrupt hillside that surrounded it.

"Pretty impressive, isn't it?" Ryan commented with a note of pride in her voice as she held the bike steady so that Jamie could hop off.

Removing her helmet, Jamie tossed her short blonde hair from her eyes and shook her head in amazement. She'd been in many large groups in her life, but never … never had she been in the midst of this many women. She guessed that there must be at least five or six thousand women already gathered, and the streets near the park continued to funnel more in, adding to the number.

"I'm stunned," she said, her expression underscoring her words as Ryan set the bike on its kickstand and came to stand next to her.

Ryan chuckled at her astonishment, then locked both helmets onto the bike before taking Jamie's hand and tugging her in the proper direction. "Let's go, my little neophyte. It's time you met the family."

When Ryan posed the idea, Jamie had been reluctant to attend. "Dyke march?" she asked, a slightly sour expression on her face. "Dyke march?" She had a hard time picturing herself in such an assembly. First off, she didn't think of herself as a dyke. Oh, she was most definitely sleeping with … well, sleeping wasn't the activity that she participated in that would cause many to characterize her as a dyke. Nonetheless, though she was having lots of hot girl-on-girl action with the lovely woman who gazed down at her, she didn't think that made her a dyke. Ryan had assured her that she was the same person she'd been before they were intimate, and she believed her completely. She hadn't been a dyke a week ago—so she was surely not one now.

Aside from the label, though, Jamie had never been to a march of any kind, and she wasn't at all sure that she wanted to break that pattern. There was something vaguely sinister about the term "march" that she was uncomfortable with. She had a strong suspicion that this gathering would not be just a friendly little "meet and greet" with other women. Having lived in the San Francisco Bay Area her whole life, she knew that the gay and lesbian communities were very willing to express their displeasure with any number of issues, often in a truculent fashion. She wasn't angry with anyone—nor did she have an interest in civil disobedience of any kind. She was mulling over her qualms when Ryan tried to draw her out.

"What's going on in that cute little head?" An elegantly shaped finger tapped at Jamie's skull.

"Uhm," she stalled, trying to think of the best way to explain her reservations. "I guess I'm just not a protesty kinda girl."

"It's not a protest. Well, it's kind of a demonstration, but not in the traditional sense."

"Huh?"

Ryan's dark hair tumbled around her shoulders as she scratched her head, chuckling at her own abstruseness. "I didn't do a very good job with that, did I?" She smiled and tried again. "It's a demonstration of the power of women in the community. It's a way to remind people that the gay community has a very large lesbian contingent. Sometimes society lumps us all together, and this is a way to say that we're different people with different agendas."

Hmm, Jamie thought to herself. *I've never had an agenda in my life … and I'm not sure I want one now.*

Ryan could see the hesitancy that was still evident in Jamie's body language, so she tried another tactic. "Okay, how about this. I'm gonna get dressed in my dykiest outfit and ride my motorcycle to meet a bunch of my friends and ex-lovers. Wanna go?" A crooked grin accompanied this statement and Jamie felt her heart melt at the woman's disarmingly charming expression.

"I'm in!" She smiled at her lover, thinking of how simple Ryan made everything sound.

As they crossed the street, Jamie held on to her partner's hand a little tighter than usual. Her reservations had diminished now that she saw the gathering was really more of a party than anything else. She squeezed Ryan's hand and said, "I had the idea that this would be some kinda angry protest march. But it doesn't look like that at all."

"Nah. I mean, it is a march, but most people don't look angry, do they?"

Jamie giggled, unable to stop herself from feeling giddy to be in such a crowd. "Hnh-uh. They look … hot," she said, sneaking a quick look to see if Ryan minded her noticing the attributes of the semi-clad women.

The taller woman laughed, a huge smile on her face. "That's my girl!"

"You don't mind?" Jamie asked.

"Hell, no! You're just figuring out where you fit. Look all you want, babe. Just remember to go home with me."

Jamie slipped her arm around Ryan's waist and gave her a hug. "There could be a million women here and I'd follow you home like a puppy."

The blonde knew that she was just starting to develop an appetite for looking at other women, but her limited experience led her to acknowledge that she was crazy about dykes. The butchier the better. Yet, every time she stopped to think about this fact, she was puzzled. It stood to reason, given her background, that she would be attracted to the slightly androgynous Armani-wearing art dealers of SOMA or the preppy lesbians who lived around Union Street. Oddly, those types of women did nothing for her. Give her a leather-jacketed woman with muscles to spare and her knees grew weak. Looking up at her partner, she had to acknowledge that she had snagged the best-looking specimen of the species that she had ever seen.

To Jamie's appreciative eyes, Ryan always looked hot. But there was something about her today that made the smaller woman question whether it was safe to be in public with her for fear that she wouldn't be able to control herself.

After Ryan announced her intention to come to the march, she'd led Jamie down to their new room to present her with a few gifts. It took a minute for the blonde to get her mind around the idea that Ryan wanted to see her in the outfit presented, but her partner had been so generous in her willingness to dress up to please Jamie that she had to give it a go.

She'd been gifted with many items of clothing throughout her life. Since her mother was more of a compulsive shopper than she, it was rare that she didn't receive a little something when she went to visit. But in all of her twenty-one years, she had never been given an outfit like this.

"Is this how you see me?" she asked slowly, holding up the scuffed brown bomber jacket and green khaki pants.

"Uhm, I'm not sure what you mean by that." Ryan hesitated, thinking that perhaps Jamie had misunderstood the purpose of the gift.

"I guess I mean that I never wear clothes like this. If this is how you want me to look, we're gonna have to do some negotiating."

Ryan crossed the room and gave her partner a gentle hug, inhaling deeply to take in another whiff of her perfume. "No, no, I don't see you this way. I don't want you to change the way you dress."

"Then why—"

Ryan interrupted to explain, "I just thought you'd feel more comfortable if you had some dyke clothes. If you wear your normal stuff, you'll stick out like a sore thumb." Seeing the hurt look that started to form, she lowered her head to look directly into her lover's eyes. "I know you don't feel like a lesbian. And I'm sure you don't feel like a dyke. I just thought you might feel more comfortable if you looked the part. It's kinda like wearing a long dress and a head covering in Iran. It doesn't mean you're Muslim, but it helps you to fit in."

"You're sure you like how I normally look?" she asked, suddenly insecure.

"I positively love how you look," Ryan said. "I love that you don't look like all of the other women I've dated. You're … special," she decided. "That's it. You're special."

Jamie's hands laced behind Ryan's neck and pulled her down for a lingering kiss. Without conscious thought, Ryan's hands slipped under the short dress and started to play.

"Unh-unh-unh," Jamie chided, as she removed the questing hands from her butt. "We've got a march to attend."

Ryan went to shower while Jamie got into her new outfit. To her amazement, everything fit perfectly. The green fatigues hung low on her waist and hugged her hips snugly, while the matching green ribbed cropped undershirt allowed a good view of Ryan's favorite part—her abdomen. She laced up the black Doc Martens, tucking her pants into the tops of the boots to complete her "basic training" look. *I wonder where the dog tags are*, she mused as she went to the closet to pick out something for her partner to wear.

When Ryan came out, the first words out of her mouth were, "No! Oh no, not that!"

The blonde head nodded slowly, intent on seeing her vision come to life.

"I don't think I can even get into that," Ryan complained, her voice taking on an uncharacteristic whine.

Another nod as Jamie approached her with the garment in question. "Oh, all right," Ryan grumbled. "I've got to put some baby powder on or we'll never get it zipped."

Looking up at her partner as they approached the crowd, Jamie had to congratulate herself one more time on her choice of attire. Besides the supple leather pants that fit like a second skin, Ryan wore a short leather vest that left a few inches of her midriff exposed. The vest was held closed by an aggressive-looking metal zipper that stopped just at the top of her attention-drawing cleavage. The top was so tight that a bra was completely unnecessary. The women even had to work together to get the thing zipped. Ryan had to bend at the waist, holding her breasts together while Jamie got on her knees to work the recalcitrant zipper, but eventually the struggling breasts behaved themselves and went along peaceably.

Pulling her partner to a halt, Jamie was compelled to toss her arms around her neck and give her a hearty thank-you, both for bringing her to this event and for agreeing to wear the chosen outfit. Ryan grinned down at her in surprise, but quickly got into the mood and returned the kiss. Seconds later she yanked away in shock as a large hand slapped her soundly on her leather-covered ass. "Hey!" she cried as she whirled around to confront her attacker.

A tall redhead wearing nothing but a big smile and a pair of jeans grinned impishly. "Candace!" Ryan cried, wrapping the half-naked woman in a hug.

Jamie immediately began to reassess her pleasure at having come to this party. Seeing Ryan holding a bare-breasted woman was not on her top ten list of favorite things to do, and she had to force herself not to let her displeasure show.

"How've you been, O?" the woman asked, using the moniker that several women on the AIDS Ride used for Ryan.

"I've been great!" Ryan said. She was filled with energy and enthusiasm, and even though Jamie didn't like to see her in a clinch with another woman, she reveled in seeing her this happy. "I'd like to introduce you to the woman who makes me great," she added quickly. "Candace, this is Jamie … my spouse."

Ryan had never used that term in public, and Jamie immediately sensed that she had chosen the term to make the nature of their relationship crystal clear to the women they would meet this day. Jamie couldn't keep the wide grin from her face as she extended her hand to greet Ryan's friend. "No shit!" Candace said as she shook

Jamie's hand. "Congratulations, girl!" She had to give Ryan another hug, but this time Jamie smiled at the scene, feeling very reassured by the introduction.

"Yep," Ryan said. "I'm off the market." She gave Candace a pointed grin and added, "Tell your friends."

"Will do," she agreed with a playful wink.

Candace slapped them both on the shoulder and started to walk away, but Ryan called out, "Hey, is Ally here?"

"No, she went to New York for their Pride Celebration. I'll tell her I saw you, though."

"Cool. See ya, Candace."

Jamie's smirk was firmly affixed to her face as they gazed at the departing woman. "That was?"

"That was Candace," Ryan said, a big smile gracing her mischievous face.

"Was she one of the lucky many to experience your charms?" It was clear that Jamie was joking, and that she was comfortable with meeting past lovers, so Ryan answered without hesitation.

"I'm charming with everyone." She had an ingenuous grin on her face that forced Jamie to admit the truth in that statement. "She, however, has been allowed to nibble on my charms." Another stingingly sharp swat on the butt was beginning to make Ryan regret wearing her leather pants.

It took a few minutes to struggle through the crowd, but Jamie finally found what she was looking for. Nearly every woman wore a bright Day-Glo sticker on some part of her anatomy, and the determined blonde had made her selection as soon as they got in the slow-moving line. She plunked down three dollars and affixed the stickers to her satisfaction. All three four-by-six-inch stickers bore the same saying, and she stuck one above Ryan's heart, another over her own and the third right above the swell of Ryan's shapely ass.

"Very funny, Jamie," her partner glowered, as she looked over her shoulder to read "Happily Married" imprinted on her butt. "Not that I disagree, but did you have to stick one there?"

"Just trying to guard my assets." Wiggling eyebrows forced Ryan to chortle along with her smirking partner. "You seem to draw an exorbitant amount of attention there, so I thought I'd better nip it in the bud."

In order to get a good view of the entire crowd, they decided to climb the bank of the small hill that surrounded the park. A few women were lounging on blankets, and several larger groups were having parties where they could spread out a little. The members of one such group recognized Ryan and waved her over. "Do you mind?" she asked Jamie before heading in their direction.

"No, of course not. I wanna meet your friends."

Giving the group a happy wave, Ryan led her partner toward them. They were still twenty feet away when the catcalls began. "It's true!" "I never thought I'd see this!" "Ryan O'Flaherty in a relationship! Not possible!" "I'm gonna faint!"

"Very funny, guys, truly hilarious." Ryan stood at her full height, hands on hips, and glowered at the group. There were about fifteen women lounging around, and they looked like they'd been there for a long while, judging from the sunburned skin, empty beer bottles, and somewhat vacant expressions.

"How'd it happen, O?" one small woman asked. "Did ya knock her up?"

"Yeah, did ya have to marry her?" another comic chimed in.

"As a matter of fact, I did." Ryan slung a long, bare arm around her partner and pulled her close. "And I marry her again every time I look into those beautiful eyes."

Jamie beamed a smile up at her partner, ignoring the groans and the retching simulations. When everyone had quieted down, she grabbed a spot on the blanket and plopped down as she introduced herself. "I'm Mrs. Ryan O'Flaherty, but you can call me Jamie."

Ryan did the honors of pointing out each member of the group as she sat down next to her partner. A woman named Molly, just to her left, looked up as she opened a fresh beer and offered, "Sip?"

Ryan took one look at the glassy eyes of the woman and accepted the icy can. Tilting her head back, she drained the entire can without pause, with Jamie and Molly watching in shock. "That's the biggest damn sip I ever saw," Molly drawled as she collapsed onto the woman next to her.

Trying to find the most sober member of the crowd, Ryan asked, "How long have you guys been here?"

"Since about noon," Wendy replied, looking at her watch in amazement. "Jeez, no wonder the beer's all gone—it's six o'clock!"

"Why don't you all take a little nap before the march starts," Ryan suggested. "They won't leave before eight."

"Damned good idea, Rock," Wendy said, as she grabbed the woman next to her and collapsed. In a matter of moments, everyone except the two newcomers was out cold. Ryan stuck her hand in the cooler and pulled the last beer from the ice, handing it to Jamie to open.

"I like your friends," Jamie said. "Sparkling conversationalists."

Ryan looked out at the group with a fond smile. "They're nice women," she said. "Most of them work at my old gym."

"I'm sure they're nice," Jamie quickly agreed, hoping that her comment hadn't been offensive. "I'm sure they're a little more interactive when they're not hammered." Just then, the woman next to Jamie started to snore loudly, and the green eyes met Ryan's as she suggested, "How about a change in scenery?"

"Not a bad idea," Ryan agreed.

They moved about twenty-five feet away, close enough to watch over the sleeping women, but far enough away to escape their sound effects. "How many more nicknames do you have?" Jamie asked when they were settled.

"Huh? Ohh ... I forgot that Wendy used that one." Ryan smiled in remembrance. "Some of the people at the gym called me that."

"Because ...?"

Ryan looked uneasy, shifting around a bit as she was forced to admit, "I uhm ... won the trainer's challenge a couple of years, and uhm ... some of the people thought I was uhm ... rock hard." She gulped a little in embarrassment, the self-effacing trait completely charming to Jamie.

She trailed the tips of her fingers down the exposed flesh of Ryan's muscular arms, lingering for a moment at the blue vein that bulged across her bicep. Leaning in close to Ryan's ear she whispered, "You are, you know. You're rock hard and baby soft, all in one big, luscious package."

Ryan's arm draped across her partner's shoulders, the scent of baby powder wafting up to make both of them giggle. "See?" Jamie teased. "You're my big, rock hard baby."

"I'll always be your baby," Ryan promised, tilting her head to nibble on the lips that called to her.

They sat in companionable silence, sipping the beer and gazing out at the assembled throng. The huge stage was slowly filling with musicians, and before long some thrumming rock started blaring from the massive speakers. Even though the music was loud, they could speak in normal tones since they were so far from the stage.

The sun was warm on this clear June afternoon, and after just a few minutes Jamie felt the day catch up with her. "I think I'm gonna go crawl onto that empty space with your friends," she said as a yawn escaped.

"Could I interest you in a little cuddling right here?" Clear blue eyes blinked over at Jamie, who smiled as she considered a lifetime of saying "yes" to whatever question this wonderful woman asked.

"Let's do it." Ryan spread her leather jacket onto the ground and lay down on half of it, extending an arm as she waited for Jamie to cuddle in. They wriggled around for a while but managed to get comfortable, and nodded off a short time later.

"Mmm," Jamie murmured as she tried to swat the annoying insect that had been bedeviling her for long minutes. No matter how quickly she slapped at the silent bug, it managed to evade her until she was fit to be tied. "Damn it!" She sat up and turned her head to find Ryan's twinkling eyes gazing up at her, a long stalk of grass between her teeth.

"Something wrong?" The grass fluttered in the even, white teeth as Ryan spoke.

Grabbing the stalk from her partner's mouth, Jamie attempted to shove the annoying stem into her skin-tight top. The work was slow, but rewarding, and both women were collapsed in a tumble of limbs when a passerby stopped abruptly and asked, "Jamie? Jamie Evans?"

All movement stopped as Jamie's head peeked out from around Ryan's armpit. "Melissa Johnston?" she squeaked out in astonishment, catching sight of Mia's erstwhile lover from prep school. Ryan lifted her arm and helped her partner sit up and compose herself as much as possible. Scrambling to her feet, Jamie continued to stammer. "W … w … what are *you* doing here?"

Melissa glanced at the "Happily Married" stickers that covered both women's breasts, the deep blush that covered Jamie's face, and the G.I. Jane outfit and lifted one eyebrow. "Same thing you are," she said with a smile.

"Hi, Melissa," Ryan said quietly, nearly causing Jamie to faint dead away.

"Ryan? Jesus, I didn't even stop to look!"

To Jamie's eternal gratitude, Melissa merely extended a hand for Ryan to shake. *Thank God I don't have to witness them kissing!* she grumbled as she fleetingly rued the day she hooked up with an "experienced" woman.

Melissa was smiling so brightly that she looked like she would burst. "Of all the people to run into! My God! Jamie Evans … and with Ryan O'Flaherty, no less! This is just too, too much!"

"Yeah, it is too much," Jamie agreed, trying to maintain her composure, but feeling sick to her stomach.

"When was the last time we saw each other, Jamie? Wasn't it our coming-out party?"

"Yeah …" Jamie had to chortle at the irony of the question. "I guess it was. So here we are again … three years later. I guess we're destined to come out again and again and again."

Both Ryan and Melissa laughed at the helpless look on the obviously flustered woman. "So how long have you two been together?" Melissa asked. "I've never heard word one about your being gay, Jamie."

"Great," she said with no enthusiasm. "I guess that won't last long, huh?"

"Ooh, not out to the family?" Melissa asked with a surprising amount of concern in her voice.

"We've just uhm … made it official," Ryan broke in. "Jamie's not out to many people yet." Ryan fixed Melissa with her most serious gaze and added, "She'd really like to be the one to tell her family."

"Oh, of course!" Melissa looked taken aback at the suggestion that she might "out" Jamie. "I'm out to my parents, but I haven't told anyone from Hillsborough. It's just not worth the trouble."

"So things are good with you and your family?" Jamie asked, trying to turn the spotlight back to Melissa.

"God no!" she laughed. "They've practically disowned me! If I didn't have a full scholarship, I'd have had to drop out of school!"

"Are you kidding me?!" Jamie was shocked at this news. She didn't know the Johnstons very well, but Melissa's mother was involved in a lot of charity functions on the Peninsula, and Jamie was sure that her mother knew Melissa's mother.

"My mother went berserk," Melissa commented dryly. "It wasn't a very long trip, I might add."

"God, I'm really sorry," Jamie said.

"No big deal." Melissa acted as though the matter really didn't trouble her. "My dad's fairly cool. He slips me some money once in a while, and my grandmother's supportive. I'm doing fine. Getting out of Hillsborough was the best thing I've ever done." She looked over her shoulder when a woman called her name. "Hey, here's my sweetie now."

A lanky blonde came over and joined the group, and Melissa introduced her. "This is Andi. Andi, this is Jamie Evans. We went to high school together. And this is her partner, Ryan." Jamie noted that Melissa omitted the fact that she knew Ryan, too. *Hmmm, I wonder if Andi is the jealous type?*

They exchanged pleasantries for a few minutes before Melissa asked in a casual tone, "Who are you living with now, Jamie? Still with Cassie and Mia?"

Jamie gave her a bright smile and nodded. "Cassie won't be back, but Mia will come home in September. She's in L.A. this summer with her boyfriend." Jamie didn't want Melissa to think that Mia had come over to the other side, too, so she thought she should add the boyfriend detail.

"Cool," Melissa said with a dampening of her cheerful voice. "Tell them I said 'hi' next time you see them."

"Will do, Melissa. Give me a call sometime—I'm listed." Ryan was surprised to hear the sincerity in Jamie's voice.

"It's a deal," the smiling woman promised. "I'd really like to."

"See ya." They both waved as the visitors strolled away, hand in hand.

"I need a list. Preferably in alphabetical order, but if you can't manage that, I'll take whatever you can give me. I want the name or the description of every woman that you've ever slept with, copped a feel from, or French kissed. I can't take another one of these surprise attacks, Ryan. I mean it."

Expecting to see anger flashing in the green eyes, Ryan was surprised and saddened to see only resigned frustration. Taking a deep breath, Ryan spoke the truth. "I didn't sleep with Melissa. I also didn't cop a feel, or kiss her—French or otherwise." Ryan's voice was subdued, and when Jamie met her eyes she looked like a small child who'd been punished unjustly.

Lying down on the leather jacket, Jamie blew out a long, frustrated breath. She knew that Ryan was telling the truth, since Ryan always told the truth, but the entire incident had left her feeling bruised and vulnerable. "I'm sorry," she said softly. "I shouldn't have jumped to that conclusion."

Ryan lay down next to her and patted her cheek gently. "S'okay. Not like you wouldn't have been right nineteen times out of twenty."

Sadness laced with regret clouded the eyes that Jamie loved, and her heart clenched in shame. "That's no excuse. It's unfair of me to assume that you've slept with every woman you know by name. Besides, even if you have, what difference does it make?" She sat up and tried to order her thoughts before speaking. Ryan was looking at her with a curious gaze, but she didn't comment. "It just doesn't matter, baby," she finally decided, and as she said the words, she knew them to be true. "All that matters is that we love each other now ... and that we're faithful to each other now. The past is past."

Ryan sat upright, her shoulder brushing against Jamie's as she did so. "I just wish–" she began in a soft voice, but Jamie placed her fingers against her lips, effectively silencing her regret.

"I wished for a wonderful mate, and I got one. That's all that matters. Really." Ryan still looked a little down, and Jamie made another try. "Look, when we were in Pebble Beach you told me that I shouldn't regret having had Jack in my life. You said that loving him made me open to loving you. I think you were right about that. But you've got to know that the same thing holds true for you."

Ryan shot her a quizzical gaze, still not speaking, but obviously waiting to be reassured.

"You are the woman ... and the lover ... that you are because of the experiences you've had." Jamie's voice had grown soft, and there was a hint of seduction in it. She lifted her hand and started to trace her finger around the outlines of Ryan's leather vest, turning the hint into a definite overture. "I know you're a very creative woman, but I bet you learned a lot from the women you've been with." Jamie's breath was floating across Ryan's skin like a warm breeze, and Ryan shuddered from the sensation. "I owe those women a debt of gratitude," she whispered. "Especially the one who taught you to do this ..."

Forcing her surprised lover onto her back, Jamie illustrated one of Ryan's favorite moves, performing a credible rendition of the fluttering tongue movement her lover had perfected through her years of experience. Ryan let out a low groan as the gentle assault continued, finding herself powerless under her partner's relentlessly probing tongue.

Coming up for air, Jamie panted out, "This is the longest we've gone without making love all week. I ... I don't know if I can control myself."

Ryan gazed up at her and stated the obvious. "We don't have to wait. We're among friends."

Her waggling eyebrow made clear just what she was suggesting, but Jamie found her head rapidly shaking. "You mean ... here?"

The seductive grin on Ryan's flushed face indicated that was exactly what she meant. "I've done worse."

Small fingers paused at the tab of the zipper that held the objects of Jamie's desire captive. A very large part of her wanted to yank that zipper down and let all of that creamy flesh spill out of the leather and into her waiting hands. But another part of her didn't want to share their intimacy with anyone, much less the dozens of women on the plateau who would have ringside seats. Ryan wasn't pushing—she had merely stated an option—but Jamie decided that she didn't want to have public sex with her partner—today or ever.

"I don't want to," she said in a quiet voice. "I mean ... I want to ... really, really badly. But not here ... not now."

Ryan wrapped her in a gentle embrace and whispered into her ear, "I'm glad. I didn't want to either."

Jamie's head shot up as she tried to focus on her too-close partner. "What? Then why did you …"

"I was just laying out the options. I've done that type of thing before, and if you wanted to, I wouldn't have objected." A gentle smile tugged at the corners of her mouth as she gazed at Jamie and softly stroked her face. "But it's not what I want … for us. Sex can be public—but making love is private. And we make love," she declared softly, kissing Jamie with a tender passion that made her body go limp.

Pulling away several minutes later, Ryan teased, "Hey, where did your muscles go?" She grasped a nearby hand, picked it up, and chuckled when it fell to the ground as she released it.

"My muscles wanna have sex," the smaller woman moaned. "The message from my brain has been completely ignored by the rest of my body."

"Poor body," Ryan crooned, running her warm hands down the sensitive flesh. She leaned over and placed gentle kisses on every part she could reach, murmuring, "Don't worry, body, you'll be taken care of as soon as we get home."

"Promise?" Glittering, desire-filled eyes begged.

"Promise," Ryan vowed, bending to kiss Jamie's lips one last time. "I think I can satisfy your body and your mind." Her flashing eyes made Jamie believe every word, and she was able to relax and settle into a long, leisurely, loving hug.

It was close to eight when the last band finished. A long string of announcements called the group to some semblance of order, and the energy started to pick up. "Let's walk around a little bit," Ryan suggested.

They stopped to make sure that Ryan's friends from the gym were awake enough to look out for themselves and then made their way down the hill. "Look, honey," Jamie enthused when they went past the large playground in the corner of the park.

"That'll be us in a few years," Ryan laughed as she came up behind her partner and clasped her arms around her in a loose embrace. They both smiled at the scene, watching women play with their young children on the various pieces of equipment. Several couples had babies in strollers or packs and, as Jamie expected, Ryan was drawn to them like a bee to honey. When they got close, Ryan pointed out a pair of women playing with a young boy on the swings. "Hey, that's Stacy and Melinda from the AIDS Ride." They dashed over and greeted the couple enthusiastically.

"Stacy, Melinda, how are you?" Ryan asked, wrapping each woman in a warm embrace. Jamie offered an equally friendly, but slightly less demonstrative welcome, smiling as her partner dropped to the sand to greet Jared, the adorable little six-year-old who was trying to touch the sky with each push of the swing.

"That's high enough, Jared," Melinda said, afraid that his small body would slide out of the seat if he went much higher.

A devilish look came over Ryan's features as she looked up at the mothers and asked, "Mind if I give him a little excitement?"

"Uhm … I guess not …" Stacy hesitated.

"She's careful with others," Jamie assured them. "She's only really wild when she's on her own."

"Okay," Melinda decided. "Go for it."

"Hey, Jared," Ryan said in her most conspiratorial tone. "Wanna make your mamas' eyes bug out?"

The small boy nodded an enthusiastic yes, even though he looked a little hesitant to align his fortunes with this tall stranger. Ryan lifted him as she sat in the canvas sling, then placed him on her lap, facing her. "Okay, pal, hold on tight," she advised as she began to pump her powerful legs. In seconds they were going higher than Jamie had ever seen a human go on a swing. Three sets of eyes stared in shock as both Ryan and Jared threw their heads back and laughed hysterically. The little boy held on as tight as his thin arms would allow, but Ryan had taken the extra precaution of wrapping her arms around the chains and then securely locking her hands around his back.

"Mama! Mommy! Look!" he cried, reassuring himself that his parents were sharing in his joy.

Both women smiled and waved at the wildly laughing boy, with Stacy saying to Jamie, "Would this be a good time to tell her he sometimes gets sick to his stomach on the swing?"

"Nah," Jamie decided, unwilling to take one moment of joy from her partner. "She's got on leather—I'll just hose her down."

"Did you have a good time, little girl?" Jamie asked when they departed the playground.

"Yep." Ryan was beaming from ear to ear, a look of such satisfaction on her face that Jamie nearly cried at her touching expression. "You go lots faster if you swing with a buddy. You spur each other on." Wiggling eyebrows showed that Ryan thought this maxim could apply to other situations also, and Jamie was beginning to wish they were at home to explore some of them. But the remarkable sights that they continued to observe made her glad they'd decided to stay.

Not the least of her pleasure came from the wide variety of friends and ex-lovers that Ryan introduced her to. It was very reassuring to Jamie that very few of the exes seemed to show anything but fond feelings for her partner.

After the AIDS Ride, she'd been a little concerned that running into former lovers would be a constant strain, with woman after woman trying to give them a hard time or even trying to cause trouble in their relationship. But this group seemed to be on exactly the same wavelength that Ryan had been on during her dating days. They seemed to be very open-minded about their sexual experiences. In fact, they seemed to be experimenting with their sexuality—trying to get and give pleasure without any major emotional commitment. Jamie knew that lifestyle would never work for her, but it had seemed to work for Ryan, and she was glad that these women were able to play the game in the same way, if that met their needs.

They were heading back toward the stage when a hand snaked out from the crowd and landed on Ryan's shoulder. "Piernuda!" called a honey-toned, lightly accented voice.

"Alisa!" Ryan said, looking genuinely happy to see her former lover. They embraced, holding on for a moment longer than Jamie would have preferred, but she was beginning to get accustomed to Ryan's near-constant hugging and kissing of practically every woman they ran into. "How've you been?"

"Good. I am good, Cariña." Alisa released Ryan and turned her head to Jamie. "Introduce me to your love, Ryan."

Jamie had seen this self-confident woman on the mountain bike ride up on Mt. Tam. They hadn't spoken that day, so her memory was vague, but seeing her again, Jamie had to admit that she would never forget her face. The strong, angular features would not be described as traditionally beautiful, but on Alisa, those features blended with her near-black eyes to create a face that was truly mesmerizing. As Alisa extended a hand, Jamie had to admit that she was happy she would never have to face her in a trial. There was something almost regal in the woman's bearing—some indescribable elegance in her carriage that made Jamie feel small and awkward and immature. "I am Alisa Guerra," she supplied before Ryan could do the honors.

Jamie grasped her cool, strong hand and nearly curtsied. It took her a second, but she got out, "Jamie Evans," even managing to add a weak smile.

Ryan was at her side, slipping an arm around Jamie's waist while she beamed at both women. "I've never seen you look so happy, Querida," Alisa said, looking at Ryan fondly. "You seem … at peace."

"Thanks for saying that," Ryan smiled. "I am at peace. I'm calmer and more relaxed than I've ever been in my life."

Jamie looked up at her with wide-eyed astonishment. "What were you like before?" she gasped, causing both Ryan and Alisa to break out in exuberant laughter.

"Don't ask!" both women supplied nearly simultaneously.

There was something about the way Alisa looked at Ryan that made Jamie feel that she was intruding. She decided to give them a little time alone, so she excused herself to go wait in the long line for the restroom.

"Are you sure you want to go alone?" Ryan asked with concern.

"Positive. You two stay here and chat. I'll come back for you."

"Okay," Ryan agreed, lowering her long frame to a comfortable spot on the ground. "I'll stay right here."

Jamie struggled through the crowd to get in the slow-moving line. Nearly everyone she saw wore some type of sticker or slogan somewhere on their bodies. *I wouldn't say most of these things to Ryan, and I DO most of them with her!* She was truly amazed at the number of women who paraded around on the streets of the city proclaiming "butch in the streets, femme in the sheets," "orgasm addict," "got lube?" "pro choice/pro pussy," or the thoughtful "breakfast included." Nevertheless, her favorite had to be the T-shirt that begged, "Dip me in chocolate and throw me to the lesbians." *Now that's one thing I'd like to try*, she thought. *But there's only one chocolate-loving lesbian I'd like to be thrown to!*

Standing in the line, Jamie mused about the crowd and the event. *I never would have believed this, but I feel pretty comfortable in this crowd. I'm not sure what it is … but I feel like … myself.* An idea struck her and she thought about it for a moment, trying it on for size. *That's it! These women aren't judging me!* As she looked around at the women surrounding her, she considered her thought. *I don't feel like I'm on display! They think I'm gay and that should make me fair game, but I don't feel like they're looking at me the way that six thousand young straight guys would!*

Aside from the lack of sexual vibes I'm getting, I've gotta admit it's weird to be with this many women and not feel like they're assessing what I'm wearing or how my hair looks. This is really odd, but it feels very freeing!

With a start she recognized that this was one of the things she most loved about being with Ryan—right from the very start. They had never—not once—spent any time analyzing anyone else. She blushed at the thought of how many times she and Cassie had sat on the Sproul steps at Cal and critiqued people as they passed through the gates of the campus. She'd thought that was what everyone did, until she began to spend time with Ryan. But Ryan was so self-assured that it would never occur to her to spend her time comparing herself to others. In a way, that behavior was beneath the confident woman, and for that Jamie was truly grateful.

As soon as she was finished, she threaded her way through the crowd to find Ryan. She was right where Jamie had left her, sprawled across the ground, head held up by one braced arm. Alisa's pose roughly mirrored Ryan's, and they were having an obviously intense discussion. The assistant district attorney was making a point of some import, pushing her finger into the softness of Ryan's breast to punctuate her words. Jamie felt a flash of irritation, but she tried to swallow the feeling before she reached the pair. Ryan, for her part, looked like she was paying attention, but Jamie could tell that Alisa's words were not really reaching her.

The blue eyes seemed to sense her approach, and they rotated in her direction, tracking her for the last thirty feet or so of her journey. Alisa sensed that her audience had deserted her, and she turned to catch a glimpse of Jamie's arrival. Her smile seemed less than genuine, but Ryan's made up for any luster that her friend's lacked. "Hi," she said, getting to her feet to welcome Jamie back with a kiss.

"Ready to go?" Jamie asked, sensing that Ryan was feeling antsy.

"Yeah, I think so." Turning to Alisa, Ryan said, "It was great to see you again. Maybe we'll catch you up on Mt. Tam some Friday night."

Jamie could see the longing in the deep brown eyes as the lovely woman said, "Maybe." She turned to Jamie and extended her hand again, gripping the smaller hand tightly. "Take care of her, Jamie," she intoned, nodding in Ryan's direction. "She's precious to me."

Jamie met the intense gaze and felt all of her normal confidence bubble to the surface. "I will, Alisa. She's precious to me, too." Both women nodded to each other, acknowledging that only one could claim this prize.

Alisa wrapped Ryan in a hug, pulling back to kiss her softly on the lips. "Hasta luego, Cariña," she whispered, then turned and strode back to her friends.

"Wanna talk about it?" Jamie asked softly as they neared the street.

Ryan had been nearly silent during their walk, seemingly lost in her reflections. "No." She shook her head briskly, running a hand through her hair to order her bangs. "I'd rather not, if you don't mind."

Jamie had a ton of questions for her partner, not the least of which was "Why is your former lover still calling you 'hottie,' 'sweetheart,' and 'dear'?" But she knew that Ryan needed some private space, so she forced herself to say, "No problem," and grasped her hand, lifting it for a gentle kiss.

Ryan beamed a smile at her, silently thanking her for her understanding. When they reached the street, the taller woman said, "I don't really feel like marching that far. Would you mind riding?"

Jamie was astounded to hear her lover plead fatigue. She stopped abruptly, pulling Ryan to a halt with her. "Are you all right? It's not like you to beg off something because you're tired."

"Mmm ... I'm not really tired. I just don't want to walk all the way to Castro. I think it'd be more fun to ride."

Jamie was actually a little disappointed. She was just getting comfortable with all of this feminine energy and she wasn't really ready to leave the protective cocoon of women. But Ryan's behavior was unusual enough that she felt the need to heed her request. "Sure. Riding is good, too."

They got on the bike and headed off, slowing severely when they reached Valencia and 23rd Street. Lined up in a neat queue stretching for nearly two blocks were motorcycles of every make and model. Most were riderless, but many held a driver or even a passenger.

"Is there some big biker bar around here?" Jamie asked over the thrumming of the engine.

Ryan flipped up her face shield and turned to say, "No ... no biker bars around here."

As they crossed the street and began to slowly make their way past the assembled bikes, Jamie was shocked to notice that every driver was a woman. She was just about to comment when she heard, "O'Flaherty! I saved you a space!"

Ryan's laugh wafted back to Jamie, and the passenger got in a good pinch to the exposed skin that lay just under her fingers. The bike slid into the space reserved for them and as they got off, Jamie stood in slack-jawed silence at the scene that stretched as far as the eye could see.

There were hundreds of bikes, hundreds of women, and a few moments after they arrived, the women began to break up their small groups and climb astride the bikes. Ryan dashed over to the woman who had saved them a space, giving out yet another kiss on the lips for her thoughtfulness. *Well, one good thing*, Jamie mused. *If we ever break up, at least I still get to kiss her!*

Before Ryan made her way back, she was stopped at least six more times for kisses and hugs. When she finally stood before Jamie, the smirking blonde grabbed her and planted a scorcher on her oft-kissed lips. The kiss continued for long minutes, with Ryan finally leaning against the bike to support her weak legs. When Jamie released her she blinked slowly and mumbled, "Is this making you hot?"

"Yes," her impish partner drawled. "But that's not why I kissed you. I'm just trying to keep those lips busy. If I've got 'em under control, nobody else can get at 'em."

"I like your style," Ryan decided, returning the favor as the bikes started to rev. Just as they got on, a bare-breasted woman ran down the street in their direction. She had painted her chest in the wide stripes of the rainbow flag, but just above her belly someone had created a perfect rendition of a street sign. It read "One Way" but the arrow pointed down into her jeans. Jamie was just about to comment when the woman cried, "Ryan!"

Just before she reached them, Jamie whispered the warning, "That street has been permanently closed!"

When everyone was ready, the lead bikes gunned their engines repeatedly, signaling that they would soon start. No one was wearing her helmet, but Jamie was still reticent to take hers off. "It's against the law to ride without a helmet," she insisted, needlessly adding, "and stupid, for that matter."

"This ride's illegal. And for that matter, the march is, too." She nodded her head in the direction of the police station they were idling in front of. At least a dozen officers stood in the parking lot, watching the assembled women. Some looked bored, some interested in the bikes; a few looked less than happy, but none of them looked like they had any intention of getting involved.

"You sure?" Jamie asked again.

"I'll pay your ticket. It's perfectly safe. I guarantee we won't go over ten miles an hour the whole time."

Feeling like a miscreant, Jamie finally tugged off the bright yellow helmet and handed it to Ryan. In return, Ryan handed her some neon orange foam earplugs. "Trust me," she intoned, and as usual, Jamie did. As soon as they had their earplugs in place, the lead bikes roared away and every other bike in the group began to rev its engine. The sound was bone-shaking as every one of the beasts let out a throaty growl that reverberated against the two- and three-story apartment buildings and shops.

Every part of Jamie began to thrum, and after a second or two she was struck by another erotic daydream of just how much leather she could leave on her partner while still having access to every vital spot.

Ryan's prediction was accurate, and they spent much more time idling than they did riding, but Jamie decided that she didn't care one bit. She was so overwhelmingly glad to be sharing this party with her partner that she didn't care if they had to push the bike the rest of the way.

Ryan and C.J., the friend who had saved them the spot, had a little competition as they rode along. The game seemed to be "see who has the loudest bike," and with what little hearing she had left, Jamie decided it was a draw. Both women had fun, though, and Jamie had to admit that as long as Ryan had fun—she had fun.

When they finally reached the last big hill leading down into the Castro, Ryan turned and shouted, "Turn around, babe." Jamie did, and practically fell off the bike as she took in the scene behind her. From the bottom of the hill to the top, the women of the march filled the street. There were so many women that they also filled both sidewalks to capacity. As the bike rolled slowly down the street, more and more marchers crested the hill—looking to Jamie like a huge invasion of women warriors. But this invasion was clearly welcome, as the assembled throng gathered on the flats began to clap and cheer for the riders and marchers.

The Castro was filled to bursting on this Saturday night of Pride Weekend. The street had been closed for hours, every recalcitrant car towed away long ago. Now the bikes rolled down the normally congested street freely, police holding back the onlookers who struggled against the restraints.

Jamie had never been greeted so exuberantly. Even the crowd at the closing ceremonies of the AIDS Ride dimmed in comparison to this. Music blared from the stage that had been set up, people yelled, bikes roared. It was a sensory overload for everyone involved.

They were led to a side street, where the police had thoughtfully provided a place to park the four hundred motorcycles. It was clear that if they got into this mess they would have to stay until the last of the revelers left, but as usual Ryan had a plan. She separated from the pack and started to wind her way through the streets and alleys of the Castro, finally finding a sliver of a spot about two blocks away.

When she killed the engine, Jamie's ears couldn't adjust to the silence for several minutes. It sounded like they were still in the pack, although much more muffled. She extracted the earplugs that Ryan had provided and gave her partner a big kiss for her prudence. "I would be permanently deaf without these babies," she marveled. "As usual, my little Girl Scout comes through again."

"Your ears are very important to me," Ryan said with a touch of seriousness. "I always want you to be able to hear me whispering how much I love you."

That merited another kiss, a long, emotion-filled one, delivered right in the middle of 22nd Street.

They didn't stay in the Castro for long. There were so many people that it was a little overwhelming for both of them, and Ryan had never been fond of huge crowds. They stayed on the periphery as much as possible, enjoying the cavalcade of diversity.

They saw nearly every permutation of leather, denim, and rubber imaginable. Jamie had never considered the leather/rubber cottage industry, but judging from this display, business was booming.

Ryan was perched on the back of a bus bench, Jamie between her thighs, when a good-looking woman walked by. She was sporting a T-shirt that read, "Vegan lesbians taste better."

Turning around to look at her partner, Jamie raised an eyebrow in question. As she expected, Ryan gave her a shrug and a small nod, adding, "I wouldn't say better, but definitely different."

"I thought safer sex prohibited that," Jamie said, turning around fully to make eye contact.

"It does, but I had a pretty wild first year out. Ally didn't knock any sense into me until I'd been around the block a few times."

"So … why is it different?" Jamie persisted. "Would you like me to be a vegan?"

"Nope." Ryan shook her head decisively. "I could tell you a lot more than you want to know, since it's all about chemistry and biology. But the details aren't important. The bottom line is that your taste is absolute perfection. I love it more than words can say, and I can't think of a reason why we're out in this crowd when I could be at home feasting upon it."

Jamie couldn't argue with that logic. She merely grasped Ryan's hand and let the sexy brunette lead her back to their new family home.

After a very quick check on Duffy, the youngest and furriest member of the O'Flaherty family, they dashed down the stairs to their room. Ryan was preparing to toss her lover onto the bed but stopped short when she noticed a huge basket filled with gourmet delicacies and a large bottle of champagne. "Jamie," she asked in surprise, "did you see this?"

The smaller woman had been thrown over Ryan's shoulder, and they both laughed as she stated the obvious. "All I can see right now is a very scrumptious-looking leather-covered butt." She reached down with her dangling arms and gave the butt in question a good swat.

Ryan placed her onto the bed gently, allowing her to see their gift. "That's so sweet!" she said. "Is there a note or a card?"

Ryan pulled off the transparent lavender wrapping paper and dug around in the items. "Here it is," she said triumphantly. The note was addressed to "Siobhán and Jamie" and was obviously in her father's handwriting. She ripped it open and read aloud,

> *This is just a small token to express our feelings for the both of you.*
> *We are overjoyed that you have found each other and we hope that*
> *your love continues to grow each day.*
> *Welcome to the family, Jamie. We love you like one of our own!*
> *Love always,*
> *Martin, Brendan, Conor and Rory*

"This is sooooo adorable," Jamie gushed. "I can't get over how thoughtful your family is. They've really made me feel at home."

"I'd like to make you feel at home, too," Ryan murmured, falling to her knees in front of her partner. Her eyes were dark with desire, and Jamie felt her heartbeat pick up again as she met and held her gaze.

"What kind of welcome do you have planned for me?" she asked softly, running her hands through Ryan's dark hair.

It was all that Ryan could do to concentrate on the question her lover posed. Her head pushed against Jamie's hands, willing the touch to continue. "Huh?" she finally murmured, lost in the sensation.

Jamie loved the little seduction games they played, and she decided to continue this one for a while. There was something so arousing about watching Ryan's normal control collapse bit by bit that she doubted she would ever tire of the game. "I asked," she whispered, as her fingers joined behind Ryan's head and started to scratch her scalp, "what kind of welcome you had planned for me."

Ryan looked like all she wanted to do was lift her rear leg and scratch behind her ear just as Duffy was wont to do when Jamie hit a particularly good spot. It was obviously hard for her to form a coherent thought, but this was when the game became particularly pleasurable for Jamie. Watching her lover struggle to speak turned her on in a way she would never have imagined. There was something unspeakably delicious about watching the normally glib woman fight to string together a two-word sentence, all because of her touch. "Welcome?" she asked, haltingly. "Huh?"

Lowering her hands, Jamie used her short nails to lightly scratch every exposed bit of skin that she could reach, starting at Ryan's sensitive neck. When she was only halfway down her bare arms, Ryan was shivering noticeably, her eyes tightly closed, relishing every touch. "Don't you want to give me a special welcome?" Jamie persisted, leaning in close to lick and suckle on Ryan's thrumming pulse point.

"Ahh," Ryan gasped, presenting her neck to her tormentor, the question never heard, much less answered.

Jamie backed off just enough to allow her victim to form a rational thought. As she pulled away, Ryan stayed just where she was—kneeling on the floor, swaying slightly as she waited for more of her lover's touch. Her eyes were closed, head tilted just a bit, lips moist and slightly parted. Jamie knew that she was near the breaking point, and she was determined to push until her lover snapped and claimed what she so badly needed.

She slid off the bed and knelt behind her partner, her knee between Ryan's so she could get close. Lifting the dark hair she started to lick and suck at the smooth, sensitive skin of the taller woman's neck. Ryan's whole body twitched with need, her shivering driving Jamie absolutely wild. The game lasted just a few more seconds until Ryan let out a sound that was as much groan as growl before claiming her need and her tormentor, in tandem.

"Is this the X-rated section?" Jamie asked idly, sometime later that night. Her finger slid down the spines of the books that rested just a few inches from her face.

Ryan rolled over with a grunt, stretching muscles stiff from the position they had been in, as well as from the unforgiving floor. "Oh, no ..." she said, "that's where I put the textbooks I want to sell back. I thought they'd be out of the way there." A small chuckle left her lips as she added, "I thought we'd be on the bed—not under it."

"Hey, you're the one who dropped to her knees," Jamie teased gently. "You started it, Buffy."

Ryan's laugh bubbled up from deep in her chest. "Yeah, that's a laugh. I'm your pawn and you can do anything you want with me—and you know it." She punctuated the last part of the sentence with a gentle jab into Jamie's exposed ribs.

A slightly embarrassed laugh acknowledged the truth of the statement. "It's ... it's just so much fun," she said rather helplessly. "I've never played like that, and I really like it."

Ryan rolled over again, wrapping her arms around her lover. "I like it too. I couldn't be happier that we play and tease each other like this. I hope we always have this much fun playing with each other."

Jamie nuzzled her head into her partner's sweet-smelling neck. "I'm so grateful that sex has been this much fun. I was afraid it'd be all serious and ... I don't know ... too emotional, maybe."

"Ohh ..." Ryan nodded, understanding her partner's worry perfectly. "You thought every time might be like merging souls or something."

Jamie giggled at that description, but she had to admit that had been her fear. "It's funny," she murmured. "Every time is a little like that ... but for just a few seconds, or a minute. Like tonight." She rolled onto her side and braced her head on her hand to be able to see Ryan's eyes. "You were poised over my body, and you held yourself there for a second ... I could see all of your muscles straining, and your eyes were like sapphires as the lamplight hit them. When our eyes met, I felt like you held my soul in your hands ... like I was yours completely. Do you know what I mean?"

Ryan bent her head to kiss the lips that were so perfectly able to express the feelings of her own heart. "I do. I felt the same way. It was very moving." She wrapped her partner in a soft embrace, murmuring, "I think we can only process a moment or two like that at a time. It'd be too much otherwise."

"Yes! That's it exactly! I was afraid it'd be like that for hours at a time. I'm so glad that it's mostly fun and play with a little bit of emotion."

"Me too," Ryan agreed, placing a kiss on her cheek. "It's been just perfect." She rolled into a sitting position and shook her hair into place. "God, it's been a long day," she moaned as she slowly got to her feet. She extended a hand to her partner, then sat on the bed and grabbed their gift basket, taking a careful look inside.

It was nearly eleven o'clock and Ryan was famished. She had eaten everything she could find in the refrigerator when she and Conor had returned home from Pebble Beach, but had not had a proper dinner, so she started pulling things out of their basket, looking for something to eat right then. "Aunt Maeve must have had a hand in this," Ryan decided.

"Why do you say that?"

"This stuff is too classy for Da or the boys to have picked out. If it was up to them, they'd bring us a couple of Italian combos as a present."

"Well, I don't really care who thought of it. I think it's about the sweetest thing I've ever seen in my life. I swear, Ryan, if you ever dump me I'm making a play for one of the boys. Yours is the nicest family I've ever had the privilege to know."

"We were just being on good behavior until we had you hooked," she said. "Now you'll see our true nature." As she lifted the champagne from the basket she shook her head slightly. "It's warm. We'll have to have this when we get to our second home."

"We do have a lot of places to celebrate, don't we?" Jamie asked with a little laugh. "I guess we'll have to christen our bed sober."

Ryan hopped out of bed and dashed upstairs. "Not necessarily," she said over her shoulder. She returned with two rocks glasses filled with ice and a bottle of amber liquor. "Irish whiskey," she said as she wiggled both eyebrows and presented the half-filled bottle of Connemara whiskey, brought back from Ireland on Ryan's last trip.

"You want to get me drunk, don't you?" Jamie teased, batting her eyes innocently. "Are you trying to lower my resistance so you can have your way with me?"

"I think I've done pretty well in the last week without any outside help," Ryan said smugly.

"Oh, you do, do you?" Jamie scoffed, narrowing her eyes to stare at her lover.

"Yep. I think I've got you hooked on me. You've got the jones now."

"So resistance is futile?"

"Completely," Ryan stated in a confident drawl.

"Okay." Jamie flung herself down on the comforter, drawing her forearm over her eyes while softly begging, "Be gentle."

Ryan smiled at her theatrics and leaned over to kiss her tenderly. "I'll always be gentle with you."

Jamie looked up at her and brushed her cheek with her hand. "I know you will." There was a slight quaver to her voice as the events of the day threatened to catch up with her. "You've only shown me kindness, and gentleness and love."

"That's the least that you deserve. You're precious to me, Jamie. I treasure you." She leaned down to kiss her softly for several minutes. As their kisses grew in intensity, their bodies began to slide against one another. With her last shred of rational thought, Ryan sat up and removed the basket from the bed. Grabbing the two glasses, she handed one to her partner, then removed the top from the bottle. She poured a small amount into each glass and lifted her glass while she gazed into Jamie's eyes. "To the keeper of my heart and the guardian of my soul. To my anam cara."

They each took a sip of the smooth amber liquid and smiled. Jamie lifted her glass and touched Ryan's. "To my one love." They sipped again, and then Ryan gathered the glasses and placed them on the table.

Jamie lay on her back, gazing up at her partner with a slightly quizzical look. "Anam cara," she murmured, rolling the words around on her tongue.

"It's Gaelic for soul friend," Ryan said softly. She lifted her hand and brushed the hair from Jamie's eyes and placed a kiss on her forehead. "It's a concept I haven't heard here in the states. It's a Celtic mindset that doesn't really fit into Western tradition." She struggled a bit as she tried to explain the amorphous concept to her partner. "I guess the best way to describe it is to say it's the one person to whom you're most bonded, but your relationship isn't limited to this life. You're joined in an eternal way with your soul friend. No boundaries of time or space separate you and your anam cara." Wrapping her lover in her arms she whispered, "That's exactly how I feel about you, Jamie." She dipped her head and captured the warm lips that smiled up at her. The taste of the liquor was still on those tender lips as Ryan ran her tongue all around the delicate mouth. They kissed for endless moments, sometimes tenderly, sometimes fiercely, but always coming back to slow, gentle, loving touches.

Ryan's gentle touch mirrored her kisses. She softly ran her hands all over her lover's body, loving her with the tenderness that their bond demanded, while slowly, but inexorably drawing her toward fulfillment. When Jamie's breath caught, Ryan increased the pace of her touch until the smaller woman was shaking with desire. As she felt her glide near the edge of release, Ryan shifted her weight so that they were face to face. Jamie struggled to stay with her, and as they gazed deeply into each other's eyes, Ryan whispered her most tender feelings of love and eternal devotion. A blissful smile graced Jamie's beautiful face as she shuddered a few times, unable to hold her eyes open any longer. Her soft cries were captured by Ryan's warm mouth, and they clung to each other as the waves of sensation and emotion washed over them both. Several moments passed as their intertwined bodies twitched slowly and then relaxed completely.

Ryan wasn't sure how much time had passed when the sound of the front door closing woke her. A quick glance at the clock showed that it was twelve-thirty, but she had no idea when they had fallen asleep. She pulled Jamie close to her body and drew the sheet over them both. Jamie stirred briefly, and tried to voice a complaint about not reciprocating, but Ryan silenced her almost comical mumblings with a gentle kiss. She reached out and turned off the light, then began to hum the tune of an old lullaby as she lightly stroked her lover's bare back. Within seconds, Jamie's breathing had settled into a familiar rhythm. Ryan lay awake for a few minutes, saying her nightly prayers. She bent her head occasionally to lightly kiss the smooth skin on Jamie's forehead and cheeks. "Go gcoinne Dia thú," she whispered as she closed her eyes, reciting the simple prayer that her mother had said to tuck her into bed at night. *May God keep you.*

Chapter Two

"**G**od, I love waking up in your arms," Jamie murmured as she stirred from her very restful sleep. "I had no idea that it could feel so wonderful to sleep so close to someone."

The smaller woman was lying on her side, with Ryan's dark head resting against her back. She could tell by the breathing pattern that her partner was awake, and the blinking eyelashes that tickled her skin confirmed her guess. "Mmm," the deep voice vibrated against her skin, sending tingles down her spine. "I've never felt so peaceful. I could stay here all day."

Just then Duffy came bounding into the room, landing on the bed with glee, and began to lick every bit of unprotected skin he could get his tongue on. "Boy, do you ever take after your mommy!" Jamie cried as she fought in vain to defend herself.

"I can't believe we forgot to close the door!" Ryan was howling as the determined dog dove for her neck, licking her so furiously that she was nearly faint with laughter.

Jamie took advantage of her vulnerability and yanked back the sheet so that Duffy could have his choice of real estate. The frantic dog was content to remain feasting upon Ryan's neck and ears, but Jamie had to point out one oddity. Ryan had wrestled the big dog into a headlock, and he calmed down immediately when she began to scratch his belly.

"Ryan," Jamie said, a teasing note in her voice.

"Yes, love?"

"Do you know that your nipples get hard when Duffy licks your neck?" Jamie's face was the epitome of innocence.

Ryan blushed three shades of pink as she admitted the truth. "Works every time," she laughed, a little self-consciously.

"And I thought I was special," Jamie huffed in mock outrage.

"Nope." Ryan laced her hands behind her head and said, "Women, dogs, makes no difference. A warm tongue in my ear and I'm yours."

The pillow that slammed into her face didn't catch her by surprise, since her reflexes were extraordinary, but the velocity did give her pause. "Nice one," she said admiringly, squeezing Jamie's bicep. "We're gonna make an O'Flaherty out of you yet!"

"The requirements for that are what?" she laughed. "Having an ability to hurt one another physically?"

Ryan considered that thought for a moment. "Hmm ... it's not a requirement, but it sure doesn't hurt your chances."

"Living here with you ruffians is gonna be a real learning experience for me," Jamie said with just a hint of worry in her voice.

"You'll fit right in," Ryan assured her. "We're not such a bad bunch when you get to know us." She wrestled Duffy aside and wrapped her partner in a firm embrace. "You're not worried, are you?"

Jamie shook her head briskly. "It's not worry ... but I feel a little odd going upstairs when I'm sure they know what we were doing last night."

"Ewww!" Ryan winced when the truth of that statement hit her. "I see your point. You're the first outsider to have an orgasm in this house since ... ever!"

Jamie drew a pillow over her face and mumbled, "Now I feel better."

"Hey ... it'll be fine. Remember, I'm in this with you. They only know you as a woman, but Da still thinks of me as his baby, and the boys aren't used to seeing me be affectionate with women, either. This is gonna be an adjustment for all of us, but it'll be fine. I promise you." Ryan's quiet confidence was deeply reassuring, and Jamie felt herself begin to loosen up.

"I guess it'll be as weird for you, won't it?" She tried to suppress it, but a giggle started to work its way out of her and before long she was laughing out loud. "I just have this image of Conor and Brendan and Rory and your father sitting at the kitchen table trying to ignore the moans and groans coming from the sweet little baby girl's bedroom." Jamie was fairly gasping for breath as this scene played out in front of her.

Ryan found it funny too, but since it was at her expense, slightly less so than Jamie did. "I guess we'd better get upstairs and see if your fantasy has become a reality."

That stopped Jamie short, and she looked over at her partner with wide eyes.

"Not so funny now, is it, sport?"

The blonde head shook slowly as the covers were drawn over her head. "I'm staying! You go up and let me know when everybody's left for the day."

"Hey, don't you want to go to Gay Pride?" Ryan stood and started to pick up her clothes.

The sheet was tossed aside as Jamie caught her partner's gaze. "Go, as in 'sit on the sidelines and watch,' or go, as in 'jump on that Harley and be on the front page of the Chronicle' kinda go?"

"Ooh." Ryan sat on the edge of the bed. "Does that worry you?"

Jamie took a minute to assess her feelings. "I'd love to go, baby. It was so much fun to do that last night, and today will be even bigger. But I'm worried about being with the motorcycle group. I know we probably won't be on the news, but I'm still worried about it."

"I can understand that," Ryan said. "They always make sure they have a few photos of the women on bikes, and to be honest, they try to find the toughest-looking ones and the cutest ones. And you, my sweet, are definitely the cutest one in the whole city, so you might be front page news."

"Thanks," Jamie said, both for the compliment and for understanding her fears.

"Running into Melissa freaked you out, didn't it?" Ryan's tone was gentle and understanding.

"Yeah, I guess it did. It was just weird having somebody from my high school see me like that." Her lips were pursed as she tried to explain the issue, but her attention was diverted when she recalled a major detail. "Hey, you never said how *you* know her."

Ryan laughed, glad that she had an innocent explanation. "She went to USF with me. She was a cheerleader and used to cheer at the basketball games."

"Ohh! That's so funny, Ryan. Did you know she was gay?"

"Nope. We didn't really talk much. I just knew her name because we were in a class together. In hindsight, I'm glad I didn't know she was gay." She wiped her brow in mock relief. "She's awfully cute, ya know!"

Jamie gave her a playful slug in the gut, as usual causing no pain at all.

"Did *you* know she was gay?" Ryan asked, quite certain that Jamie had never mentioned knowing any lesbians from her social circle.

Jamie really wanted to tell Ryan about Mia's sexual encounters with the homecoming queen/cheerleader. But she admired Ryan's policy about not revealing everything she knew, and she'd decided to try to emulate it. Besides, even though Mia hadn't asked her not to tell, she thought it likely that she wouldn't want Jamie to talk about her dalliances, even with Ryan. "Uhm … I didn't know a thing in high school. She and Mia were good buddies because their boyfriends were pals, but I didn't know her well. I did hear some rumors about her having a fling with another girl, but I certainly didn't know she was a card-carrying lesbian."

"Yeah, it looked like old Andi was punching her card regularly," Ryan joked.

"It was nice to see that she's found someone. But it did freak me out to have even a lesbian see me there. I really don't want to be in the newspaper, Ryan." She looked up at her partner, trying to think of alternatives. "I do want to go, though. Would it bother you to just watch?"

"Hard to say," Ryan mused. "I've never just watched the parade." She pondered the question for a moment and decided, "I think it'd be hard for me to sit for that long, to tell you the truth. We'd have to be there by nine or so to get a good spot, and the parade will last until at least two."

"Hmm." Jamie didn't want to disappoint her partner, but she really felt nervous about the motorcycle group. "I wouldn't mind being in the parade if we were with a less visible group."

Ryan's eyes lit up at this suggestion. "Really? No problem, babe. Pick the group you feel comfortable with and we'll do it!"

"What?" Jamie was shaking her head in surprise. "How do we do that?"

"I was invited to join at least ten different groups this year. You decide which one you want, and we'll do it!"

Jamie continued to shake her head as she regarded her industrious partner. "You always have a backup plan, don'cha?"

Jamie was in the middle of picking up her scattered clothing from the night before when she asked, "How did you know what size to buy me? These clothes fit perfectly."

"Thank you," Ryan said. "That's a hard-earned skill." She was waggling an eyebrow as Jamie tossed one of the heavy boots at her.

"Come on, tell me how you do that."

"Okay," Ryan acquiesced. "I went to the store and found a helpful sales clerk. I showed her what size you were, and we found pants to fit."

"You 'showed' her what size I am?" Green eyes twinkled with mirth as Jamie tried to guess how that particular verb was appropriate.

"Yep."

Ryan looked completely pleased with herself, and Jamie had to know the details. "Go on ..."

Standing next to her partner, Ryan closed her eyes. She took her hands and held them at about waist level on Jamie, and moved them apart until she was satisfied. "Okay, grab those pants, zip them up, and hold them up to my hands."

Furrowing her brow in question, Jamie did so. To her amazement, the pants, when tugged into shape, extended just to each of Ryan's hands. Even with her eyes closed, Ryan knew she had done it again, and her smile indicated her pride.

"That is truly remarkable," Jamie marveled.

"I can do it with your bra, too, but that'd be more embarrassing than even I could tolerate!"

The first hints of breakfast were starting to waft down the stairs, and Ryan grinned widely when she noticed them. "Ooh, Da's home," she said with considerable glee. "Even better—he's making breakfast. Let's get some breakfast and get going."

"Aren't we going to shower first?" Jamie asked, since that was their habit.

"I told you we were on our good behavior before," she teased. "You're in for a rude awakening."

Ryan rummaged through her drawers to find some cotton knit pajama bottoms and a matching long-sleeved knit shirt. "Do you have any pajamas?"

"No, I didn't think I'd need any in Pebble Beach ... and I was right," she reminded her. "I'll just grab my sweats." Ryan was waiting to go, but Jamie hated to be rushed so she urged her to go ahead. "You run on up. I want to make a phone call first, okay?"

"Okay, but you'd better hurry. I'm particularly hungry, and I think Conor is up, too. Food disappears fast when we're together."

"I've noticed," Jamie observed dryly, giving her partner a pat on the butt as a send-off.

Ryan dashed up the stairs, pleased to find Martin, Brendan, and Conor enjoying a big breakfast. "Brendan!" she said with pleasure as she threw her arms around his neck and gave him a kiss on the cheek. "I had no idea you were here. When did you come over?"

"Just a few minutes ago," he said. "I thought I could snag a decent breakfast before church."

"When are you going?" she asked as she moved about the table, kissing Conor and her father.

He looked at his watch and replied, "I could make eight o'clock. But I think I'll stay and chat with you both and then go to nine-thirty."

"Cool. We have to get going soon, but we can spare a little time to chat."

"And just where would you two be off to so early? I assume you're not going to give thanks to God?" Martin asked, a teasing grin belying his gruffness.

"I give thanks to God every morning," Ryan replied honestly. "But my God makes house calls." She was already leaning over her father to kiss his cheek, and was unprepared for the sharp swat to her butt. "Yow!" she cried, rubbing the stinging flesh as she shot an outraged look his way.

"I'll have no such sacrilegious talk in my house on the Lord's day," he scowled, and Ryan realized that he was only partially kidding. "You're not too old for me to take you over my knee, Siobhán."

Ryan gave him another kiss and took her place at the table. "No, but it's a little late to start now, Da. If you were going to beat us, you should have started when we were easier to control."

He laughed at her guileless expression and said, "Luckily, I have an ally in keeping you in line now. Where's my daughter-in-law, anyway?"

"Yeah, we wanted to harass you both at the same time," Conor chortled, drawing a blush from his sister.

"Give her a break, Conor," Brendan chided, unable to hide a grin.

"It's not every day we get a new victim," Conor said logically. "It's pretty sweet, really. We get to torture Ryan about sex, and we get Jamie thrown in to boot!"

Just then a pale blonde head poked into the dining room and popped back out just as quickly. Ryan spotted the movement and called out in a soothing tone, "Come on in, honey, I'll thump 'em if they give you too hard a time."

"Hey!" Brendan cried. "I'm on your side, sis!" He looked over to see Jamie once again peek into the room. "There's my favorite sister-in-law," he beamed. "Come over here and give me a hug."

She broke into a big smile and came up to the table as he stood and wrapped his arms around her. "I'm really happy for you both," he said.

Martin hopped up and offered a similarly warm embrace. "You're the first addition to our family in almost twenty-four years, Jamie," he murmured, holding her close. "I guess it's true that good things come to those who wait."

She struggled to hold back the tears as the powerful arms released her. Brendan tried to lighten the mood by teasing. "Conor and Rory are really gonna have to work to come up with a better sister-in-law than you, Jamie."

Conor held up his hands in surrender. "We both concede," he said. "Ryan wins, hands down."

Jamie was blushing deeply as she remarked, "I think I'm the lucky one. I told Ryan just last night that if she ever dumped me, I'd make a play for one of you."

Ryan got up and slid her arm around her partner's shoulder as she said, "Don't get your hopes up, boys. We're in this for the long haul."

Martin smiled at the two of them, a lump forming in his throat as he witnessed their obvious joy. "Sit down and have some breakfast before it gets cold, you two. Now where did you say you were off to, Siobhán?" By the time he finished his question he was already bustling around noisily, getting breakfast ready for the female members of the family.

"I didn't say," she replied, raising her voice just enough for her father to hear her in the kitchen. "You started beating me before I could get a word in."

At Jamie's shocked look, Martin shouted back, "Don't listen to a word she says, Jamie. It's the devil in her talking this morning."

"I'm just now becoming familiar with that little devil," Jamie called back, leaning over to place a gentle kiss on the devilish cheek. "To answer your question, Martin, this little devil is taking me to my first gay pride parade."

"Oh, is she now?" he laughed, exiting the kitchen with platters full of steaming hot food balanced along his arms.

"Are you sure you're up for that, Jamie?" Conor asked. "She used to run with a pretty wild crowd, you know."

"Like you would know," Ryan scoffed, quite certain that Conor's opinion was based more on fancy than fact.

"I've learned an awful lot about Ryan's past over the last couple of weeks," Jamie laughed. "I don't think she can shock me much at this point."

Ryan just grinned at her, sharing a wink with her mischievous brother, whose fantasies were actually close to the truth.

"So are you ready to lead the parade?" Conor asked. "If you don't have an outfit picked out, I'd recommend the recent trend of a tiny little X made of electrical tape that you put over your nip–" The rest of his wish was cut off by his father's large hand clamping over his mouth.

"I'll not have you two harassing poor Jamie in this house," he decreed.

"Two?" Brendan cried. "Don't paint me with that brush, Da!"

"Fair warning to the lot of you. Jamie's not used to that kind of talk, and I'll not have it!"

"It's okay, Martin," she assured him, feeling much more comfortable now that the boys were teasing her like a member of the family. "I can take whatever Ryan dishes out; I'm sure I can handle anything Conor might throw at me."

Conor's bright blue eyes lit up at this opening, but before a single syllable could form on his lips his father's hand was once again covering his mouth. "Dishes!" he ordered. "Now!"

While Conor went to serve his punishment, Jamie looked at the remaining men and said, "We can't thank you all enough for the wonderful presents you left for us last night. It really made it special to come home to."

"We relied on Maeve's expert guidance to help us put that together," Martin admitted. "How did we do?"

"Everything looks great," Ryan said, carefully avoiding the question. Conor was carrying dishes into the kitchen, and he shot her a smirk, picking up on her evasion. "We haven't tried everything yet, but we'll give you a full report when we do."

Ryan tore into breakfast like she hadn't eaten in a week. She cleaned every morsel of food from every platter, shifting her eyes from plate to plate to ascertain that no one had left a spare bite. The boys stared at her in shocked silence, but Martin just got up and went into the kitchen. They heard the pans rattling around as he called out, "How many and how do you want them?"

"Three. Sunny side up," Ryan replied with a grin. "Do we have any bagels?"

"Rye or poppy-seed?"

"Both," she said decisively, to the continued stare of her brother. "I'm hungry," she said rather defensively as she shrugged her shoulders.

"Being in love sure hasn't hurt your appetite," Brendan marveled.

"Don't tease your sister," Martin's voice boomed from the kitchen. "Jamie's just got some weight back on her, I'm pleased to see. But you still need to add a few more pounds, darlin'."

"This morning ought to take care of at least five pounds," Conor joked as he reentered the dining room. Before he sat, he leaned down and whispered into Ryan's ear, "You didn't have a bite of food last night, did you?"

Her deep blush was her only answer.

When they returned to their room, Jamie looked at the list Ryan had made and chose the group that held the most meaning in her heart. Ryan looked over her shoulder and nodded, having had a very good idea of her choice. "Our buddies won't recognize us on our mountain bikes," Ryan laughed softly, thinking of how easy it had been on the AIDS Ride to spot Jamie on her bright orange bike.

"I had no idea that a group from the AIDS Ride participated in the Gay Pride March," Jamie said, now getting very excited about the day.

"Yep. And if the logistics work out, we'll have time to join another group or two if you want. We might as well indoctrinate you fully!"

Their racing bikes were somewhere between L.A. and San Francisco, sent via bus after the ride. Luckily, both mountain bikes were at Ryan's, and since those were better for riding on city streets anyway, everything was working out well.

An hour later they were gliding down a steep hill, rolling onto Market Street in the light early morning traffic. Jamie had never gotten used to riding in the city, so Ryan stayed behind to give her a small illusion of safety. The morning was cool, but amazingly clear, with not a wisp of the usual morning fog.

They both wore their purple, long-sleeved AIDS Ride shirts and black bike shorts, and Jamie added a light jacket against the morning chill.

They were about three blocks from 1ˢᵗ Street when they started to hear the first sounds of activity. It was a faint thrumming that grew and grew as they drew closer. Jamie turned to give her partner a startled look as the noise level evened out at a dull roar. Turning a corner, they were hit with a burst of color and noise that almost caused the smaller woman to fall off her bike.

Stretched out in front of them, as far as the eye could see, were floats and bands and classic cars, and groups of people on horseback, motorcycles, bicycles, and of course, on foot. At first, it looked like complete chaos, but after a moment of staring in open-mouthed amazement, Jamie began to see order within the chaotic jumble.

When she looked closely, each group was standing or sitting by a large poster board sign that identified them by name and number. Some groups wore T-shirts that further identified them; as she took it all in, she felt a comforting hand on her back. "Overwhelmed?" a soft voice asked.

"I've seen pictures in the paper, but … I had no idea," Jamie murmured slowly.

Ryan chuckled a little at the look on her partner's face. "This is just the early call. Our group is the second one out, so we have to be here early. New groups will be arriving every half hour or so until this street is filled and cleared at least six times."

Jamie turned slowly and tried to express herself clearly. "Are these all *our* gay people?" she asked, rather inelegantly.

Ryan cocked her head slightly, trying to discern the meaning of the question. "Our gay people?" she repeated slowly, then realization dawned. "Oh! I get it! You mean are these all locals?"

"Yeah. It seems like an awful lot of people to just be from San Francisco. I mean, people joke that everyone here is gay, but given this crowd …" she trailed off, having already stated the obvious.

"People are mostly from the Bay Area, but that's a pretty big area, as you know. Beside locals, though, there are lots and lots of visiting groups, mostly from Northern California, but there are some people from around the country, and even from other countries."

"Wow," she muttered, leaning against Ryan as well as she could given her position, still atop her bike. "That's still a lot of people." After staring for another moment she asked, "Do other cities have this?"

"Yeah," Ryan said. "Lots of cities around the world have pride events. Ours and New York's are the biggest, though."

"That's nice," the smaller woman said decisively. "We shouldn't get to have all the fun."

Well, well, well, Ryan mused as they walked their bikes the rest of the way to better observe the crowd. *It seems like my little neophyte is acclimating pretty darned well.*

At ten-thirty on the dot, the motorcycles started to rev their engines, as they waited impatiently at Market and Beale. The traditional leaders of the parade, the group now formally known as the Women's Motorcycle Contingent but constantly referred to as "Dykes on Bikes," were given the signal and they roared away, two by two. Ryan felt a small stab of longing, having ridden with her buddies since she was eighteen. But the fleeting wish in no way dampened her deep satisfaction at being able to share the parade with her partner.

She had often taken a date to the parade, and had once gone with Ally, but she'd never shared the event with anyone who really mattered to her. While they waited to get the signal, she decided that being a part of the parade with Jamie made all the difference in the world. She was now able to view the event through her partner's novice eyes, and she found that it was a deeply satisfying experience.

For the past hour and a half, Jamie had been a veritable whirlwind of questions, exclamations, and exhortations. They walked around investigating every little cache of people, and Ryan proudly introduced her partner to everyone that she had even a passing acquaintance with.

Now, as they awaited their send-off, Jamie turned to her with a luminous smile and said, "Thanks so much for making this safe for me. I'm so glad I didn't chicken out."

"You're up!" the coordinator shouted before Ryan could say a word, and their group started to roll. Rounding the corner onto Market, the thunderous applause that greeted them brought tears to the eyes of most of the riders, who were spread across the street, six abreast.

When they met up with their group, Jamie was amazed to see so many familiar faces from the just-finished AIDS Ride. They walked through their pack just before they took off, so that Jamie could count everyone. She lost count at 105, and Ryan was unwilling to start over, so she satisfied herself with the knowledge that more than one hundred of her peers had come out to join in the festivities.

Much to their surprise, Karen Joncas had come over from Sacramento, and they were able to spend a few minutes giving her a honeymoon update.

"I don't really need to ask how it went," she laughed when she took in the beaming duo. "If you two looked any happier you'd be illegal!"

Giving Jamie a healthy squeeze, Ryan agreed. "This should be a controlled substance. In the wrong hands this could be lethal!"

"I'm just glad that it's in your capable hands, O," she said with genuine affection, as she ruffled Ryan's hair. "It couldn't happen to a better person."

As they rolled down the wide street, Jamie considered how grateful she was that they didn't have their road bikes. Those temperamental lightweight frames not only didn't fare well over potholes, they also responded much too quickly to steering corrections. Since she felt absolutely compelled to wave to nearly every person on the route, she knew she would have been eating pavement if she hadn't been astride the more forgiving mount.

Looking over at her partner, Jamie was once again struck by Ryan's simple beauty. Right before they took off, Ryan removed her helmet and clipped it to her handlebars, pulling out a traditional, cotton racing hat, this one a bright yellow. The hat bore a black Campagnolo logo, which surprised Jamie, since Ryan hated to use her body to provide free advertising. But her musing stopped when Ryan settled the cap on her head, backwards, of course. *Does she just look fantastic in every hat in the world, or does she only wear the ones that show off her gorgeous face?* This question had flitted through her mind on many occasions, and she considered it for a moment. As well as she knew her lover, she didn't have a feel for how conscious Ryan was of her looks. Even after all of the time they'd spent together, she had never seen Ryan try to look attractive, but she always managed to.

Today's millinery choice was a perfect example. Jamie had seen dozens of people sporting the tiny style of cap that Ryan now wore, but most looked totally silly, at best. However, something about Ryan's strong face and square jaw allowed the hat to accentuate her bone structure, and Jamie was very glad that she had chosen to wear it. *Although I can't for the life of me see what the point is of wearing a tiny hat like that backwards*, she laughed to herself. Nonetheless, Ryan looked fantastic, and Jamie decided that she didn't much care whether or not Ryan secretly fussed over her appearance. The effect was fabulous, no matter the motivation.

They didn't have the opportunity to speak much since they were about twenty feet away from each other. Even if they'd been riding tandem, Jamie doubted they would have been able to hear each other, since the crowd was so incredibly vocal. Time after time she had to swallow a lump in her throat from the outpouring of emotion from the massive crowd. It seemed as though every single person on the route was familiar with the AIDS Ride, given the thunderously enthusiastic reception they received.

After a few blocks, Jamie decided that the only way she would be able to focus well enough to finish the route was if she avoided looking at her partner. Every time she cast a glance at the childlike, exuberant face she nearly wept, and she was afraid of hitting a pothole or another rider if she couldn't focus properly. She couldn't, however, avoid one last look at the terribly appealing woman.

Ryan had many "looks," and Jamie loved every one of them. She had the ability to express more with a twitch of an eyebrow or a hint of a grin than most people could convey with a prepared speech. Jamie considered that, of all Ryan's looks, the one she wore at the moment was perhaps the most fetching of all.

A smile wide enough to expose her molars graced her lovely face, and her eyes flashed with glee. She was sitting tall in her saddle, holding on with only her right hand, while her left waved enthusiastically at the crowd. Her bright blue eyes zeroed in on one member of the crowd after another, making each lucky recipient feel that her smile was for them alone. Jamie's smile grew wider as she observed that Ryan seemed to reserve her most enthusiastic waves for the small children that she effortlessly picked out of the massive crowd. She held their gaze until the child matched the intensity of her own smile, often gifting them with a wink or a blown kiss.

I have got to stop looking at her! Jamie shouted to herself as she narrowly avoided striking a parade volunteer. Her internal warnings went unheeded, however, and after another near miss she crossed the street as soon as there was an opportunity, and slid into the empty space in front of her partner. She tossed a wave over her shoulder at what she knew was a puzzled look, and got down to the business of focusing on the crowd, rather than the devastatingly charming woman who rode right behind her.

The parade route was long, covering quite a bit of Market Street, and Jamie expected it'd take a long time to complete. To her surprise, they reached the end rather quickly. Parade volunteers indicated a place for the riders to park their bikes, but they had other plans and quickly turned away from the pack. It took a few blocks to be far enough removed to hear each other speak, but soon Jamie was chattering away nonstop.

Ryan beamed over at her, pleased that her partner had enjoyed her first parade so much. Nearing Beale again, they securely locked their bikes to a couple of street signs, threading their helmets through the Kryptonite locks at the same time. Ryan pulled two pairs of khaki shorts from her backpack and they each slipped a pair over their bike pants. Baseball caps were added next, Jamie's worn in the traditional manner, Ryan's not. After tinkering with their look in the window of an office building, they headed back to the holding area for the next groups.

It didn't take long to find the one they were looking for, but Ryan nearly fainted from surprise when she spotted a most unexpected participant. "DA!" she cried from a good fifty feet away. Bobbing and weaving through the crowd, she threw her arms around her father, nearly crushing the sturdily built man with her embrace. "I never expected you to come!"

Jamie came running up a moment later, pleased beyond measure to find Martin locked in his daughter's robust embrace. "Maeve," she chided, "you didn't let the cat out of the bag when we called you this morning!"

Ryan's aunt laughed gently, rubbing her niece's back. "I didn't know he wanted to come until after I spoke with you, Jamie, or I might have. I'm no good at all at keeping a secret."

Ryan sniffed away her tears and reluctantly released her father, stepping back just enough to grasp her aunt in a gentler, but no less fervid hug. Martin kept one hand on her back while he stretched to offer his other arm to Jamie. "When Siobhán said you were coming to your first parade, I decided it was about time I made an appearance myself. I called my helpful sister-in-law and made arrangements to join her and here we are."

"This means so much to me, Da," Ryan murmured as she grabbed her father once more.

"I would have been here before, but you were always riding that infernal motorbike," he reminded her. "This was the first time we had the opportunity to join you."

"I can't thank you both enough for being here with us," Jamie said, grasping Maeve for a hug. "It really makes me feel like part of the family."

"You are part of the family, Jamie," the older woman assured her.

Jamie was struggling with her own emotions when she heard Ryan moan, "Oh no! Not you, too!"

Brendan came loping up to the small gathering, flashing the patented O'Flaherty grin. "We had a hell of a time finding a place to park," he began, but did a double take when he saw he was alone. "I can't believe I lost him again!" he groaned, standing on his tiptoes to look around.

"Conor's here too?" Ryan asked, amazed that her brothers would make the effort to join them.

"Of course," Brendan said, as though this were their normal habit. "But he's carrying a distraction with him that keeps delaying him."

Seconds later, a smiling Conor popped out of the crowd, carrying a giggling Caitlin on his shoulders. "Just my luck," he groused. "Every woman at this darned thing runs over to see the baby—and every one of them is a lesbian! I can't catch a break!"

Ryan nearly knocked the breath out of him with the hug she enveloped him in. "You are the best brothers in the world," she whispered fiercely.

"We would have come before, but you were …"

"Always on the motorcycle," she finished for him.

"Plus, we had to bring Caitlin to her first parade." Ryan reached up and snatched the giggling baby, holding her in front of her body to carefully observe her. The youngest member of the clan wore a pink T-shirt emblazoned "Baby Woman," recently purchased for her by her beaming cousin.

"Got your new shirt on, don'cha baby?" Ryan cooed to the adorable tot.

Making like she understood the thread of the conversation, Caitlin giggled and slapped at Ryan's face, making both participants laugh together.

Maeve went to talk with one of the leaders of the group and came back with T-shirts for the boys. "I think you two might want to wear these." She chuckled as she held them up for inspection. One read, "My sister's gay and that's okay," while the other proclaimed, "Straight, but not narrow."

Conor immediately grabbed the latter, insisting, "I've been cruised more times than I can count, just walking over here. I want to make things perfectly clear!"

Ryan laughed at his antics, knowing that her brother's popularity wouldn't be dimmed one bit by his proclamation that he was straight. In fact, some of her closest male friends were attracted exclusively to straight men. *You can run, but you can't hide*, she silently smirked.

A few minutes after noon, they were given the signal to take off, marching together as a family under the banner "Parents and Friends of Lesbians and Gays."

The ovation they had received on their bikes paled in comparison to the reception they now received. PFLAG was one of the most beloved groups in the entire community, and the enthusiasm of the crowd certainly supported that claim. Maeve had been a member since the year Michael disclosed that he was gay, and she remained very active in the local chapter even now, eleven years after his death. She often told Ryan that the group was the major factor in getting her through the pain of his illness and death, since so many other mothers in the group were struggling with the same issue. Martin had never joined, mainly since he didn't struggle much with the news of his daughter's lesbianism. But seeing the impact the group had on the assembled crowd, he began to rethink his decision. Leaning over to his sister-in-law he commented, "I think I just might have to join you at your next meeting, Mrs. Driscoll."

Startled by this declaration, she smiled up at him and said, "It would be my pleasure, Mr. O'Flaherty."

The parade route seemed significantly longer on foot than it had on the bikes, and by the time they reached the Civic Center they were all exhausted, except for the youngest member of the crowd. Caitlin had ridden on every pair of shoulders except for Maeve's, so she was as fresh as a daisy.

The boys both had things to do, so they were anxious to get going. They agreed to take the bikes home in the truck so that Ryan and Jamie could just hop on Muni for the ride home.

Logistics settled, the five remaining participants sat down in the shade of the trees that lined the long promenade in front of City Hall. The main stage was in full gear, with an energetic salsa band beating out a fierce rhythm. Ryan took off to buy Italian ices for everyone, and when she returned, she chuckled at the extemporaneous entertainment that Caitlin was providing.

The tiny tot was dancing to the music, swaying her little hips as well as could be expected for a ten-month-old. Jamie was holding one chubby hand to provide stability, while the baby kept remarkably good time to the beat. As Ryan sank to the ground next to her, Martin related, "I was just telling Jamie about your dancing career."

She covered her face with her hands, shaking her head in embarrassment. "Can a woman have no secrets around here?"

"Of course not, dear," Maeve joined in. "How can we embarrass you if we don't dig into the archives?"

"Let me get this straight," Jamie chortled, trying to keep a straight face. "You … Ryan O'Flaherty … wanted to be a cheerleader for the '49ers?"

"Umm … I liked football?" Ryan was blushing furiously, and Jamie couldn't help but prolong her agony.

"Then why didn't you decide to break the sexual barrier and *play* for the team?" Green eyes blinked ingenuously.

"Fine," Ryan huffed, giving up on the pretext. "I liked the girls! I liked football, but I loved the girls in those tight outfits!"

"Siobhán!" her father cried. "You were no more than four years old!"

She shrugged her broad shoulders and gave him a helpless smile. "I was a prodigy!"

As usual, Jamie was carrying her cell phone, and when Conor got near the Civic Center, he called her to announce his whereabouts. After a bout of hugs and kisses, Martin, Maeve, and Caitlin headed on home, leaving Jamie and Ryan to enjoy the rest of the festival.

They wandered around the various booths, with Jamie doing a little shopping, as usual. Approaching the "Good Vibrations" table, Ryan called out greetings to her friends who were working the booth. "Still going strong, huh, O?" one of the women grinned.

"Permanently partnered," Ryan beamed back at her. "No more dates in the try-on room."

"Hey," Jamie nudged her with a hip. "You can still take me there!"

"Excellent point, as usual, love." Ryan shot her a grin so high-powered that her friend couldn't help but join in.

"You are so whipped, O'Flaherty."

"And I've never been happier," Ryan replied absently, her attention focused on the sparkling green eyes that looked up at her with total devotion.

"I think his booth should be right around here, somewhere ..." Jamie scanned the area until she focused on the banner that heralded "The Episcopal Archdiocese of San Francisco Welcomes You." "Poppa!" she cried when she made eye contact with the senior member of the Evans family.

Ryan was pulled along forcibly as Jamie dashed the last twenty-five feet to greet her grandfather. "Jamie, Ryan," he murmured, wrapping each woman in a hug. "It's so good to see you both looking so healthy and happy!"

"Happy?" his gleeful granddaughter cried. "Happy? I'd have to be severely depressed to only be happy. I've never been happier, Poppa," she insisted, shaking her head at her inability to convey the depth of her joy.

"That's obvious, sweetheart," he said, clutching her to his chest. "You both look completely blissful." Holding her at arm's length, he offered an apology. "I'm sorry I wasn't able to walk with you in the parade, girls. Even though I'm on my sabbatical, I needed to conduct the services today. My associate priests are far younger than I am, and they both wanted to march with our gay and lesbian group, so I filled in for them. But next year, I hope you'll join our group. We could use a vibrant pair like you two."

"We might just do that," Jamie said, looking to Ryan for approval.

"It's a date," Ryan said. "It'll be nice to have an organized religion welcome us with open arms."

"Oh ... we have our struggles with the issue in both the national and the international church," Rev. Evans said. "But the archdiocese is very supportive, and my congregation has been extraordinarily foresighted in its outreach to gay men and lesbians."

"Thanks to you," Jamie said, smiling.

"No, no, that's not true at all," he insisted. "I'll gladly take credit where it's due, but the members of my congregation are light-years ahead of me on many social issues. I just try to keep up."

"It's so nice to have your support," Ryan insisted. "It's meant an awful lot to both Jamie and me."

"You'll always have it," he replied confidently, grasping Ryan's shoulder and giving it a gentle squeeze. "I'll help you both in any way possible."

"Maybe it's just the day and the freedom I feel, but I think I'm going to tell my parents soon, Poppa," Jamie said.

"You are?" Ryan blinked in surprise.

"Yeah … I don't see any point in waiting. You're my life, and they need to either accept that, or get out of the way and let us start our lives together. I think they need to know."

Ryan continued to blink at her, unsure of what her response should be. Rev. Evans patted Jamie on the back and offered, "Let's get together and strategize before you do that. I can offer you some tips that you might not have thought of."

"Okay, Poppa," she agreed immediately. "I'm not quite ready, and I haven't really discussed it at any length in therapy, but I want to do it soon. Let's get together for dinner. Is Friday okay?"

"Yes, I can make Friday," he said. "Is that good for you, Ryan?"

"Sure. My schedule is all about Jamie," she said, grinning.

"Excellent. Call me later in the week and we'll decide on the details, okay, honey?"

"Will do, Poppa," she agreed, giving him another hug. "We'll see you then."

Walking away from the booth, Ryan asked, "Do you happen to have a feather on you?"

"A feather? Ahh, why would I need a feather?"

"I just wanted to see if you could, in fact, knock me over with one," Ryan mused, giving the question serious consideration.

"Does it really surprise you that I want to tell my parents?" Jamie stopped and tugged Ryan to a halt beside her. "I guess I should have asked you first, but it didn't dawn on me."

"No, no," Ryan soothed, fluffing the golden bangs that framed Jamie's face. "I don't want you to ask me for permission to do what you need to do. It just took me by surprise, that's all."

"Do you think it's a bad idea?"

The taller woman took a deep breath, letting it out slowly as she considered the issue. "No, I don't think it's a bad idea. I guess I'm afraid that it's going to be stressful, though. A large part of me wants to maintain this euphoria that we're in for as long as possible." She had such a wistful, lovesick expression on her face that Jamie just had to kiss her tempting lips. They stood in a tender embrace for a long while, oblivious to every person that passed.

"I didn't think of it like that," Jamie murmured as they broke apart. "It's a good point though. I'll wait until the euphoria dies down, then I'll tell them."

"Now, honey," Ryan said, "let's not get carried away. The average life expectancy for a man is only seventy-five. I think we should tell them before that!"

"You are soooo cute!" the smaller woman cooed, holding Ryan's face in such a tight squeeze that her lips went from their normal horizontal orientation to a vertical one.

Jamie placed a few more kisses on the newly oriented lips, deciding that she couldn't get enough of the pink flesh, no matter how it was placed.

By the time late afternoon rolled around, they had seen every booth and said hello to most of the gay and lesbian population of the San Francisco Bay Area. Once again, Jamie was taken aback by the sheer number of people that her partner knew. "It still boggles my mind how you know all of these people and remember their names," she said as they walked toward one of the dance floors.

"Well, I am pretty good with names, and I didn't just meet most of these people once or twice. I worked at the largest gay gym in the whole Bay Area since I was seventeen, and tons of people belong there. I met lots more on the AIDS Rides, and got to know lots more through women that I dated. It all starts to add up."

"Add to that a few thousand women who've known you in the biblical sense, and you get an even better picture," Jamie teased, sneaking her fingers just underneath Ryan's ribs, a lethal spot.

Ryan slung an arm around her partner's shoulders and guided her toward the dance floor. A nice, slow number was playing and as they began to sway to the music, Ryan commented, "You know, I was worried about how you'd be with the women I've 'known' before. You've actually surprised me quite a bit. You seemed jealous of them before we got together, but now you seem fine with it."

"I really was jealous then," Jamie laughed, only slightly embarrassed by her behavior. "It's just that I had all of these feelings for you, and I couldn't express them or even think about them much. I think they came out as irrational jealousy."

"And now?" Ryan's deep voice burred against her ear as the taller woman leaned over and let the tip of her tongue caress the outer edge of her partner's ear.

"Huh?" Several moments had passed, and Jamie sensed it was her turn to talk, but she didn't know about what.

"And you're not jealous now ..." Ryan prompted, taking a swipe at the tempting ear once again.

"Honey," Jamie's voice floated up to Ryan, "if you want to have a conversation, you have to stop that."

"Which would you rather have?" Ryan queried. "This ..." another long swipe of her warm tongue, "or conversation?"

"Umm ... can I get back to you on that?" Jamie's somewhat breathless voice replied. "I'm concentrating on something right now." She craned her neck just enough to allow Ryan full access to her other ear. "Continue," she commanded, while sliding her arms around Ryan's trim waist, holding her close.

Jamie lost track of how many dances they shared, but when they finally stopped they were both sweaty and tired. "You are so cute!" the smaller woman said as they left the dance floor to grab a beer.

"Why am I so cute today?" Ryan grinned in reply.

"You're cute every day, goofy. But it's adorable how you turned down all of those women who wanted to dance with you."

"Hey, I said nothing but the truth," Ryan insisted.

"You told every woman that you'd promised the next dance to your spouse," she teased, recalling that Ryan used the same line every time.

"And that's the truth," Ryan repeated, her blue eyes darkening as she grew serious. She turned to face Jamie, holding her hands up to her lips, where she kissed each one reverently. "Every dance, for the rest of my life, is promised to my beloved spouse."

While they enjoyed a cold beer, they relaxed in the grass to listen to the music from the main stage. It didn't take long for the events of the day to catch up with both of them and in no time they were sound asleep, curled up together like newborn pups.

Their impromptu nap lasted almost an hour, and they were both relatively refreshed when they woke. "Ready to head home?" Ryan asked.

"Yeah." Jamie stretched and yawned for several moments, getting all of the kinks out. "I guess we'd better. It's a long walk from Muni."

"I think I'll page Conor from the station and see if he'll meet us. I'm beat!"

"Thank God for large families," Jamie agreed wholeheartedly. "There's almost always someone at home!"

Conor immediately agreed to fetch them, giving his sister pause. "That's odd," she muttered when she returned to the station platform. "He didn't make me promise to do anything to pay him back. I usually have to at least wash his car for a ride somewhere."

"Maybe he's being particularly nice because it's Gay Pride Day," Jamie suggested.

"Yeah … that sounds like him," Ryan agreed with a good bit of sarcasm in her voice.

The Muni was exceptionally crowded for a Sunday afternoon, but a train arrived after just a short wait on the cool, damp subway platform. The closest stop to the O'Flaherty home was Castro, but Ryan knew it'd be a madhouse in the neighborhood, so she suggested that Conor pick them up at the stop just prior to that. They weren't able to find seats together, so were forced to claim aisle seats, one in front of the other. Jamie was still buzzing from the energy and excitement of the day, and she continually perched on the edge of her seat, leaning close to speak into Ryan's ear.

Ryan was quite a bit calmer than her partner, having experienced the parade and festival many times, but she recalled how she felt the first time she participated in the event, and she happily shared in Jamie's enthusiasm.

Unconsciously, the smaller woman played with Ryan's dark hair, pulling stray locks from the collar of her T-shirt as she kept up her running commentary on the day. Her actions were more nervous habit than sensual, but she couldn't stand even the foot of separation between them, and the gentle caresses helped calm her.

Ryan, as usual, soaked up the touch greedily. Her eyes fluttered closed as her head dropped onto the plastic handrail on her seat back, allowing Jamie greater access.

Even though her partner didn't verbally respond much, Jamie kept up her rambling chat, covering many of the sights and events that had captured her imagination throughout the day. Looking around, the smaller woman commented, "It's so odd to see so many gay people on the train, isn't it?"

"Umm-hmm," Ryan responded lazily, silently hoping for the delightful head scratching to continue. "S'nice."

"I think you're placating me," the masseuse giggled, leaning in just a few inches to place a very gentle kiss onto the crown of Ryan's head. She added a few more scalp scratches, then sat back into her own seat, looking around the crowded car some more. Several same-sex couples were holding hands or snuggling a bit, and a few leather-clad men were striking poses as they held on to the overhead rail. As her eyes trailed past a young mother with a four- or five-year-old girl on her lap, she was shocked to get in return the most hate-filled look she had ever received. Her mouth dropped open and her stomach flipped queasily as she made, and held, eye contact with the young woman. The woman looked to be about her own age, and she gave no clear indication that she was a tourist, but there was something about her that gave the impression that she was not a native of the city. Her style of dress was more conservative than most young San Franciscans, and behind her venomous glare Jamie detected a stark fear of … her. *She's afraid of us!!* Her mind reeled from the combination of blatant hostility and obvious fright that covered the young woman's face, twisting her plain but attractive face into a gruesome mask.

Their gaze only held for a moment before the woman shifted her daughter so that the child faced the window, obviously trying to protect the girl from … whatever it was that was disturbing her so profoundly.

They were nearing their stop, and Ryan snapped out of her haze to struggle to her feet, casually sticking her hand out to grab Jamie's. For the first time in their short union, the blonde felt a flash of embarrassment at accepting the nearly automatic gesture, and she just gave Ryan a quick pat to let her know she was behind her.

The woman had obviously been trying to banish her fear, and she was plainly successful, for as they passed she looked up at Jamie and spoke in a clear voice. "Godless heathen! Repent before you are damned for all eternity!"

The train was coming to a stop as the words left her mouth, but Ryan heard them, and she whirled to face the woman, catching a glimpse of Jamie's wounded look. "What did you say?" she spat out, freezing the woman with one fierce look. Jamie pushed past and grabbed Ryan's upper arm firmly, tugging her toward the door as a few other people struggled to exit.

Ryan flicked her gaze from Jamie to the now-terrified woman several times, softening her features when she saw the pleading look in her lover's eyes. Immediately deciding where her priorities lay, she followed her partner out the door, not bothering to engage in a battle of wits with a narrow-minded homophobe.

Ryan tugged Jamie onto a bench on the cool, acrid-smelling subway platform. "What happened?" she asked gently.

The words came out in a rush. "She was staring at me, because ... because I was touching your h ... h ... hair." The smaller woman shook her head roughly, trying to make sense of the encounter. "I've never, ever had anyone look at me with so much hate in her eyes."

Ryan's heart clutched in her chest at the injured, fragile green eyes that looked up at her. Her eyes fluttered closed with the memory of the first time she had been treated with the same venom, all because she had the temerity to love a woman. "I would do anything," she whispered, her voice sounding strangely loud on the near-silent platform, "anything to spare you from that type of intolerance." Her broad shoulders slumped in defeat as she admitted the truth. "But I can't, Jamie. God, I wish I could, but I can't." Her head dropped onto Jamie's shoulder, and they held each other tenderly for a moment, until they heard footsteps scampering down the stairs. They broke their embrace, neither up to another encounter at the moment. Slowly, they walked to the escalator, standing close enough to brush shoulders, but not holding hands in their usual manner.

Conor was waiting patiently in the truck, and with a conspiratorial glance, the women silently agreed not to mention the incident. Caitlin was still in his care, but she was none too happy to be in her car seat. He was turned around in his seat, running through his normal tricks to calm her, but nothing was working. Jamie hopped into the front as Ryan opened the rear passenger door of the king-cab pickup and climbed in. The crying paused for one blessed moment, but resumed immediately. "What's the problem?" Ryan asked, launching into her usual baby-pacifying repertoire.

"She's cranky and needs a nap," Conor said over the baby's rising cries.

"Why didn't you say so?" Ryan asked. "You didn't have to come pick us up."

"Well ..." he began, his blue eyes betraying an impish look. "I kinda have plans and I thought you could ..."

"Ohh ..." Ryan scoffed, now understanding her brother's willingness to fetch them. "The sooner I get home, the sooner you get to leave."

"Uhm ... something like that," he admitted, flashing his most winning smile at his little sister.

"Can the charm, boyo." Ryan returned his smile and flicked the back of his dark head. "We'll all take a nap together."

"Thanks, girls," Conor replied, adding another grin in Jamie's direction, even though it wasn't required.

Minutes after they entered the house, all three women were stripped down to their T-shirts and underwear, settling down in the king-sized bed for a nap. Ryan knew they needed to have a little discussion about the encounter on the subway, but she thought they would both be more lucid after a nap. Jamie didn't bring the subject up either and, in fact, was barely speaking at all. Ryan climbed into the middle of the bed, with Jamie on her left and Caitlin on her right, tucking a long arm under each blonde head. Her nap-mates immediately cuddled up to her sides, enveloping her with the warm comfort of their tender embraces. *This is what matters*, Ryan mused as her eyelids grew heavy. *This is all that really matters. Having this love is worth any amount of bullshit we have to put up with.*

Chapter Three

The shrill ringing of the phone woke Ryan from a perfectly lovely dream. She reached out blindly and inadvertently woke her tiny blonde companion, who greeted the affront with an equally shrill cry. Jamie also sat bolt upright, and for a brief moment Ryan felt like joining in on Caitlin's plaintive cry. "This is so not how I wanted to wake up," she grumbled, grabbing the offending telephone. "H'lo," her ragged voice croaked.

"Ryan?" The voice on the other end was deep and masculine.

"Oh, hi, Tommy," she said, yawning.

"Is Cait being ornery?" he asked somewhat sheepishly.

"Nah ... we were all asleep and the phone woke her." Ryan smiled up at Jamie, who had scrambled out of the tangle of sheets to pick up the still-squawking baby.

"Jeez, I'm sorry, buddy," Tommy murmured. "I just called because Annie's home, and we wanted to come get the baby so we could have dinner together."

"No prob," she said, tossing her long legs off the bed to stand up. She was unable to resist her compulsion to stretch, and did so from the vertical position, much to Jamie's amusement. She felt short fingernails scratch her back while she stretched, and as she leaned into the contact, she nearly hung up without saying good-bye.

"Ryan?" Tommy's voice held a note of amusement also, and Ryan knew that his hazel eyes were likely dancing impishly. "You okay?"

She forced herself to swallow the pleasured groan that was about to escape, and tried to concentrate. "Fine ... just fine," she drawled. "Jamie's just helping me wake up."

"I'm not gonna have to deprogram Caitlin, am I?"

"Nothing she hasn't seen before," Ryan assured him. "All G-rated." The baby was now calm, and she struggled a bit to go to Ryan. "Talk to Jamie," she said, handing the phone to her partner as she accepted the baby.

"Hi, Tommy," the slightly hesitant voice began.

"Hey, Jamie. Good to have you guys home again. Wanna join us for dinner? I know Martin's working tonight, so your cook is gone."

"Sure," she said immediately, not even bothering to check with Ryan. She was confident that her partner would never turn down the opportunity to spend some time with the Driscolls. "We'll get dressed ... I mean we'll uhm ... put our pants back ... I mean ..." She was blushing furiously, and Tommy rescued her immediately.

"I take Caitlin into the shower with me, Jamie. If that hasn't scared her to death, seeing you two half-dressed won't scar her, either."

"Good point," she mumbled, feeling relieved but still slightly embarrassed. "We'll be over in a few."

"See ya then," he said. "Don't forget your pants."

"This level of openness is gonna take some getting used to," she muttered, dropping the phone in the cradle and flopping onto the bed.

A little after six, the threesome started off for the walk to Caitlin's home. The Driscolls, like the rest of the family, lived in the Noe Valley. Their small rented house was on the edge of the business district running along 24th Street, while the O'Flaherty brothers and Maeve lived in Upper Noe and enjoyed the very hilly terrain of the area nearer to the Castro. Conor had not bothered to bring the baby's stroller, and the car seat was still in the truck, so Ryan placed Caitlin on her shoulders for the six-block walk.

Jamie smiled at the pair as they made their way down the steep pitch of Noe Street. "You look like one of those mules in the Grand Canyon," she said. Ryan was walking carefully, her natural gait greatly slowed—almost ambling with the baby astride her shoulders.

"Brrrrrrhhhhh," the lanky pseudo-donkey replied as she shook her head playfully. Caitlin, of course, loved this sound, and she jumped and slapped at Ryan's head to get her to repeat it. It didn't take long for Ryan to get into the game and begin acting more like a frisky filly than a donkey, and Caitlin couldn't get enough of the fun. They cantered a few dozen yards, then galloped back up the hill, to the delighted laughter of both rider and pony. Jamie urged them on, cheering for them both until the pony was gasping for breath.

"No more," Ryan cried, bending over at the waist to gasp for air. Jamie pulled Caitlin off and settled her on her own shoulders, mentally preparing herself for a more casual hairdo than she usually wore.

When Ryan was rested they took off again, with Caitlin only slightly dissatisfied with her new, slower mount. Ryan slipped her hand around Jamie's, giving it a gentle squeeze, but she felt just the slightest hesitation from her partner. "Wanna talk about it?" Her voice was slow and calm, and Jamie knew that the invitation could be declined without bothering Ryan.

"I suppose." Her voice betrayed her lack of enthusiasm, but Ryan moved forward anyway.

"It's a pretty bad feeling, isn't it?" Empathetic blue eyes met and held Jamie's gaze.

She briefly nodded. "It … caught me by surprise, I guess. That was the first time I've ever felt that kinda hate."

Ryan's brow furrowed at that declaration. "What about that time we went to the Hillsborough Tea Room? You were treated pretty shitty there."

Jamie shook her head as well as she could with Caitlin's chubby fingers threaded through the golden strands. "No, you were treated shitty. I was just an observer."

Ryan considered this for a moment, then the light dawned. "Ohh … you didn't identify with being gay, so you didn't feel like you were being criticized."

"Right. I was outraged by how we were treated—but I was outraged for you. The woman today was talking to me … about me."

"Gotcha," Ryan said, understanding that the difference was critical. "What about Cassie? Didn't you feel judged by her?"

Blonde brows knit together for a moment. "No … not really. I know her pretty well, and she isn't really antigay."

Ryan's mouth gaped at this revelation. "She sure coulda fooled me!"

"No, really. I think she suspected something between us from the beginning, and she was convinced that you were trying to turn me into something I'm not. It was stupid and narrow-minded, but she has gay and lesbian friends, and she treats them well. I think she just hated *you*."

"Oh … well … that's understandable." Ryan was wearing one of her adorably goofy grins, and Jamie couldn't help but give her a pinch.

"No, it's not!" she said. "I never want to see her again, but I still say that she's not really homophobic."

"Okay," Ryan agreed, deciding to let the matter drop, even though she didn't agree with Jamie's assessment. "Today's little episode was from a homophobe, and it was directed at you, and you have every reason to feel hurt by it."

"Yeah …" Jamie was staring at the pavement, walking carefully because of her cargo. "I was hurt. It really got in … do you know what I mean?"

"Yeah, I do," Ryan said. "Sometimes things like that just surprise you so badly that they get past your defenses."

Jamie looked up at her with a completely quizzical expression. "I don't think I have defenses."

"I think you do," Ryan said, looking thoughtful. "I've seen your whole personality change when you're interacting with men."

"Huh?"

"You put a damper on your openness, your friendliness. When you're around guys you don't know, you don't show all of your most adorable qualities."

"Really?" Jamie looked completely stunned.

"Yeah, you do. I thought you did that so guys didn't get the wrong idea and start hitting on you."

"I … I don't think I do that consciously," she said, not refuting that she did tone her personality down when she was in the company of available men.

"I don't put up my defenses consciously either," Ryan said. "They just come up when I'm in public, or with people that I don't know well. You've seen my defenses up full force around Jack and Cassie."

Jamie thought of the few times she was with Ryan and Jack. "Yeah … I guess I see what you mean. You were very reserved around him. I didn't know you that well when you were around him and I thought you were just shy."

"Nope. I haven't been shy since I was a kid. I knew that he had an issue with me, and I tried to give him as little ammunition as possible."

"Do I have to do that?" Jamie looked crestfallen at the thought of having to hide her love for the wonderful woman who was so gently holding her hand.

"No, no, you don't. You'll figure out what you're comfortable with."

"How do I know?" Jamie asked, looking confused and wary.

"You have to …" Ryan pursed her lips, obviously thinking. "You have to make a decision about how to act given where you are and who you're with."

"I do? All the time?"

"No, babe, not all the time." Ryan could see that this wasn't settling well, but she didn't have a better spin to put on it. "I'm willing to put up with some harassment from strangers—so I act pretty normally around you in public. But when I'm in a situation where I could be physically harmed I pull back and try not to give off any lesbian signals at all."

"Have you always been like that?"

Ryan's face grew dark as a flash of pain crossed her face. "I got much more careful after I was gay-bashed last year," she said. "I haven't been to the bars or clubs in the marginal neighborhoods since then. Some very violent guys know there are gay and lesbian clubs there, and they sometimes go looking for victims."

A shiver ran down Jamie's spine as her mind automatically created a mental image of her partner lying on the street in a pool of blood. They hadn't spoken about the incident since Ryan had first mentioned it, and judging from the look on her lover's face, it was best left alone for the moment.

Jamie didn't like the message Ryan was giving her, but she tried to lighten the mood to get Ryan's mind off the attack. She adopted her fiercest look and muttered, "Nobody will mess with you now, babe. They'd have to get through me first."

The smile returned to Ryan's face as she paused to assess her protector. Sunny, open features, a wide smile, and dancing green eyes were topped by a jumble of fine blonde hair and one giggling baby. "I wouldn't mess with you two," Ryan said in a somber tone. "You could cute a person to death!"

"I'll show you cute!" Jamie leaned over just enough to allow Caitlin to reach Ryan's eye level. "Get her, partner!" Amazingly, Caitlin seemed to understand the attack command perfectly. She slapped her tiny hands at Ryan's face, while the tall woman playfully bit at each little pink hand.

"I give! I give! You win, Cait. I know when I'm up against a born fighter."

Jamie straightened and patted the champ's little leg. "Ya did good, Rocky."

Caitlin seemed to agree, and her joyful laugh echoed off the cozy little Victorian houses lining the streets of the Noe Valley.

As they reached the front walk of the Lilliputian house that Tommy and Annie rented, Ryan cast a quizzical glance at her partner, noticing a large number of voices coming from inside the house. "Who else is coming?" she asked, hefting Caitlin from Jamie's shoulders.

"Search me." Jamie shrugged her shoulders, partly in reply and partly to loosen them up after carrying her burden.

The door was locked, which in itself was strange, and the women shot one another puzzled glances when the house grew quiet as soon as Ryan banged on the door.

Seconds later the decibel level grew beyond the previous high when the assembled crowd saw them enter. "Surprise!" they all called out in unison. All of the cousins and aunts and uncles were jammed into the small living room around a very beautifully decorated cake that read "Congratulations, Jamie and Ryan." Colorful balloons and streamers flew around the ceiling, and the table was laden with cards addressed to them.

They were both staggered by the welcome, and Brendan came over to swoop the baby from Ryan's arms. He leaned over and kissed her, then leaned farther and gave a kiss to Jamie. A big smile played across his face as he needlessly asked, "Are you surprised?"

They both nodded, still in shock over the outpouring of affection from the clan. Jamie resorted to her normal reaction and tears began to flow down her cheeks. Ryan quirked a grin in her direction as she slid her arm around her shoulders and hugged her firmly. "You're really a member of the family now. You've gotten your first cake!"

One by one the various members of the family came over to hug and kiss each of the still startled women. A few bottles of champagne were produced, and everyone held up their filled glasses as Martin proposed a toast. "To my most precious daughter and her beloved Jamie. May your love bring you joy and peace and sustenance all the days of your lives. We love you both, girls. And we couldn't be happier for you."

As the glasses were raised in a group cheer, Jamie looked up at her lover, the tears still glistening in her eyes. "I love you, and I love your family."

"Our family, Jamie," she corrected her as she placed a delicate kiss on her trembling lips. "It's ours now."

The party was a rousing success by any standard. Caitlin, of course, was certain that she was the guest of honor, being of the belief that every part of every day revolved around her. Ryan and Jamie did their best to make her believe that such was the case, even letting her cut the first piece of cake with their assistance. After everyone had at least one piece of cake, the confines of the small house got to be too much for both Ryan and Caitlin, so they decided to go out to the postage-stamp-sized backyard and let Caitlin practice her walking.

The baby still needed the security of a hand or a leg or a piece of furniture in order to feel confident in her ramblings, and her babysitters were only too happy to aid her quest. They both delighted in her determined face as she scrunched up her little brow in concentration and began to scamper toward whatever object took her fancy. She walked with a stiff legged gait, with most of her weight over her toes. She kept her arms at her sides, not yet understanding that they could be helpful in maintaining her balance. She didn't fall often, but when she did, they just helped her up and sent her on her way again. She took her little tumbles in stride, barely stopping after each one, but around seven o'clock she took a relatively minor fall and stayed down. She lay face down on the grass and cried pitifully until Ryan picked her up and cuddled her, cooing into her tiny ear until the sobs subsided. Jamie went to get a bottle as Ryan did a quick diaper change, and after a bit she settled down in Ryan's arms to enjoy her dinner.

The early evening sun provided a warm cloak as Ryan relaxed in a spring chair, rocking the baby slightly as she ate. Jamie went back in once more to grab some tidbits to tide the big baby over, and when she returned, a mildly struggling Caitlin was being held firmly by her big cousin. Ryan was smiling at her and quietly singing a song which eventually got her attention. She stopped her struggles and lay quietly in Ryan's embrace, looking up at her with a look of pure adoration. "That's just how I feel when you hold me," Jamie said quietly from over her lover's shoulder.

Ryan beamed up at her and blushed a tiny bit at the compliment. "Are you having as nice a day as I am?"

"I don't think I've had a bad day since I realized I was in love with you." Her blissful smile was testimony to the sincerity of her words, and she leaned over to kiss the still-pink cheek before she sat down. "But I'd say that this has been a particularly lovely day."

"They really do love you, Jamie," Ryan said as she nodded her head toward her gathered family. "You believe that, don't you?"

"Knowing your family, they'd try to make me feel welcome even if they didn't *like* me," she said with a grin. "But I really do feel their love. They all make me feel like I've known them for years. It's so hard to believe that it's only been seven or eight months since I met them."

"You understand how hard it's going to be for me to leave here, don't you?" Ryan's eyes filled with tears as she considered their move to Berkeley.

Jamie got up and squatted on the ground next to her partner. "Ryan, if there's any part of you that doesn't want to live in my house, I want you to tell me. If you want to stay here, I'll call my father and tell him to sell it."

Ryan smiled down at her lover, and ran a hand through her tousled hair. "No, no. I really do think it's best for us to have some time alone. I just don't think I realized how much it's going to affect me until today. I hope you can be patient with me if this makes me kinda nuts."

"Sweetheart, I want you to promise me that if you get homesick, you'll let me know. I've actually been thinking about when we might like to buy a house over here," she said, surprising Ryan completely. "As much as I love my house, I'd much prefer to live in a place that you and I pick out together. I really don't see any reason why we won't make the Noe Valley our home." She looked down at Caitlin's half-closed eyes, as she gently touched her head. "There's no way I want to miss seeing this little one grow up."

Ryan's eyes filled with tears again as she choked out, "I'd really like that, babe." She rested her dark head against Jamie's and revealed the real reason behind her emotional display. "I'm just so used to seeing Caitlin two or three times a week, it's really going to be hard to just see her on the weekends. I can't express how much she means to me, Jamie. I know she's just my cousin, but I feel a bond with her that's …" She shook her head, unable to come up with words to express her love for the child.

"She feels it with you too." Jamie's earnest face and tone of voice showed just how much she understood Ryan's pain. "The look on her face when she first sees you is one of pure joy. She looks like I feel when I see you after we've been apart for a few hours. I know it's hard, honey, but please don't let this bother you today. If it doesn't work out, we'll come back. That's a promise."

"Thanks for understanding," Ryan said softly, taking a deep breath to calm herself. "I can't tell you how important it is to me that you really understand my feelings for my family."

"I've only known them a few months, and I'm not sure I can stand to be away from them either," she said with a smile. "Let's go inside and soak up some O'Flaherty magic, okay?"

Ryan gave her another appreciative smile and stood up with her now sleeping bundle. Jamie wrapped her arm around the lithe waist, and they walked into the party together.

They didn't return home until nearly eleven. They had planned on spending some of the evening packing up for Berkeley, but they were both too tired.

Ryan flopped down on the bed and let out a groan of pure exhaustion. "One good thing about being in Berkeley during the week," she moaned. "I might be able to get a little rest. As much as I love my family, they sure do take a lot of energy out of ya."

Jamie knew her partner was mostly teasing, but she had to admit that the sentiment was accurate. The O'Flahertys were closer than any family she had ever encountered, but that closeness came with a price—the almost total loss of privacy. They had nearly no boundaries—and it was unthinkable to refuse a request that you were able to fulfill.

The cousins were currently helping Niall renovate a small house that he had purchased in the Sunset District, and nearly every male member of the family had devoted at least one full day of each week for the last three months to the renovation. Ryan had already been making noises about joining in, and as Jamie considered the eleven other single men in the family, she hoped that the rest wouldn't decide to buy homes for many, many years. *The only chance I have of having time alone with Ryan is if we're in Berkeley. We've got to make the most of our time alone this year, 'cause when we move back here our privacy will be shot!* She laughed to herself as she thought of the fact that the O'Flahertys didn't lock their doors during the day, and that no one knocked before entering. *That's one area where I'm putting my foot down! I'll not have the cousins walking in on what I hope will be near-constant lovemaking!*

Joining her partner on the bed, Jamie began a light scratching of her belly. "Do you honestly think that I'm gonna go easier on you than your family does?" She continued to tease Ryan's skin as Ryan rolled onto her side to provide new territory.

"I hadn't considered that," Ryan mused sleepily. "Maybe I should get my own apartment so I can get a few hours' rest."

"I'd track you down, Tiger. You're mine now, and I'm gonna exploit every one of your luscious natural resources."

"How do you know all of my resources are natural?" Ryan teased, rolling onto her back once again. She hefted one of her breasts and gave it a squeeze. "These might be augmented, you know."

"God, I hope not," Jamie murmured as she pulled the purple T-shirt from Ryan's shorts. "'Cause I'm gonna give 'em such a workout, there's a good chance an implant would burst!" She dove in with gusto, catching Ryan by surprise. But after a few moments, she relaxed and let her partner fulfill her wishes.

Running her hand through Jamie's fine blonde hair, Ryan bit back a gasp as the voracious touch grew fiercer. "Honey, honey," she soothed. "I don't think they're guaranteed against puncture."

An embarrassed smile covered Jamie's flushed face as she looked up and met her partner's loving gaze. "Sorry. I got carried away."

"Hey … nothing to be sorry for. I was just teasing you. I like it when you threaten to consume me bodily." A sexy smile combined with impishly twinkling blue eyes as Ryan suggested, "Let's put 'em to the torture test."

"We'll start our own twisted version of Consumer Reports," Jamie giggled as she bent to her pleasurable task.

Stupid, stupid, stupid! She cursed herself for showing her hand too early and taking out only one of the toughs.

Two of the men … *boys really*, she thought with disgust, grabbed her by her wrists and applied pressure to her elbows from behind. The pain was excruciating, but she couldn't fight back, since they could easily dislocate her elbows. Kelly lay at her feet, moaning continuously—a keening, low tone that set Ryan's teeth on edge. As the stocky young man approached her he gave her a sickeningly evil smile, saying conversationally, "You're gonna regret the day you were born, bitch." Then he hit her—a dull thud to the ribs with a heavy length of lead pipe. Every molecule of air flew from her lungs—leaving her unable to even cry out.

As he unleashed another brutal blow, her mind turned to her teacher, the gentle but lethal soul who had often warned, "Never reveal your abilities if you cannot disable your attacker." *I screwed up, big time*, she thought as the pipe whistled through the air, aimed for her head. *If I live through this, I swear I'll never make that mistake again.*

Am I in a strait jacket? This must be the hospital … oh shit! I can't move my arms! She struggled roughly, thrashing about frantically as she tried to assess her injuries.

"Honey … Ryan, wake up. Come on, it's okay."

Warm, comforting arms enveloped her, and she sucked in a deep breath of relief. *At least Jamie's here.* Her heart calmed its racing beat as she considered how that was possible. With a start, she sat up as her head flew from side to side, amazed to find that she was in her own bed. "Jamie?" Her scratchy voice was higher than normal, reflecting the fear that she'd been gripped with just seconds before.

"I'm right here, honey," her partner soothed, brushing hair from her damp forehead.

Ryan glanced down to find her purple, long-sleeved T-shirt wrapped around her elbows like a tourniquet. Her sports bra was shoved up over her breasts, restricting her ability to take a deep breath. Looking down her body, she saw that her underwear and khaki shorts both clung to one ankle, socks and shoes still laced up tight. "What in the holy hell?" She roughly kicked her clothing from her foot and yanked her shirt and bra off, rubbing her arms to restore feeling to them. "Jesus Christ, Jamie, we've gotta stop doing this!"

Finally meeting her partner's eyes, she saw the flicker of hurt that her sharp words had caused. She fell back onto the bed and draped her arm across her eyes, trying to sort out her tumultuous feelings.

A soft hand trailed down her ribs, stroking her belly while she composed herself. "I'm sorry," Ryan finally said. "I didn't mean to snap at you. I just … I was having a nightmare, and being trapped by my clothes made me think …" She shook her head roughly, not wanting to go into the dream. Her voice softened, and she removed her arm so that she could look into her partner's eyes. "I'm sorry."

"It's okay. Don't worry about it. You were half-asleep."

Trusting green eyes calmly gazed at her, and Ryan suddenly felt even worse. She'd been quite awake, and she knew that she was just venting her fear at her partner. "That's no excuse. I really do apologize."

"You wanna talk about it?" Jamie's tone was soft and somewhat tentative, but her eyes held Ryan's firmly.

"No. I really don't." Long, bare legs slid off the bed, and as Ryan stood she glanced down at her feet and shot her partner a half-smile. "Since I've already got my shoes on, I might as well go do my run."

"Want me to go with you?" Jamie could tell that her grumpy partner needed some space to regain her normal attitude, but she didn't want to abandon her if she needed companionship.

"Nah. I know you don't like to run, and I feel like going on a long one today. Why don't you just stay in bed?"

"No thanks." Jamie slid out of the messy pile of sheets and came to stand by her partner. "You're even taller with your shoes on," she teased, placing a small kiss on her breast.

"Hey … that's how this whole thing began, sport." Ryan's tone was lighter now, and Jamie accepted the teasing in the jocular manner that it was intended.

Another gentle kiss followed the first, as Jamie's arms slid around her partner's waist. She rested her cheek against Ryan's chest, letting her strong, steady heartbeat calm her completely. "You can't blame me for being unable to resist your luscious body."

"Same goes for me, love," Ryan agreed, placing a soft kiss on the crown of Jamie's tousled hair. Released from the embrace, Ryan got back into her sports bra and T-shirt and found a pair of nylon running shorts to finish her outfit. "I'll be back in about an hour."

"Can I use your computer to check my mail?" Jamie asked.

"Sure. You're a Mac person too, aren't you?"

"Yep." Sitting down at the desk, Jamie asked, "Any special requests for dinner this week? I want to make a shopping list."

"I've never had a bad meal from you. Anything you want is fine with me."

"Hey," Jamie called when Ryan was halfway up the stairs. "Let's invite your father and brothers over for a barbecue this week."

Ryan flashed a luminous grin at her partner, amazed at how just a few moments with Jamie could make a bad mood vanish. "Great idea. Da's off on Wednesday."

Jamie smiled back and blew a kiss as Ryan took off again, a little bounce now in her step. *She's soooo easy,* Jamie thought with a smirk.

By the time Ryan reached the top of the stairs, she could hear Duffy begin to whine from the other side of the stairwell door. As she cracked the door open, his shiny black nose peeked through, snuffling to get a whiff of her scent. Laughing gently, she opened the door fully, and was greeted by his joyous face and always energetic tongue. She pushed at him weakly, giggling uncontrollably when he reached her ears.

Jamie's amused voice carried up the stairwell. "You sure have done a fine job of training that dog, Ryan."

Grabbing his eight-foot leather leash and two plastic bags, Ryan rubbed his big head affectionately and offered a stage whisper for her partner's benefit. "You can't help it that I'm irresistible, can you, boy?" Jamie's laugh reached her ears as she needlessly asked, "Ready, Duff?" His fiercely wagging tail was answer enough.

It took a few minutes for the computer to boot, and while she waited, Jamie pulled one of Ryan's T-shirts from the large net bag where she kept her dirty clothes. Sniffing delicately, she mused, *Not the cleanest thing in the world, but I just can't stand to work at the computer in the nude.*

She logged on to her remote mail server and was surprised to see a short note from Jack. Cringing as she read it, she thought, *This is a pretty polite way to ask if I've lost my mind.* The note was ostensibly a thank-you for the graduation present, but he managed to ask if she was all right, and also mentioned that he was concerned about how upset she had seemed on Saturday. *He probably thinks I'm a mental patient after the way I acted.*

She hit "reply" and wrote,

Dear Jack,

I'm glad that you liked the gift. Thanks for writing to say so.

I'd like to apologize for my near-meltdown on Saturday. I obviously had some unresolved feelings about our breakup, and I'm sorry they came out during your celebration. I want to assure you that I'm perfectly fine and am doing very well, and I'm glad that you are too.

Take care this summer. Good luck on the bar exam. I hope to see your name in the paper come Thanksgiving.

Fondly,

Jamie

She surveyed the message for a moment, trying to make sure she was giving the correct impression. *I think it's pretty clear from this that I don't want to have an ongoing relationship. I wish him well, but I don't really want to hear from him again. I know I'll check with Daddy to make sure he passes the bar, but that's really the next time I'd like to hear his name.* Satisfied that the message was clear, she hit "send."

As they huffed up and down the hilly streets of Upper Noe Valley, Ryan reflected on her dream and how she had woken up. *God, that freaked me out*, she mused as a chill ran down her spine. *It felt so real—and that hasn't happened for months now.* She recalled with a grimace how frequent the nightmares had been, remembering the times she woke in her father's arms after her cries had roused him from a sound sleep. *The doc told me I might have another bout when the anniversary came around*, she recalled. *Guess I'm gonna have to ride it out.* She knew that she had to share her fears with Jamie, but she just wasn't willing to dampen their still-joyous mood with the details of the attack. "Maybe that'll be the last one," she said with more confidence than she felt.

Banishing thoughts of the dream, she allowed herself to laugh a bit at the state of her dishabille when she woke. *I've got to have a little more discipline here. God knows I love having "little frisky" love me senseless, but I've got to at least figure out a way to get my teeth brushed!* She mused thoughtfully for a second, smiling to herself when she considered, *If I tell her I call her "little frisky," she'll leave me alone at night. Heck, I might not ever have sex again!* Trudging up a particularly steep hill, the idea hit her. *That's it! I'll brush my teeth every time I eat something in the evening! Ha!* She laughed at her cunning solution, figuring that a few more bouts of brushing would be a lot better than doing without.

She had traversed most of the streets near the house and now found herself in front of Douglas Playground, a small but attractive little plot where she was first introduced to the joys of playing on the swings. She could still remember tugging on Brendan's hand every afternoon, looking up at him and begging, "Bwen, can we go thwing?" Her big brother would look down at her with remarkable patience for a nine-year-old, grasp her little hand, and allow her to drag him down the street, where he would spend a good hour pushing her until his arms ached.

A choked cry caught her attention before she realized that the sound had come from her own mouth. A flood of memories washed over her, nearly drowning her with their weight. Her entire life had consisted of roughly one square mile of real estate, and she suddenly realized that she didn't want to go to Berkeley … not today … not ever. The Noe Valley was more than her home—it was her birthright. Every member of her family in America lived within walking distance. She knew almost every person by name and considered many of her neighbors to be extensions of her family. She and Duffy had met every dog within five miles, and she really enjoyed their social interactions at the park on cool summer evenings. She knew every employee at the local coffee shop, and she relished the thought that, without a word, her latté was waiting for her when she got to the front of the line. The guys at the pot pie restaurant constantly teased her about her legendary appetite; Jacob at the newsstand always saved a copy of the Sunday *Dublin Mail* for her; even the mail carrier, Hector, would stop and chat for a few minutes during his busy day. It wasn't exciting, it wasn't even very interesting, but it was home, and she was physically ill at the thought of leaving it.

She'd slowed to a walk, and Duffy immediately sensed her mood. He sat at her feet, cocking his big dark head, and when she made eye contact with his sad eyes she nearly lost it. *I've gotta get home*, she decided, taking off again at a very fast clip.

"I don't know how you're gonna do without this in the morning, Duff," she said aloud as they huffed up and down the hills. Her father had already assured her that he didn't mind taking him for a walk in the morning, but he was clearly not interested in running with him. Conor was a good runner and he put in about five miles most days, but he did so at night, and that's not when Duffy had his burst of energy. Rory was away so much that he didn't figure into the equation, so Duffy would have to expend his morning energy in some other way. She knew that most dogs didn't get the kind of exercise that Duffy was used to, and she assumed that he didn't really need as much as he got. But he was very used to their morning ritual, and she knew it'd bother him to not have it any longer. "We're just going to have to see how it goes, boy," she said as they ran along. "If you can't stand it, we'll bring you over to Berkeley." The big dog looked up at her with his trusting brown eyes and she felt her reasoned façade begin to crack once again. "I'm worried about your not being able to stand it," she muttered aloud. "It's me that probably won't be able to function without you!"

They covered almost ten miles, and were both exhausted when they returned home. Ryan had a rather difficult time catching her breath as they stood outside the family home, and Duffy was panting heavily. They climbed the stairs and were both surprised by the door being opened from the inside. Martin was grinning at them both as he took in the sight. Ryan was drenched with sweat, her hair plastered to her face and neck. Sweat ran down her face, dripping from her chin and trailing down her neck. Her bright red T-shirt was stained a dark crimson from the collar to her breasts. She forced a crooked grin at her father and asked, "Do we look as tired as I feel?"

"Duffy looks none the worse for wear, sweetheart, but you look like you've been leggin' it!"

"I guess we did go a little farther than normal," she said. "I just wanted to make sure he was tired."

Her father looked at her with a gentle concern on his face. "You're already trying to make sure we can survive without you, aren't you, darlin'?"

Ryan felt her lower lip start to quiver.

"I think you might have to take him with you," he said. "I don't think he'll be happy without you." After a beat he added, "I know I won't."

The fragile control that she'd managed burst apart immediately upon hearing this expression of emotion from her father. She threw her arms around his neck and cried in a way that she hadn't done in years. He embraced her tightly and held on as sobs wracked her body. It took a while, but she finally was composed enough to choke out, "I don't know if I can stand to be away, Da. Even though I think it's the right thing for us to do, it's incredibly hard for me to leave."

"Shh, shh, sweetheart," he said as he patted her back and rocked her slowly in his arms. "It'll be okay, Siobhán. You'll be fine once you get settled in with Jamie. If you really don't like it, you can always come home. You know we'd love to have you back any time."

Ryan pulled back and tried to swipe away some of the tears from her eyes, wiping them with the handkerchief her father handed her. They finally went inside so she could get something to drink before she showered. She'd managed to make herself somewhat presentable by the time they reached the kitchen, where she nearly ran into Conor. "What's wrong?" he asked immediately, his voice full of concern.

"Your sister's having a tough time of it," Martin responded, leaving it to his daughter to share her feelings if she chose to.

"What is it?" Conor asked again, squatting down a bit so they were eye to eye. "Can I do anything to help?"

His obvious concern brought another flood of tears as she leaned against her brother, who glanced up at Martin with a look of total confusion on his handsome face. Martin just shook his head as he stood next to his children and again patted her on the back. Conor was also rubbing her back and uttering soothing words as she continued to cry against his shoulder. After a long while she lifted her tear-streaked face and said, "I'm sorry I'm being so emotional about leaving."

"Siobhán," her father said in a serious tone. "Don't you ever be ashamed about showing how much you love us. This is going to be hard for all of us, and it helps us to see that leaving has an impact on you too. How do you think we'd feel if you just upped and took off without a care?"

She gave him a small smile, pulling away from Conor's embrace. "You're right, Da," she said. "This has made one thing clear, though. I'm only applying to graduate schools in the Bay Area. I've learned that I'm not the kind of woman who can be too far from home."

"That's the best news I've heard all week," Martin said as he gave her another hug. "Now I'm off to work, or they'll have my head." He gave her a kiss on the cheek and a quick hug before he turned abruptly and headed for his room. Ryan started after him, and heard him quickly open and close a dresser drawer. He emerged with a clean handkerchief, and as he headed down the stairs she could hear him sniffing away his tears.

Conor had followed his sister into the dining room and he slid his arm around her when he saw that another round of tears was on the way. He held her again as she tried to compose herself, but the emotion flowed from her unabated. He breathed a small sigh of relief when Jamie's blonde head poked up from the stairwell. She made eye contact with Conor and indicated that she'd take over, and he turned the shaken woman to gently guide her into Jamie's open arms. He indicated to Jamie that he would go make breakfast, then left them alone in the dining room.

Jamie sat down on one of the old mahogany dining chairs, and tugged Ryan down on her lap. *My God! How much does she weigh?* The chair groaned from the demands placed on its construction, but to her great relief it held firm. The dark head fell onto her chest, and Jamie spent long minutes rocking her and whispering words of love into her flushed ears. Ryan was overheated from her run, and the outpouring of emotion caused heat to radiate off of her body in waves. It reminded Jamie of Caitlin when she was very tired and very cranky, and she smiled just a bit when she considered how childlike her partner often was. *I'd love to be able to let my feelings show in front of my family just once*, she wished silently. *Maybe someday ....*

The sobs had now turned to sniffles, and when Jamie suggested a shower, Ryan nodded compliantly. Jamie urged her to her feet and took her clammy hand and led her to their room. She guided Ryan into the bath and started to wrangle her out of her wet clothes, but Ryan mumbled, "I can do it myself."

"I know you can, but I'd like to baby you a little bit today. Do you mind?"

Jamie's look was one of pure empathy, and Ryan couldn't refuse her request. She sniffled a little and shook her head just a bit to indicate her agreement. To aid her partner, she sat on the commode to provide better access to her long frame. As soon as they were both undressed, Jamie led Ryan into the shower and let the warm spray rejuvenate her spent lover. Moving behind her, she lovingly washed her dark hair, then moved down her body, cleaning her with a tender, loving touch. Ryan soaked up the affection, not speaking a word, but obediently moving in whichever direction she was tugged.

When they were both clean and dry, Jamie led Ryan over to her desk chair and slowly freed her hair of all of its tangles and blew the dark tresses dry, pulling them into a long braid. As usual, the gentle brushing and braiding relaxed Ryan, and Jamie knew it wouldn't take much convincing to take her right back to bed. But they had too many things to accomplish today, and she knew Ryan wouldn't wish to put them off.

This time, Jamie sat on Ryan's lap and drew her into an embrace and held her until she seemed to have regained her equilibrium. Ryan finally looked up at her. "I can't talk about it now. Can we just go have breakfast? I'm starved with the hunger," she said in her brogue, invoking a phrase that Jamie assumed was familial.

"Sure. You don't have to talk about it at all, if you don't want to. I think I know what's troubling you."

Ryan smiled at her and went to her chest of drawers to pull out an outfit. She chose a pair of well-worn jeans and a red cotton tank top, drawing on a white oxford-cloth man's style shirt over it. She buttoned the shirt halfway and rolled the sleeves a few times, exposing her tanned, muscular forearms. *Boy, she cleans up nice*, Jamie mused as she surveyed her lanky form. Ryan took a quick glance into the mirror, shook her head briefly, and tucked both shirts into her jeans, adding a wide black belt. A pair of black penny-loafers completed the look, and as she took another glance she caught Jamie's head nod in concert with her own. She spared a smile at her observer and placed a small kiss on her lips. "I'll go help with breakfast while you get dressed, okay?"

"Okay. I'll be right up."

Ryan came up behind Conor as he was spooning oatmeal into a big bowl. She slid her arms around his waist and rested her head on his broad, muscular shoulder. "Thanks for the support," she said gratefully. "I had no idea this would be so hard for me."

"It's hard for all of us," he admitted as he looked over his shoulder. "I think breakfast will be the hardest time for me. I really look forward to starting the day by spending a few minutes with you and Da. It always cheers me up to see you and Duffy come bounding in the front door first thing in the morning."

Ryan felt like her composure was slipping yet again, so she grabbed the oatmeal and took it into the dining room. Conor had already set the table, so she set about assembling the condiments for the cereal. By the time all was ready, Jamie had come into the dining room and cast a quick glance at her lover, who still seemed shaky to her experienced eye. When Conor entered the dining room Jamie asked, "Are you free on Wednesday night?"

"I don't have any plans yet."

"I'd like to have you all come over for dinner if you're free," she said with a quick glance at her lover. Ryan was gracing her with a sweet smile, and her mood seemed a bit lighter.

"I'd love to come, and I'm sure Da would too. Should I ask Brendan?"

"No," Jamie replied. "I'll call him. He should have a proper invitation."

They ate their meal quickly, the turmoil having caused Conor to run late for work. Jamie insisted that she and Ryan would clean the kitchen since he'd done the cooking, and he gratefully agreed. He came over to his sister and squatted down by her chair, making eye contact when he said, "We're gonna miss you, but we'll be okay. Da and I will do our best to take your place in the mornings with Duff. I know we can't give him the kind of workout you do, but I think he'll be fine."

Ryan wrapped her arms around her brother's neck and squeezed him firmly. "Thanks, Conor," she said as the tears threatened again. "I'll see you on Wednesday."

He stood up and bent over from the waist to kiss her cheek. "See you then," he said, moving around the table to give Jamie a kiss and a hug. "Thanks for the invitation, Jamie. I'll see you soon." As he left the dining room Ryan burst into tears again, dropping her head onto the dining room table with a thunk as the sobs shook her body.

"Honey, honey," Jamie cooed into her ear as she pulled a chair up next to her. "Tell me why you're so sad."

Ryan struggled to sit up and forced herself to take some deep breaths to calm down. "God! I hate being such a baby about this! I'm gonna be home every weekend, for pete's sake!"

"Hey …" Jamie ran her hand through her partner's bangs, fluffing them gently. "Don't be angry with yourself. This is hard for you, and that's all that matters. Now, come on, and tell me how you feel."

Ryan sucked in a shaky breath and got to the heart of the matter. "I know this sounds crazy, but this feels like … well, like death to me."

Jamie tried to hide her shocked look. It had never occurred to her that Ryan would equate the move of a few miles with death. She began a slow, rhythmic stroking of Ryan's back to help calm her, and after a few moments she was able to continue. "It's hard to express what it was like to lose my mother. She wasn't just a person, she was the center of our home, and when she died some of that role fell to me. There's a part of me that feels like I'm abandoning them, like she did," she choked out as another wave of emotion surged over her.

"Oh, sweetheart," she whispered, "I had no idea that's how you felt."

"I wasn't really aware myself until yesterday," she said through her sobs. "They really do depend on me for some emotional stability. I'm just afraid that the boys might leave too, and that would kill Da."

"Oh, honey," Jamie said soothingly. "I don't think Conor or Rory has any intention of leaving home. I know they'll miss you, but it's only for this year."

"I know," she said shakily. "I just feel overwhelmed. I haven't felt this sad in a long, long while."

"Is this what your nightmare was about?"

"No." Ryan shook her head, deciding that she had to come clean. "Thursday is the anniversary of when I was gay-bashed. The nightmare was about that."

Jamie's eyes fluttered closed as she considered how many things her partner was trying to cope with at once. "No wonder this is so hard for you right now," she soothed. "Do you want to wait a few weeks before we move?"

Ryan closed her swollen eyes and considered the offer. After just a few moments she shook her head confidently and said, "No. We planned to do this now so we'll be close for summer school and work. I think we should go ahead and go. Once we're over there, I'm sure I'll be fine."

"Ryan," Jamie said softly, holding her face in her hands. "I hope you believe me when I promise you that we'll come home if this is too hard for you. I'm almost ready to tell my parents about us, and I could tell them to sell the house at the same time. Might as well make it a huge announcement!" she said with a twinkle in her eye.

A soft laugh escaped from Ryan's lips and she rested her head on Jamie's shoulder. "Let's table that idea for a little while, okay? My stomach's in a knot already."

Jamie nodded, standing to grasp her hand. As they went into the kitchen to clean up she said, "I want you to know that I think it's a wonderful thing that this is so hard for you. Twenty-five years from now, I want our kids to feel the same way when they're ready to leave our home."

"At the rate I'm going we'll still be here, and they'll be crying over leaving Grandpa and Uncle Conor and Uncle Rory!"

"That would be fine with me," Jamie declared, standing on her tiptoes to place a kiss on her partner's flushed cheek.

After kitchen cleanup, they repaired to their room to pack enough for the week. "Don't you feel like you've been living out of a suitcase for weeks?" Ryan asked as she tossed clothes into her bag.

"We have been for a couple of weeks," Jamie said. "And I was here for a couple of weeks before that, so yeah, it does feel like we haven't been home in a while."

"I'm only planning on bringing enough to get me through Friday," Ryan said. "Not much more than this bag will fit into the Porsche."

"That's fine. We can slowly bring things over that we need. Other than clothes, I have everything that you might need, like a hair dryer and toiletries. Is there anything else you can think of that I don't have?"

Ryan gave her the first genuine smile of the day. "Not unless you want me to bring something from my little bag of tricks."

Jamie was a bit taken aback. She knew that her partner had played with lots of toys, but for some reason, she had never considered that she was the owner of any of them. But she loved the twinkle in the blue eyes that gazed at her, and she wasn't willing to dampen it. "Lemme see what you've got."

Ryan pulled out a gym bag from the bottom drawer of her dresser, setting it on the bed to unzip it. Jamie stuck her hand in and pulled out all manner of latex, rubber, and leather accessories. Her eyes grew wide as she stared at the assortment, some of which left her clueless as to their purpose. "I seem to remember that you said you didn't want to experiment with toys," Ryan said with a crooked grin. "But you seem to have loosened up considerably since that little talk. Does any of this pique your interest?"

"I don't have any idea what some of this is," she said. "But I can certainly imagine that some of this would be kind of fun to try. Pick out a few of your favorites and bring them along, but leave some for here, too. I don't want to have to transport this stuff every weekend."

Ryan sorted through the items and picked out three that she thought would be fun to try. She grabbed another small bag and tossed them in with a big smile firmly affixed to her face.

Now I know another key to chasing the blues, Jamie smirked to herself as they finished their packing.

Chapter Four

By the time they reached Berkeley, it was nearly ten o'clock. During their honeymoon, they had decided that it made sense for Jamie to take some classes during Ryan's work hours. That would allow her to take a lighter load during her senior year, which would allow her to try out for the golf team if she decided to pursue that goal. The classes she wanted were not terribly popular, but she wanted to make sure she got enrolled, so she decided that she needed to get going. If she was successful, she would be at class from one to three, then she had an hour to kill until her four o'clock therapist appointment. "I hate to leave you here all alone," she said, standing in the doorway with her arms around Ryan's neck.

"I'll be fine. I'll just snoop around for a while and then head over to the gym. I'm scheduled from one to four."

Jamie tweaked her lover's nose, smiling when Ryan twitched it like a rabbit. "It's not snooping. Everything here is yours. This is our house now."

Ryan nodded. "I'm just teasing, but I've never been here alone, so I'll spend some time trying to feel at home. Where should I put my clothes?"

"I thought you'd take Cassie's room. There's a big closet in there and some built-in drawers for your folded clothes."

"I get my own room?" she asked with a quizzical but pleased grin.

"Sure. I want you to have a place that's yours alone. We've got the room, so why not use it? Oh. There are two medicine cabinets in the bath. I use the one on the right, so you get the one on the left. Okay?"

"Sounds great. I'll get my stuff squared away and head on over to the gym. I'll have my pager on, so call if you need anything."

"I need you," Jamie said. She looked up into Ryan's eyes, finding it very difficult to let her go.

Sensing her reluctance, Ryan said, "I don't want to be away from you all day. Sure you don't wanna drop out of school and lie in bed all day?"

"I'm sure that's exactly what I want to do," Jamie said. "Don't even tempt me!"

Ryan bent to kiss her, keeping it brief. "Get going now," she said, giving Jamie a gentle hug. "I'll expect you home at about five-thirty. Do you want me to have dinner ready?"

"Let's get carryout and drink our champagne. We need to christen this house, too, ya know."

"I anxiously await your return," Ryan said as she bent to kiss her tenderly one last time.

Nice room, Ryan mused as she placed her bag on the queen-sized bed in her new quarters. She had never been in Cassie's old room, and she smiled a little as she considered the chain of events that led her here. *It'd frost old Cassie's ass to know that I took over her room. I'll have to make sure she finds out*, she thought with uncharacteristic vengefulness. *I wonder if I should have Father Pender come over and do an exorcism before I put my stuff in here?*

The room was located on the other side of the shared bath, and overlooked the driveway, rather than sharing Jamie's view of the backyard. There were windows on only one wall, and Ryan guessed that the room wouldn't get the nice cross-breeze that Jamie's room was afforded. *But I bet this room is warmer in the winter. Maybe we'll have to move over here on really chilly nights.*

It didn't take long to organize the little clothing she'd been able to bring, and when she was finished Ryan started poking around the big house, trying to feel at home. She spent a few minutes looking at the items neatly organized in the bathroom cabinet. *Hmm ... I've never used any of these products ... but Jamie always smells great so it shouldn't be a problem to share them until I bring my usual stuff over*. She removed some of the items and looked at them more carefully. *Where does she get this stuff? I've never seen deodorant with the label in French.* Upon closer inspection, Ryan realized that she had never heard of any of the manufacturers of Jamie's personal care products. *I have a sneaking suspicion that my sweetie doesn't just go to Costco and buy whatever's cheapest.*

Heading into Jamie's room, she paused to take in the compulsively neat space. Every book was lined up one inch from the edge of the bookcase; every knick-knack was held down with a small dab of earthquake putty; the computer, printer and scanner were arranged on the desk to provide maximum accessibility. *We'll get along just fine*, Ryan mused confidently. She snuck a look at the wicker laundry hamper, relieved that it was completely empty. *Gotta love a girl who does her laundry before she goes on a trip.*

A good-sized television and VCR were located on a shelf in the built-in bookcase. Noticing that neither device was plugged in gave Ryan another cause for enthusiasm. *Thank you, God, for not making her a TV addict!* Surveying the twin towers of CDs next to the ultra-elegant Bang and Olufsen stereo, she amended her praise, *You could have given her better taste in music, God, but I'll forgive you for one little error in an otherwise perfect package. At least she has a lot of classical selections. I don't know much about classical music, but I'm sure I'd like it a lot better than the rest of this stuff!*

She was halfway down the stairs when the rear doorbell rang. Although she sped up, by the time she reached the door a delivery van was already pulling out of the drive. A double deadbolt was installed on the sturdy door, and it required the use of a key to open it from either side. *That's a good idea for preventing burglaries, but a bad idea for fires or earthquakes*, the firefighter's daughter mused. *With only two exits on this floor you could be stuck in here if your keys were upstairs. Ahh*, she amended, spotting a key hanging from a hook just far enough away so that a burglar couldn't break the window and reach it. *My princess already thought of that little detail.* Slipping the key into the lock, she swung the door open and a bag of groceries practically fell into the house. *What the . . . ?*

Stooping to pick up a pair of bags, she hefted them into the kitchen and placed them on the counter, repeating the action until all six bags were retrieved. Each bag was clearly labeled "Web Van.Com." *She buys groceries on the Internet? Oh no*, she decided immediately. *That's got to be more expensive than going to the store.*

She set about getting all of the purchases organized, with the job taking quite a while, since she had to learn where everything was kept. But when she was done, she felt much more familiar with everything, and she was happy that she'd had a little time alone to snoop.

By this time it was nearly noon, so she decided to get dressed for work and take off. *Why didn't I bring my motorcycle? It's a good two and a half miles to the gym. Now I've got to run and then I'll be sweaty all afternoon. Damn, I don't even have my Roller Blades.*

Grumbling about her lack of foresight, she headed up to her room to change into running clothes. Stripping quickly, she was in the middle of hanging up her jeans and white shirt when she heard Jamie fumbling with the lock on the front door. *Darn, she must have been too late registering to get the classes she wanted.* She padded out into the hall, stark naked, calling out, "Miss me?"

"AAAAHHHH!!!!" cried the shocked young Latina who stared up at her.

"AAAAHHHH!!!" Ryan cried simultaneously, slapping her knees together as she tried to cover her nakedness with her arms. "Who are you?"

"Quien es usted?" the young woman cried.

That doesn't sound like Gaelic, Ryan thought as she considered the only foreign language in which she was fluent. *Why couldn't I take Spanish like all the other kids in high school? No, I had to take Latin.* After a beat she asked herself, *Why are you standing here having this discussion with yourself, while a stunned woman is staring at your naked body?* She dashed into her room, struggling into some Lycra shorts and a sports bra, adding her "Women Power" polo shirt. Grabbing socks and her shoes, she ran back to the hallway, surprised to see the woman standing in the exact same spot, still staring up at her.

She approached the poor woman carefully, almost amused at the wide eyes that still looked a bit glassy. Extending her hand, she pointed at herself and said, "Ryan."

The woman nodded, looking more composed as she parroted, "Maria Los," and accepted Ryan's handshake.

"Do you speak English?"

"Not very good," she haltingly replied. "Habla usted Español?" the young woman asked.

"No," Ryan replied, offering the same regretful look. Trying to communicate without words, Ryan mimicked putting the key in the door. "Do you have a key?" she asked needlessly, since that was the only way the woman could have gained entrance.

Regrettably, Ryan was no Marcel Marceau, and Maria Los had no idea what she was attempting to ask. "Lo siento, pero no entiendo," she offered. "Vengo a limpiar la casa," she said, lifting her bucket filled with cleaning cloths. "Es usted la … amiga … de la Señorita Jamie?" The young woman wasn't sure if this tall stranger was another roommate or just a visitor. It was clear that Cassie, the blonde devil, had departed the house some weeks earlier, and she sincerely hoped that this woman didn't share any of the other one's personality traits.

Ryan nodded, understanding that the woman was there to clean, recognizing Jamie's name as well as the word "friend". "Sí, Jamie's amiga," she agreed, figuring the full extent of their relationship was not something Maria Los needed to hear.

Now both women nodded and offered smiles, their scintillating conversation at a standstill. Ryan was just about to say "adios" when she heard her partner's tread on the stairs. *Jamie … you got some s'plainin to do*, she thought to herself in her admittedly awful Spanish accent.

The grinning blonde burst through the door, smiling sheepishly at Ryan and offering a quick, "Sorry," as she greeted Maria Los affectionately. The young woman began to babble, "Lo siento mucho, Señorita Jamie. No sabia que tenia visita. Entre a la casa sin tocar y sorprendi a su amiga." *I'm very sorry, Miss Jamie. I didn't know you had a visitor. I entered the house without knocking and I surprised your friend.*

The young woman was blushing furiously, and Jamie spared a glance at her partner who was rocking back and forth on her heels, whistling a little tune as she rolled her big blue eyes at the ceiling.

"Esta perfectamente bien, Maria Los. Esta usted bien? Se ve molesta." *That's perfectly all right, Maria Los. Are you all right? You seem upset.*

"No, no," she said quickly. "Es que su amiga … no estaba … ella no estaba … preparada para visita." *It's just that your friend … she wasn't … prepared for a visitor.*

Her blush deepened, and Jamie's mind reeled at the possible scenarios that flashed before her. *Please, God, let it not be something that will scar Maria Los for life!* "Que es, Maria?" Jamie asked gently, placing a reassuring hand on her shoulder. "Que paso?"

Ryan was tired of being left out of the conversation, and she could tell just by their body language that they were discussing her, so she decided to cut to the chase. "I was naked, Jamie. I heard the key in the door, I thought it was you, and I came out into the hall completely naked." Now her blush rivaled Maria Los's, and Jamie bit back a laugh.

"Completely naked?"

Ryan nodded.

"Completamente desnuda?" she repeated in Spanish.

Maria Los nodded.

"Bueno! Eso le dara algo para decirles a las muchachas cuando llegue a la casa en la noche!" *Well! That will give you something to tell the girls when you get home tonight!* Jamie laughed easily, and her relaxed posture allowed Maria Los to shed some of her anxiety.

The young woman laughed nervously saying, "Nunca he visto a una mujer como ella … es una actriz?" *I have never seen a woman who looks like that … is she a movie star?*

"No," Jamie laughed. "Ella es estudiante tambien. Pero es bastante extraordinaria, no es asi?" *She is a student also. But she is extraordinary, isn't she?*

"Oh, si!" Maria Los nodded enthusiastically, relieved that Jamie was taking this so well. "Su amiga tomara el lugar de Señorita Cassie en la casa?" *Oh please, oh please*, she prayed. *Will your friend be taking Miss Cassie's place in the house?*

"Si, Maria Los. Cassie se fue para siempre." *Cassie is gone for good.* The young woman's smile became nearly radiant, and Jamie wondered again what had transpired between the two women. Maria Los would never reveal the source of the tension that obviously existed between them, and Cassie's flippant remarks about the young woman were not revealing either. It was obvious, however, that Maria Los was jubilant about the change. "Ryan es una mujer muy, pero muy amable. Le garantizo que no tendra problemas con ella." *Ryan is a very, very nice woman. I guarantee she will treat you well.*

"Eso es muy bueno para saber, Señorita Jamie. Se ve que es muy amable." *That is very good to hear, Miss Jamie. She seems very nice.*

Ryan was shifting back and forth, uncomfortable with the glances she kept receiving from the two women. "Ryan, let me introduce you properly," her partner finally said. "This is Maria de Los Angeles Gallegos."

Ryan once again shook hands with the young woman, who now looked much less nervous. "Pleased to meet you," she said, flashing a wide smile.

Jamie didn't translate these few words, knowing that Maria Los would understand them perfectly. "Maria Los, this is Ryan O'Flaherty."

"I'm pleased to meet you, Miss Ryan," the young woman said in precise, but heavily accented English, rolling the "R" in Ryan's name.

"You don't need to call me 'Miss'," Ryan began, but stopped abruptly when she realized that they were now conversing in English and that Maria Los couldn't understand her.

Jamie explained. "Maria Los feels more comfortable using that term, honey. We've discussed this before."

"Okay, no problem," Ryan agreed, not liking it one bit, but acceding to the young woman's wishes.

"How about I offer you a ride to work?" Jamie asked her partner.

"I'll never make it if you don't," Ryan said, checking her watch.

After a much more relaxed good-bye, the twosome hopped into the Boxster for the trip to the gym. "Have you eaten?" Jamie asked.

"Nope. I was gonna get something before I left, but your little friend took up all of my available time."

"It's only 12:20, why don't I drop you off at that little falafel place by the gym. I don't want you to go to work without anything in that tummy."

"Best idea you've had all day," Ryan agreed, settling down in the seat for the short drive.

Traffic was slow, as usual, and as they progressed through town Ryan finally broke the silence. "Today sure was full of surprises." She had an unreadable expression on her face, and Jamie had a sneaking suspicion that she was referring to more than Maria Los's appearance.

"I bet Maria Los is thinking the same thing." Jamie laughed, trying to gauge her partner's mood.

Ryan just nodded, obviously not willing to share everything that was on her mind. They were nearing the restaurant, and she turned to face Jamie. "I've got a few questions about the house and how you manage things. Can we talk about that tonight?" She certainly didn't look angry, which reassured Jamie a bit, but there was something behind those blue eyes that was a little disquieting.

"Are we okay?"

"We're fine." Ryan smiled and leaned over for a kiss. "I just want to figure out what's going on in the cabeza."

Jamie pulled back and furrowed her brow a bit before a quick laugh burst out. "I think you mean cabaña. Cabeza means head."

Ryan shrugged her shoulders amiably. "Your head ... your house ... I'll settle for finding out what's going on in either of them."

Jamie had a sneaking suspicion that they were going to have another go-around on their finances. Even though she didn't look forward to these discussions, she realized that they were part and parcel of building a partnership, so she tried to swallow her anxiety over the issue. Ryan leaned in for another kiss and Jamie couldn't help but tease her a little bit. "Bye-bye, my little movie star," she hummed seductively.

"Movie star?" Ryan asked, puzzled.

Jamie just laughed as she pulled away from the curb, offering a quick wave over her departing shoulder.

Ryan ran up to the house at around four-thirty, stopping short when she spotted a well-used pickup truck in the driveway. *Now what? Is our cook here? The masseuse?* Her questions were answered when she got close to the truck and saw the staggering array of rakes, shovels, lengths of PVC pipe, lawnmowers, and leaf blowers neatly arranged inside the battered truck. A pair of young Latinos was just getting into the truck, and each waved and called out, "Buenas tardes, Señorita!" when they spied her heading up the walk.

Ryan pasted a smile on and waved back. "Buenas tardes ... Señors," she replied, using up most of her vocabulary.

They drove off, the ancient truck sputtering as several cylinders misfired. *A yard the size of a postage stamp, and she hires a gardener? This has got to stop!* She strode into the house, determined to set things right before nightfall.

When Jamie returned home an hour later, she wasn't sure what to expect. She thought that Ryan might be a little miffed to learn that she employed a housecleaner, understanding that was not the O'Flaherty way. It actually took a few minutes to find Ryan; there was no sign of her presence anywhere in the house. Poking her head out the back door, Jamie came upon the sight she hoped would greet her every day for the rest of her life: her lovely mate, sitting on the teak bench that rested under an arbor covered with fragrant white "Lady Banks" climbing roses.

Her breath caught as she took in the beauty of both the setting and the woman who held her heart. Ryan was freshly showered, judging by the still-wet hair slicked back off her face. Her skin glowed pink from what Jamie assumed was a combination of recent exercise and a good scrubbing.

The sun was low in the sky, the garage angling the rays so that they caught only the top of her dark head, creating a riot of highlights of gold and burgundy in the glossy tresses. The afternoon was warm, and only the briefest of khaki shorts covered her upper thighs. A black linen camp shirt draped attractively across her broad shoulders. Her feet were bare, and one long leg was drawn up so that her unshod foot could rest on the bench. A hardbound book rested on the raised knee, the intense blue eyes focused on the passage she was considering. Her eyes lifted, and she stared into space for a few moments, obviously deep in thought. Jamie decided right then that she could happily spend a few dozen hours just watching her beloved think.

The sparkling intelligence that was always apparent, but often slightly veiled, came to the fore when she was deep in thought. Jamie could practically see the synapses firing in her agile brain as her eyes flicked back and forth just a micrometer. Her dark brows knit together just a bit, as her head tilted a few degrees. With a blindingly white smile, the dark head nodded as some nugget of information became clear, and her eyes returned to the book to continue her study.

Unable to resist the lure of those blue eyes, Jamie descended the stairs and walked up to the bench. Ryan heard her coming and closed the book, placing it on a small table she had drawn close. A relaxed, warm smile covered her lovely face as her arms opened to welcome her partner home.

Climbing onto her lap, Jamie tilted her head to bestow a few gentle kisses on tart-tasting lips. "Umm ... you made lemonade," she breathed, allowing her face to stay right where it was.

Ryan's deep voice burred against her lips. "Somebody bought a dozen lemons. I figured that was a good way to reduce the stockpile."

Jamie pulled back and reached for the sweaty glass of the pale yellow beverage. "Ooh, this is good." She smacked her lips together for a moment, tilting her head as she assessed the drink. "You put orange juice in this, too," she decided.

"Yep. One orange really makes a difference," Ryan said. "Adds sweetness without adding as much sugar."

"It's divine," she decided. "Just like you." A few more kisses followed, with Ryan finally pulling away, to Jamie's regret.

"We need to talk, little one, and I'm not going to have you make me lose my rational mind again tonight." Startled green eyes looked down at her and Ryan quickly amended her statement. "Yet, that is. You can knock me senseless later, of course."

Now placated, Jamie slid off her lap and sat next to her on the bench. "So … what happened today? It's obvious something's bothering you."

"Are you hungry?" Ryan asked, off topic.

"Yeah, but I'd like to know what's bugging you first."

"Let's sit at the table and munch on a few tidbits, okay?"

Jamie turned her head and caught sight of the attractive presentation that her partner had arranged upon the glass-topped dining table. Most of the items from the basket Martin and the boys had given them were arranged on small plates, all of them covered by wire mesh domes to keep the insects away. An ice bucket held the chilled bottle of champagne, and a pair of crystal flutes waited to be filled. "You've certainly familiarized yourself with the kitchen, haven't you, Tiger?" Jamie was delighted that her partner had taken the time to prepare such a nice repast, and she expressed her gratitude with a few more kisses.

They walked the short distance, hand in hand, and Jamie smiled sweetly when Ryan pulled out one of the heavy chairs for her. Ryan sat down, drawing her chair close enough so that their knees touched. "Would you open the wine? I'm not very skilled in the champagne arena."

"Let's do it together," Jamie suggested. She indicated that Ryan should hold the cork while she gently turned the bottle. After half a turn the cork popped quietly, nary a drop of wine spilling. "Teamwork, buddy," she said.

Ryan poured the wine and clinked her glass against her partner's. "To the life we'll build in our house." She used the term they had decided on for the Berkeley dwelling, acknowledging that the O'Flaherty home was now both of theirs also.

"Mi casa es su casa," Jamie agreed, drawing the conversation back to the issue she thought was bothering her partner.

Ryan smiled, knowing that her lover was allowing her an opening. She took a sip of the wine and said, "A few things caught me by surprise today. The grocery delivery, the cleaning woman, and the gardener. What order do you want to take them in?"

Jamie started to reply, but a truck pulled into the drive just as she was opening her mouth. A slight grimace covered her face as she said, "You'd better put the car detailing service on the list as long as you're at it."

After conversing with the young men who had arrived to clean her car, Jamie came back to the table and took her seat. Once again, Ryan's gaze was unreadable, so rather than try to figure it out she took the bull by the horns. "Okay, here's the whole story.

We've had someone clean the place since we moved in. Neither Cassie nor Mia would do a damn thing around here, and I wasn't going to clean up after those two."

Ryan offered a small smile at the vehemence in her partner's tone. Jamie took a breath and continued. "We decided to hire someone to come in three days a week ..." She paused as Ryan's eyes grew very wide. "And since there were three of us, we each paid for one day. It's worked out well, and I don't see the need to change anything."

Ryan's brow furrowed and she interrupted. "Can I jump in?"

"Sure. Anytime."

"Okay." Ryan drew in a breath and held it for a moment, in a move Jamie had come to realize meant she was trying to remain calm. "I don't mean to judge you, Jamie, but it's a pretty sad state of affairs when three able-bodied women can't keep a house clean. It's just not that hard!"

Jamie bit back the sharp remark that threatened to burst forth and calmly muttered, "Thanks for not judging me."

Ryan's heavy sigh showed she was having a tough time staying cool, so Jamie jumped in with more facts. "Let me finish the whole story, and then we can discuss it, okay?" Ryan gave her a curt nod and she continued. "I wasn't happy with the first woman we hired, and over the next two years we ran through three more housecleaners. Most of them couldn't stand Cassie's demands, but some of them just didn't seem reliable enough for me to give them a key."

There she goes with the keys again! Ryan silently fumed. *What is it with the Evans clan and giving out keys? I've got to have an inventory of the key holders before I can sleep soundly in this motel!*

Jamie did her best to ignore the frown on Ryan's face as she continued with her explanation. "I know I've told you about Marta, our housekeeper and cook." Ryan nodded, recalling Jamie's fond recollections of the woman, and the important role she served during Jamie's childhood. "For as long as I can remember, she's worked at her church, teaching English to Spanish-speaking immigrants. Last year her church started a program where they provide seed money to members of the parish who are trying to become self-employed. I know Marta would never give her time to something that wasn't worthwhile, so I've been supporting the program financially."

Ryan cocked her head at this news, having never heard Jamie speak about how she made her charitable donations.

"A few months ago, Marta asked me if I would consider hiring some of the people from the program to do some jobs around here. That's how I met Maria Los, and Zaragoza and Estaban and Ramundo."

"So all of these people are just starting out?" Ryan asked, now both interested and somewhat pleased.

"Yes. Maria Los is just nineteen. She emigrated from El Salvador just after Christmas this year. She's a darling woman, and I think she's sweet on Zaragoza, the car detailer. She lives with two other women from the program in East Palo Alto."

"Does she work for other people too?"

"No. She's in class or studying the other two days. I pay her well and she can afford to only work three days a week until she's more skilled in English."

"She's been here how long?" Ryan asked.

"Since January," Jamie replied.

"Uhm … I hate to break it to you, but she doesn't know a bit of English."

Jamie slapped her on the thigh, seeing the gentle tease behind the impish grin. "She does just fine, smarty-pants. You just shocked the English right out of her with that scrumptious body!"

"Well, I don't know about that, but she does seem like a nice woman. You said that Estaban and Ramundo are the gardeners?"

"Yep. They don't know that I know it, but they're lovers," Jamie said quietly, in case Zaragoza could hear them speaking.

"Really?" Ryan wasn't sure why this surprised her, but the thought of the two sturdy young men being gay was startling. "Are they in business together?"

"Uh–huh. They're together all day. They work together and they live together. Two of Ramundo's cousins live with them too, and I think they're gay too."

"That's cool that they're there to support each other," Ryan said thoughtfully. "I assume it's not okay to be gay where they're from?"

"Yeah. Marta tells me they were basically banished from their town near Puebla in Mexico. Their families don't speak to them at all."

Ryan shook her head for a full minute, ruminating about the cruelty of families. "So … having all of these people work here is helping them build lives in the U.S."

"Yep." Jamie's smile was nearly radiant, and Ryan knew that she was trapped without an argument for letting any of them go.

"Hey …" Her brow contracted as she came upon the flaw in the logic. "Which one of these recent immigrants owns Web Van?"

Jamie blushed as she admitted the truth. "Uhm … that one's just because I'm lazy."

Satisfied that she had won at least a tiny bit of turf, Ryan decreed, "From now on I'm in charge of grocery shopping. Web Van can serve every other yuppie in Berkeley, but they'll never darken our door again!"

Zaragoza finished up by seven, and as Ryan observed her partner converse with the young man she reminded herself, *You never asked how she learned to speak Spanish so well!*

When they were once again alone, Ryan tugged her partner into her lap and asked, "Did you take Spanish in school?"

"Yeah, a little in grammar school," Jamie informed her. "But Marta taught me most everything. She had a rule—I couldn't help in the kitchen unless we spoke Spanish."

"Smart woman," Ryan murmured, nuzzling Jamie's sweet-smelling neck. "Better than my Granny's method—'Go to your Gaelic lesson, Siobhán, or you won't get dinner!'" Both women laughed, knowing that food was always a sufficient motivator for Ryan.

"Yeah, I'm really grateful to Marta. I was bilingual by the time I learned to speak, and it's sure come in handy quite often."

"I'd like our kids to be at least bilingual," Ryan agreed. "By the time they're adults, the majority of Californians will probably be Spanish-speaking."

"It's a deal," Jamie decided. "I'll teach 'em Spanish, and you teach 'em Gaelic"

"Great," Ryan muttered. "They can hate me for making them learn a language that almost no one in America speaks!"

"True, but we've got to make your Granny happy," Jamie reminded her, green eyes dancing.

"Good point," Ryan nodded, smiling broadly at the thought of her grandmother's happiness upon having her great-grandchildren speaking the native tongue.

The sun was just a memory as the two reclined on twin chaise longues, pleasantly buzzed from the champagne and partially sated from the delicacies in the gift basket. They were holding hands and softly sharing their hopes and dreams of the future, while the cooling breeze wafted over their skin. "I feel a lot better about living here," Ryan murmured, leaning over to place a gentle kiss on Jamie's cheek.

"Why's that?" The pace of her reply was much slower than normal, and Ryan was fairly sure the alcohol was to blame for that.

"Not sure," Ryan replied lazily, holding her wine glass up to gaze at the moon through the bubbles. "Maybe because I got settled and spent some time checking the place out. Maybe because it was really convenient to have you get home in ten minutes. It's so nice not to have to cross the Bay Bridge during rush hour, too," she added as she let the last drops of the slightly warm liquid slide down her throat. "But I guess the number one reason is because I can do this ..." In the blink of an eye she was lying upon Jamie's prone body, her weight pressing heavily into her smaller partner.

Jamie looked up at the glittering eyes that held hers and immediately decided that she didn't care if Ryan weighed more than the offensive line of the 'Niners. She needed to be crushed by the coiled power that lurked just under the surface of the baby-smooth skin that she reached up to taste.

"Wanna go to bed?" Ryan asked softly, her desire boldly displayed on her lovely face.

"I can't ever imagine saying no to that request," Jamie murmured breathlessly as she captured the rose-tinted lips that hovered over her.

As all rational thought began to seep from Ryan's brain, she got to her shaky feet and held out a hand. "Bed." Her demand was clear, and Jamie willingly complied, taking her hand for the short trip to the house. A quick glance at the table brought the adult in Ryan to the surface, and she stopped to swoop up the little plates and wire domes. "Ants," she intoned seriously, nodding judiciously at Jamie's giggles.

Once again, their evening ablutions were cast aside, neither woman willing to delay the expression of her passion for another moment. "I love you so much." Jamie's endearingly sincere expression as she spoke made Ryan's heart swell with love for the woman who rested upon her body.

Hands shaking with desire lifted to run through the golden locks that had shifted forward, nearly covering the sea green eyes that she so loved. "I love you, too," Ryan murmured, finding that her voice was rough with emotion. "I'll never stop loving you, Jamie."

A slow smile spread across the smaller woman's face, and she dipped her head once more to taste the lips that held her in their sway. "Forever," she whispered, repeating the word that best expressed her love. "It doesn't matter where we live. It only matters that we're together." Another series of achingly tender kisses followed, causing a low groan to escape from Ryan's slightly parted lips. "Always together."

The slowly building passion had risen to irresistible proportions, and Jamie felt the demands of her body increase exponentially. She shifted just a bit, allowing her legs to spread when she felt Ryan's muscled thigh press against her need. She sucked in a short breath, lifting her head slowly as her eyes fluttered closed.

Ryan's head swirled with want, and the ache in her belly grew as Jamie's tongue peeked out of her parted lips and slowly, teasingly, traced all around their outline, wetting them just enough so they glistened in the candlelight. It was an unconscious gesture, but Ryan's addled brain considered it one of the sexiest things she had ever seen. "Kiss me," Ryan whispered, her need for the moist lips undeniable.

Jamie gracefully granted her wish, putting all of her tender feelings into the touch. She continued to move against Ryan, now sliding easily against the firm thigh, while their mouths met and merged.

The blonde head lifted once again as a shudder rolled through her body, sending chills down Ryan's spine in response. "Ooh," she moaned softly, continuing to drive her hips against her partner. "I had no … idea … it could ever be this … wonderful." Her voice was rough with desire as she gasped out the words. Her skin shimmered in the candlelight, droplets of perspiration threatening to slide down her flushed face. Tiny flecks of gold and amber glinted in her verdant eyes as she struggled valiantly to hold them open.

Ryan's hands slipped down to her lover's hips, holding her securely. Jamie was beginning to strain now, her eyes tightly closed as her thrusts became rougher—more demanding. "Let go," Ryan cooed softly. "Come on, let it go. Let everything out. Tell me—show me how it feels."

"I … love … you," she gasped, speeding the beat of her hips in a wild fury. She blindly reached out and grasped Ryan's firm breasts, anchoring herself to her partner.

Covering Jamie's trembling hands with her own, Ryan whispered, "I love you, too, Jamie … so much."

Watery green eyes fought to open as she felt herself drown in the ocean of blue that gazed up at her with pure devotion. "For … ever," she gasped as waves of sensation buffeted her body, rolling over and over her as she cried out softly.

Ryan pulled her down, gasping in surprise at the wildly beating heart that pounded against her breast. The smaller woman was nearly limp in her arms, the heat radiating off her body. Shudders continued to rock her, each one causing a catch in her still-labored breathing.

"You're so incredibly beautiful," Ryan murmured, running her fingers through the damp golden locks splayed across her chest. "Your face ... your body ... the way you look at me when I'm loving you. So beautiful." Her voice was wistful and soft, and the slow, calming cadence was a powerful lure to Jamie to drift off. But her need to touch and taste her beloved was far greater than her need to sleep, and as she began to run her hands over her lover's body she felt her energy return.

"I want to show you how I feel," she murmured, her voice capturing the slow, sensual tone that her partner had used. "I want to show you with my hands, and my mouth and my tongue. I want you to know how much I love you."

Ryan gazed at her with a combination of deep love and nearly painful desire. "Love me," she murmured in a voice as soft as a breeze.

Never had a request been so willingly granted, and their bodies spoke for their hearts deep into the warm summer night.

The sun was just beginning to give evidence of the new day when a muffled voice that sounded like it was being forced out of a pair of lungs compressed under a heavy weight croaked out, "Has anybody ever told you that you were a load?"

Ryan chuckled at her partner's choice of words, her laugh constricting Jamie's chest even further. "Others have mentioned that." With another laugh she rolled from her perch atop her smaller partner's body and gently examined her for signs of damage. "No harm done, sweet pea. I don't think I was on top of you for long."

Jamie's fingers tangled in the dark hair that was draped across her chest. "I like you on top of me," she murmured lazily. "It just astounds me how heavy you feel, though. I don't crush you like this, do I?"

"Hardly. You're just a little heavier than Caitlin."

"Funny, very funny." A few good tickles made Ryan retract her statement.

"Well you're heavier than you look. Jack wasn't even ..." she began, but cut herself short before she could finish the thought.

Ryan knew that her partner was trying to censor herself from bringing up a loaded topic, but she felt no need to be protected. "I doubt that Jack weighed as much as I do," Ryan offered, trying to show that she wasn't bothered by speaking about him.

Jamie lifted her head to get a better look into her lover's eyes. "Of course he did," she protested. "Guys weigh lots more than women do."

Ryan laughed at this generalization. "Not when the guy is really lean, and the woman is ... sturdy," she concluded, trying to find the correct term for her impressive musculature.

"Honey, I think he weighed about one seventy-five or one eighty. How much do you weigh?" In all their time together, they had never discussed this bit of trivia, which was slightly surprising to the smaller woman.

"Guess," Ryan teased, climbing astride her once again.

As the air was squeezed from her lungs, and her ribs felt like they were going to poke out of her back, Jamie gasped, "Six hundred pounds!"

Rolling off again, Ryan scoffed, "You're way off. You'll never make a living guessing weight at the carnival."

"Come on ... tell me," Jamie begged.

"I'm really not sure," Ryan said. "I fluctuate a lot, and I haven't gained back what I lost on the ride. I'm still pretty low."

"You sure don't feel low," the smaller woman mused, hefting a weighty thigh in both hands.

"We can check, if you have a scale," Ryan said. "I might need the information later today, anyway."

"Huh?"

Ryan hopped out of bed, stretching sensually while Jamie watched her in fascinated silence. "I might need to know how much I weigh," she said absently as she bent to stretch her lower back.

"Huh?" This time, Jamie's confusion was mostly from her fascination with her lover's flexing body.

Ryan caught the difference in tone and chuckled at the look on her partner's face. "Let's hop in the shower."

"No running today?" Jamie asked, getting up to do a few stretches of her own.

"Nope. I need my strength. I'm trying to arrange for an appointment this morning that'll use up a lot of energy." She wandered into the bath and got onto the scale, nodding to herself as the needle settled down.

"One hundred eighty-five pounds!" Jamie was bent over the display, and when she stood her face reflected her surprise. "You weigh one hundred eighty-five pounds?"

"Told you I was way down," Ryan said.

"Down? Did you say down?"

"Yeah, I like to be about two hundred, but I've only been there once this year."

Jamie looked rather weak, and she sat on the edge of the tub for a moment, gathering her thoughts. "Having a baby with O'Flaherty genes might actually kill me," she said.

"Nah," Ryan reassured her easily. "My mother was very slight and she popped all of us out without a problem. 'Course, she was in labor with me for twenty-four hours ..."

"Adopting. We're definitely adopting." The tone was firm, but Ryan detected the teasing in her eyes.

"You're the boss," Ryan said.

"Yeah. Wouldn't *that* be nice," she quipped, slapping her grinning partner on her muscular butt.

They were in the process of drying each other with fluffy white towels when Ryan's pager went off. She looked up at Jamie and said, "That might be my call now."

"I'll get it," Jamie said as she walked into the bedroom to pick it up. "It's a local number, but I don't recognize it," she said as she handed it to Ryan.

"Yep, this is the call I've been waiting for." Ryan sat down on the bed and dialed. "This is Ryan O'Flaherty," she announced in her confident tone. "Thanks for calling me back." She nodded a few times and replied, "I'm very interested. Do you need someone with my skills?" Another series of nods and then, "Is that the only time you have?" Pursed lips and a clouded expression gave way to a sigh, "No, I'd rather see you today. I'll be there."

"What's going on, Tiger? Who besides me needs your skills?"

"That was Coach Greene. I've got to go over to campus for a while. Want to come with me?"

"Who is Coach Greene, and why is he interrupting our lovemaking?" she asked, placing her hands on her hips and narrowing her eyes at her lover.

"Hmm," Ryan mused. "I wasn't aware that we were making love."

"Honey, we're either making love, on the verge of making love or on the verge of being on the verge. Get used to it." The charmingly confident expression on Jamie's face made Ryan grin from ear to ear.

"I'm never going to argue with that logic," she agreed. "I'll call back and say I've become permanently indisposed."

"*Who is he?*" Jamie's curiosity had reached the boiling point, just the effect Ryan was seeking.

"*She* is the women's soccer coach. I heard they had some open positions, and I thought I might fit in."

"You play soccer well enough to play at this level?" She knew that Ryan was gifted athletically, but playing a varsity sport in college was a very big deal.

Ryan shrugged her shoulders and replied, "I guess I'll find out. She can meet me in twenty minutes. Are you interested?"

"Do I get to see your cute little butt in those shiny, checkerboard-patterned soccer shorts?"

"Sure, if that makes you happy; I've probably got a pair in with my workout clothes."

Jamie dashed into Ryan's room and rummaged through the drawers. She finally picked a pair of red soccer shorts and an old white jersey with red lettering that read "Sacred Heart".

She came back into her room and held up the jersey. "Is this from high school?"

"Yeah," Ryan said. "I forgot I still had that. It must have been hidden in with the shirts I packed. I wonder if it fits." She shrugged into the jersey and decided that even though it was a bit snug, it still looked presentable. Jamie came up behind her and helped tuck the jersey into the red shorts, grabbing a few handfuls of her favorite real estate in the process. Ryan had obviously prepared for this trip in advance, since she went to her room and retrieved a pair of white knee socks and some shin guards, which she snugged into place while Jamie got ready.

There was no time for breakfast, but Ryan got a couple of bananas and a plain bagel down while she was waiting for her partner. While Jamie drove the short distance, Ryan went to work on a quart of Gatorade, managing to polish it off by the time they pulled up to the soccer field.

Ryan started on an energy bar as she loped across the grass to greet the coach, Jamie following behind at a more leisurely pace. It was obvious that the two women already knew each other—rather well. The coach was clearly interested in Ryan, looking her over appraisingly. Jamie hoped her interest was purely professional, but one could never tell with her lover.

Coach Greene looked like she was in her mid-thirties. She was not very tall, maybe 5'5" or so, but she had a very muscular build. She looked like she could be on the field herself with her Lycra shorts and tank top barely covering her tanned and toned body.

Jamie approached and was immediately pulled into the conversation by her grinning lover. "Coach, this is Jamie Evans," she said proudly. "Jamie, this is Coach Greene."

"Pleased to meet you, Jamie," she said with twinkling eyes. "Have a seat on the bleachers while I put Ryan through some drills."

Ryan and the coach went to the goal nearest where Jamie sat. After a few minutes of warm-up, Ryan took her position as the coach began to try to get the ball past her. *She's a goalie? I swear, one day I'll find out she was a rodeo clown or a trapeze artist.*

Watching Ryan defend her goal was closely akin to watching a wild animal safeguard her newborn pups from a predator. With a glare in her eyes that Jamie had never seen before, she prowled along the goal line, daring the coach to make a move. Her laser-like eyes never left the ball, ignoring all of the stutter steps and feints that the coach tried to lure her with. She bent at the waist and flexed her powerful thighs, weight balanced on the balls of her feet, so that she was poised to move in any direction at any time, and she easily moved her body at the same second that the ball moved toward her. Working at close quarters like this, the coach was able to get quite a few balls past Ryan, but she had to really work for every one. There was a wide smile gracing the older woman's face by the time they stopped, and she tossed her arm around Ryan's neck to give her a rough hug.

They came back to the bleachers laughing and joking with each other. "She hasn't lost a step," she reported to a very interested Jamie. "As a matter of fact, I think you're quicker now than you used to be."

"I think I am too," Ryan said. "My legs and my butt are a lot more powerful now, and I think that helps me get a bigger burst when I move."

"What do you weigh now?" The coach's eyes roamed up and down Ryan's body, pausing momentarily on some of her more ample curves.

"I'm down to one eighty-five, but I'm trying to add a few," she said. "I have more stamina when I'm over one ninety."

Oh God! Jamie shrieked to herself. *She'll kill me with any more stamina!*

"I don't know what you've been doing to keep in shape since you left USF, but you look absolutely fabulous," the coach marveled.

"I do a lot of weight training and I run. That's about it," she said modestly, omitting the twenty other things she did to keep herself fit.

"Have you ever injured your knees?" the coach asked, looking up as Ryan shook her head. She squatted down to move her kneecap gently. She continued to move her leg, trying to determine how much flexibility there was in the joint. Getting to her knees, she grasped Ryan's leg with both hands and tried to move her knee while instructing Ryan to keep her foot planted. She nodded to herself and moved to the other leg, accepting Ryan's hand for a boost when she was done.

She told Ryan to sit down on the bleachers as she performed the same ritual of flexing and testing her range of motion with each ankle. As she moved from body part to body part, Ryan answered negatively to each question about injury. Finally, the coach looked up and asked, "Haven't you ever been hurt?"

That brought a burst of laughter from both Ryan and Jamie. "I'm more into broken bones and concussions," she said with a smile. "But I've been really lucky. I've never injured a joint."

The coach had her squat down and leap as high as she could, gauging her explosiveness. She asked Ryan to tense her legs and felt all along her quadriceps and then her hamstrings, her nimble fingers poking and prodding deeply into what Jamie considered her exclusive territory. But Ryan didn't seem fazed in the least by the examination, and Jamie controlled herself from barking out a protest.

When the coach had finally stopped groping her, she flashed Ryan a wide smile as she firmly slapped her butt, shaking her head in amazement. "You are absolutely rock hard, Ryan. How much do you work out?"

"An hour or so a day," she said, minimizing greatly. "I ride my bike a lot, too— about a hundred miles a week. I try to run five to ten miles every day, and since I live, or lived," she corrected, "in the Noe Valley, I do a lot of hill work."

"Well, you just look great," she said with her hands on her hips, a big smile covering her face. She turned to Jamie and asked, "Doesn't she look great?"

A thin smile covered Jamie's mouth but didn't extend to her eyes. "Great," she agreed tersely as she watched the coach's eyes linger on her lover's sculpted body.

"I can't think of another test I could give you," she said as she shook her head.

"You could count her teeth," Jamie said only slightly under her breath.

"Pardon?" Coach Greene asked. "Did you say something?"

"No, I was just agreeing with you," she said sweetly as Ryan rolled her eyes.

"We start practice next week, Ryan. I don't have a scholarship to give, but I guarantee we could use you. Are you interested?"

"I'll have to think about it," she said slowly, a small frown gathering between her brows. "It's an awfully big time commitment, and without a scholarship ..." She shook her head slowly, deep in thought. "I would like to play a sport this year, so I'll give it some serious thought. I'm going to talk to a couple of other coaches this week. I'll let you know by Friday."

"I hope you decide to join us, Ryan. I've seen you play in all of your other sports, and I've always thought that soccer was your most natural game."

"Actually, that's not true," Ryan said with a cocky grin. "But I'm glad you think so." She shook the coach's hand, and as the compact woman gathered her equipment, Ryan asked, "Can I keep a ball to play around with for a while?"

"Sure. Those are old practice balls. You can keep one," she said, tossing one to Ryan. After she had assembled her equipment, she waved good-bye and trotted off the field.

"Well, I have no idea why, but I am amazed," Jamie said as she looked up at her lover in admiration.

"What do you mean?"

"I don't know why it surprises me that you can play any sport so beautifully. You are just the most graceful athlete I've ever seen," she said.

"Thanks. But it's mostly genetics. My size and my speed enable me to do a lot of things, and they were gifts from God."

"Being given the gift is one thing. Making use of it is quite another," Jamie corrected her.

Ryan dropped the ball to the ground and started to kick it around in a lazy fashion. "Have you ever played?" she asked her lover.

"Sure. I was on a team when I was a little tyke. But I was never very good. I guess my hand-eye coordination isn't very good."

"No way, babe," Ryan said quickly. "You can't play golf without excellent hand-eye coordination."

"Well, I admit that I didn't apply myself very much. I just liked putting on the uniform and running around."

"I agree that the uniform is an important part of the game," Ryan teased. "I bet you looked adorable in yours. Do you have any pictures?"

"I'm sure we do. I'll ask Mother when she gets home. How about you? Any pictures of you in action?"

"Yeah. A couple of hundred or so," she said, laughing. "You know how Da is about family pictures." She started to play a little game with the ball, and Jamie quickly caught on that the purpose of the game was to keep the ball from touching the ground. She watched in awe as Ryan spent a good fifteen minutes juggling the ball with every part of her body, save for her arms, of course. Her balance was so perfect that she could easily stand on one foot while she used the other leg to repeatedly tap the ball. She would lightly touch it with the toe of her cleated shoe, then her shin, knee, shin, toe, then knee again. She effortlessly switched legs and began the routine again. When she tired of that drill she spent a few minutes tapping it with one knee, then the other, bringing her knees up so that her thighs were perpendicular to the ground. When that became too easy, she made the game a little tougher by striking it just hard enough to fly above her head.

To Jamie's amazement she tapped the ball with various parts of her head at least twenty times, sending it to the exact same height with each tap. Jamie finally asked, "Can you talk while you do that?"

Ryan shifted her eyes, never moving her head from the level plane it was on, and easily replied, "Sure, why not?"

"I thought maybe you, oh, I don't know, had to concentrate or something!" she said with exasperation.

"I *am* concentrating," she said as she started to hit the ball with each shoulder in turn. "But I'm not using my mouth to concentrate, so I can talk."

"You're something else, Ryan O'Flaherty. I'm not sure what, but it's definitely something else."

"Wanna see me show off a little?" The blue eyes were glittering with mirth, and Jamie couldn't imagine who would be foolish enough to say no to that request.

"Uhm ... showing off starts when?" she grinned, wondering what her partner called the impressive array of tricks she had already performed.

"Now." Ryan popped the ball in the air a few times, getting a nice height on it. Suddenly, she leaned back precariously and kicked straight up in the air with one long leg, sending the ball darting over her head like a bullet. She hit the ground lightly, rolling as she touched down so that she was back on her feet before Jamie could blink.

Wide green eyes just stared at her, Jamie's open mouth preventing any comment.

"Didn't you do drills like this when you played?" Ryan asked in what appeared to be a serious question.

"Ahh, no," Jamie replied. "We had to kick the ball around little orange cones, but that's all I can remember doing."

After retrieving the ball, Ryan popped it high in the air, catching it on her instep, and quickly pulled her foot up so that the ball was firmly wedged between her foot and her shin. "No wonder you never enjoyed it. Playing little tricks and games with the ball is half the fun." She abruptly tossed the ball in the air with her leg and in the same instant, kicked it to Jamie, who caught it from a purely defensive posture.

"Hey, you almost clipped me!"

"Gotta look alive when you're on the field," she teased as she walked over to the bench to grab their things.

On the way back to the car Jamie asked, "Was soccer your favorite sport?"

"Uhm, that's hard to say. I think my favorite was always the one that was coming up next. But I did love soccer. When I was in grammar school I don't think I ever went to school without my ball. I kicked it all the way there and all the way back every day."

"Bu ... bu ... but you had to climb those massive hills to get to school," Jamie stuttered as she recalled the thigh-busting streets between the O'Flaherty house and St. Philip's.

"Don't I know it," she said with a laugh. "But I think that's how I developed my ball-handling skills. I had to run down the hills backwards to control the ball, and that exercise really helped my footwork."

"Well, I would guess so!" Jamie's mouth gaped slightly in amazement as she imagined her young lover running down the hills, with her books tucked under her arms while she tried to control a soccer ball. "You said the next sport was always your favorite. What other sports did you play?"

"You'll just have to wait and see," she teased, snatching the ball and tapping it along the ground in a dazzling display of footwork that once more left Jamie standing in place with her mouth dangling open.

On the way home, Jamie glanced over and asked, "Coffee?"

"Ooh, I'd love some, but I didn't bring my wallet."

As the green eyes rolled, Jamie said, "No problem. You can just watch *me* have breakfast."

"Okay," Ryan muttered, a little embarrassed that she'd been caught in one of her habits. "I'm just not used to relying on other people for money. It's gonna take a while for me to adjust."

"It's an adjustment for me too," Jamie reassured her. "I've never wanted to take care of someone financially."

"Not even Jack?" Ryan was amazed at this little revelation, and she realized that they had never discussed how money was handled during their engagement.

Jamie laughed rather ruefully as she pulled into a parking space only four blocks from Sufficient Grounds. "Especially not Jack," she admitted. As they walked along the quiet streets, she added, "I'm embarrassed to admit this, but I don't think I paid for one thing while we were together. I bought him presents, but only for his birthday and Christmas. Even then I never went overboard. I guess I wanted to make sure that he was with me for me rather than my money."

Ryan squeezed her hand, grateful that Jamie was revealing something that seemed hard for her to admit. "Why doesn't it bother you with me? I assume that you aren't bothered, that is."

"Not in the least," she said with a serious expression. "It's actually important for me to be able to share my money with you. It means a lot to me."

"But not with Jack?" Ryan asked, once again.

Jamie shook her head, obviously trying to understand the dynamic herself. "Maybe it was because he was a guy, and I bought into the stereotype that he should provide for me. I'm really not sure. I mean, we did so little that it wasn't hard for him to provide everything. I bought dinner if I picked up carryout, but that's about it. Other than that, we just hung out at his apartment."

Ryan mulled over this scenario as they walked along, finding it difficult to reconcile her energetic partner with the woman who was content to sit in an apartment and watch her fiancé study. It seemed much more like a pattern that an old married couple would fit into, and she knew that it would never make sense to her.

Jamie took a big sip of her latté and broke off a piece of her chocolate chip scone for her partner. "Remember the last time we did this?" she asked with an exaggerated rolling of her eyes.

"Yeah … I seem to remember the 'face of evil' causing quite a scene over how familiar we were with each other."

"I am so glad that she's in New York," Jamie mused. "I hope she likes it so much she never comes back."

"It's gonna be weird seeing her around campus," Ryan agreed, wondering if Jamie would be more open about their relationship by the time Cassie returned in the fall.

"Only at first," Jamie said. "She only has power over me if I give it to her."

"True," Ryan nodded, pleased that her partner recognized the truth of that statement.

"Hey, would you mind if I didn't go to summer school?"

"Huh? I thought you were all set? What happened?"

"I got into two classes, but they're real duds. I hate to give up my afternoons just for the hours. We didn't get a chance to talk about this yesterday, but I stopped by the golf coach's office yesterday and he agreed to talk to me about trying out for the team."

"Really?" Ryan's eyes were wide with excitement, and Jamie offered up a silent prayer of thanks for her partner's unfailing support.

"Yeah. I'm gonna meet him at noon today and he's gonna take a look at my game. I think I'd rather spend my afternoons practicing than sitting in class."

"I think it's a perfect plan." Ryan smiled, taking Jamie's hand and placing a gentle kiss on it. "I'd always rather be active than sitting in class."

"I've just decided that if I'm going to do this, I'm going to do it right. That means three or four hours of practice a day. It just seems like the best time for that is when you're at work."

"Sounds like a deal," Ryan beamed. "I'll put some thought into how we should change your workout to focus on golf muscles."

"Great. If you don't mind, I'll try to go out with you in the morning a couple of days a week. I think I have a plan for how you can still have solitude while I'm with you." Waggling pale brows showed that Jamie was pleased with her idea, and Ryan was looking forward to hearing it.

"I can't imagine how I could ever concentrate when you're in sight, but I'm willing to try," she promised with a trusting smile.

Chapter Five

Later that morning, Ryan continued to fuss over her partner, nearly driving the smaller woman to distraction. "Do you have a snack in your bag in case you get hungry?"

"Yes, Mom."

"Let me check your neck to make sure you have enough sun block on."

"Ryan, I'm sure I have enough," Jamie said. "I'll be fine, sweetie."

"I just hate that I can't come to watch you." Since this was at least the twentieth time she'd voiced this complaint, Jamie acknowledged that this was the true source of her partner's anxiety.

"I know, but you can't miss work and you know it. Besides," she said as she slid her arms around Ryan's waist, "I might not be able to concentrate with you watching me."

"But I can come to your matches when you make the team, can't I?"

Jamie couldn't resist the childlike hopefulness on her face, and she leaned in for a slow kiss. "Of course you can come. *If* I make the team," she amended gently.

"Oh, you'll make it, all right."

Ryan's confidence was contagious, and Jamie allowed herself a moment to agree with her optimistic prediction. "Now, you know that this isn't a real tryout. The coach just wants to see me play a round. If he thinks I'm good enough, I can try to play my way onto the team in August."

"I know." Ryan's patient tone belied her excitement and enthusiasm. "But I also know that you'll make the team. You're really good, and I know that you'll work hard this summer to be even better."

"I'm gonna have to play a lot, Ryan. A whole lot. Are you sure you won't mind playing on the weekends?"

"Honey," she drawled, lacing her hands behind Jamie's neck, "I'd play tiddly-winks all weekend if you were going to be playing with me."

Jamie's mouth opened for a rejoinder, but instead she smirked slightly while shaking her head. "Too easy. That was just too easy."

After her workday was finished, Ryan walked home, mulling over the possibility of playing soccer. *Damn, I'd love to play again ... but it just toasts me that I can't get a full ride. I know Jamie will never be able to understand this, but that scholarship means more to me than I can say. It's not just the tuition. Even though the money is important, the most important thing is that giving me the scholarship is an acknowledgment that they gave up on me too soon in high school. Of all of the coaches from Cal who recruited me, Coach Greene knew me the best. She had to know that I could shoulder the work here. It wouldn't have been that big a risk for her to take. Hard to believe that one bad semester in high school made her ignore everything I'd done up until then.*

She had been walking a long while before she realized that she had gone quite a bit out of her way. Providentially, she found herself near the large farmers market, and she stopped to load up on organic fruit and vegetables. Nearly every stone fruit found its way into her backpack—peaches, plums, apricots, and nectarines. Stopping by an herb stand, she chose fresh basil, oregano, and thyme, then decided that she might as well make tomato sauce for dinner since she already had most of the ingredients. The heirloom tomatoes were too beautiful to resist, and she added six of them, after grabbing a couple of pounds of Romas. Quickly adding some red, yellow, and orange peppers, she headed toward home before her empty stomach demanded anything else. *I think I'm gonna have to have Conor bring my bike tomorrow*, she grumbled as she struggled with her purchases during the rest of the long walk home.

When Jamie pulled into the drive at four-thirty, Ryan was sitting on the front porch, clutching a beer and looking anxious. The impatient golf widow bounded off the porch and opened the car door before Jamie could even get the key out of the ignition. "How did it go?"

Jamie smiled up at her as she got out of her car. "It went well."

"Tell me!" Ryan demanded.

Jamie laughed gently at her partner's impatience, grateful to have such an enthusiastic reception. "Okay, okay. Let me get out of the car." While she slid out of the car, Ryan ran around and grabbed her golf bag, running back to slide her arm snugly against Jamie's waist.

"You're out of the car," the taller woman whispered, nudging Jamie's hip with her own.

"Okay, I give! Let's sit down right here and I'll start at the top."

They sat side by side on the stone steps of the porch, with Jamie taking a long pull from Ryan's beer. Ryan's eyes were wide open and she leaned forward a little in anticipation.

Jamie laughed at her posture. "I've got to tell you, it really makes me feel special to have you so interested in this."

With a pleading expression that only the coldest of hearts could ignore, Ryan asked, "Shouldn't you reward that interest by telling me what happened?"

"Yes, I should. The coach met me at the course and we spent a couple of minutes talking. He seems like a nice guy. He's about thirty or so, married, with a baby girl. He was very laid back. Asked me to call him Scott."

"What questions did he ask?"

"He wanted to know how long I'd been playing, where I usually played, if I'd been in much competition. You know, the usual background stuff."

"Then what?"

"We went out to the driving range and he had me work through my bag. I must have hit a hundred and fifty balls. I was kinda tired when I was done. But he seemed pretty impressed. I was really glad that I'd spent some time working with Chip because he asked me to fade and draw the ball about two dozen times. It seemed to surprise him that I could do both pretty well."

"That's 'cause you're really good!" Ryan bounced around excitedly on the edge of the porch, beaming at her partner.

Jamie smiled again and continued, "Then we played nine holes. He had his clubs, but he only played one or two holes. Luckily, I hit some really nice drives today. I was afraid I'd be too tired to boom them after all that time at the range, but I was really smokin' 'em," she said, wiggling her eyebrows.

Ryan lifted her open hand and slapped Jamie's loudly. "You're a stud."

"You're the first person I've ever dated who's called me a stud," she said with a laugh.

"Well, you are a stud."

"When we were finished, he said that he was really impressed with my game. Then he said he hoped I'd come out in August and try to make the team."

"What were his exact words?" Ryan asked, brow furrowed.

"Hmm, I think he said, 'I'm really impressed with your game, Jamie. I hope you come out in August and try to make the team.'" She stuck her tongue out and Ryan tried unsuccessfully to grab it.

"Then what?"

"I asked how many spots he had on the team. He said he could carry twelve. There are already nine scholarship players, so he has three spots to fill. Last year about twelve women tried out for two spots, so I guess the competition is pretty tough. I'm really gonna have to work to be ready." Her voice and face became more serious as she considered her chances.

"I'll help you in any way that I can. I gave some thought to your program, and I think we should do a lot more work on your shoulders and back, and we should keep working your legs. If we can get you in top shape, that'll really give you an edge."

Jamie got to her feet and extended a hand to her partner. "You give me an edge, Buffy. Just knowing you're there to support me is all I could ever ask for."

When they entered the house, Jamie turned and gazed at her partner with a puzzled grin. "Did Martha Stewart come by here this afternoon?"

"Whatever do you mean?" Ryan batted her eyes ingenuously, trying to play dumb, but failing.

Jamie looked at the neat piles of laundry folded on the dining room table, caught the tangy scent of tomato sauce bubbling away in the kitchen, and marveled at the simple, elegant arrangement of gladioli on the coffee table. "I had no idea you were this domestic," she said, just a hint of teasing in her voice.

"It's just laundry, tomato sauce, and a bunch of flowers." Ryan's head was cocked a bit, trying to figure out why Jamie was so surprised. "I've been cooking and doing laundry since I was seven."

For reasons that she couldn't understand, Jamie was a little taken aback by this fact. She sat down rather heavily on the sofa and made an admission. "I've never done laundry in my life."

"Sure you have, babe," Ryan said. "You washed our bike clothes out when we got back from the ride. Remember?"

"Oh, I've washed things out in the sink when I've traveled, but I've never sorted a bunch of clothes and figured out how to use a washer and dryer." She was blushing, and Ryan knew there was something going on in her head, but she could not, for the life of her, figure out what it was.

"And that bothers you … why?"

Jamie sat back and looked at Ryan for a few moments, finally lifting her hand to gently tuck some stray hairs behind her lover's ear. Her touch was very tender, and she gazed deeply into Ryan's eyes the whole time. "It's never really hit me how it must have been for you," she said softly. Her eyes filled with tears, and a few drops slid down her cheeks, where they were caught by Ryan's fingertips. "I've never really considered how many adult tasks you had to take on. I was a kid, but you were a little adult."

Ryan wrapped her arms around her partner and tenderly kissed her head, finally coming to her forehead, where she swept the fine blonde hair away with her lips. "It wasn't that bad," she soothed. "We had lots of help—my aunts and my older cousins were over every day when I was little. Besides, I wanted to help out. I wanted to do my own laundry and help with meals. It made me feel like I was a part of the family, you know?"

Jamie nodded her head slowly. *I never had that*, she thought to herself. *I never felt like I contributed in any way.* The distance she felt between herself and her parents seemed to grow larger just by thinking about it. "I'm sorry for going off like that," she finally murmured, not ready to share her thoughts. "I feel kinda shaky this afternoon."

Ryan brought her hand up to feel Jamie's forehead. "You haven't looked quite right since you got home. Tell me what's wrong."

"Nothing big." Jamie got up and ran her hands through her hair, shaking her head a bit to clear it. "I got my period today, and I'm a little crampy and a little emotional."

Slipping an arm around her shoulders, Ryan pulled her partner close and gently rubbed her back. "My poor baby," she soothed. "Let me take care of you tonight, okay?"

Uncharacteristically, Jamie shrugged off the offer and pulled out of the embrace. "It's no big deal." She got to her feet and offered a smile to her puzzled partner. "I started to feel twinges when we were on the golf course, and I didn't have any pain pills with me. I'm sure I'll be fine after I take some ibuprofen."

Ryan remained seated on the couch, casting a thoughtful glance at Jamie's departing form, while the smaller woman went up to her bedroom. *That was odd. Either something else is bothering her, or she doesn't like to be touched when she's feeling under the weather.* She shook her head and got to her feet. *Guess I'll find out eventually.*

A few minutes later, Jamie came into the kitchen wearing one of Ryan's oversized tank tops and a pair of her roomy cotton boxer shorts. The bright blue shirt was so huge that it nearly covered the pink striped shorts, and Ryan toyed with her by ostentatiously peeking into the armholes to observe her bare body.

"Nice look for you, sparky," the brunette said conversationally.

"I like big clothes when I don't feel well. You don't mind, do you?"

"Nope. You can start wearing my jeans if you want." *The fact that you want to wear my clothes lets me know you're not mad at me. That takes one possibility off the list.* "Did everything go okay today?"

Jamie was leaning against the counter, legs crossed at the ankles, looking more like a five-year-old than her true age. She nodded, sparing a small smile. "Everything's fine. Really." Her tone was friendly, but it was clear that she didn't want to converse any more about her mood, so Ryan tried a different tactic.

"Why don't I bring in one of the chaise longues, and you can sit down and have a glass of lemonade while I finish dinner?"

Pushing away from the counter, Jamie walked over to the stove and stirred the delicious-looking sauce. "This looks absolutely great. Thanks for working so hard."

"No problem," Ryan assured her. "Uhm … do you want me to bring in that chaise?"

Although her lover's back was turned to her, the taller woman could see the sigh that caused her shoulders to rise and fall. "Honey, I have cramps. I've been getting them since I was thirteen. It's no big deal." Jamie turned to face her with a slightly exasperated look on her face. "I took some pills, and that's all that can be done."

Ryan crossed the room and put her hands onto Jamie's hips. "No, it's not," she said softly, rubbing her thumbs across the cotton material that engulfed her lover's torso. "I could give you a massage, or get you a heating pad. I'm sure you'll feel better if you lie down until your pills start to work, too. I can tell by the way you move that it's bothering you, Jamie. Why won't you let me help?"

She dropped her head onto Ryan's chest, embarrassed that she was acting so hardheadedly. "I don't like to give in to minor little aches and pains," she said. "I try to ignore them, you know? It kinda seems like they go away faster if you don't acknowledge that they're there."

Ryan considered this tactic for a moment, finally agreeing that it had some merit. "That works for me if I'm out in public and don't have time to think about pain. But once I get home and relax, it always comes back full force. Then I pamper myself a little."

Jamie cocked her head and gave her a slightly puzzled look. All at once it became clear to Ryan that her partner really had no idea what she was talking about. "Weren't you pampered when you were sick?"

"No, not really," she said, looking a little embarrassed.

"Well, you're going to start now," Ryan said, the tone in her voice allowing no argument. "Go get your mail while I get you set up here. I swear, you get more mail than my whole family does. Go on." She shooed her out of the kitchen, smiling at the puzzled look she got as Jamie left the room.

When Jamie returned, one of the chaises from the yard was sitting in the kitchen. A little wrought iron table was placed next to it with a cool glass of lemonade just waiting to be savored. "This is kinda weird," Jamie said as she plopped down on the lounge chair, but she looked immediately grateful when she allowed her cramping body to relax against the thick cushion. Ryan bustled over with some pillows from the living room and spent a few minutes making sure that her lover was completely comfortable.

"I like being pampered when I don't feel well, so I assume you'll feel the same way once you get used to it," she said, as she bent to kiss her tenderly.

"Were you really pampered when you were ill?" Jamie wasn't sure why she thought this, but she had assumed that the O'Flaherty household would be filled with Spartan ideas about dealing with illness.

"Oh, yeah. If Da couldn't be home to watch me, Aunt Maeve would come over. They'd make me cocoa and play cards with me, or read to me if I was really sick. The boys would even take a turn at nursing me back to health as they got older. How were you treated?" she asked, slightly afraid of what she might hear.

"Not much nursing," she said. "Elizabeth didn't think it was good to coddle a sick child. She said it gave you no incentive to get well. She'd provide the bare necessities, then give me little rewards when I'd get out of bed."

Ryan suddenly was hit with the image of little Jamie in an observation room, with Elizabeth watching her through a one-way mirror, taking notes about the experiments she was conducting. "Well, you're going to be coddled from now on, princess. This is one more area in which Elizabeth had her head up her ass!"

"Of all the places that I can picture Elizabeth's head, that is one that I cannot begin to imagine," she said with a laugh. Ryan went back to her chores and Jamie looked up at the stove again. "Where did you learn to make spaghetti sauce?"

"My father *is* a cook, you know. You can't serve only Irish stew and soda bread to a bunch of hungry firefighters. He has a quasi-international range," she said.

"Your father is an excellent cook," Jamie agreed. "I'm really a little nervous about cooking for him tomorrow."

"You could serve peanut butter sandwiches and Da would rave about them. He's quite over the moon with you, you know."

"If he likes me half as much as I like him, I'm doing well," she said, grinning. "And, speaking of liking people, Ms. O'Flaherty, tell me all about this soccer thing."

Ryan crossed her arms and leaned back against the counter, a relaxed grin covering her face. "Sure, what do you want to know?"

"I didn't even know you played soccer seriously, Ryan. Now I find out that they want you to play for Cal. That's a very big deal!"

"You know I'm athletic," she said. "I told you I played basketball at USF."

Blinking, Jamie asked, "And that means I should assume you played soccer?"

"It's a different season, honey. Soccer is a fall sport, and basketball is in the winter." The slightly puzzled frown crossing her face indicated that this should have been obvious to Jamie.

She blew her bangs off her forehead in frustration. "I swear, Ryan, sometimes it's like playing twenty questions with you."

"I'll tell you anything you want to know," Ryan said, surprised by her partner's comment. "I just don't always volunteer stuff. It's how I was raised. Da always told us it's impolite to brag about our accomplishments."

Jamie nodded slowly, recognizing that her partner was always going to be a bit reticent about blowing her own horn. "Okay, let's start over. I want to know everything, so I'll just cross-examine you."

Ryan's grin brightened as she assured her partner, "You can examine me in any way you want, hot stuff."

"Right. Don't try to distract me, now. I've got business to conduct here." Her stern tone didn't extend to her eyes, and Ryan was happy to see the sparkle return to them. "Tell me how you know this Coach Greene."

"Oh … I've known her since I was a freshman in high school. She practically lived with us during my junior year."

"*What?*" Jamie's mind reeled from this information. *Wait a minute … Martin wouldn't allow that!*

"Don't take that literally, honey. She recruited me to play for Cal when I was in high school."

"Yeah …" Jamie nodded, assuming that was the case. "But why was she at your house all of the time?"

Ryan laughed a little and set the record straight. "I was exaggerating, babe. NCAA rules are very tight on how many home visits you can have, but you can call and write and attend games that the recruit plays in as long as you don't have any contact with her. So she called me every day for almost two years. She attended every one of my soccer games, and she sent me a handwritten note after every game. She'd tell me how my performance that day would have fit into the Cal system, and all that type of nonsense. Since she had a little more free time during the winter, she'd come watch my basketball games too. We'd be playing some team down in San Jose, and I'd look up and she'd be sitting in the stands—watching me like a hawk."

"Wasn't that weird? I don't think I could perform well if someone was watching me all of the time."

Ryan thought about that for a moment and nodded. "It's hard at first. But you get used to it after a while."

"So it doesn't bother you now?"

"Nope. It actually helps my focus if there are a lot of distractions. I go deeper into my concentration. Kinda funny, huh?"

Jamie nodded, slowly beginning to understand some of the many factors that made Ryan such a gifted athlete. "So, you saw this woman a lot, but you didn't really speak that often, right?"

"Kinda," Ryan said. "If you're on a high school team, you can go to all of Cal's home games without charge. So some of my teammates and I would take BART over here for the home soccer games. I'd say that we saw nearly every game my freshman, sophomore, and junior years." Ryan had a wistful look on her face, remembering the carefree days of her youth. "No matter where we were sitting, at the end of the game she'd always catch my eye and give me a smile or a thumbs-up. It was kinda nice."

"When did you see her last?" By the sad look in her eyes, Jamie knew something was bothering her partner, but she was a little reluctant to bring up bad memories. But Ryan looked like she wanted to talk, coming over to sit on the edge of the chaise. Jamie began to gently stroke her back as a small sign of encouragement.

"I played in two games during my senior year." Her flat monotone was very uncharacteristic, giving evidence of how difficult it was to talk about this period of her life. "She was at both of them. In my final game we had a shoot-out. You know what that is, don't you?" Blue eyes shifted to look for confirmation.

"I'm not sure," Jamie said. "Is that when each team gets to take a shot?"

"Yeah, that's pretty much it. Five players get to try to score with only the goalie defending the goal. Anyway, it was tied four to four when my team made their final score. I made a pretty good save and we won because of it. It was pretty cool, and everybody came over to congratulate me. I looked into the stands for Da, but I saw Coach Greene before I caught sight of him. She gave me a smile that I still remember, and … it meant a lot, Jamie. It just meant a lot." The uncharacteristic slump to Ryan's shoulders reflected the burden that she still bore over the entire incident.

"Then what happened, honey. What did she say when you quit the team?"

Ryan barked out a bitter laugh, shaking her dark head slowly. "She said nothing."

"What do you mean, nothing?"

"She said nothing." Ryan got up and went to the refrigerator, pulling out a beer and taking a moment to open it and take a long pull. "After I quit the team, she fell off the face of the earth. Not one phone call, not one letter. No one from Cal called to try to figure out what happened. They just abandoned me." Her head dropped a little, the dark hair shifting forward to drape around her regret-filled face. "When it was time to make my choice about college, I called her, and she said she'd decided to offer the scholarship to another girl."

"But why?" Jamie was off the chaise immediately, wrapping her arms around her partner. "Why would they do that?"

"I don't know," Ryan said. "They must have figured I was doing drugs or something. I mean, my grades did plummet … I did stop playing all of my sports … I did start acting pretty wild, and I'm sure that information got back to the Athletic Department. I guess they were just being cautious."

"Is today the first time you've talked to her since then?"

"No, she called me last year when she heard I transferred. I couldn't play then because of NCAA transfer rules, plus I wouldn't have been given medical clearance because of my head injury. But she told me then that she wanted me to try out for this year's team. She called me several times last year, actually. It felt like she was recruiting me all over again." She gave a small, bitter laugh as she added, "I told her I wasn't interested, and she finally quit calling."

"How do you feel about her?" Jamie had to admit that she was puzzled by Ryan's behavior. She'd treated the coach as a best friend, rather than a person who'd betrayed her.

"Okay, I guess," she said. "We talked about it last year when she called me. She said she couldn't give me any details, but that she was really sorry how things had worked out. I have no way of knowing everything that went on then, so I just chose to believe her." Ryan looked up with one of her guileless expressions, and Jamie felt the emotion well up in her chest as she once again considered how Ryan tried to see people in the best possible light.

"Could you play for her?"

"I think I could." Ryan took another pull on her beer, and stared up at the ceiling for a moment. "I'm trying to get past that part of my life, and in some ways I think this might help me."

"Okay, that makes sense. But it seems like there's another part of you that doesn't want to play. Tell me about that."

"I guess I don't want to give them the satisfaction of being able to blow me off and then get me for free. It really irks me that they still won't give me a free ride."

"Is that it? Really?"

"Yeah. I'm just pissed."

"Okay, why *do* you want to play?"

"I love to compete," she said simply. "And for women, playing at the NCAA Division One level is usually the highest level of competition. Obviously you could go higher and be on a national team or the Olympic team, but the NCAA is still pretty good. I also think I'd feel proud of myself to be able to walk on and play when I'm nearly twenty-four years old. I like being able to kick the butts of younger women."

Jamie looked at her partner for a few moments, going over in her head the things Ryan had spoken of. "It sounds to me like you really want to play. It's only to get back at someone if you don't, and that doesn't sound like you, honey."

"You're right," she said as she let out a frustrated breath. "I'm letting my pride get in the way. But then I have the money issue. I can't work and study and play soccer. I'd have to quit my job. Then I'd have to take out loans to get through the year."

"Can you try to ignore the money issue for the time being?" she asked. "You know there are many ways we can take care of that."

"Okay," she slowly said. "If I ignore money, I guess I need to decide if I want to play, and if I do, I need to just throw myself into it and ignore the side issues. But my next problem is that I can't decide what I want to play. If I'm not able to get a scholarship anyway, I might choose to play a sport that doesn't award scholarships. Maybe I need to talk to those coaches too, and see which sport fits my current life the best."

"What other sports are you talking about?" Jamie asked, looking puzzled.

"All in due time, my dear," Ryan teased, patting Jamie's cheek as she guided her back to her sickbed.

As the dinner preparations continued, Jamie watched with delighted interest as Ryan made a salad, layering sliced tomatoes, mozzarella, and fresh basil, and then topping it with some balsamic vinegar and olive oil.

The dryer buzzed and Ryan dashed over to it to take out the last of the laundry. As she meticulously folded each piece, Jamie commented, "Maria Los does laundry. You should leave it for her."

"No, thanks. I've been doing my own laundry since I was a kid. I like to do it myself."

"But ..."

"Jamie, I prefer to do my own. I'll do yours too, if you'd like, but I don't want a stranger cleaning my clothes."

"She knows how ..." she began again, but Ryan cut her off.

With a no-nonsense look, the brunette said, "I know it sounds odd to you, but I'm not gonna change my mind, so you might as well drop it. I'm going to clean my own room and do my own laundry. I'm not sure I can ask Maria Los to stay out of my room without resorting to drawing pictures, so I'd appreciate it if you'd mention it to her."

"Okay." Jamie realized there would be other, more important disagreements down the line, so she gave in gracefully. "I'll tell her tomorrow."

"Thanks, babe. Oh, how much do I have to chip in for Maria Los?"

"Well, nothing if she's not going to clean your room or do your laundry. Mia and I'll just split it."

"No, that's not fair. She'll clean the rest of the house, and I'll benefit from that. So I'll pay my share."

Once again, Jamie gave up quickly. "Seventy-five dollars," she said, wishing she'd lied when she saw Ryan's eyes bug out.

"Seventy-five dollars?" Each syllable had been enunciated so perfectly that Jamie was certain Maria Los would have been able to understand the question perfectly.

"Honey, if she's not worth that to you, I don't have a problem in the world with paying two-thirds myself."

"No, no, don't worry about it," Ryan assured her. "I just didn't realize it cost that much. I can handle it." *It comes out to forty-five minutes of work after taxes. Don't be such a Scrooge.* "While we're at it, how much do I owe for my share of the gardeners?"

"One hundred dollars a week will cover both, honey." This was only a tiny fib in Jamie's book, and one that she felt entirely justified in telling. "How much do I owe for the groceries you bought today?" she asked, trying to catch Ryan in her own trap.

"Nothing," Ryan said. "I'll pay for groceries until I balance out what you paid to Web Van. I still have ninety-six bucks to go until we're even."

Damned math major, Jamie grumbled to herself while Ryan went back to check on the sauce.

Now that her domestic duties were done, Ryan asked, "Would you like to go sit outside for a while? I could open some wine and make us some appetizers."

"Do you ever have a bad idea?" Jamie got to her feet and stretched a bit, getting out all of the kinks from a long day of golf. Pausing to take a long appraising look at her partner, she smiled at the very appealing look that she was sporting. Ryan was wearing the cute red and white board shorts that she had purchased for her in Santa Cruz. Tucked into the waistband was a tight white tank top with spaghetti straps. She obviously was not wearing a bra, and when Jamie grabbed her by the rear to pull her in for a kiss, it became obvious that she had also neglected to wear panties. "Didn't you ever hear that you're not supposed to go out without clean underwear?" she teased, palming the firm cheeks to good advantage.

"I honor every word," Ryan murmured as she maintained the tiny distance between their bodies. "But I only have about four pairs of panties, and they're all dirty. My regular underwear would stick out of the bottom of these little things," she said as she tugged on a leg of the shorts. "So rather than flouting one of the tenets of womanhood by wearing dirty underwear, I decided to go without."

Jamie smiled up at her as she gripped the muscular flesh. "I like this a lot," she whispered. "I might throw out all of your underwear when you're not looking."

"You sound like you feel better," Ryan said as she pulled away and held her lover out at arm's length to gauge her appearance.

"My cramps are just about gone," she admitted. "I come home to a gorgeous woman, a good dose of pampering, and I'm gonna have a great meal soon. I think I like having a wife," she mused as she leaned in for another hug.

With a send-off kiss, Ryan patted her butt and guided her toward the back door. She strolled outside and sat in the still-bright sun while Ryan scrambled around in the kitchen, trying to find everything she needed. She came out a few minutes later carrying a tray filled with the last items from their welcome-home basket along with a loaf of crusty Italian bread that she'd picked up on the way home. The tray also carried a crisp Pinot Grigio and two chilled glasses.

After she set the tray down, she dashed back inside to bring the chaise back out and set it in place. They chatted about their respective days, and after a few minutes, Jamie began to feed some little tidbits to Ryan. She reciprocated, and soon her fingers were being drawn into Jamie's mouth as she handed her each bite. Mere seconds later they were both on the same chaise, making out furiously. After several minutes of passionate groping, Ryan tore herself from Jamie's voracious mouth and announced, "No matter what, I'm having dinner tonight! I swear you're trying to starve me to death. I've missed more meals in the last week than I have in my whole life!"

Jamie pulled her back down and answered her with a torrid kiss. They rolled around on the narrow surface of the chair for a few more minutes before Ryan sat up again. "I'm not kidding, Jamie. I'm gonna eat dinner tonight!"

"I know what I want for dinner," she rasped out in reply. "It's tasty, and delicious, and decidedly Irish." A few more minutes of passionate wrestling made Ryan forget her vow completely. Jamie had unlaced her shorts and was beginning to tug them down when Ryan pulled away one last time to dash up the stairs and turn off the sauce. She looked longingly at it and shook her head as she ran back down the stairs to Jamie's eager mouth.

Ryan stood at the edge of the chaise and unlaced her shorts completely. Her hips swayed sexily and the fabric began to slide from her body of its own accord. As the shorts fell, she crossed her arms in front of herself and grasped the hem of her tank, but Jamie shook her head briefly. "Let me," she murmured, her gaze never leaving the blue eyes that she so loved.

"My pleasure," Ryan whispered as she gingerly climbed astride her partner to once more express the love that they shared.

"If we're gonna do this very often, we've gotta get some wider chairs." Ryan bit back a groan as she slid off the chaise, landing on her knees. Her head slipped down Jamie's body until it rested on her upper thighs. "I think we'd better move inside to continue this discussion," she murmured against the soft cotton of her lover's boxer shorts.

Jamie ran her fingers through Ryan's damp hair, smiling as her lover's pulse point throbbed against her leg. "I'm not up for it, baby," she said softly. "I'm still feeling too crummy."

The dark head tilted until Ryan could make eye contact with her partner. "Really? You seemed pretty interested a few minutes ago." Her hand had begun to tickle the baby-soft skin on Jamie's thigh, and the involuntary shiver that chased across the smaller woman's body belied her claimed disinterest.

"I was, silly," she laughed. "I was very, very interested in making love to you. I just don't feel like being on the receiving end right now. I'm more interested in getting some dinner and taking more pills. If I really knock these cramps out tonight, I should feel fine by tomorrow."

"Okay, babe," Ryan said, getting to her feet and offering a hand to Jamie. "Let me go rinse off, and I'll get you fed." She picked up her clothes and took Jamie's hand as they crossed the small patch of grass that made up the backyard. "I could be convinced to administer my one hundred percent guaranteed cure for cramps after dinner if you're in the mood."

Jamie turned to make eye contact, and it became clear just what that cure involved. Ryan's eyes were twinkling, and her wolfish gaze was roaming up and down Jamie's body in a very proprietary fashion.

"I just bet you would," Jamie laughed, slapping Ryan's bare butt. "I should have known that all of your home remedies would involve getting me into bed."

"Not all of them," Ryan started to protest, but then thought better of the denial and corrected, "Okay … that's true, but how many doctors can claim that they've never been sued for malpractice?" Her confident smirk was too irresistible for Jamie, and she had to pull her partner to a halt to reward her with a kiss for her bedside manner.

Just a little after nine Ryan was curled around her soundly sleeping partner. *I've never seen a person sleep through a massage. She was out like a light before I reached her lower back! I have a feeling that my little princess is not often plagued by insomnia*, she mused as she let the slow, steady cadence of Jamie's breathing lure her into a similarly sound sleep.

Ryan was amazed to open her eyes and find Jamie's green orbs gazing at her. "Wow, I didn't know you could open your eyes before six-thirty," she said slowly, blinking her eyes into focus.

"When you put me to sleep at nine o'clock, it's amazing how early I can wake up," she said as she leaned over to give her lover a little kiss. "Can I go out with you today?"

Ryan gave her a broad smile, and replied, "There's nothing I'd like better than that. Do you want to run?"

"I can't keep up with you, and I don't want to slow you down. I had the thought yesterday that it might work if I rode my bike and stayed in your general vicinity while you ran. Luckily I still have my school bike here. Wanna try it?"

"Sure," she said. "I don't know the neighborhood very well, so you can lead me through some of your favorite streets."

"It's a deal." Jamie hopped out of bed, feeling completely normal and very well rested. A few moments later she was dressed in her bike shorts and an emerald green jersey, watching from the doorway of their bath while Ryan chose an outfit. Jamie was vigorously brushing her teeth when Ryan finally decided on her attire, and Jamie realized that she was lingering just to watch Ryan get dressed.

As Ryan stepped into a pair of bright blue running shorts, Jamie marveled at how much of her long legs were exposed beneath the lightweight nylon. When Ryan bent over to pick up her shoes, her curious lover could see the white liner peeking out from the back. She crept up behind her and slid both of her hands up the legs of the tiny shorts, rubbing the firm buttocks that were so easily reached. Ryan maintained her bent position and slowly twitched her hips, causing her nylon clad cheeks to slide against Jamie's hands. "Umm," she moaned after a few seconds of this tender caress. "Are you sure you want to go outside? We could probably work up a sweat without leaving the house."

Jamie stood and slapped her rather forcefully on the butt, causing Ryan to snap to her full height. She rubbed her cheek while giving Jamie a narrow-eyed glare. "That's gonna leave a handprint," she accused.

"When we get home, you're going to have my prints all over your luscious body," she whispered as she wrapped her lover in a firm hug.

"We're going to bed early every night if this is how you wake up," Ryan teased. She pulled her sports bra over her head and then yanked on a white nylon singlet, tucked in her shirt, and twirled around once asking, "How do I look?"

"Good enough to eat," Jamie said with a leer. "I think those are the sexiest shorts I've ever seen you in. But you don't normally wear running shorts, do you?"

"Not very often. It's usually cold or foggy, so I wear compression shorts to keep my thighs loose. But I don't see any fog today, so it's probably warm. It's going to take me a while to get used to the different weather here. There's rarely a bright morning in the Noe Valley."

"You're also going to have to get used to running on level ground," Jamie reminded her. "Unless you want to go up into the hills, that is. That would let me get in some more strenuous riding while you stressed those pretty thighs."

"Let's do that later in the week. Today I want to retain a little strength in my legs. I might need it when we get home," she said, waggling one eyebrow.

"You're going to need every ounce of strength you can marshal," Jamie promised, her leering gaze promising lots of fun.

They started off slowly, but within a few minutes Jamie was racing down the street and doubling back to fly by her grinning lover. Ryan found it rather difficult to get into her normal cadence with the near-constant distraction from her partner, but she reminded herself that it was a small sacrifice to make to have the companionship of her beloved.

She watched as Jamie went flying down the quiet street, butt twitching as she left her seat and mashed the pedals hard. *There is something so appealing about her body,* she thought, as she admired the departing form. *I don't think I'll ever get tired of looking at her.* She felt a familiar tingle begin to grow and she laughed at her reaction, *I don't normally get aroused during my morning runs, either. I guess living together will produce all sorts of unexpected surprises.*

Jamie looked down at her odometer and was surprised to see that she had already gone five miles. She was getting a pretty good aerobic workout since she was, in essence, doing sprints. She hadn't slowed down since they started, so she lagged a bit and rode behind her lover for a few minutes. *God, she has the best-looking ass in the Bay Area,* she thought as she watched Ryan's running form. Her hair was gathered in a high ponytail, and Jamie loved watching it twitch back and forth as she ran. It reminded her of a horse's mane as it slowly swayed across her broad shoulders in time with her steps.

Jamie didn't know a lot about running, but it was obvious that Ryan's form was very natural, as well as efficient. She had a long stride that seemed to eat up distance, and it seemed that she came down lightly on her feet. It looked as though she spent a lot of time with both feet off the ground, even though that seemed physically improbable to Jamie. In fact, it looked like she was gliding along three or four inches off the ground with an occasional touchdown for propulsion. *Her heels barely hit the ground at all*, Jamie noticed from her position directly behind her lover. The lanky woman seemed to just lightly push off with the balls of her feet, rolling gracefully through her stride until the toes of one foot lifted from the pavement as the ball of the other foot touched down.

Jamie also noted that her attitude was slightly forward. Rather than standing completely upright, her whole body was tilted a few degrees. Oddly, it didn't appear that she was bending from the waist. Rather, it looked more like her momentum carried her forward a bit, allowing her to slice through the wind aerodynamically. Jamie was studying her so intently that she nearly ran into her as she slowed to a stop. Ryan turned around with a look of shock on her face at the closeness of the bike. "Did you almost hit me?"

Jamie blushed as she admitted, "I was watching your butt so closely, I didn't notice that you were stopping."

"Jeez! You're either going to love me to death or run over me! You're really randy today, aren't you?"

"I guess I am," Jamie agreed with a little blush coloring her cheeks. "Don't know why, but I'm really focused on you."

"Hey," Ryan panted. "Don't misunderstand, babe. I'm not complaining in the least. Nothing I like better than to have you chasing me around the streets of Berkeley with love on your mind."

"Oh, it's on my mind," Jamie agreed with a wink. "I'm gonna rock your world as soon as we get home."

Ryan beamed up at her as she leaned in and gave her a small kiss. "I'm very ready to be rocked," she replied. As she looked down the quiet, tree-lined street, her mouth quirked up into a grin as she asked, "Wanna do some speed work?"

"Sure," Jamie replied happily. "What do you want to do?"

Ryan pointed to a deep red house about fifty yards down the street. "Let's race to the number painted on the curb. Since you have an advantage, I'll take off and you start at the count of three. Agreed?"

"Yep. Are you ready?"

Ryan got down in a three-point stance. She adjusted her feet until she felt they were properly centered under her body, then twitched her butt until she was a mass of coiled energy waiting to be unleashed. "Ready, set, go!" She burst from her start and quickly found her stride. Jamie noticed that her heels didn't touch the ground at all when she sprinted. She was watching her so intently that she nearly forgot to count to three for herself. But she rallied and took off as quickly as she could. Ryan was well ahead of her, but her bike allowed her to eat up ground far quicker than Ryan's feet could manage. She thought she had her, but just as the finish line came up Ryan leaned forward as she raised her arms and stuck out her chest. She had nipped her partner by just a few inches, but from the little "whoop" she gave, it was obvious that the victory was important to her.

"How did you do that?" Jamie marveled, panting as much as her partner.

"I used to run track," she admitted, sucking in a deep breath. "It's just a trick to get a few more inches at the finish line."

"Is there any sport you can't do?" she asked with a grin as she started to pedal in a slow circle around her lover.

Ryan thought about that as she bent forward from the waist and rested her hands on her knees in order to fully catch her breath. Finally she looked up with her face deeply flushed and said, "Polo."

"Are you serious?" Jamie asked with a laugh.

"Yeah," Ryan said rather defensively. "I've never been on horseback, so even though I could probably swing the mallet pretty well, I wouldn't have any idea how to work in conjunction with the horse."

"No, silly," Jamie said, amazed that her partner had given the matter some deep thought. "I'm not surprised you can't play polo, I'm surprised that you think you can play every other sport!"

"I'm not good at every other one, but I've played almost everything at some time or another in my life. There really aren't that many differences between the major sports. You either need hand-eye coordination, or speed, or quickness, or agility, or stamina, or power from some particular body part."

"That's a lot of attributes, honey," she teased. "But I have no doubt that you possess all of them."

The flush had still not left Ryan's face and she finally mumbled, "You don't think I'm bragging, do you?" She was staring at the ground, and Jamie expected her to start kicking the dirt with the toe of her shoe any minute.

"Of course not," she insisted. "You never brag, honey. Well … you brag a little, but only about sex."

Ryan's head shot up to find the teasing grin affixed to her partner's face. "It's not bragging if you can back it up," she drawled, blue eyes dancing. "Got any claims in particular that you'd like to dispute?"

"Never! You're the real deal, hot stuff. Now let's go again."

"Thought you'd never ask," Ryan readily agreed.

They sprinted through their fifty-yard course at least eight more times. When they finished, they were both panting from the effort, and Ryan was covered in sweat. She decided that she needed to run home at a pretty good clip to avoid tightening up, so they got home in good time.

When they got into the house, Jamie went into the bath to start the shower, but Ryan went into her room, lay down on the floor, and started to stretch. "Want to shower together, babe?" Jamie called out.

"No, I've got to stretch. You go ahead."

Jamie hopped in and let the hot water remove the stiffness from her fatigued muscles. Her cramps had not returned, and she felt amazingly good. *I guess that's what love will do for you,* she mused happily.

She lingered much longer than normal in the shower, but to her surprise, when she got back in the bedroom, Ryan was still on the floor, doing some particularly painful-looking contortion. She was on her back, with one foot resting on the floor, and the other foot propped against the raised knee. Grasping the top leg with both hands, she pulled it across her body until the tendons in her hip stood out in stark relief.

Ryan looked up to see her partner staring at her in slack-jawed silence, her look a mix of desire and amazement. "You okay, babe?" Ryan asked, drawing her out of her trance.

"Wha … oh … yeah," she said weakly. "I've just never seen that muscle stand out like that on another human being."

"Muscle? Which muscle?" Ryan ran a hand down her leg, trying to identify the muscle her partner spoke of.

"Do it again," Jamie asked.

Ryan did so, and nodded when Jamie touched the part in question. "That's not a muscle, babe. That's my iliotibial band. It's a ligament." She rolled over onto her stomach and did a series of leg/arm lifts that looked particularly painful, causing her pelvis to be the only part touching the floor. "The strength and flexibility of my hips are probably the main reasons I can play most sports," she grunted out as she lifted both arms and legs simultaneously.

"Really?" Jamie was fascinated by this tidbit of information, having no idea what separated the gifted athletes from the rest of the population. "Why is that, honey?"

"I get most of my speed, balance, and thrust from my hips. I was blessed with a really good set of wheels, and they let me do things that a lot of people can't."

Jamie nodded, thinking that Ryan's synopsis might be true, but that it also minimized the reality of her work ethic. "Do you always stretch this much when you run, babe?"

"Mmm … not always … but almost always. Stretching after I exercise has been a lifesaver for me."

Jamie looked at the clock and realized that Ryan had been at it for over twenty minutes. *God-given talent is one thing, Ms. O'Flaherty. Working your butt off to exploit that talent is quite another.*

Ryan had just exited the shower when a pair of hands gripped her around the waist and began to guide her to the bedroom. "Hey, I'm still dripping wet," she protested as she was tossed onto the bed.

"Your point?" Jamie growled, climbing astride her hips. "You're gonna be dripping wet in one way or another for the next hour, hot stuff."

Ryan chuckled at the determined look of lust on her partner's face. "You don't look like you could be dissuaded anyway, so I surrender." She tossed the towel onto the floor and prepared herself for a full frontal assault.

"Smart girl," Jamie murmured as she bent to claim the spoils of war.

Thirty minutes later, Ryan was stretched out spread-eagle across the bed, badly in need of another shower. "Did anybody get the license number of that truck?" she muttered slowly, almost unable to form words.

"JDSE 211," her partner giggled, reciting her own license plate number. "It's about to back up for another run, so you'd better fasten your seat belt, baby."

"Whoa, whoa," Ryan drawled. "I need a serious rest after that little overhaul. It's your turn now, big talker."

To Ryan's amazement, Jamie rolled over, shutting off her view of her favorite parts. "I'm not up to it right now, honey."

"Not up to it!" Ryan gaped in incredulity. "You're about ready to slide off the bed, baby. You're obviously terribly turned on. Why don't you want to?"

"I don't really like to have sex when I have my period. It kind of bothers me."

"During your whole period?" Ryan asked, eyes wide with alarm.

"Umm ... yeah."

"But you *do* feel desire, right?"

"Yeah ... it's not that. I get turned on, I just think it's gross."

"But aren't I the one who should decide what's gross when I make love to you?"

Ryan's logic was, as usual, correct and irritating. "I suppose, but I don't think I could relax enough to enjoy it."

"Do you want to abstain while I have my period, too?" Ryan had shimmied up the bed so that her back was now resting against the headboard.

"I guess I didn't think that far ahead. But now that you mention it, I guess I thought that we would."

"You realize that when our cycles don't match we could be abstaining for ten to twelve days out of the month, right?"

"I guess I didn't do the math," she admitted, slightly embarrassed.

"Do you mind giving up a third of our opportunities?"

"That does seem like a lot, huh?"

"That it does," Ryan murmured, pulling Jamie up against her chest. "I don't want you to feel uncomfortable, honey, so we'll just do without. It's not that big a deal."

"Really?"

Her small voice carried a large dose of doubt, and Ryan quickly sought to reassure her. "Of course, love. If you're not one hundred percent into it, we'll hold off. We're not animals, you know. It won't be that difficult to abstain."

"You are so sweet, Ryan," she murmured. "Thanks for not making fun of me because of this."

"I'd never make fun of you. I want sex to be nothing but enjoyment for you. If you're uncomfortable about something, we just won't do it."

Jamie's blonde head nuzzled tenderly against Ryan's chest. "Thanks," she whispered. "Thanks for making me feel like I'm so special to you." She scooted up just a bit and gave Ryan a few kisses to thank her for her patience. A few turned into a bunch, and before long she was flat on her back, Ryan pressed tightly against her body.

"I think you're trying to compromise my position," she murmured, coming up for air.

"I think you're right," Ryan whispered. "Do you want me to stop?"

"N ... n ... no, I want you to keep going," she said as she leaned in for another torrid session. After another few minutes of searingly hot kisses, Jamie pulled away again, her unfocused eyes carrying a hint of panic. "I don't know if I can do this, Ryan. I feel funny about it."

"Tell me exactly what bothers you about it," Ryan asked in a calm, neutral tone.

"It's messy and it smells bad. It'll get all over the sheets. And I ... I ... I'm afraid you'll be grossed out and you'll be funny with me."

Ryan rolled over and sat up straight, looking at her carefully. "Did something like that happen with Jack?"

Jamie blushed deeply and nodded just a bit while she bit her bottom lip.

"Tell me what happened," Ryan soothed, pulling her close, and wrapping her in a gentle hug.

"This is kind of embarrassing," she whispered, hiding her head against Ryan's chest.

"Take your time, babe. Just tell me what you feel comfortable sharing."

"Okay. He wanted to have sex once when I had my period and I didn't want to, but he finally talked me into it. He tried to take my tampon out and he couldn't ... of course. I don't know what is so complicated about taking out a tampon but he practically took my uterus with it. When I got it out he acted like it was radioactive or something. I honestly thought he was going to call in the HAZMAT team to scrub the place down. As soon as that tampon was out, his ... well, let's say that his desire deflated, and he suddenly had to go to sleep. I swear that ever since then he was weird about using his mouth on me." She added in a timid voice, "I just don't ever want you to be grossed out by something and have it affect how you feel about me."

Ryan gave her a gentle squeeze. "I don't mean to brag, but I think I have more experience in this area than Jack had. I've made love to women at every stage of their cycles, and I swear I have never been grossed out. There's nothing mysterious about it, Jamie. It's just another part of you. How could I find a part of you distasteful?"

"But it smells funny," she maintained, just the hint of a whine in her voice.

"No, it does not," Ryan said patiently. "I don't find the scent offensive in the least."

"I don't know, Ryan. I don't want to disappoint you but ..."

"No, no, no, honey," she said firmly. "This isn't about disappointing me. I want to help you get over this, but not for me. I think overcoming these little phobias is good for your self-image. But if you don't want to, please tell me and I'll drop it."

"I guess I'm more worried about your reaction than my own. Are you sure you want to do this?"

"Yes," she replied solemnly as she gazed steadily into her partner's eyes. "I'm sure."

"Okay," she finally said. "I'll try."

"Would you feel more comfortable if I could guarantee that I couldn't taste or smell you?"

"Er ... how on earth could you do that?"

"Trust me, I'm a doctor," she teased. "Plus I can guarantee that we won't make a mess ... at all."

"That's a pretty good guarantee, Doc. Are you sure you can deliver?"

"I haven't lost a patient yet," she said with a wiggling eyebrow. "You go change your tampon; I'll be right back." Ryan gave Jamie a final kiss and dashed into her bedroom.

When she returned, Jamie was lying in bed, looking more like a woman waiting for the oral surgeon than her lover. "Ready if you are," she said gamely.

Ryan gave her an encouraging smile and held up her hand. She waved a good-sized sheet of latex at her partner, waggling her dark eyebrows as she did so. "I'm already salivating," she smirked, harking back to the declaration she had made on their honeymoon that dental dams made her hot.

"Why do I ever doubt you?" Jamie mused with a giggle as her partner climbed into bed.

"Search me." Ryan shrugged her broad shoulders and snuggled in close. "Now, did someone around here call a doctor?"

Chapter Six

Some time later, Ryan heard a low groan come from Jamie's open mouth and leaned down, placing her ear close. "I told you I couldn't relax enough to enjoy that," Jamie said with a weak smile.

A gentle laugh caused Jamie's head to bounce a bit, given its position atop Ryan's chest. "I assume the moans were signs of your reluctance?"

"Yes," she drawled, enjoying the tease. "I was moaning from tension."

"How about the little gasps and groans?"

"Same thing," she murmured, playfully scratching Ryan's exposed tummy. "Tension ... tension."

"Hmm, that may fly, but let's see you explain away the hands laced through my hair, the thighs locked around my neck and the commands that I touch you 'harder' and 'faster'?" Ryan's hand had been idly resting upon Jamie's waist, but as she asked her question she got in a lightening-quick tickle of her sensitive ribs.

"Yow!" Jamie cried, curling up in a ball to prevent further attacks. "No fair! I was in a very vulnerable position!"

"Speak the truth," Ryan intoned, "or face my torture!" Her wiggling digits underscored her threat, and Jamie knew a loser bet when she saw one.

"Oh, all right," she huffed dramatically. "Once again you've proven your mettle between the sheets, Tiger. One more phobia down the drain."

"That's my goal," Ryan crowed. "I'm really an operative from the American Psychological Association. We're going to stamp out sexual phobias—one woman at a time."

Cuddling up contentedly against her talented lover Jamie murmured, "I'm just glad I'm near the front of the alphabet."

"Señorita Jamie?"

"Yikes!" Jamie flew out of bed, scampering across the floor to close the bedroom door. Out of the corner of her eye she caught Ryan throwing her clothes on faster than she would have thought humanly possible. "It's okay, sweetheart," she soothed, smiling a bit at the wild look on her partner's face. "I'll go ask Maria Los to start on the first floor." She slipped on a robe and gave Ryan a wink as she left the room.

Jamie returned a few minutes later, puzzled to find that Ryan was still sitting on the bed, her singlet haphazardly pulled over her head. "I don't like having strangers in the house, Jamie." Her tone was slightly regretful, but there was a steely determination in her eye that Jamie was not used to having directed at her.

The smaller woman let out a heavy sigh and came to sit next to her partner. "What do you want to do about that?" Jamie's expression was neutral, her posture open. Ryan had expected her to be defensive, and this attitude caught her by surprise.

"Umm ... I don't know," she said somewhat hesitantly. "I uhm ... I guess I'd like to fire her."

"Okay." Jamie stood and tightened the closure of her robe. "I'll go tell her now." She took a step toward the door, but was stopped by Ryan's hand grabbing her wrist firmly.

"You'd just fire her?" She was staring at Jamie with an absolutely stunned expression on her face. "With no notice, or anything?"

"Well, no," she admitted. "I'll continue to pay her until I find her another job. It's not her fault that you don't want her in the house."

"Aww, jeez, Jamie, you're making me feel like a jerk." Ryan had fallen into full-on pout mode. Her arms were crossed over her chest and her chin was nearly touching her folded arms.

The smaller woman came back to join her partner on the bed. "I certainly don't mean to, honey," she soothed. "But if you're adamant that you don't want her here, I don't see how a compromise is viable."

"Well ... why do *I* get the final vote?" Blue eyes peeked out from too-long bangs, and Jamie had a perfect image of Ryan as a five-year-old.

"For the same reason that you told me I'd have the final decision on what we do sexually," she said softly as she rubbed her hand across Ryan's bare thigh. "If something bothers you, or makes you uncomfortable, your vote wins."

Her mouth quirked involuntarily into a sardonic smirk. "I hate it when you use my own logic on me." Jamie ruffled her bangs, but said nothing, waiting for Ryan to decide what to do. "Will her feelings be hurt?" It was clear that Ryan was having a tough time with this, but Jamie honestly didn't know how to reach a compromise.

She pondered this for just a second, knowing the answer immediately. "Yes, honey. Her feelings will be hurt. She's very proud of the work she does here, and I think she'll assume that she offended you on Monday."

"Damn!" Ryan got up and paced in a small circle. "I don't want to hurt her feelings, Jamie. I just don't want someone coming and going without warning."

"Well, we have warning," she offered. "She comes at ten on Mondays, Wednesdays, and Fridays, and she leaves at three."

Ryan nodded, and crossed her arms against her chest. She was silent for a moment before she offered a compromise. "Since Mia's not here, I don't expect the house to be very dirty. I want to do the laundry, so that will save her a lot of time. Until school starts let's have her come from noon to three. We'll pay her the same amount, of course—tell her it's like a little vacation."

"And that would work better because ...?"

"Because that's when I'll be at work. This will be easier for me to adjust to if I don't have to be at home when she's here. Plus, I want to spend most mornings making love to my best girl, and I hate to have my concentration ruined." The sparkle was back in the azure eyes, and Jamie shot her a grateful grin for her willingness to give a bit on the issue.

"I'll go talk to her now." Jamie started toward the door, anxious to get the issue settled. Once again she was pulled back by Ryan's grip.

"Nah. She's here now," Ryan reasoned. "Tell her this starts on Monday. That way she won't think anything's wrong."

"You're a very sweet woman." Jamie slid her arms around her partner and gave her a generous hug.

"I have my moments," Ryan admitted with a grin. "But don't let it get out."

"Your secret is safe with me." Jamie placed a few kisses on her smiling face before leading her into the bath for their second shower of the morning.

Jamie flew in the front door at 5:20, struggling with two large grocery bags. Ryan jogged over to relieve her of her burden, and she gratefully relinquished both bags, ogling her partner as she did so. Ryan was wearing a red baseball cap which was backwards, as usual. Her hair was clipped loosely and stuck out beneath the bill of the cap. Only faded overall shorts covered her long frame. "Nice outfit," Jamie commented as Ryan turned to take the bags into the kitchen.

"Thank you," she responded over her shoulder. "It was as close as I could get to your request of this morning."

Jamie thought about that for a second and then laughed as she followed her lover into the kitchen. She recalled mentioning that she wished she could keep her partner naked at all times. Slipping up behind her visual delight as she put two six-packs of beer in the refrigerator, Jamie slid her hands in the unbuttoned sides of the jeans and tantalizingly stroked the nearly naked body for several minutes. Ryan's eyes fluttered closed, and her head fell back against Jamie's shoulder as she luxuriated in the feel of her lover's hands. "I love the look, Tiger, but you didn't quite follow orders."

"It's cold today!" Ryan protested. "I was naked until the fog rolled in and my nipples got so hard they could have snapped off!"

"Oh, you poor thing." Jamie's voice dropped to its lowest register as she moved around to the front of her body and locked eyes with Ryan. She slowly unhooked a shoulder strap, smiling seductively as one pink nipple was revealed when the oversized garment sagged down Ryan's body. A fervid stare caused it to pop up immediately, and Jamie bent over to pull it into her warm mouth. Ryan's hands immediately rose to rest on her partner's head and a soft moan fell from her lips. After a few minutes of attention, Jamie pulled back to inspect the object of her affection. "It doesn't seem to have gotten any softer," she said with a questioning glance. Her index finger flicked over the pebbled flesh, creating goose bumps all over the taller woman's torso. "Is it still cold?"

"Unh-uh," Ryan said slowly, her own voice taking on a seductive tone. "It's warm, and getting warmer all the time. The other one's still cold though."

"We can't let the other one feel left out," Jamie purred as she unhooked the second strap. The overalls dropped to the floor as her mouth warmed the other hard nipple. After a few minutes of this loving care, she straightened and looked up at her lover, a playful grin flitting across her features. "Are any of your other parts cold?"

Ryan slowly shook her head. "All of my parts feel very warm right now. Actually, some of them have grown decidedly hot in the last few minutes."

"Is there much we have to do before your family gets here?"

"Unh-uh," she said as she shook her head again. "I've made a salad, I've shucked the corn, and I just started the fire. We've got a good thirty minutes to kill."

"Hmm, I wonder what we should do … thirty minutes … Maybe we should lie down for a little nap. Would you like a thirty-minute nap, love?" Her hand had traveled to Ryan's bare ass, and she lightly patted the smooth surface with her open palm.

"I think I could do with a five-minute nap," Ryan growled as she bent down to bestow a series of torrid kisses upon her lover.

Thirty minutes proved to be more than enough time for Ryan's favorite kind of nap. Jamie ignored her invitation to make it speedy, and she teased the poor woman until she was nearly mad with arousal. When she finally allowed her release, Ryan actually needed a more conventional nap, but she struggled to stay awake and luxuriate in the delicious sensation of being held in Jamie's tender embrace. At six o'clock sharp they hopped in the shower, and by quarter past they were both dressed and in the kitchen tending to dinner.

The family wasn't due until seven, but since they were never late, there was a good chance they would be early. Martin always liked to allow for a few major accidents and a natural disaster or two when he planned his departure time; true to form, he rang the doorbell at six-thirty on the dot. Ryan looked at Jamie and gave her a little shrug along with an adorable grin, having warned her partner that the proposed time was the outermost limit of when the family would arrive. They went to the door hand in hand to welcome the clan to their house.

Brendan and Martin stood on the deep porch wearing smiles and bearing a bottle of wine. They were pulled inside and welcomed with a surfeit of hugs, Ryan providing more than her share. Just when they were about to go into the kitchen, Conor arrived and was treated to the same welcome.

"Isn't this just grand," Martin said as he looked around the living room. "How many of you are there living here, girls?"

"Just us this summer, Da. One of Jamie's roommates is in L.A. right now, but she'll be back this fall."

"My, but this is a large home for three girls," he commented as he continued to look around. "I don't mean to pry, but however will you afford it, Siobhán?"

"Jamie's father owns the house, Da," she said by way of avoiding the direct question.

"Oh, I see," he said, although he obviously didn't. "Well, but you'll be paying your share of the rent then, won't you?"

"Let's talk about this during dinner." Ryan dodged an answer once again as she led them on a quick tour. Connor was particularly effusive about the redwood covering the floors and the exposed beams in the craftsman-style home. He pointed out a number of elements that Ryan had never noticed, making her a little uncomfortable when he went on and on about the quality of the workmanship. It was becoming obvious, even to Martin, that this was not a rental home that a trio of typical Cal students could afford, and she noticed that her father grew more pensive as they continued the tour. When they were done making appreciative comments, they all went out into the small, enclosed yard and watched while Ryan got the grill ready.

Martin went back into the house to offer his help to Jamie. "Would you be needing any assistance?" he asked, blue eyes sparkling.

"No, Martin. Everything's set. Your daughter is quite proficient in the kitchen, I've come to find out, and she got everything ready while I was playing golf this afternoon. But you could set the kitchen table with the things I laid out."

As he walked by her he asked in a low tone, "How is she faring?"

Jamie turned and smiled up at him. "She's doing great. I think the hardest part was leaving on Monday. Since then she's been fine. I've been keeping a close eye on her, though. We actually went running together today—of course, I had to ride my bike to keep up with her."

Martin laughed at the accuracy of that statement. "She's as quick as they come," he admitted, smiling fondly as he spoke of his daughter.

Jamie caught the hint of sadness in his deep blue eyes and grasped his arm lightly. "How are you doing, Martin? This is really hard for you, isn't it?"

He turned his back, appearing to study the detail work on the redwood cabinets. "The child is twenty-three years old, Jamie. I have to let go of her sometime."

The sad tone of his voice indicated just how much he hated that prospect, and Jamie flashed on the difficulty Ryan would have letting their own children leave the nest. Jamie came up behind him and wrapped her arms around his waist for a hug. He patted her linked arms, grateful that she couldn't see the tears in his eyes.

Ryan came bounding up the stairs announcing, "The fire is ready. Let's rock." When she entered the room, Jamie was just pulling away, and she immediately guessed that her father was having a tougher time than she was with this adjustment to their living situation. "I knew it!" she cried, trying to lighten the moment. "I knew you were using me to get to the prize of the O'Flaherty family!"

Jamie laughed at her efforts, protesting her accusation. "If I had remained on the straight and narrow, Martin would have to fight me off," she agreed, "but I'm pretty happy with the distaff side of the O'Flaherty clan."

With a heavy sigh, Martin turned and joined in the teasing. "Jamie's already claimed the prize of the family, Siobhán, and though I have not met the Evans family, I predict you've done the same."

"Well, the latter part of that statement is true for sure, Da." She wrapped her partner in a hug from behind and gave her a flurry of kisses, tickling her neck and ears thoroughly. "Hey, why didn't you bring Duffy? He usually handles this for me."

"I didn't want to confuse him, darlin'. I think it would be hard for him to see you, but not have you go home with us."

"That makes sense," she agreed, wishing once again that Cal was in San Francisco.

"Let's get dinner started," Jamie suggested as she handed Ryan a big platter of chicken and a bowl of barbecue sauce. "Would the boys like a drink?"

"Hey, fellas," Ryan called down the stairs, "would you like a beer?" Receiving two enthusiastic affirmatives, she turned back to Jamie and indicated the tray. "The boys are thirsty, love. Put three on here, will you?"

"I'll carry the drinks," Martin insisted, always the cautious parent. Ryan was greatly aided by all three men giving her advice on the proper way to grill chicken, and she accepted and ignored the advice with good humor. Jamie had come down to join them, and they all stood by the grill, soaking up the last rays of the weak sun while the hot fire warmed them.

When the chicken was ready they sat down to dinner, where everyone made appropriately glowing comments on Ryan's abilities as a grill cook. They tried to compliment Jamie, but she had to admit that she hadn't done a thing. "She really is a fabulous cook, though," Ryan said with pride.

"I'll second that," Conor said. "That meal you made down at Pebble Beach was killer!"

"You were starving, Conor," she reminded him with a chuckle. "It was just an Italian omelet."

"Whatever it was, it was killer," he insisted, unwilling to back down from his praise.

"So tell us how you've been spending your days, girls?" Martin asked.

"Yeah, Ryan." Conor's mischievous blue eyes twinkled, and it was clear that he was about to put his sister on the spot. "Tell us how you've been spending your time."

"Don't you go prying into your sister's business," Martin warned.

"I just asked the same question you did, Da." The handsome face was the epitome of innocence as he gazed at his father.

"It's not the question, lad, it's the inference." He narrowed his gaze and reminded his son, "The girls are still on their honeymoon, and they don't need to be cross-examined about their sex life."

"Sex? Who said anything about sex? Jeez, Da, that was the furthest thing from my mind."

Jamie was ready to crawl under the table, and Martin backhanded his son across the shoulder. "You've embarrassed Jamie again, boy. Now behave yourself, or they won't be invitin' us again."

"It's okay, Martin," the still-blushing woman assured him. "I'm getting used to being teased almost around the clock. Your daughter is the worst one of the bunch."

"Hey! I ..." Ryan started, but then decided that she might as well be honest. "You're right." She beamed a smile at her partner and added, "But you love me anyway."

"This is true." Jamie gave her hand a squeeze and directed the conversation back to the original question. "Ryan gave me quite a little surprise yesterday morning," she informed the men, sparing a grin toward her lover.

"How so?" Martin asked, turning to his daughter.

"Well, I wasn't going to say anything until I'd made up my mind, but I had a tryout for the soccer team."

"Soccer team?" Martin's features grew dark, and his voice took on a low, rough tone. "With the phantom Coach Greene?"

Oh-oh ... I guess absence didn't make the heart grow fonder. "Come on, Da," Ryan urged. "I hadn't signed my letter of intent yet. We really weren't bound to each other."

"Letter of intent?" Jamie asked, trying to keep track of the conversation.

"Yeah." Ryan cast a quick glance at her partner, then another at her father. Deciding to answer Jamie's question, she informed her, "Once a high-school athlete signs a letter of intent, you're bound to that school. If you decide not to attend, you can't go to another school and participate in your sport. I hadn't signed with Cal when they dropped me, so I was free to play somewhere else if I wanted to. The bottom line is that they didn't actually harm me by dropping me as a prospect."

Martin looked like he was going to burst, so Ryan quickly turned back to him. "They did, in reality, hurt me a lot, Da. But it was my feelings and my self-confidence that they hurt. All I'm saying is that they didn't take anything tangible away from me."

"I'd kick a soccer ball right up her butt," Brendan growled, his dark face mirroring his father's.

"Hear, hear!" Martin agreed, shocking everyone at the table with his approbation of Brendan's uncharacteristically salty language.

"Hold on, guys," Ryan urged, trying to get the conversation under control. "I love soccer, and I've missed it ... a lot. I know I could play in a rec league, but the competition is really good in the Pac-10, and that's what I love. It's only hurting myself to let my anger keep me from doing this."

The assembled men let her words sink in for a minute, finally agreeing that she had a good point. "Are you sure you can trust her, darlin'?" Martin still wasn't sold on the idea, but he wanted his daughter to feel free to do whatever gave her pleasure in life.

"No. I'm really not, Da. Before I give her an answer, I'm going to check out a few other sports and talk to some of the players on the team. I promise I won't agree to do this if it'll give her a chance to hurt me again."

Jamie piped up helpfully, "Since they don't have a scholarship for Ryan, she might choose to play one of the non-scholarship sports."

"*No scholarship!*" all three O'Flaherty men cried at once.

Ryan cast a sickly smile at her partner and muttered, "Thanks, pal. I owe you one."

When dinner was finished, and everyone had been calmed about the scholarship issue, Brendan and Conor got up to start on the dishes. Ryan stood too, but Jamie insisted that since she had done the cooking, she couldn't clean. Martin had not been able to hide his worried frown for most of the night, so Ryan took the others up on the offer and asked her father to join her for a beer in the backyard.

The night was really too cold to be called pleasant, and the fog obscured every star, but neither of the naturally warm O'Flahertys was bothered by that fact. They each sat in a comfy chaise and acted as though they were watching the stars for a few minutes. "Jamie certainly has a lovely home," Martin finally said.

Here it comes ... three ... two ... one ...

"I don't know much about this side of the Bay, but in the city a place like this would cost a very pretty pence."

"Umm-hmm," Ryan agreed, waiting to see where this train was headed before she decided if she wanted to ride it to the end of the line.

"I can't imagine that Jamie's father bought the house to provide free housing to her friends, Siobhán."

Ohh ... now arriving at "Guilt Trip Station"! I think this is my stop. "I've offered to pay for half of the ... incidentals, Da." She didn't think this was the best time to bring up the cadre of service personnel affiliated with the house.

"Aren't you taking the place of one of the girls who was here before, darlin'?"

"In a sense," she agreed. "But I hope my position is a little bit more permanent than 'housemate'." She said this in a light, joking tone, but there was a note of hurt in her voice as well.

"Now, now," he soothed, understanding the tone. "I didn't mean to make light of your commitment to one another, Siobhán."

"But you are, Da. That would be like you asking Jamie for money to live with us on the weekends."

He mulled that over for a moment, but had to disagree with his daughter. "That's not so, sweetheart. We've welcomed Jamie into the family. The Evanses haven't had the opportunity to do that for you. Living here without their permission or even their knowledge is not how I would expect you to act."

"But I'm not creating any more expense for Mr. Evans ..."

"No, but you are taking income away from him, love. If not for you, Jamie would likely find another roommate to take the other girl's place. Mr. Evans is losing that income by having you here."

Ryan thought about that statement for quite a while, mulling it over in her mind from every angle. Try as she might, she could not really punch a hole in the logic. "Okay," she finally sighed. "I see your point."

"Don't sound so glum, sweetheart," he urged. "You'll feel better about being here if you do everything aboveboard. Once they know about you, you can all come to some agreement about finances."

"So … you wouldn't be disappointed in me if I let Jamie support me this year?"

"Completely support you?" The surprise in his voice was evident. "Siobhán! Do you know how much it costs to support you?"

"Yes, Da, I know," she insisted. "But it's the only way I can play a sport and keep my grades up."

"But she doesn't work! How on earth …"

"She has family money, Da. It's more than enough to support both of us."

"Ohh … I see …" he said slowly.

For the second time in the evening, Ryan was quite sure that he did not.

"Da's worried that feeding me will send you to the poorhouse," Ryan murmured into her partner's sweet-smelling hair. They were snug in bed, the chill in the house forcing them to cuddle for warmth as well as emotional succor.

"Oh, I think I can handle you," Jamie murmured, almost asleep. "I'll apply for government cheese if things get too bad."

"We do need to work out some finances, baby." Ryan was still wired from her evening, and she couldn't let the issue go.

"We will," Jamie mumbled. "G'night, sweetie."

Ryan placed a soft kiss right above her ear and pulled her limp body even tighter against herself. "'Night, love," she whispered, hoping that they could come to an agreement over the financial issues that were beginning to cast a cloud over their lives.

"Jamie?" Receiving no answer, she raised her voice and tried again. "Jamie?" Ryan looked around on the first floor, trying to find her elusive lover. From the scent of espresso wafting through the house, it was obvious that she was up, but exactly where she was up, Ryan did not know.

A faint voice reached her ears. "I'm outside, babe."

Ryan walked out onto the rear landing to see her partner sitting on the attractive wooden garden bench, *The New York Times* spread out over the small wrought iron table that was pulled up to her knees. She was wearing headphones, and her Walkman lay on the seat beside her. A cup of coffee, or more precisely latté, if Ryan's guess was correct, shared space with the remaining sections of the newspaper.

"Now this is the picture of a woman starting her day out in the manner to which she has become accustomed." The truth of the matter was that Jamie did, in fact, look absolutely content. A short discussion had taken place when they woke, and she had admitted that, as much as she loved being with Ryan in the morning, she was beginning to miss her pre-Ryan routine. Seeing the contented look on her face, Ryan was very happy that her partner had decided to get back to it this morning. "Are you listening to music?" she asked, leaning over to kiss Jamie's cheek.

The tousled blonde head shook briefly, and she removed the headphones to reply. "I listen to 'Morning Edition' on National Public Radio. The day doesn't feel like it officially starts if I don't hear Bob Edwards say good morning to me." Her sunny face was crinkled up in a playful grin, and Ryan got an even better indication of how important this routine was to her partner. Jamie started to get up, offering, "Let me make you some breakfast, Tiger. You look like you've burned off a couple of thousand calories already."

"No, please," Ryan insisted, lightly touching the tops of the terrycloth-clad shoulders. "I want you to sit right here and enjoy your coffee. I still need to stretch, and then I prefer to take a shower before I eat." Jamie smiled up at her and sank back down onto the bench, tucking her mint green robe around her legs to ward off the morning chill. "Anyway, since breakfast is the meal I do best, why don't I cook in the morning, and you can handle the evenings?"

A soft laugh and a teasing smirk were Jamie's reply. "That would be fine, Buffy, but you've cooked every night so far. If that's gonna be the plan, you've got to let me do my part, too."

Ryan lay down on the dew-soaked grass, a hiss of pleasure escaping as she let the cool moisture absorb some of her body heat. She started on her stretching routine, looking thoughtful as she did so. "On second thought, maybe you should be in charge of lunch," she suggested. "I get home before you do if you play a full round of golf in the afternoon, and I really do need to eat by six or so. Think you can stand my cooking?"

"I love your cooking," Jamie assured her, "but let's see how it goes for a while. I don't want you to wind up doing too much around here. You're already in charge of laundry .... If you add breakfast and dinner to your list of chores I won't have a darned thing to do."

"Hey," Ryan grunted, nearly pulling her leg over her head in a painful-looking stretch, "being my sex slave takes a lot of time too, ya know. That's your most important job around here."

Jamie grabbed the section of newspaper that she was working on and held it up close to her face. "If I don't stop watching you stretch, we're gonna miss another meal, Buffy. That routine of yours is definitely rated NC-17!"

Over breakfast Ryan commented, "Did this morning work better for you, babe? You looked pretty darned content out there, reading your paper."

"Yeah ... it did work better. I mean, I kinda feel bad to want that time to myself, but I've been doing that since I was six, and it just feels right."

Ryan cocked her head, her spoonful of cereal stuck halfway between the bowl and her mouth. "What part of your routine did you perform when you were six?"

"All of it," Jamie blithely replied.

Ryan laughed, thinking of her partner sitting at the kitchen table, tiny little feet dangling high off the floor, reading the *New York Times*. "What ... you read one of your little storybooks while you ate breakfast?"

"No ... I read the *New York Times*."

"When you were six?" The disbelief was evident in Ryan's tone, if not the question.

"Yeah ... is there an age limit that I'm not familiar with?" Jamie's green eyes were dancing, obviously enjoying the teasing.

"So you'd sit at the table and read the paper while you had your juice and your cereal?"

"No ... I'd read the paper while I had my latté and my jam and bread. While listening to 'Morning Edition', that is." Now she was unable to hide her grin, finally breaking into a laugh at the astounded look on Ryan's face.

"That's ... that's ... Are you serious??"

"Yes, babe. I didn't understand ten percent of what I read, but my father read the *Times* while he ate, so I read the *Times* while I ate. It was a nice time for us," she said softly, looking rather wistful. "I'd ask him questions about words I didn't understand, and he'd quiz me on different things that he thought I should know about. I was probably the only six-year-old who could have competently cast a vote in the 1984 presidential elections." Ryan was staring at her with a rather stunned expression still gracing her face. "I just find that unbelievable," she muttered, thinking of the thick-paged, small-word picture books she'd read at age six. "That doesn't explain why you were eating bread and drinking latté, though. That sounds like some strange form of yuppie child abuse!"

Jamie laughed at her partner's hyperbole. "That was one of mother's eccentricities. She thought breakfast cereal was a horrible thing to put into a child, so we ate more like the French. Marta would go to the bakery in the morning and buy brioche or a baguette, and we'd just have some fresh bread and a little jam. I guess I started drinking latté to imitate mother. I couldn't drink espresso, because it was way too strong, so Marta added steamed milk until it suited me. I probably had a half-ounce of espresso to twelve ounces of milk, but it made me feel very sophisticated." Her smile faded as she admitted, "Both of my parents paid more attention to me when I acted like an adult."

Ryan grasped her hand and chafed it a bit between her own hands, "How do you want to handle breakfast with our kids?" She knew that talking about their future family always lightened Jamie's mood, and today was no exception.

"I'm not sure," she admitted, her smile returning. "I kinda liked being treated like I had a brain. They never treated me like a dumb kid, and that really helped my self-confidence and independence. But I think I like breakfast at your house a lot better."

"Let's compromise," Ryan suggested. "We can have porridge and back bacon with latté and the sports section of the *Times*."

"Best idea I've heard all day," Jamie agreed happily, picturing their future family sitting around a breakfast table that looked amazingly like the one in the O'Flaherty manse.

"I will never understand how taking a shower together takes three times longer than showering separately." Ryan was grumbling, mostly under her breath, as they jogged through the corridors of the brand-new, partially finished Haas Pavilion. Jamie didn't take her grousing very seriously, knowing that her partner loved their communal cleanup. Ryan just hated to be late, no matter how pleasurable the reason for the delay.

They arrived at the office they were looking for less than five minutes after their scheduled time, but Ryan was apologizing to every person she made eye contact with. "Hi, I'm Ryan O'Flaherty," she said to the receptionist, speaking her name with just the barest hint of an Irish accent. "I've an appointment with Coach Placer, but I'm late. Is he still available?"

The woman looked at the large clock on the wall, then glanced at her appointment book. "It's 9:03, honey. Take a chill pill."

Ryan shoved her hands into the pockets of her chinos, and started to rock back and forth. She looked about ready to jump out of her skin, and Jamie placed a calming hand on the small of her back, giving her a light scratch. Ryan took in a breath and held it for a moment, feeling some of the tension leave her body. "I ... uhm ... I just hate to be late," she admitted.

"Three minutes is not late, honey," the woman laughed. "Three hours ... three days ... three weeks ... now that's late." Her laugh floated behind her as she walked down a short corridor and poked her head into an office. Stepping back toward the reception desk she motioned Ryan and Jamie forward. "Come on, honey, he's on the phone, but you can come in."

Ryan gave her a grateful nod, and strode into the office, Jamie right at her side. She smiled at the man sitting behind the desk, and they both sat when he motioned them to. Rich Placer was a good-looking, dark-haired young man, about twenty-eight years old. He had been hired the year before to take over from the coach who had wooed Ryan when she was in high school. He finished his call and stood, extending his hand. "Ryan?" he asked.

"Good to meet you, Coach. I've brought someone with me. Is that okay?"

"Sure," he said easily, offering his hand to Jamie. "Rich Placer."

"This is Jamie Evans, Coach. She's my lifemate."

"Life-mate, huh?" His eyes were twinkling as he sat down and regarded the pair. "I like that term, Ryan. Life is a lot more pleasant with a mate to help you through it, isn't it?"

Ryan grinned at him, his stock rising dramatically in her book with just those few words. "Life is wonderful with the right mate," she said, sparing a meaningful glance at her partner.

The coach pulled a legal-sized manila folder into the center of his desk and tossed it open. He started thumbing through the two-inch-thick pile, smiling to himself as he scanned the notes. "So, I read the file that Coach Nichols made about your high school career. He was obviously very impressed with your game to recruit you when you only played his sport for one year."

Ryan nodded, thinking about her reply to that comment for a moment. "It always bothered me that I had to choose between sports, but when two of them are at the same time, you have to pick. During my freshman year, I got a slight head injury playing soccer. They wouldn't let me play the rest of the season, so I finagled my way into an open spot as an outside hitter. I really only played six games, so I was surprised to learn that Coach Nichols was interested in me."

Rich Placer smiled at the self-effacing, confident young woman who smiled back at him. "Well, I remember you from USF, even though you only played one year there too. You tend to make a rather lasting impression on a coach, Ryan." He smiled at the slight blush that traveled slowly up her cheeks, charmed to be able to speak to an athlete who didn't think they had invented their sport. "I don't think there's any question that you can play. Check that. There *is* no question that you can play. Obviously your grades have been superb since you've been in college, but I'm really puzzled by the path you've taken. Tell me what happened in high school."

Ryan took a deep breath and decided to tell it all. It wasn't really much of a risk at this point in her life, but she still felt a little nervous about talking about her personal life with a stranger. "As you can probably tell, I had three great years at Sacred Heart. But during the summer after my junior year, I fell in love. With another woman." She waited for a beat, then continued. "Things didn't work out quite like I had hoped, and she ... freaked out," Ryan said, minimizing the incident as much as she could. "She stopped speaking to me and that was really hard, but I could have lived with it. However, I guess she told someone at school that we had sex, and within a week the entire school knew."

Coach Placer looked puzzled by this part of the story, and he asked for clarification. "Why would she do that, Ryan? If she was freaked out, why tell everyone?"

"To this day I have no idea, Coach. All I know is that everyone knew, and she and I were the only people involved. I know I didn't tell ..." She shook her head sadly, still unable to understand the betrayal. "It's actually worse than it sounds, to be honest," she said softly. "I don't know what she said, but the other girls definitely had the impression that our time together was not entirely consensual."

Ryan looked like she was about to cry, and her voice had grown so quiet that Jamie had to lean toward her to hear the last of her sentence. She reached out and grasped Ryan's hand firmly, shocked at this stunning revelation. Ryan's face was set in a grim mask of pain, and most of the color had drained from her skin.

"That's not uncommon, Ryan," the coach said softly. "Sometimes kids deal with their own guilt about something like this by trying to blame the other person. I'm sure that the people who knew you didn't believe it."

Her dark head lifted slowly and Jamie could see every bit of pain and dismay from those days settle onto her face. "That's what nearly destroyed me," she whispered. "Everybody did believe it. Within days there wasn't one girl who would take the risk of talking to me in public. This happened at the end of junior year. I got through the end of the term, and spent the summer in Ireland with my family. I honestly thought things would blow over after the summer. But after the second game of the soccer season, some of the most talented players accosted me in the locker room and told me that they wanted me to quit. They said that they didn't want to have a predator watching them getting dressed and taking showers."

The color was back in her cheeks now, but it was the deep flush of shame that showed on her face. "I relied on these women. We were teammates," she said simply, still unable to process the hurt. "We had won the state championship the year before, and we still had an excellent team. But they were so afraid of being associated with me that they demanded I quit."

Both Jamie and Coach Placer were taken aback by this revelation. They both stared at Ryan for a long time, until Jamie silently reached for her partner's hand again and grasped it tightly. Ignoring the coach, she lifted the hand and brought it to her lips, placing a gentle kiss on the soft skin and whispering, "I'm so sorry, sweetheart. I'm so very sorry that happened to you."

Ryan just nodded her head briefly, her lower lip caught between her teeth in her characteristic effort to stave off tears. "It was horrible," she agreed, her voice no more than a whisper. "In one of the most gay-friendly cities in America, in 1993 …. It still boggles my mind."

"It makes perfect sense that you quit," Jamie murmured, still holding Ryan's hand close to her face. "Nobody should have to put up with that kind of treatment from their teammates."

"I didn't quit immediately," Ryan amended softly. "I guess I was still naïve about the ways of the world. I went to the coach of my soccer team. We had always been close, and she had made me the team captain at the end of the previous year. I told her that the other girls wanted me to quit, and I asked her what she thought I should do. She said that she couldn't 'take the risk' of standing up for me. She said that it would probably hurt the team if I stayed on, so I finally realized that I couldn't stand up to the whole school by myself, and I quit."

"Did it eventually get better?" Coach Placer asked, causing Jamie to gasp as she remembered where they were.

Ryan shook her head again, defeat clouding her features. "Once I gave in, it actually got worse and worse. I had disgusting notes taped to my locker and my bike was vandalized more than once. I couldn't concentrate in school and my grades just plummeted. I was considering dropping out and just getting a G.E.D., but my family finally got me to tell them what was happening, and they were a tremendous help in getting me back on track. By the second semester my grades were back to normal, but I was never treated any better by the students. Only two or three girls were openly hostile to me, but nobody else had the guts to talk to me in public. I spent the entire second semester without a single word being said to me socially."

Coach Placer asked, "The file I have here says that you decided not to pursue playing for Cal. Why was that?"

Ryan barked out a bitter laugh. "That's a lie, Coach. I desperately wanted to come to Cal, but every one of the coaches here dumped me. I hadn't signed my letter of intent yet, and my soccer scholarship, which I thought was a lock, disappeared. I was pretty bitter about it for a long time, but I think I'm over it now. I decided to not let my animosity rob me of my goal of graduating from here. I'm happy that I transferred, and now I want to play a varsity sport. Mostly I want to do it for myself, but partly, I want to show those coaches that they should have taken a chance on me."

Coach Placer silently stared at the ceiling for a long minute. Finally, he gave Ryan a big smile and said, "You do know that my predecessor is now at UCLA."

She found this an odd path for the conversation to take, but she acknowledged his statement. "Yeah, I do."

"There's no team I'd be happier to beat," he said with another grin.

Ryan understood his point immediately, and answered him with a beaming smile. "Death to the Bruins!"

As they left the office, Ryan reached over and took Jamie's hand. They walked together down the long corridors until they found their way back to their car. "He certainly seemed excited about having you play—whatever sport it is that we're talking about," she said as she pinched Ryan in the ribs.

"I thought you were a detective," she teased. "Use your deductive reasoning."

"I could, but I might as well wait until you go back to work out for the whole coaching staff. I guess we'd better get to bed early tonight, huh, Tiger."

"I wonder what poor souls he's going to make show up to play against me at seven in the morning?"

Jamie squeezed her hand and offered, "I could play against you. You'd look a lot better if I was your competition."

Ryan laughed a little at Jamie's offer, but reminded her, "You don't even know what sport we're talking about, remember, babe?"

"I know. But whatever it is, I'm sure you could whip me at it."

"Maybe," Ryan agreed, "but you get to whip me when we play golf on Saturday. Did you make arrangements?"

"Yeah. I called the club and got us a tee time for eight. Is that good?"

"Perfect. I'll call the boys and let them know."

"Do you mind if I play on Sunday with my father?"

"No. I can spend the day with the baby. We have a week's worth of bonding to make up for."

Ryan slipped her key into the lock and slowly opened the back door, sticking her head in tentatively. "Anybody home?" She turned to Jamie, who was right on her heels and instructed, "Now you ask the same thing in Spanish."

"You goof!" Pushing her partner into the house, Jamie restated the schedule. "Maria Los comes on Monday, Wednesday, and Friday, babe. The others are Mondays only. We're completely alone on Thursdays."

"Can't be too sure," Ryan insisted. "I'm still sleeping with one eye open just in case you've given out any other keys to the house."

Jamie laughed at her exaggerated caution, but suddenly stopped short. "I think Cassie still has a key."

Without a word, Ryan stood and walked to the door, noting the manufacturer of the lock. She purposefully strode to the small desk by the telephone and pulled out the yellow pages. Thumbing through the listings, she found what she was looking for and made eye contact with a puzzled-looking Jamie as she dialed.

"Hi, I need a locksmith to come over and change out some Medeco locks for me."

Jamie pulled into the parking lot of Women Power at three-thirty. Ryan wasn't expecting her, but since her partner was planning on working out after her last client she knew that she would still be there.

They hadn't had the opportunity to discuss the revelations Ryan had made to Coach Placer, and although she had put on a happy front, Jamie knew that the issue would linger in the background until they could speak about it. The gym wasn't the place to have this discussion, but Jamie thought that Ryan could use some extra attention, so she cut her time at the golf course short to be with her.

The gym was fairly deserted at this point in the afternoon, and Jamie spotted her partner immediately upon entering. Ryan had removed her gym-issued black polo shirt and was working out in a black sports bra and a pair of long, black Lycra tights. She was obviously in one of her little "zones" because she didn't notice Jamie enter, and the smaller woman indulged in the guilty pleasure of watching her lover for a few minutes.

Ryan was apparently working her trunk today, and Jamie marveled at the single-minded determination that she brought to the task. She dropped to a mat and began to perform a horribly tough-looking series of crunches. Ryan had grabbed a forty-five-pound weight plate from a rack, and as she prepared to work she grasped it with both hands and held it a few inches above her breasts. Her knees lifted a few inches and she crossed her ankles just to help hold her legs together, then she began to perform the crunches, using just her torso to move the upper and lower halves of her body together. It didn't take long for the veins near her temples to start to throb, and Jamie was actually a little concerned by the flush that covered her face and neck, but she assumed that Ryan knew what she was doing, so she continued to watch silently.

After a few sets of that exercise, she hopped to her feet and went to a pull-up bar. The bar was hung almost six feet up the wall, and Ryan had to stand on one of the conveniently placed wooden boxes to get to the right height. She slipped her forearms into a pair of heavy black slings which supported them in the correct position, then she crossed her feet at the ankle and lifted her knees until her thighs were parallel with the floor. Supporting her body weight with just her upper arms, she began to torture her abs by twisting her lower body until her knees nearly touched the wall behind her— first to the right, and then to the left. Jamie watched in fascinated silence as beads of sweat trickled from nearly every pore of her lover's body as she put herself through this self-inflicted torture.

She had no idea what was going through Ryan's mind, but her partner was obviously trying to exorcise some internal demons. Jamie had seen Ryan work out on numerous occasions, but she had never seen her look so determined to inflict pain upon herself. Ryan didn't look like she was even keeping track of how many of the contortions she did. It looked to Jamie like she was just going to continue to torment her body until she dropped. Ryan was now grunting audibly with each rep, and the few other women present were giving her surreptitious glances as they worked. Turgid blue veins were standing out sharply against her flushed skin as her arms shook heavily, obviously nearing failure. She completed her last rep in an uncharacteristically ragged fashion, letting out a strangled groan as she did so. Her legs searched for the step and she stood atop it for just a moment, clearly trying to make sure that her legs would hold her before she slid her arms from their supports. She took a few deep breaths and hopped off the step, finally making eye contact with Jamie as she did so.

"Been here long?" she asked quietly as she crossed the short distance between them.

Jamie just nodded, unable to conceal the worried look that she knew was betraying her concern.

"Wanna toss the medicine ball at my gut while I do some crunches?"

It took a second for Jamie to realize that her partner was serious. "No, I most certainly do not!" Her hand came to rest on Ryan's slick arm, and she said in a low tone, "I think you've done enough, honey. How long have you been working out?"

Ryan checked her watch and nearly did a double take. "Wow! I guess forty-five minutes is enough time for just my abs, huh?"

"Yeah … I think it's more than enough." She grabbed a towel from the stack near the wall and handed it to her lover. "Do you have any other clothes here?"

Ryan looked down at herself and noticed that her clothes were nearly dripping with sweat. "Yeah. I've got a pair of shorts and a T-shirt or two."

"You go change, babe. We're gonna go pamper ourselves a little bit."

Ryan dutifully went to do her lover's bidding, not even asking for clarification before she walked into the office.

A half hour later they were relaxing in a eucalyptus-scented hot tub located in one of the new day spas that had opened up in North Berkeley. They were the only two women in the large tub, since it was too late for the lunch crowd and too early for the after-work crowd. "Wanna talk about it?" Jamie asked after ten minutes of silence had passed between them.

"'Bout what?" Ryan asked lazily, the warm water rendering her nearly unconscious.

"'Bout what you were thinking about while you were trying to burst a blood vessel at the gym." There was no accusation in her tone, but it was clear that she was determined to get an answer.

"That obvious, huh?" Ryan sat up a little and looked like she was trying to make up her mind about something. She finally turned to Jamie and said, "It pisses me off that I'm still so pissed off."

Jamie shook her head a little, not getting her partner's point.

"I'm mad at myself for still being so upset about things that happened six years ago!" The frustration in her voice was building, and Jamie was afraid she was going to start yelling.

"Okay, baby, it's okay," she soothed in a calming tone, trailing her hand down Ryan's arm.

"No, it's not okay," Ryan growled, her building anger clearly evident. "I'm letting a couple of small-minded kids still get to me over something that happened when I was barely old enough to drive, for Christ's sake! It pisses me off that I can't control my mind any better than that! Jesus, Jamie, I practically cried today in front of a total stranger that I was trying to impress!"

"Honey, honey." Jamie spoke in a very low, soft voice, trying to let her reassuring tone reach the angry part of her partner. "It doesn't do you any good to try to minimize what happened. You were treated terribly by the girls in your school, and when you add the betrayal by your own coach, it makes it twice as bad. But I know you, babe, and I believe that you would have gotten over those wounds quickly if the whole thing hadn't been started by Sara. The fact that she was the source of all of your trouble had to be a hurt that you just can't let go of."

Ryan took a deep breath and scooted forward a little. She leaned back and lowered her head into the steaming water, letting her dark hair float around her for a moment before she sat up abruptly, water streaming down her face. She didn't verbally acknowledge the truth of Jamie's statement, but she turned to her and asked, "So ... how *do* I let go?"

Jamie gave her a sad smile and palmed her cheek, tenderly brushing her lips with her thumb. "I'm not sure, baby, but I know that it can be done. Have you spent much time talking about how it felt?"

A very rough headshake indicated that very little time had been spent in this pursuit. "Since I had no friends left, that wasn't an option." She let her head loll back against her shoulders, finally adding, "Bringing up Sara's name at home wasn't a real smart idea. I was truly afraid that Da or one of the boys might go ballistic."

Jamie nodded slightly, acknowledging that the O'Flaherty men had a very hard time remaining passive when Ryan's happiness was threatened. "They let their love for you get in the way of being there for you to talk about things sometimes, don't they?" she asked gently.

"Yeah ..." Ryan started to slap at the water with the flat of her hand, trying to see how hard she could hit it without having it splash her in the face. Jamie recognized this as another nervous habit that she used to distract herself while talking about painful issues. "I wind up keeping things to myself because they get so angry. I almost had to physically restrain Da from going to Sara's house to berate her." She shivered with the memory of the terribly tense scene, and recalled how out-of-control the whole house was on the day she revealed everything that had happened. "To this day, he doesn't know that my soccer coach told me to quit for the good of the team, he doesn't know about my bike being vandalized, and he doesn't know about the vile notes I got at school."

Jamie felt her heart clench with sadness for the young girl who'd had to keep her feelings bottled up to protect the people who loved her the most. She slipped her hand underwater and lightly rubbed Ryan's thigh, trying to send a supportive message that Ryan should keep talking if she wanted to.

Ryan let out a bitter laugh and revealed, "He doesn't know this, but the biggest reason I didn't go to Cal was because I couldn't bear to be there and know that Sara was on that soccer team, and that I wasn't. It didn't matter that I could have gotten an academic scholarship. I know this never made sense to him, but I just couldn't be on the same campus as she was. It just hurt too badly."

"Why not Stanford, honey?" Jamie had long wondered why her lover didn't accept the scholarship to play soccer at Stanford.

Ryan looked at her like she was crazy. "And play Cal twice a year? See Sara in the blue and gold uniform that I'd been dreaming about since I was a kid?"

"I'm sorry, love, I didn't think it through. Of course you couldn't do that."

This obviously sincere apology ameliorated Ryan's pique and she relaxed again, the tension visibly leaving her body. "I couldn't bear the commute either," she said softly. "And I just couldn't leave home to live in Palo Alto right then. I needed Da and the boys too much. I just turned inward and stayed close to my family. That's why I decided to take time off from school—it just seemed like the only way to put it behind me."

"But you haven't really put it behind you, baby. You've just stopped talking about it. That's not the same thing." Jamie was a little afraid of setting Ryan off again, but she felt strongly about this issue, and she felt that she needed to make her views known.

Ryan nodded, realizing that her partner had a very valid point. "I'll try to talk about it more, Jamie. Really I will. It's much easier to talk about with you than it is with Da, and that will really help."

"Okay, love," Jamie agreed quietly. "We don't have to do it all at once. I just want you to feel that you can talk to me when the issue comes up."

"I do." Ryan stood, the water sluicing down her body in rivulets. She extended her hand and pulled her partner to her feet. "I'm getting light-headed from being in here too long. Let's go before I pass out."

"Can I interest you in a massage?" the smaller woman asked as they climbed out of the tub.

"Sure." Ryan's grin indicated just what she would like to have massaged first.

"I mean a professional massage, you goof. I think both of us could use a little attention on our sore muscles."

"But I could …"

"I know you could, Tiger. But I can't do a competent job on you. So just relax and let me pamper you a little bit." Without a moment to allow for argument, she grabbed a towel and went to arrange for the massages.

Have I won an argument yet? She paused for a beat, and answered her own question, smirking to herself as she did so. *Do I care?*

Chapter Seven

An hour later they were lying on fully reclined chaises allowing the just-applied mud that coated their bodies to dry a bit. "This is too weird," the taller of the two mud-women muttered.

"But your skin feels soooo good when you wash it off," Jamie assured her.

"How could it not?" Ryan chuckled at her own joke and Jamie smiled over at her, pleased that her sense of humor was returning. They were still the only patrons in this part of the spa and when Ryan heard a pager go off, she knew it had to be hers. She got to her feet, grimacing when the mud began to audibly crack as she moved. "This is gross!"

"You'll live," Jamie insisted. "I bet you were nearly this muddy on a daily basis when you were little."

"I wish I could disagree, but you know me too well, sprite."

Jamie flung one of her shower sandals at her partner for using today's favorite term of affection and was amazed to score a direct hit on her butt.

"Not bad," Ryan said absently as she retrieved her pager from the little basket where they had stored their things.

"Who is it, babe?"

"Can I use your phone?" Ryan was already dialing, and she shot as much of a smirk as she could at her partner while the call went through. "I think I'm being recruited again. Hi," Ryan said when the call was connected. "No, I haven't made any decisions yet." After a long pause, she began to nod her head. "That probably would make me lean toward playing, but where did you get it?" A slow scowl began to form on her face. "Have you told her yet?" Pursed lips accompanied another slow nod. "Upperclassman?" Slight pause. "In state?" Another pause. "Okay. Yes, I do understand." Longer pause, more nodding. "I'd appreciate it if you didn't do anything on this yet. I'll get back to you by tomorrow afternoon. Yes, I do realize that." She was nodding thoughtfully, but there was an unreadable expression on her face that Jamie couldn't wait to have explained.

Ryan placed the phone down and flopped back onto the chaise. "Shit!" she muttered as she crossed her long legs at the ankle and rested her head on her linked hands.

"What's wrong, honey?"

"Coach Greene offered me a scholarship." Her voice carried a heavy dose of bitterness.

"But I thought that's what you wanted?" Jamie asked, totally confused by Ryan's attitude.

"I do, but she's yanking it away from another player. She has a player who hasn't been contributing as much as she'd like, so she wants to kick her off the team and give me her scholarship."

"Can she do that?" Jamie asked incredulously.

"Sure. There are all sorts of restrictions on how you dole out scholarships, as you might expect. I actually called Coach because I read in the school paper that their best goalie was declared academically ineligible. When that happens, they can't reuse that scholarship, so she's light one ride this year. But if they kick you off the team because of your performance they can award the scholarship to someone else."

"Light a ride?"

"Oh … sorry. A scholarship is sometimes called a ride …. You know, like a free ride."

"Got it," Jamie said. "Okay, so she has one less than normal anyway, so she wants to make sure every one that she does have is used for the best player, right?"

"Right," Ryan agreed.

"But I'm guessing you don't feel very good about benefiting from someone else's misfortune."

"Right," she said quickly. "Been there, had that done to me."

"Do you think she would have kicked this woman off if you weren't interested?"

"I doubt it. They start practice next week and I assume her roster is set. So I'm guessing the only thing between this other woman and her scholarship is me," she replied glumly.

"What did she tell you about her?"

"She's a junior and she's from out of state. If she loses her scholarship, she'll have to pay a load for tuition. I just don't think I can accept this knowing that some other woman will probably have to drop out because of me."

"I see your dilemma, babe, but if she really isn't cutting it, maybe she doesn't deserve the scholarship."

Ryan nodded absently and started to pick at the flaking mud on her belly. "That's probably true in the abstract, but this is a real person who will have her life turned upside down because of me. I don't think I can be responsible for that."

"Okay. I can understand that, baby. I know this is hard, but I want you to tell me exactly why the scholarship is important to you. How much is about pride, and how much is about money."

"I was thinking about this yesterday afternoon," Ryan remarked. "I'm going to have a pretty difficult schedule this fall. If I play soccer, I'll have to practice every afternoon, run every morning, and spend more time in the weight room than I do now. I don't know if I'll have the energy to do all of that and be available to you." She gave her lover a fond smile. "I figure I need to save at least two hours a day for lovemaking, so my time would really be stretched. I just don't know if I want to have to take out loans for the privilege of running myself ragged."

"How does a scholarship fit in?"

"If they paid for my tuition, books, and fees I could live on what I saved last year. It wouldn't let me have much left after the school year, but I could get by."

"I have a simple solution to your problem, honey," Jamie said softly as she bridged the distance between them and grasped Ryan's hand loosely.

Ryan rolled her eyes and muttered, "I was hoping to delay this conversation for another year."

Jamie rolled over onto her side, facing her lover fully. "You want to play, Ryan. Either soccer or one of your other sports-to-be-named-later. You don't want to contribute to ruining someone else's plans, and I admire that about you. But I don't want you to deprive yourself of the pleasure of competition just because of money. And I don't want you to be horrendously busy every moment of every day. Let me support you this year, Ryan. There is nothing I'd like better than for you to be able to just relax and enjoy your last year of college. It breaks my heart to think of how hard you've had to work to get this far, honey. I would truly be grateful if you would let me help you."

Ryan gave her a bemused grin, "Grateful, huh?"

"Yes. I would be grateful that you were willing to put aside your reservations about this issue and allow me to help you. It'd give me more pleasure than you can imagine to let you have another chance to fulfill some of the dreams of your youth. It'd make me feel like I was helping you heal some of your wounds. I swear it means a lot to me, baby."

Years of indoctrination flashed through her mind, and Ryan had to struggle to not immediately refuse. She didn't want to be hardheaded, and she knew this was important to Jamie, so she gave her partner another shy grin and offered a compromise, "How about we make it a loan?"

Jamie breathed a heavy sigh, grateful that Ryan was willing to budge, but not terribly happy to be loaning her spouse money. Seeing the determined look in Ryan's eyes, however, made her realize that this was probably the best deal she was going to get out of the negotiations. "Okay, that would work. I'll loan you the money for tuition, fees, and books. I'll even have a loan agreement drawn up. I will not, though, under any circumstances, put a repayment date on it. You can pay me back as slowly as you need to after you're finished with school."

"That's fair," Ryan agreed, grateful that Jamie was allowing her to maintain her principles. "Now, I won't be able to contribute much to our household expenses if I don't work. I want you to keep track of what we spend this year and add half of that to the loan, too."

Jamie pursed her lips and shook her head firmly. "Unh-uh. No deal," she insisted. "School is sort of optional, and I can understand that you feel like it's a big expense. But you need to eat, and you need to have some entertainment, and you need some spending money. I am your partner, Ryan. I pledged to take care of you just like you take care of me. I will not have you feel indebted to me for providing you with the essentials of life."

"You sound like me father," she said softly, lapsing into her brogue.

"Well, that makes sense, since he and I both love you dearly. But why do I sound like him specifically?"

"Because he won't allow any of us to contribute one dime toward household expenses. He says it's a parent's duty and honor to support the household."

"He's absolutely right. I'm in a position to provide for our financial security. Because I can do that, it's my duty to do so. So play nice, and I won't have to hurt you."

Ryan laughed at her mock threat. "You almost broke my neck last night, and that was while you were loving me. What would you do if you really wanted to hurt me?"

"You'll find out," Jamie muttered as she narrowed her eyes, the scowl looking sillier than normal because of the mud masque.

"Well, this will be an interesting experiment, Ms. Evans. It's going to take a lot of adjustment for me to be comfortable, but I will do my best to allow you to deplete your fortune in order to keep my belly full."

"That was less than poetic, sweet pea, but I truly appreciate your willingness to work with me on this. Compromising like this is what being life partners is all about, babe."

"You're right, hon, but I gotta tell you, most couples would trade their problems for ours in a hot minute. Most people don't argue about having too much money."

"Good point, Ryan. I certainly hope that this is the most contentious issue we ever face."

Ryan smiled at her partner, knowing that her wish was entirely fanciful, but hoping that the inevitable problems that they would experience were a long way off.

A few minutes before seven, they drove the short distance to the Recreation and Sports Facility, where the tryout was to be held. "I think I know what sport this is," Jamie said, a confident smile on her sunny face.

"Oh, is that deductive reasoning kicking in?"

"Yep. I reason that women only play two sports at Haas, so I've got a pretty darned good idea what today's sport is." Jamie had carefully attended to Ryan's choice of attire, and the odd shoes that she wore indicated that they weren't going for a basketball tryout. "Those funny shoes with the built-up soles don't look like any I have, so I think I have a pretty good idea."

"You're much too quick for me to ever pull a fast one," Ryan agreed. "I'm a little nervous about today, to tell you the truth. You heard the coach mention that I haven't done this in a long while." She looked contemplative for a long moment, and Jamie was just about to step in to reassure her when Ryan mused, "I sure hope I don't have any trouble with the pommel horse. That's my worst event."

"Isn't that in gymnastics?" Jamie asked in a stunned voice.

"Yeah. You don't think my feet are too big for the balance beam, do you?" Her blissfully innocent face didn't prevent her from getting a hard slap to the belly, and she rubbed the spot with a dramatic flair.

"Very funny, Ryan," Jamie growled playfully. "You never tire of setting me up, do ya?"

"No, I can't imagine getting tired of that," she happily agreed. "You are such a perfect victim—that sincere little face that just wants to believe every word I say is too easy a target to waste."

"I always thought I was missing something, growing up as an only child. Little did I know that I would marry into a whole family of teasers and comedians that would extend my childhood indefinitely."

"Yep. You've jumped into the O'Flaherty fountain of youth." Ryan's smile showed just how happy she was with the chain of events that had led to Jamie's joining the family.

"You're only young once, baby. But you've proven that you can be immature forever!" They shared a smile at that, both women silently reflecting on how much fun it was to be immature together.

Coach Placer was waiting as promised. As soon as they caught sight of him, Jamie's guess was confirmed: Ryan was there to try out for the volleyball team. The coach had set up the net and coerced three other women to attend the early morning workout, none of them looking very happy about the early hour. His two assistant coaches were there as well, but since they were dressed in khaki shorts and Cal golf shirts, they obviously were not planning on playing. He introduced Ryan to his assistants, Ken and Erin, and to the other players, Stacy, Ashley, and Anna, and they spent a few minutes warming up by just tossing the ball back and forth, all of them on the same side of the net.

When the coach decided they were sufficiently warmed up, he signaled one of the players to stay on Ryan's side and sent the other two to the opposite side. It was clear that they were going to try to play the two-person game on the big court, even though the large area was an awful lot of ground for two people to cover.

Ryan was wearing an outfit that Jamie was very fond of, and the other players were somewhat similarly dressed. She had on a pair of bright blue Lycra shorts, but they were amazingly short—Jamie guessed that the inseam was no more than two inches. Acres of long, lithe, lean leg were exposed to Jamie's appreciative gaze, and she decided that she liked volleyball better than soccer without even seeing the ball go over the net. The other players wore similar shorts, but all three sported T-shirts. Ryan had gone for a different look and Jamie was very pleased that she had done so. She wore a print tank top with the blue of her shorts, a bright yellow and white pattern. Even this was not her usual tank—it looked more like a compression top, or even a very long sports bra. It obviously gave her a little extra support since it was so tight, and Jamie reasoned that she would be able to be very active without fear of her bra riding up.

All of the other players were tall, lanky women, and they each looked very athletic. Jamie wasn't sure if her partner had chosen her outfit to display her impressive musculature, but whether planned or inadvertent, it did just that. The other women looked a little gawky next to her—they looked as tall as they were, while Ryan looked shorter until she stood right next to one of them. Her body was so perfectly proportioned that it continually surprised Jamie how tall she was, until she had to stand on her tiptoes just to get her arms around her neck.

As the ball was tossed into play, Jamie had to remind herself that she had seen her lover play this game on the beach in Santa Monica. Playing on a large hard court changed the game so much that it seemed like an altogether different sport. The players moved so quickly, and covered so much ground, that they were literally throwing their bodies all over the court. Fortunately, Ryan wore both kneepads and elbow pads, and Jamie was thankful that she had, or her body would be acquiring a mass of bruises. Ryan's tight braid flew around her back and shoulders as she dove for ball after ball, making a play on most that she tried for, and giving an all-out effort on the ones she missed.

Within a very few minutes, Ryan was clearly dominating the game. She had a vertical leap that was hard to believe and her power was truly intimidating. The first time that she rose into the air to spike the ball into the other court, she let out such a powerful yell that the players on the other side froze for a second. Jamie couldn't help but think of the Celtic warriors she had read about who beat their opponents with their bloodcurdling war cries and physically intimidating style as much as with their skills in battle.

Ryan's powerful back muscles flexed as she brought her arm back to slam the ball onto the opposite court, sending it into a dizzying spin as it curved toward an open space on the floor. Jamie could see the women on the other side occasionally flinch as her arm came back and even to her unschooled eye, that didn't seem like a good tactic for returning the ball. After about ten minutes, they were dodging out of the way to avoid being hit by her powerful slams, another approach that seemed counterproductive, but understandable. The coach was getting frustrated with the two women and he finally asked Ryan's partner to switch with one of them; after getting hit a few times, she was looking for a safe haven as well.

The coach had finally seen all that he could stomach. He called a halt to the slaughter and called Ryan over. He spoke with her quietly for a few minutes and patted her on the back before he gathered the other three into a little group and spoke with them. She came back over to Jamie and flopped down onto the bench next to her. "That was kind of embarrassing," she admitted, rubbing her wet face with a towel.

"Were those varsity players?" Jamie asked.

"No, they were walk-ons like me. I think the roster is pretty well set at this point. My guess is that he's only got one or two spots to fill this late in the year."

Jamie pulled the towel from Ryan and carefully dried her back, lifting her braid to get to her very wet neck. "It was really woman against girls, honey. You looked All-World."

"I feel bad for them, though," Ryan admitted a little sheepishly. "They're trying for a spot, too."

"I know, baby. But you still had to do your best, even if it made the others look bad."

"Did they really look that bad?" she asked, turning to look directly into Jamie's eyes.

She fluffed the wet bangs out of the bright blue eyes that gazed down at her and wished that she could kiss her partner for being so concerned about the other women's performances. She just nodded slightly, acknowledging that they did, in fact, look horrible, even in her uneducated view.

"I guess I can't let that bother me," Ryan agreed. "But to tell you the truth, I liked the days of youth league where everyone got to play the same amount of time no matter how bad you were."

Unable to resist her need, Jamie leaned over and kissed her partner's steaming hot head. "I love that you care about those women and how they feel about this, love. You have such a good heart."

Ryan gave her a shy, almost embarrassed grin and went back to drying the rest of her body. When she was finished she stayed right where she was until Jamie finally asked, "Are we waiting for something?"

"Yeah, Coach Placer asked me to hang around for a few minutes. I think he wants to talk to the other coaches."

After a few more minutes Coach Placer came back onto the court and motioned Ryan to follow him. "Come on," she said to Jamie.

"Are you sure?" she asked as she trotted alongside. "Maybe he wants to see you alone."

"I don't want to go alone, so that's settled," she said with a smile. "We're a package deal, honey."

They followed him down the hall to his office where the other coaches were already perched on whatever furniture they could fit on. They took the two chairs as the coach went to sit at his desk. He gave Ryan a broad smile and said, "I think it's clear after that little exhibition that we'd like to offer you a spot on the team."

Ryan smiled back and nodded, waiting for him to continue. "I know you only played volleyball for one year, but what else did you play at USF?"

"I played soccer for one year, volleyball for one, and basketball for two. The other things I did were just club sports."

"You were a busy girl, weren't you?" he teased. "What years did you participate?"

"'96 and '97."

"That should leave you with two more years of eligibility since you sat out last year. We'll check the records at USF and make sure everything is square with the NCAA. If it all checks out, we'd like to have you with us. Are you interested?"

"Yes. I'm definitely interested. But Coach Greene wants me to play soccer this year and I'm considering one other sport."

"Are you just doing this for fun, Ryan, or is a scholarship important to you?"

She smiled at Jamie and said, "It's important, but I'm not going to let it be a deal-breaker. I've decided that I need to play the sport that appeals to me most."

"Well, I don't mean to put pressure on you, but I'd like to be able to let the other girls know as soon as possible. If you don't join us, we need to offer one of them a spot."

Jamie piped up. "Are you offering Ryan a scholarship?"

"Why, yes, of course. We have one left to give. We've been working those three women out for weeks trying to determine which one we'd give it to. Luckily Ryan came along and made the decision easy for us."

"Were any of them scholarship players last year?" Jamie asked.

"No. They were all walk-ons from this year. Why?"

"I just wondered if any of them would lose a scholarship because of Ryan."

"Oh no. I don't yank a scholarship unless there's a compelling reason. If I convince a girl to come here to play, I feel like I have to keep my end of the bargain. If she comes to practice and tries hard, she keeps her ride."

Ryan smiled and said, "That's good to hear, Coach. I do have a few questions. Do you think it'll be a problem that I'm openly gay?"

"Not for any of us," he said easily. "The only problem I've ever had is when two players are dating each other and they break up or have a fight. I trust that won't be a problem for you, will it?" he asked with a grin as he looked from Jamie to Ryan.

"Nope," she said happily. "I am permanently partnered. Would you have a problem if Jamie went on road trips with me?"

"We couldn't pay for her airfare, and she'd have to get her own room, but we don't do bed checks, so ..." He smiled at the pair and shrugged his shoulders, indicating that his policy was to not get too involved in his players' personal lives.

"I'm thinking of playing a winter sport too," Ryan said, surprising Jamie completely. "Would you mind if I had to practice with another team during the end of the volleyball season?"

He shook his dark head and said, "We had two players who played two sports last season. We didn't have any trouble working out the schedule. But I would ask that you focus more on volleyball since that is the most important part of our season. You might have to miss an exhibition game or two, but I'm sure we could work it out."

"When do you start practice?"

"Next week," he said quickly, his excitement building. "Can we count on you?"

Ryan pursed her lips, obviously not quite ready to commit. "I've got an appointment with Sandra Johnston at nine. After we speak with her, I really need to think about it for a while before I'm ready to commit, Coach. Jamie and I need to spend a little time making sure that I make a decision we can both live with. Can I call you late this afternoon?"

"Sure. Here's my home phone number," he said as he wrote his number on his business card and handed it to Ryan. "Is there anything else I can do to help you make the decision? Would you like to talk to some of the players from last year?"

"Yes. That would be helpful. Could you have one or two of them call me?"

"Absolutely. What number should I use?"

"Just have them page me." She recited her number. "I'm going to be in and out today, and that's the surest way to reach me."

"Will do, Ryan. I'll make sure it happens. Anything else?"

"Yeah," she said slowly. "Would you be comfortable talking about the paperwork that you have on me from when I was recruited in high school?"

He shifted a little in his seat, but answered her honestly. "I can't share anything that's confidential, but I'll answer anything I can."

She fixed him with a level gaze and asked, "Did the teachers from my high school go to bat for me?"

He let out a heavy sigh and said, "They didn't do you any favors, Ryan."

Ryan maintained her steady gaze and finally asked just one more question. "Coach Ratzinger sold me out, didn't she?"

He looked very pained as he just nodded his head a slight bit. "I think she made the coaches here doubt your emotional stability."

"Emotional stability? Being a lesbian in San Francisco calls your stability into question!?" Jamie nearly shouted.

Ryan smiled indulgently at her partner and explained to the coaches, "She's my little champion."

"Well, Jesus, Ryan, someone needs to be! It just slays me how chicken sh—" she began, but Ryan gently covered her mouth with her hand.

"There's nothing in here about Ryan being gay, Jamie. Now, it's possible that my predecessor just didn't put that in the file, but this indicates that Ryan just quit for no good reason."

"But she didn't!" Now Jamie was shouting, and Ryan felt her stomach start to clench as the tension in the room rose sharply.

"It's okay, honey. I just need to know the facts to put it behind me once and for all." Turning to Coach Placer she said, "I appreciate that you were honest with me, Coach. That means a lot." She got up to shake his hand, nodded to the assistants and shook each one's hand as she made her way toward the door. "I'll call you late this afternoon."

After they walked a few feet down the dark hallway, she pushed Jamie gently against the wall and gave her a very sincere kiss of thanks. "What was that for?" the startled woman gasped.

"For loving me, and trying so hard to defend my honor."

"I do love you, Ryan, and it makes me irrationally angry to see what a bunch of asshole adults did to a fragile young girl. I'd do anything to take that hurt away."

"I know, babe, but it can't be done. We just need to move on now."

As they walked down the hallway, Jamie pulled her to a stop in front of a large display of color pictures of the previous year's team. She smiled up at her and said, "I know that you haven't made up your mind, but I choose volleyball."

"He was a nice guy, wasn't he?" Ryan said thoughtfully. "And I'm really excited about getting a scholarship."

"Ryan, Ryan, you're not focusing on the important things," she chided as her face broke into a gleeful smile. "Look at these outfits!"

They drove to the coffee shop and spent an hour sipping lattés and munching on scones. Ryan's next interview was at nine, and she assured Jamie that her current outfit would be acceptable for the next sport as well. "Aside from the outfits, what did you think?" Ryan asked, sharing a teasing smile with her partner.

"I liked the coach a lot," Jamie said. "He seemed like the kind of guy you could really get along with."

"I think so, too," she said thoughtfully. "Telling me the truth about my coach at Sacred Heart boosted his stock way up in my book."

"I can well imagine," Jamie agreed, knowing that Ryan despised being treated like a child.

"Well, it's time for the last of the interviews," she said, standing to stretch. As she did so she winced a bit, but kept right on doing it.

"Hey, what was that war cry you let out when you were slamming that ball at those poor girls?" Jamie was laughing at the memory, but Ryan just shook her head.

"That wasn't a war cry, babe," she insisted. "That was an 'oh my God, I feel like my abs have been cut by a razor blade' cry. That'll teach me to work out my frustrations on my own body!"

"Where to this time, honey?" Jamie asked as they approached the Boxster.

"Do you know where Kleeberger Field is?"

"No. I've never heard of it."

"Then I'll drive," she said with a grin as she slipped the keys from Jamie's hand.

About fifteen minutes later they were striding across a well-tended field to meet the stocky woman who was obviously waiting for them. Ryan approached her and stuck out her hand. "I'm Ryan O'Flaherty," she said in her warm alto voice.

"Good to meet you, Ryan, I'm Sandra Johnston." She turned to Jamie as Ryan made the introductions. "I don't know much about you, and I didn't have time to go through my predecessor's recruiting files, so tell me a little about your background."

Ryan began, "I played at Sacred Heart in San Francisco from '88 to '91. We had a pretty good team …"

"Pretty good! Sacred Heart was the state champ in '90! Hey … wait a minute … I remember you!" The coach was now bubbling with enthusiasm. "Didn't you play under a different name then?"

"Kinda," Ryan admitted. "My given name is Siobhán, and that's how I was listed."

"I tried to recruit you," Coach Johnston said, narrowing her brow in concentration. "I was an assistant at Santa Clara then, but as I recall, you didn't have any interest in moving up to play at the college level. What happened?"

"Long story," Ryan said dismissively. "I took off a few years and went to USF for a couple of years. I'm just now thinking of getting back into it."

The coach pursed her lips and rocked back on her heels. "That's an awfully long time to be away from the sport, Ryan. What makes you want to try it again?"

"My financial circumstances have changed, and I'm able to participate in sports this year instead of having to have a job. It's my last year of college and I really miss the competition. I want one more chance to be on a team before I have to join the real world," she said with a grin.

"You look like you're in great shape," the coach said, as she looked her over from top to bottom. "What do you do for a workout?"

"I do a lot of weight training, and I run five to ten miles a day, usually in the hills. Oh, and I ride my bike about one hundred miles a week."

"I'd give my eyeteeth if I could get some of my girls to do that much in a week," she said with a laugh. "You certainly sound like you're able to motivate yourself. I'm willing to give you a tryout, if you want."

"Sure. I am talking to some of the other programs, but I'm very serious about playing some sport this year."

"Do you want to do it now or do you need to prepare?"

"Let's go," Ryan said with a grin.

Jamie still had absolutely no idea what sport they were talking about. *It's obviously not swimming—no pool; not basketball—no court; not softball—no diamond. I don't think they'd let women try out for football—but with Ryan, you never know.*

Ryan walked over to a bench and peeled off the thin nylon warm-up pants that she had put on after her volleyball workout. She rummaged around in her gym bag and took out a pair of black leather shoes with plastic cleats and a pair of knee socks. Before she pulled the socks up, she inserted a pair of shin guards, adjusting the inserts until they were just so. To Jamie's regret she tugged a T-shirt on over her tank, but she had kept the tiny shorts on, so Jamie was still relatively satisfied with her look.

While Ryan fussed with her shoes and socks, Jamie took a moment to observe the coach. As a newcomer to the lesbian club, she found that she spent a lot of time trying to guess sexual orientations—something that surprised her a little, since she had never done so before. Ryan had assured her that this was a passing phase and that most people did it when they first "came out," but Jamie was still uncomfortable with her unconscious habit. She tried her best to refrain from labeling every woman without a man draped all over her as a lesbian, but assessing Sandra Johnston caused her to immediately place her into the "definite" category. The coach was short, stocky, and remarkably butch, giving the impression of a pit bull as she strutted around the field, loosening up her ample muscles. Her hair looked like she had placed a bowl on it before she cut it, and her features were compressed on her pugnacious-looking square face.

Sandra went to her long nylon bag and pulled out a pair of varnished wooden sticks with hooked ends and two small, hard white balls. *Field hockey?* Jamie gaped, before she reminded herself that field hockey was just about the only sport that was left after all of the others had been eliminated by her deductive reasoning.

When Sandra was standing still she looked quite bulky, but as she started to warm up Jamie noticed that she moved with the confident, graceful strides of an athlete, and she quickly saw how her compact body was perfectly suited to the game. Her short, powerful legs let her stop and turn quickly, and her small stature allowed her to take a full swing at the ball without bending at all.

Ryan, on the other hand, was so unusually tall that she had to bend quite a bit to hit the ball with the rather short stick. That didn't seem to slow her down much, though, Jamie had to admit, as she dashed around the field.

When they were both limbered up, Coach Johnston tossed one of the balls down on the ground and she and Ryan began to pass it back and forth, using their sticks to direct its movement. After giving quite an impressive little display, she had Ryan run the length of the field several times, controlling the little ball with her stick. Jamie was astonished at the dexterity that her lover showed in this exhibition. She could move the ball around so effortlessly that it looked as though it were glued to her stick. She knew that the stick was perfectly flat, but the way Ryan played it sure didn't seem so.

After she had shown that she could control the ball, the coach tried to run along with her and take the ball away. For seven trips up and down the field, Ryan never relinquished her control of the ball. Jamie was pleased that, as the workout went on, the coach's smile grew bigger. She finally threw her stick up in the air and shouted, "I give!"

Ryan bent over and rested her hands on her knees for a few moments, but she quickly caught her breath and jogged back over to Jamie with a big smile on her face. "That's my most natural sport," she said with a cocky grin.

"If you want to play, we'll find a spot for you," the coach said as she gasped for air. "Shit! I didn't even ask you what position you play." She looked up at Ryan from her bent position and let her face curl into a smile. "Does it matter?" she asked with a laugh.

"Not really." Ryan blushed modestly. "I can be a pure defender or a goalie but I prefer to be a midfielder. I like to score, but playing defense really gets my juices flowing."

"I seem to remember that you were going to play soccer, weren't you?" the coach asked, still slightly out of breath.

"Yeah. I'm still considering it," she admitted. "Plus there's a spot on the volleyball team I'm considering."

Sandra looked a little crestfallen, knowing that her small, non-scholarship program didn't have much of a chance against the big sports. But she summoned a bright smile and said, "We'd love to have you, Ryan. If you want to talk to any of the players I'd be happy to hook you up. My assistant coaches would be glad to talk to you, too. Boy, when I left the house today I told my husband that I had to go waste an hour. I'm awfully glad I was wrong!" she said as she shook Ryan's hand firmly.

As they walked across the field to their car, they waited until the coach was out of earshot before they looked at each other and simultaneously shouted, "Husband?"

While Ryan took another shower, Jamie prepared a massive lunch for her favorite athlete. Ryan came down just as she placed a large vegetable salad at the table for her to begin munching on. "Oooh … this looks good," Ryan purred, casting a lingering glance toward her lunch while she dutifully hugged her partner from behind.

Jamie grasped both of the arms that circled her waist and took a moment to breathe in Ryan's sweet, clean scent. She couldn't resist turning in her embrace for a few kisses, releasing her partner only when she felt Ryan's attention start to flag. "I can tell you're thinking more about your lunch than you are about me, chow hound, so go on." She swatted her firmly on the butt. "Go to your first love."

Ryan scampered across the kitchen, attempting to look contrite. "My stomach has a mind of its own, honey," she insisted. "It's the most dominant part of my psyche."

"Sure it is, sweetheart," Jamie said in mock agreement. "Next time you want to make love, I'm going to remind you of that and give you a sandwich instead."

Ryan knew she'd been caught in a major lie, so she quickly switched the subject as she dug into the crisp vegetables with their light poppy-seed vinaigrette dressing. "You are the best cook in the universe," she gushed, an innocent look plastered on her smiling face.

"I'm glad you think so, love," Jamie soothed as she bent to kiss just above Ryan's ear. "Then you won't mind when I feed you rather than f …"

Ryan whipped around in her chair and inserted a baby carrot into her partner's mouth. "Jamie! I think you were going to say a very naughty word!" The shock she was trying to affect was ineffective on her grinning lover.

She bit down sharply on the carrot and smiled as she chewed. "Fondle, babe. I was going to say fondle."

"No matter what you were going for, neither is acceptable," Ryan insisted. She pulled Jamie onto her lap and kissed her tenderly, the kisses growing in intensity until Jamie's breath caught. "Touching you and loving you are the most important things I do. I would gladly starve if I had to choose between that and eating."

Jamie knew there was more than a little hyperbole in this statement, but she appreciated the sincerity in the big blue eyes that gazed at her lovingly. She rested her forehead against Ryan's and whispered, "We'll never starve as long as we can love each other. Our love is completely life-sustaining." Their lips merged in another bout of achingly tender kisses, neither making a move to break the contact until Ryan pulled away as she sniffed delicately. "Is something burning?"

"Umm hmm," Jamie murmured, leaning in for another scorcher. "Yipes!" She jumped from Ryan's lap and dashed for the range, turning off the burner under the butter she had been melting. "I bet Wolfgang Puck doesn't have to work with these kinds of distractions!" Switching pans, she paid attention to her work, ignoring Ryan's amused chuckles as she prepared an egg white, chili, and cheese omelet for her partner.

When the meal was ready Jamie sat next to her partner and munched off her plate while Ryan talked about the decision she had to make. "I'm in a bit of a quandary," she admitted.

"Tell me what you're thinking about, hon," Jamie urged. "Tell me which sport is your favorite, ignoring every other concern."

Ryan thought for a minute and said, "Soccer is my favorite, I guess. I like that it's played outside, I love being a goalie, and the pace is just right for me. I can watch the whole game from my position and I like the level of concentration I have to maintain to defend my goal. I can also express a lot of emotion as a goalie. It's really fun to make a great save and be able to celebrate. There aren't that many other activities that give me the personal satisfaction of saving a goal."

"That sounds pretty important. Is there anything you don't like about it?"

"No. I love soccer, but there are other factors that I can't ignore. I'm still a little bit afraid of having to hit the ball with my head. The neurologists I consulted don't think I'll have any permanent damage from my concussions, but they all said that the effects of trauma are cumulative. I don't have to use my head much as a goalie, but it does happen. And when a ball is coming at you at forty or fifty miles per hour, hitting it with your head really gets your attention."

"Honey, if there is any chance that you can injure your brain by playing …"

"I know, Jamie. It's not worth the risk," she said quietly, forcing herself to acknowledge that her head injuries had finally caught up to her. She paused for another few seconds before she continued. "You know, even if that wasn't a consideration, I don't think I'd play. As much as I wish I wasn't, I'm still angry with Coach Greene. I hated the way she treated me, and it really pissed me off when she offered to yank a scholarship for me."

"Those seem like pretty good reasons to not play."

"They are," she admitted. "But I really love soccer," she said wistfully. "It's hard to admit that some things that mean a lot to me are simply out of my reach now. I guess this is part of growing up." The sad look on her face made Jamie wish she could make the reality of the situation go away, but she knew it was unthinkable to risk Ryan's health for the sake of a sport.

"Maybe soccer is on my mind more because of the World Cup coming up. Would you like to go to some of the matches? The first-round games are at Stanford."

"I'd love to," Jamie said, smiling at the flicker of a grin on her partner's face. "You can explain some of the strategy to me."

"That I can do," Ryan agreed confidently. "So … if we narrow it down between volleyball and field hockey I still have a tough choice. Field hockey is truly my most natural sport. It feels effortless when I play, and my instincts just lead me to the ball. The other plus is that they only play sixteen games and there are only two road trips."

"I keep forgetting about road trips. How many does the volleyball team make?"

"Probably five or six and then the NCAA tournaments, if the team gets that far."

"Hmm … that is a lot," she agreed. "Which sport do you like better?"

"Field hockey," Ryan said firmly. "I like volleyball, but I don't love it. Plus it's really hard on my knees. They ache like a bitch after a five-game match."

"Then you should play field hockey," Jamie urged.

"There are a few more factors that are important to me," Ryan said. "And one of them is kind of embarrassing."

"What could be embarrassing about field hockey?"

"No, not the sport. I'm embarrassed that one of my considerations is that nobody cares about field hockey. There are usually fewer than twenty people who come to a match. It feels more like you're just running around with a bunch of your friends. I think that's one of the things I like best about it. But on the other hand, if I'm going to devote a ton of my time to a sport, I'd like to get some recognition for it."

"And it embarrasses you to feel that way?" she asked gently, touching Ryan's hand softly.

"It's pretty self-serving. I wish I didn't need the approval of fans, but I do. And part of the reason that I want to play is to get the full experience of playing a major sport at the Division One level. Field hockey won't give me that."

"I think I see your point. Do you like volleyball enough to dedicate yourself to it?"

"Oh yeah. I like volleyball a lot. It's just not my favorite. I prefer beach volleyball because it's outside, but I don't think I would have a hard time gearing up for it." She sat for a few minutes in pensive silence. "Plus I can't ignore the scholarship. This is another self-serving trait, but it makes me feel really good that they think enough of me to give me a free ride."

"I can understand that, honey. It validates that you're important to the team and to the school."

"But I think we need to make some decisions about how we want to live our lives this year. How do you feel about my playing any of the sports?"

Jamie sat back in her chair and acknowledged that they hadn't really discussed the time any of the sports would take away from their time together. "Do you have any idea of how much time volleyball will take?"

"I can only assume it is run like the program at USF. There we practiced about two hours a day. You were supposed to spend at least three days in the weight room, and they had us run as a team three mornings a week. They play about thirty games, so that takes up two or three nights a week. Most of the games are on Friday and Saturday nights so we wouldn't have a date night until December at the earliest. And if I played basketball next, I'd be busy every weekend until March."

"That's not a small sacrifice," she agreed. "But let me ask you a question. If you were single and were offered a scholarship, would you play?"

"Yes," she said immediately.

"Then I want you to play," Jamie replied just as quickly. "I know there are times when our relationship will cause you to give up things that you like, but this doesn't have to be one of them. I think we'll be able to adapt to your schedule, especially if you quit your job."

"What have I had to give up for the relationship?" Ryan asked with a confused look.

"Having sex with tons of women, for one," she replied with a smirk.

"That was kind of fun," Ryan said wistfully. "But you're proving to be more than I can handle, so it's not much of a sacrifice. Speaking of which, have we scheduled today's two-hour lovemaking session?"

"No ... we'll be at our home tonight, so as long as we can get rid of Duffy we can get started as soon as dinner's over."

Just as Jamie was going to seal the deal with a kiss Ryan's pager went off. "Hold that thought," she said as she went to the phone.

She spent nearly twenty minutes on the phone, giving the poor woman on the other end a thorough cross-examination. Jamie began to wash the dishes, and Ryan tucked the portable phone under her chin and took over the drying duties while she talked. Jamie laughed to herself as she heard Ryan ask every possible question that could influence her choice, but her ears perked up when Ryan asked, "How do you think the other players would feel about having a lesbian on the team?"

She recognized the smirk that immediately covered Ryan's face, and instinctively knew that the woman on the other end was flirting with her partner. "Yeah, I'd say I'm decent-looking," she drawled, whipping around as Jamie tried to grab the phone from her hand. "That's good to know," she laughed. "I'll tell my lover that you'll cast a vote in my favor." Jamie stopped her attempt to join in on the conversation, now that Ryan had covered the most important point. "Yeah … I'm happily married," she added, further reassuring Jamie. "That's great. Thanks a lot for your time, and I guess I'll see you on Monday." Ryan paused again and let the smirk cover her handsome face. "I'll let my partner do that for you." She handed the phone to Jamie and said, "Jordan wants to know what I look like, honey. She wants to make sure she welcomes me to the team."

Jamie laughed and took the phone from her partner, "Hi, Jordan, this is Jamie." She paused a bit, poking her tongue out at Ryan before she said, "She's very tall, has very dark hair, gorgeous blue eyes, the whitest teeth you've ever seen, and a short blonde bulldog hanging on her leg most of the time."

As Jamie drove her partner to work Ryan said, "I think I'll call the coaches and give them my decision as soon as I'm done with work. The good news is that you get to see me in your favorite outfit."

"My favorite outfit would be if you joined the hot oil wrestling team," she teased. "But volleyball is a close second."

When Jamie showed up to pick Ryan up for the ride to the city, Ryan took Jamie's cell phone and spent the next twenty minutes making her calls. Jamie had so many questions that she fervently wished they had a speaker phone, but she waited as patiently as possible for Ryan to finish. The last call was to Coach Placer, and when Ryan hung up she had a very happy grin on her face.

"I take it that Coach Placer was happy?" Jamie smiled.

"Yeah, he seemed pretty happy. I'm surprised you couldn't hear him yell," she admitted.

The usual Friday night traffic had slowed them to a crawl as they tried to get across the Bay Bridge, and Jamie stared at the skyline of the city for a few minutes, letting the fresh breeze waft over her skin. "What did Coach Greene say after you turned her down?"

"Oh, she had to put down the volleyball program. They did really poorly last year, and she claims that even with me they'll have a hard time making the NCAA's. She said that soccer was the current sports vogue, and that I still had a chance to make the national team if I played for her and all that kind of crap."

"Is that true?" Jamie asked, slightly incredulous.

"If I had come here originally and was only twenty-two now I think I could have had a chance. I played against some of the women on the U.S. team and I could hold my own against them. But it didn't turn out that way. I don't think there's any way they'd add a twenty-four-year-old to the team, so I think she's just trying to lure me back."

"I'm so glad you decided not to play for her. I don't think you would have been happy."

"I'm glad too," she admitted. "Oh, and Coach Johnston gave me a good tip. She said that since I had only used two years of eligibility, I could play next year."

"But you will have graduated."

"Doesn't matter. As long as you're enrolled in undergrad or graduate school you can play if you have eligibility left. So I could play field hockey next year if I get into grad school here. That would really be ideal. The schedule is less demanding and it'd let me play my best sport!"

"That sounds great, honey. But that reminds me, we've got to sit down and make some decisions about next year, and then start applying to grad schools."

"Since we've both taken the GRE and I've finished with the MCAT, we can send in our applications anytime. Do you want to do that next week?"

"Yeah. Doing all that, as well as two hours of sex a day, should fill our week!"

As they slogged through the heavy Friday night traffic, Ryan called Conor from the cell phone. "Hey," she said in their standard greeting.

"Hi, Ryan," he replied in a happy tone. "Are you guys coming home?"

She smiled at his use of the term. "Yeah, we're on the bridge. Traffic is crawling, so we won't be there for about forty-five minutes. Are you going to be home for dinner?"

"No, I've got a date. I need to leave home by six or so, and Da's at work, so no one will be here when you get home."

"Oh, okay," she said with just a touch of disappointment coloring her words. She had spent dozens of Friday nights alone, but she was looking forward to reconnecting with her family, though she had seen them just two days ago. "We're playing golf at eight tomorrow, okay?"

"Yeah. Where are we playing?"

"It's a surprise. But rest assured we'll be the poor relations," she said while she wriggled in her seat as Jamie tried to find enough flesh to pinch.

After she disconnected, she turned back to her partner and said, "Conor and Da are both out. Maybe we should just get off and have dinner downtown."

Jamie blanched noticeably and said, "It's Friday! I told Poppa we'd have dinner with him today!"

"Whoa," Ryan laughed, wiping her forehead with the back of her hand. "Good save, Jamers."

"Jamers?" The smaller woman blinked and tried to get a handle on this newest nickname. "Where did that come from?"

Ryan shrugged her broad shoulders and gave her partner a helpless grin. "I've got no idea. It just seemed like your name at that particular moment. Do you mind?"

"You can call me anything you want, sweetie, as long as it isn't 'late to bed'."

Ryan shot her partner a sincere smile and assured her, "That will never happen, buddy. Bedtime would lose its cachet if you didn't join me."

Fifteen minutes later they pulled up in front of the neat little church that Rev. Evans pastored. Following the flagstone walk up to the small house provided by the congregation, they waited just a moment for the distinguished-looking man to answer the door. He wrapped Jamie in a warm hug, squeezing her tightly, then gave a slightly more reserved hug to Ryan and welcomed them both in. They chatted for a few minutes, then decided to walk to a local restaurant since he had no car and theirs couldn't accommodate all three of them.

It was just six o'clock, and the summer sun was still prominent in the sky, assuring them of several more hours of light. As they walked along, enjoying the cool evening air that whipped around them, they talked about the Ride and their stay at Pebble Beach. Rev. Evans asked a few questions, but was mostly a very interested listener. Ryan reflected that his style seemed to be to allow his companions to talk, and then react thoughtfully to their issues. When they reached the restaurant, they were immediately seated at a small table near the front. After they had perused the menus and ordered, they sat back to enjoy a glass of wine. Jamie's face took on a thoughtful look as she asked, "Poppa, I've been thinking about telling my parents about Ryan. I know we've discussed the topic in general, but I thought you might have some specific things I should watch out for."

They hadn't discussed the issue much in the past week and Ryan still felt it was too soon for her partner to make this revelation, but she didn't think it was her place to discourage her if she was intent on doing so. Rev. Evans sat quietly for a moment before he said, "Mmm, that is a big one, Jamie. Do you think they have any suspicions?"

"Mother does, but I think Daddy will be stunned," she admitted. "Mother actually came to my house one day this spring and asked me if Ryan and I were lovers."

He tilted his head slightly and gave her an interested look, not directly asking what her reaction had been, but welcoming her to give it if she so chose. "I lied to her," she said softly, blushing with shame as she acknowledged her actions.

Rev. Evans nodded his head, giving his granddaughter a fond smile and patting her hand gently. "I'm sure that you felt that you needed to, Jamie. You don't lie easily."

She smiled back and agreed. "I don't want to get better at it either, Poppa. That's why I want to tell them as soon as possible."

"What do you plan on telling them?" he asked.

"I want to tell them that I've fallen in love," she said as she looked over at Ryan. The candlelight made her partner's skin glow bronze, and her eyes looked a very deep blue. "I want to tell them that I've met the woman that I'm going to spend the rest of my life with." She reached across the table to grasp her hand.

He smiled at the two young lovers and waited a moment to ask his next question. "Do you think of yourself as a lesbian, Jamie?"

She paused for a moment before she answered, taking a deep breath before she spoke. "I guess I'd have to say that I am, based on my behavior, but I don't think of myself that way. Does that make any sense?"

Both Ryan and Rev. Evans nodded simultaneously. Ryan spoke first: "That's not uncommon, honey. You might never feel like a lesbian. It's really not that big of a deal."

"I agree with Ryan, Jamie. But I asked the question because I think that it'll come up during your discussion with your parents. I just want you to give some thought to how to answer that question. I don't mean to frighten you, but if you tell them you're not sure you are a lesbian, it might give them hope that you'd go back to 'normal' if Ryan were to disappear."

"You don't mean that literally, do you?" Ryan gulped.

"No," he laughed, clapping her on the shoulder. "I don't think they'll resort to violence. But I want Jamie to be well prepared for this. I have seen this issue come up time and again for parents, so I assume it might happen here."

"What do you suggest, Poppa? Should I tell them that I am a lesbian even if I don't feel comfortable with that label yet?"

"I'm not urging you to lie, Jamie. I just want you to be prepared for the types of things that can come up. You should think about your answer and feel comfortable with whatever it is. Until you feel right about it, I would urge you to wait to tell them."

"But what if I never have a term I'm comfortable with?" Her eyes were round with surprise and he hastened to reassure her.

"I don't mean to say you have to have a term, honey. I'm just warning you that your parents will want you to have one. It's perfectly acceptable to tell them that how you refer to yourself is none of their business. All I'm trying to do is alert you that they will probably ask."

"Okay, that's good advice. What else should I expect?"

"I assume they'll be disappointed. Maybe not with you, but with the loss of some of their expectations for you. I know they expected your life to mirror theirs. That's hard for many parents to deal with."

"Yeah," she sighed. "I know it'll be hard for Mother to have me doing something that is socially undesirable."

"Don't assume that it won't bother your father too, Jamie. He definitely got a lot of pleasure out of having you and Jack together."

"You're right," she agreed, remembering how proud her father was to take the two of them to social functions at the firm. "Okay, what else?"

"I think the odds are good that they'll believe Ryan coerced you into this," he said softly, true regret coloring his words.

The color rose on her cheeks as she said, "That couldn't be further from the truth!"

"I know that, honey. And when they get to know Ryan, they'll know that too. But that will probably be their initial reaction."

"How do I make them see that's not true?" she asked. "Do I have to spell out how I pursued her?"

"No, I don't think you have to and I don't think you should. This is one area where you should maintain your privacy. It's no one else's business how you came to be lovers, and if you don't want to reveal that, you shouldn't. I think you should tell them that there was no coercion involved and leave it at that."

"What else?" she asked glumly, now regretting her inclination to tell them at all.

"I think they might assume that Ryan is after your money," he said softly.

"Oh please!" she said, her voice rising. "I have to beg her to let me buy her a pair of shorts! The only fights we've had have been because she can't stand to have me spend money on her!"

He laughed at this detail and Ryan blushed a bit. "I know it's not true, honey. But I am certain the thought will cross their minds. I suggest you remind your father that the Smiths thought the same thing about him when Catherine brought him home."

"I didn't know that," she said with a small laugh.

"It's a very common reaction from people who have great wealth. They assume that everyone wants a piece of it."

"Okay, other than seducing me for my money, what else will they think of Ryan?"

"They won't like that she's older than you are, or that she's been with other women before you. That will just reinforce their thoughts of her coercing you. But I think the biggest problem will be their difficulty in dealing with the loss of their dreams for you, Jamie. That's usually the biggest problem for secular, liberal parents."

"Yeah, I guess they can hardly throw the Bible at me," she agreed with a laugh.

"That would be a stretch," he said, sharing her smile.

"So, do you think I should tell them at all?"

He took a sip of his wine and gazed into space for a moment, carefully considering his reply. "I think you need to feel comfortable with why you want to tell them. Are you trying to come out at them or to them?"

"What do you mean?" She had never heard the issue framed that way, and it gave her pause.

"Some people tell their parents because they know it'll drive them crazy. They want to create some drama and hurt their parents with the news."

She shook her head violently. "I want to tell them because Ryan is such an important part of my life," she said sincerely. "This isn't a passing fling. I'm not just trying out lesbian sex because everyone else is doing it. Ryan means everything to me,

Poppa," she said as she squeezed her hand tightly. "If I don't tell them about her, they can't really know me. She's a part of me now," she said simply.

He smiled at her and patted her cheek with his hand. "That's a wonderful reason, Jamie, and if they have any sense at all, they'll thank God that you care for them enough to share your life with them."

She smiled up at her grandfather as she said, "It's nice to know that no matter what happens, you'll always be supportive of me."

"You can count on that, Jamie," he said with a broad smile.

Chapter Eight

As they raced up the hill, Ryan yelled ahead to Duffy, "Hey, no fair, you've got four legs. I should get a head start." As though he understood her entreaty, he crested the hill and waited patiently until his mistress caught up. "Thanks, pal," she said fondly as she bent over to ruffle his fur.

They had been trudging up and down the hills for nearly an hour. It was just past six now, and Ryan's stomach was growling fiercely. "We'd better head home, boy. With any luck, Conor's started breakfast."

To her severe disappointment, not only had Conor not started breakfast, he was nowhere to be found. *He'd better show up on time. I need to warm up a little bit before we play,* she groused. Her sour mood lightened appreciably when Jamie's sleepy head poked up from the lower stairwell.

"Hi, honey," she mumbled, scratching her head absently. "Did you have a good run?"

Ryan walked over to the stairs and greeted her lover with her second kiss of the day, this time to a sentient being. "Yeah, we did. My legs were really dead by the last few miles, though." She looked down at her uncooperative legs as if they would provide the reason for their reluctance to attack the hills with their normal gusto.

"I think it might be your workouts, honey," she opined, laughing to herself at Ryan's inability to acknowledge that she'd had a killer of a week.

Ryan gave her a little smirk, acknowledging that she had been putting a different kind of stress on her body. "Maybe I'm too old to do this."

"Yeah, right. You did three major workouts this week, baby, and two of them were on the same morning! That would knock most people out. I think you should be pleased that you're just a little slow today."

"I didn't say I was slow." Ryan shot her a nearly petulant look, a bit offended by the mere suggestion. "I said my legs felt dead. Just because they didn't feel right doesn't mean I demanded any less from them."

Jamie took her hand and tugged her into the kitchen, smiling to herself at her partner's stoic nature. She urged Ryan to sit at the counter while she poured her a large glass of juice. As she handed it to her, Jamie leaned over and kissed each of the cool, damp thighs. "I'm sorry she's so rough on you, guys. I'll try to make it up to you later with a nice massage."

"Don't spoil 'em," Ryan laughed, slapping at each muscled leg. "They'll start expecting it." She laughed at her own inability to go easy on herself, but she had a genuine worry that she might not be able to perform as well as she used to, and she felt that she needed to give voice to that fear. "I know you're teasing, but I have to be realistic, Jamie. I don't have the same body that I had in high school, and I think I'm going to have to learn to demand a little less from myself."

Once again wishing that she had known her partner years earlier, Jamie said, "That works for me." She walked over to Ryan and slid her arms around her wet body. "I have a lot of demands to make on this gorgeous body, and I'm not willing to accept a poor performance. I need you to get as much rest as possible to meet my high standards."

"You have really turned into a stern taskmistress, haven't you?" Ryan smiled up at her grinning face as she returned the hug.

"You have a coach to keep you motivated in your other sports. I'm just taking over in the bedroom."

"Now those are the outfits that *I* really like," Ryan said with a big smile.

Conor came barreling into the kitchen, stopping short when he saw the embrace they were locked in. "Jeez, do you two ever give it a rest?"

"And you were out doing what all night?" Ryan asked innocently.

"Aahh, good point," he admitted. "Who's making breakfast? I'm starved."

"Let's get ready and have breakfast at the club," Jamie suggested. "They have a really good buffet."

The siblings exchanged quick glances as they each took off for their respective showers, leaving Jamie standing in the middle of the living room. "I guess that was a yes?" she called out to the empty room.

At 7:50 Jamie tried to drag the siblings away from the breakfast buffet. "All you can eat isn't necessarily a challenge," she finally said in exasperation.

"Almost done." Ryan grinned up at her, cheeks still as full as a chipmunk's.

"Maybe we could just skip golf and stay here and eat," Conor suggested hopefully.

"Do they have doggie bags?" Brendan's eyes wandered up and down the lavish buffet, truly upset that he didn't have the opportunity to sample each dish.

"Let's go, you gluttons." Jamie's chiding tone didn't match the fond grin that covered her face, and the O'Flaherty siblings knew that she was merely teasing them. "I thought you wanted to warm up this time, Ryan."

"I'm plenty warm from jumping up every two minutes to get more of these little muffins," she admitted with a grin.

Conor was finally allowed his long-held wish to witness Jamie's swing. But after the match, he admitted he should have been happy to merely hear about it. "If we'd been playing for money, you would have cleaned me out!" he moaned as they sat in the Grill waiting for their lunch to be delivered.

Jamie just smiled and soaked up the praise. She was extremely pleased with the way she had played, and she felt confident about her plans to try out for the team. She reached over and patted his hand as she said, "I just had a good day, Conor. I'm sure you'll take me next time."

"I don't think so, Jamie. I'm going to have to get used to my sister beating me in almost every sport and my sister-in-law beating me in golf. It's a darn good thing I'm secure in my masculinity."

Brendan chuckled at that. "Does my kicking your butt threaten your masculinity?" His bright blue eyes were filled with mirth, and it made Jamie smile to see how the gentle teasing never seemed to bother any of the O'Flaherty children.

"Not a bit," Conor insisted. "You're my older brother—you should have some of the privileges of seniority."

As Jamie got up to go wash her hands, she leaned over and wrapped her arms around Conor from behind. She gave him a playful hug, rubbing her cheek against his twelve o'clock shadow. "You just ooze masculinity, Conor," she teased. Her hug had mussed his hair a bit, and she neatened it up, placing another kiss atop his head when she was satisfied. As she turned to walk away, she felt a hand upon her back. Spinning around, she stood face to face with her father. "Daddy!" she cried as she threw her arms around him.

"I had no idea you were playing today, honey," he said as he squeezed her back. "We've missed you, Jamie," he added softly.

"I've missed you too, Daddy," she said sincerely. "Can you sit with us?"

"I have a few minutes," he said as he moved around to meet the boys. "I'm Jim Evans," he said, shaking Conor's hand. All three of the O'Flahertys had risen when Jim appeared, and Ryan extended her hand also.

"These are my brothers, Conor and Brendan," she indicated as he shook each man's hand in turn.

"I think I would have guessed that if I'd had a moment, Ryan," he said with a grin. Looking between Ryan and Conor he asked the inevitable. "Are you twins?"

"No, sir. Conor is significantly older than I am." She gave her brother a playful pat on the back as he rolled his eyes dramatically.

"Ryan insults me, and Jamie humiliates me on the course. I'm beginning to get a complex."

Sitting down, Jim smiled at his daughter and asked, "I take it your game is doing well?"

"Yeah, it's coming along pretty well," she said modestly.

"Don't let her get away with being modest, Mr. Evans," Ryan began, but was quickly interrupted.

"You agreed to call me Jim, Ryan, remember?"

"Right. I'll do that, Jim." She returned his friendly smile and relaxed a bit, the tension starting to fade from her body.

Conor joined in, "I play pretty well, Jim, and Jamie thrashed me today. We played from the white tees and she out-drove me on every hole. I've never played with a woman who can hit it like she did today."

Jamie blushed furiously under the weight of this praise. "Since I've gotten stronger, I have a lot more power," she said frankly, but humbly.

"Well, I can't wait to play tomorrow," Jim said. "Nothing would make me happier than to have my little girl beat me at my own game."

"Unless you're ready for the Tour, you should be downright giddy by tomorrow afternoon," Conor warned.

Jim got up to leave when he saw his playing partners enter the room. He gave them a wave and held up a finger, indicating that he would be right with them. "Did everything go well down at the beach, girls?"

Both women nodded enthusiastically. "I had a marvelous time, Jim. I can't thank you enough for your hospitality."

"Did you give my cars a workout?"

"I sure did. I spaced them out over two days to prolong the pleasure," she admitted. "Conor came down to give me a ride home on Saturday, and he got to share a little of the enjoyment."

"Excellent! I love being able to share them with people who appreciate them."

"I've never met anyone who appreciates cars more than Ryan," Jamie said.

"But I taught her everything she knows about them," Conor said as he patted his sister's hand.

"You'll have to come down and hang out in my garage someday, Conor. I'm always looking for another aficionado."

"That would be a thrill," he said sincerely, his eyes dancing at the thought of being able to hang out with someone who could afford the toys he had always dreamed of.

"Well, I've got to get moving, but it was a pleasure to meet you both and to see you again, Ryan." He shook each sibling's hand, and gave Jamie a kiss on the cheek. "I'll see you tomorrow morning, cupcake. Is eleven o'clock okay?"

"Sure. I'll see you then, Daddy."

As he walked away in search of his playing partners, Conor stared after him with the lovesick look of an adolescent girl. "Gosh, he's dreamy," he said wistfully, just managing to duck the quick backhand his older brother sent his way.

"I hate to disappoint you, Conor," Jamie teased, "but if he was going to be a sugar daddy I think he'd choose a woman."

Keep your face neutral, Ryan. Don't you dare let on how much truth there is in that statement!

By three o'clock they had showered and were resting in their room. Ryan had on her board shorts and one of her undershirts, this one in white. Jamie was wearing a tiny little cotton batik dress in shades of tangerine and white that showed off her tanned, toned legs. They had taken a power nap as soon as they got home, so they were rested as well as clean. "What do you want to do for the rest of the day?" Jamie asked over the whine of the blow dryer as she finished her hair.

Ryan was lounging on the small chintz love seat that sat opposite her bed. She had both feet up on the cushion, with her arms wrapped around her shins, the pose vaguely reminiscent of Caitlin. "I don't know. I guess we should get to work on our graduate school applications. I have all the stuff here." Her tone conveyed her lack of excitement at the prospect, but Jamie knew that Ryan rarely let her feelings about a task be a factor in whether she tackled it or not.

"That doesn't sound like much fun. Is that really the best that you can come up with for a Saturday afternoon?" She went over to sit next to Ryan on the love seat and rested her hand on Ryan's knee.

"No, I can think of lots more. We could go get the baby and take her for a long walk—I'm sure she misses both of us. We could take Duffy to the park and throw his tennis ball for a while—he's got to have a lot of excess energy stored up. We could wash Da's truck—I usually do that if I'm free on a Saturday. We could take our bikes out of the shipping cartons. We co—" but she was cut off by a pair of lips plastered against hers.

"Can't you think of anything we could do inside?" The invitation was plain in Jamie's voice, as well as in the way that her hands began to slide slowly up and down Ryan's bare arms.

"We could start dinner," she said, being intentionally obtuse, just because she felt like playing.

"Think harder," Jamie purred as she pulled her head over for another deep kiss.

Ryan blinked as she sat up, and smacked her lips together to get her mouth working again. "We could do some laundry."

"Unh-uh," Jamie purred in her deepest voice. "Let's do something down here."

"I haven't dusted down here in weeks." Ryan's innocent look encouraged Jamie to continue the game—now determined to wipe that look off her partner's face.

"Nope. Doesn't appeal to me," she whispered, her breath tickling Ryan's neck as she leaned over and sucked on a tender little earlobe.

Ryan drew in a sharp breath, and she felt her nipples tighten, but she kept her focus. "I have the fall schedule on my desk. We could make sure our course work fits together well."

"Not even warm," Jamie breathed as she started at her exposed collarbones and licked a wet path up to her chin.

The trail beneath Jamie's foraging tongue not being the only place that was getting wet, Ryan gulped audibly, but she managed to squeak out, "Clean the bathroom?"

Jamie pushed Ryan's feet to the ground as she slid onto her lap, straddling her. She was not wearing a stitch under her dress, and Ryan gasped as she felt silky, damp curls slide over her thigh. Jamie grasped her head with both hands and held it steady as she devoured her mouth with deep, probing kisses, not lightening the intensity until Ryan began to whimper under the assault. Jamie pulled away with an audible "smack" as she broke the suction between their mouths. "I want to do something where we get hot, and wet, and messy," she whispered seductively, her warm tones causing chills to run up and down Ryan's spine.

"We could give Duffy a bath," she replied weakly, her voice quavering from the strain of her arousal.

"No dogs. Just you and me," Jamie murmured as she bent to lick her way across Ryan's collarbones and down her shoulders, stopping to suck in a bit of skin as she blazed her trail.

"Hot and wet and messy, huh?" she rasped out. "I'm stumped." Ryan was nearly ready to hurl her lover to the bed and ravish her, but she enjoyed being seduced in such a playful way. She was doing her best to hold on as long as possible, but she knew it wouldn't be too much longer.

Jamie gave her a final kiss and slid off her lap. She sat down on her side of the love seat and raised her legs, imitating Ryan's earlier position. "Do I have to spell it out for you?"

"'Fraid so," she said regretfully, as she grabbed her shorts to pull them away from her throbbing vulva, her fingers lingering just a moment longer than was absolutely necessary. "I don't have a clue."

Jamie gave her a sultry look as she slowly spread her legs apart. Ryan practically spasmed from the completely erotic vision of her lover in that tiny little dress with her legs splayed apart lewdly. Jamie's gaze commanded Ryan's attention and she watched, transfixed, as her normally more conventional partner slid one hand between her legs to hold herself open, while the other slowly trailed up and down her deep pink folds. Her half-closed eyes stayed locked on her lover's but she was obviously having trouble maintaining the gaze. "Does this give you any ideas?" Her voice was rough and deep with need, and it took every ounce of Ryan's self-control to slowly shake her head, finding it devastatingly erotic to watch Jamie excite herself this way.

"No ideas at all?" she whispered, her eyelids fluttering closed as she sucked in a ragged breath. Her index finger was drawing teasing patterns all over her shiny pink skin, and Ryan leaned over a little to be able to watch more closely, fascinated by the way her partner was touching herself. Her long, dark hair brushed against Jamie's thighs and green eyes shot open at the contact. Seeing Ryan's fascinated stare brought a smile to her lips and she asked again, "Still not coming up with anything, baby?"

Ryan cleared her throat and murmured, "I must be hungry again, 'cause all of a sudden my mouth is watering."

"You go get something to eat," Jamie gasped, as her index finger was joined by two more of the lucky digits, and her pace picked up noticeably. "I'll be right here when you get back." Her hips tilted just a bit, and she bit her lip and let out a ragged gasp as her finger slipped lower and played lightly at her opening.

All resolve left Ryan's body and she jumped to her feet and yanked her shirt off, then unlaced her shorts in a blur and kicked them off roughly. As she sat back down next to Jamie she started to place her hand next to her lover's to join in the exploration. But Jamie pushed her away, gasping out, "I've got it, honey. You can go wash the dog."

Ryan sat up in surprise at this development, but she was more than willing to alter the rules of their little game at any time. She immediately snatched the bait. "Let me touch you," she begged. "I promise you'll like it."

"I'm sure I would," she got out with some difficulty. "But ... unh, I'm doing fine," she said as her fingers began to stroke a little more quickly.

"C'mon, baby," Ryan whispered in her ear, stealing a quick taste of the sweet earlobe. "Let me ... you know you love my touch."

"Sure I do," she gasped, "but I'm almost there ..."

"C'mon, Jamie," she said as her arms slid around her waist and nuzzled her neck. "Let me touch you. Give it up for me, baby."

"*Unh!*" she huffed as her hips began to thrust firmly against her blurring hand. Ryan dove for the floor and grabbed her legs, pulling them toward herself until the pulsating flesh was pressed against her mouth. She dipped her head and began to firmly lick and suck on the now throbbing clit. Within moments she felt the second climax build in her lover's body. She held her tight and kept up the pressure until she exploded again, much more vocally this time. But Ryan was still not satisfied. She waited until the spasms had stilled, and then she bent to taste her again. She started off much more slowly, gently laving every sensitive inch of flesh. Jamie urged her on enthusiastically, grasping her head and grinding it against herself as her hips jerked and thrust. Ryan focused her attentions on the center of her pleasure, loving the little nub with her determined tongue. After she sucked her entire clitoris into her mouth Jamie's body became rigid for mere seconds. Her voice started low in her chest and increased in volume and pitch as she screamed, "Oh baby, oh baby! Yes! Yes! *Yes! Oh, God!*"

Her body shook and quivered as she continued to move her hips against Ryan's face. The crinkly hairs tickled the larger woman's nose, but she doggedly fought the urge to sneeze. She held completely still and let Jamie control the pressure, smiling inwardly as her lover continued the gentle movement, just barely rubbing herself against Ryan's happy mouth.

After a long while, she relaxed completely, and Ryan tried to imagine how they must look. Jamie was slumped down so completely that her hips were no longer on the seat. Her legs were hanging over Ryan's shoulders and her dress was pooled up under her breasts. Ryan was completely naked, kneeling on the floor with her face still trapped between Jamie's thighs. She was almost certain that her lover was spent, but just for good measure she ran her tongue up her swollen inner lips. The soft tongue was nearing the locus of Jamie's pleasure when firm hands grabbed Ryan's hair and held her head in a vise grip. "Don't even think about it," came the stern command. Ryan chuckled and delicately dried her mouth on Jamie's wide-open thighs.

She got to her feet with a groan, her muscles complaining about the uncomfortable position she had forced them to maintain. As she rose, she grasped Jamie's limp hands and pulled her to her unsteady feet. A small moan of protest escaped from her lips, but she went along quietly when Ryan stooped to pick her up. Ryan carried her precious bundle to the bed, settling her softly onto the worn quilt that covered the surface. Holding Jamie upright with one hand, she efficiently tugged her dress over her head before she allowed her to collapse limply. Ryan smiled fondly at her partner, not surprised that she was nearly sound asleep already. She snuggled up next to her and pulled her close to her body, holding her in her arms until she sank into a deep sleep.

A half hour later, Jamie blinked her eyes open to find Ryan's smiling face looking down at her. "Hi," she said, a yawn escaping her mouth along with the greeting. "Whatcha thinking?"

"I was thinking about how incredibly happy I am," she said with a gentle smile, trailing her index finger across Jamie's features, following each dip and curve.

"How happy are you?" Jamie asked, letting out a little grunt as she turned over and rested her chin on her palms.

"I'm happier than I think I've ever been," Ryan said honestly, lying down flat on the bed and gazing at the ceiling contemplatively. "I was lying here with you in my arms, all cuddled up tight. There was a gentle, warm breeze blowing over us and the sun was making pretty little patterns on your skin. I'd just made love with you, and I could smell your delightful scent every time the breeze blew by my face. A feeling of complete and utter contentment came over me. It was kind of a God moment," she said softly, smiling down at her lover. "Do you know what I mean?"

Jamie gave her a warm smile and said simply, "Yes, I think I do." She turned toward Ryan and placed several delicate kisses on her lips. "I've had moments where I feel … like I'm experiencing some kind of peak sensation. Like a form of … perfection."

Ryan nodded slightly, pleased that her partner understood what she was speaking of. "It was a perfectly peaceful moment, Jamie. I felt completely loved … completely happy. There wasn't one thing that I could add to make the experience more perfect. It felt like I imagine God intended us to experience love."

Jamie was too touched to speak, so she rolled over onto her back and lifted her arm, urging Ryan to rest her head against her chest. She slid her fingers into the long, black hair and massaged Ryan's head for a few moments, humming softly as she did so. "I have those moments too," she whispered after a long while, finally trusting her voice. "I've never thought about them as God moments, but that describes them perfectly. It's a wonderful gift you've given me, Ryan … letting me see God in you."

Ryan graced her with a beatific smile, tucking her head back down after their eyes had shared the moment. Jamie continued to stroke her head, the tune coming back to her as she once again hummed softly into her lover's ear. It didn't take long for the soothing head rub and the gentle song to lull Ryan to sleep, her left hand rising unbidden to gently cover Jamie's breast.

Ryan didn't sleep long, but she still needed to complete her entire stretching routine, to the delight of Jamie's appreciative gaze. She was almost finished when her frisky lover pushed her onto her back and fixed her with a devilish gleam in her eyes. "Now where were we?" she asked as she started to attack her lover's lips.

Ryan returned her kisses and softly grasped Jamie's hands when they started to stray. "I'm gonna need a little longer to reload," Ryan said with a slight blush coloring her cheeks.

"But ... I didn't ..."

"I did," she admitted with a guilty little smirk as she shrugged her shoulders. "I couldn't help myself."

"Oh, you poor baby," she said as she rubbed her hand down Ryan's arm. "I fell asleep on you when you were all turned on. I'm so sorry, honey."

"I didn't mind," she said happily. "It's been weeks since I flew solo. It was kinda nice."

Jamie tweaked her nose and gave her a mock scowl. "Are you implying that you can live without my talented hands?"

"Nope. I need your hands like I need air. But touching myself reminded me of when I was young and used to race home from school to do it."

"This was when?" Jamie asked, an impish grin covering her face. "Kindergarten?"

Ryan rolled her eyes at her partner's exaggeration. "No, wise guy," she laughed. "I'd say sixth grade."

Jamie laughed at that little fact. "I'm quite sure I didn't know that I even had a clitoris in sixth grade. You've got me beat by at least three years."

Ryan gave her a satisfied smirk and declared, "I'm an overachiever."

"Of that I'm certain," Jamie agreed, getting a good tickle in on her partner's ribs. "Why do you think touching yourself made you think of that?"

"I used to daydream about having someone I loved in bed with me. Today I had just what I'd dreamed of."

"Tell me about your dreams," Jamie begged, fascinated by this revelation.

Ryan stared at the ceiling for a moment, trying to summon her inner twelve-year-old. "I didn't have real specific dreams," she recalled. "I just dreamed about being held and kissed. I wasn't really sure what people did in bed, but I knew there had to be a lot of touching involved, and I was all in favor of that."

They both laughed at this scenario, silently acknowledging that Ryan's tastes hadn't strayed far from that fantasy. "Were your fantasies always like that?" Jamie was absently playing with the soft skin on Ryan's forearm, tracing the faint blue veins that barely showed under the skin.

"Hardly." Ryan laughed, assuming that her partner was joking. When she saw that she wasn't, she explained. "My fantasies changed as I grew up, honey. I'd have to say that I generally fantasize about something I'd like to do, but haven't been able to accomplish."

"Like?" The look on Jamie's face was one of pure fascination, and Ryan smiled at the interest her lover was showing in the smallest details of her life.

"Like ..." Ryan drawled, "I'd think about touching a woman's breasts when I was in high school. I didn't make the connection that I was gay—they just seemed very erotic to me."

"Me too," Jamie happily agreed.

Ryan smiled at her, acknowledging the truth of that statement. "My fantasies just kinda kept pace with what I did. The last few years I'd usually fantasize about having unprotected sex. God, I missed that!" She barked out a laugh that slowly turned to a confused look, then into shock. "Shit!" she cried, sitting up completely, her eyes wide with alarm.

"Honey, what's wrong?" Jamie sat up also and placed her hand on Ryan's arm, trying to figure out what had her partner so spooked.

"Shit!" Ryan cried again, hopping out of bed to pace in a tight circle. "I can't believe I did that!"

"Ryan ... *Ryan!*" That got her attention, and the agitated woman stopped and stared at her partner with a resigned look of self-contempt.

"I lied to you, Jamie. I told you I hadn't had unprotected sex in years—I lied to you."

She looked so bereft that Jamie went to her and wrapped her in a hug. "Tell me, baby. Tell me what happened."

Ryan was obviously very angry with herself, and she shrugged out of Jamie's embrace and nearly flung herself onto the loveseat. "You know about the incident," she muttered. "It was that woman in the vintage clothing store on Telegraph. Remember?"

Jamie nodded, clearly recalling Ryan's description of the extremely casual sexual encounter with the shop owner. "Go on," she urged.

"I had unprotected sex with her," Ryan muttered, providing no useful information at all.

"I understand that," Jamie said, sitting down on the bed to give her partner some space. "I just don't understand why you're so upset about it."

Ryan looked at her like she was daft. "Because I lied to you!"

"Ryan," Jamie soothed. "Did you intentionally lie to me?"

"Of course not," she muttered, acknowledging that she would never do such a thing about an important issue. "It ... I ... I'm just mad at myself for doing something stupid like that. I just wasn't in my right mind at the time."

Now Jamie was puzzled. She distinctly remembered that Ryan had told her this encounter took place in the store, right before school started last year. She also remembered that the woman didn't touch Ryan sexually, so she couldn't understand the comment about not being in her right mind. "Were you drunk?"

"Drunk?" Once again, Ryan gave her a puzzled stare. "It was the middle of the afternoon, Jamie, and I haven't been drunk in years."

"Were you doing drugs?" They had never discussed drug use, but Jamie was nearly certain that Ryan wouldn't abuse her body or her mind with untested substances.

Now Ryan's puzzlement grew. "Drugs? I've never done drugs in my life!"

"For God's sake, Ryan, then will you tell me what in the hell you're talking about? I'm out of guesses!"

Ryan rubbed at her face with her hands, realizing that she was being unresponsive, but not really wanting to talk about this issue right now. "I'm sorry, honey," she said softly, as she patted the seat next to her. "Come sit by me and I'll explain."

Jamie did as she was asked, placing her hand on the top of Ryan's spine when the taller woman leaned over to brace her forearms atop her knees. "It was right before school started," she said softly, providing facts that Jamie already knew. "I hadn't … been with anybody since the … accident."

Jamie nearly asked what accident Ryan was referring to, but she quickly realized she was talking about being gay-bashed. Remembering that the attack occurred just after the AIDS Ride, Jamie murmured, "That was a long time, baby."

"I know," Ryan conceded. "It happened around the third week of June, and I didn't feel like having anyone touch me for at least six weeks. I couldn't work, of course, and I kinda lost my normal support network since I didn't see my friends at work or at the clubs. It's hard to explain, Jamie, but I didn't feel like myself for a very long time. It wasn't just the pain or the discomfort—I felt like those guys took something very important from me."

Thinking of what an attack like that would do to her, Jamie posited, "Did they take your sense of safety and security?"

Ryan shook her head. "No, they took my confidence. I didn't feel confident about myself, or my abilities. I started to doubt that I'd ever feel sexual again." She closed her eyes and shook her head harder, her long dark hair cascading down her shoulders as she did so. "I had absolutely no interest in seeing any of my buddies, and meeting someone new was actually terrifying for me. I just spent a lot of time reading and sitting at the park—I had totally turned inward."

"What snapped you out of it?" Jamie asked, recalling the supremely confident woman she'd met in late August.

Ryan laughed ruefully, as she admitted, "Being with that woman in the shop, to be honest. I didn't have time to think, or worry, or be afraid that she'd want to talk about it."

It became clear to Jamie why her partner didn't take solace with any of her regular "buddies." They were obviously worried about her, and would have naturally wanted to see how she was doing—something that Ryan apparently hadn't been able to handle. "Then you should be glad that you had that encounter with her," Jamie soothed, running her hand up and down Ryan's back.

"I guess I am," she admitted. "I'm just mad at myself for having unsafe sex. I didn't even stop to think about it, to tell you the truth. I'd spent years counseling kids to avoid the situations where they feel out of control, and the first time I'm in the same situation, I give in immediately."

"Honey, don't be so hard on yourself," Jamie soothed. "Do you remember what you were thinking?"

Ryan nodded. "I needed the intimacy," she said softly. "I needed to touch someone in the most intimate way I could. I needed to taste another living being to remind myself that I was alive. I didn't just want to give her a sexual release, I needed to fill myself up with her taste—even though I didn't know her. The mere fact that she was alive made me feel more alive." She flopped back against the cushion and gazed at Jamie with a pathetically fragile look on her face. "Does that make any sense?"

"Perfect," Jamie whispered, pulling Ryan against her chest and running her fingers through her hair again, inadvertently feeling the small knot of scar tissue that would always mark her head. "Please don't be angry with yourself, Ryan. You did the best you could at the time."

"But I put myself, and you, at risk, honey," she started to protest, but Jamie silenced her by placing two fingers upon her lips.

"You didn't put me at risk, Ryan. You had yourself thoroughly checked out before we made love. And while I understand that it's risky to have oral sex without a barrier, you weren't harmed, so give up the guilt, baby."

Ryan nodded, much relieved that Jamie didn't think less of her for being so cavalier with her health. "Thanks for understanding, Jamie. I just want you to know that being with that woman like that was really rare for me. I might not have known some of the women I was with very well, but they were usually friends of friends or people that I knew at least a little. I had very little anonymous sex."

"It doesn't matter, Ryan," Jamie assured her. "The past is past and you can't change it now. All that matters is that we're together now ... and that we will be for the rest of our lives."

Ryan offered a small smile, once again feeling her equilibrium return. "That's an undeniable truth," she whispered, placing a tender kiss upon her partner's lips.

"Are you sure that you want to do this?" Ryan cast yet another puzzled glance at her partner, searching her eyes for any sign of hesitancy.

"Why is it so surprising that I'd want to go to church with you and help watch Caitlin?" Jamie asked, finally tiring of Ryan's persistent questioning.

The taller woman gave one of her adorably incongruous adolescent shrugs and looked slightly embarrassed at being caught in an insecure moment. "I guess I assume that you'd want to go to your grandfather's church, honey. You've been going there your whole life, and I know you really enjoy it."

Jamie approached her partner and fluffed her dark bangs, smiling at their current propensity to land in her blue eyes. "You've been going to St. Philip's since you were born, Ryan. Switching to my church would be a big change for you, too, so don't act like you wouldn't have to sacrifice to go with me."

"But it's your grandfather's parish," Ryan whined, unwilling to let go of her concern.

"I know that, love," Jamie agreed. "But your whole extended family goes to St. Philip's, and I think that's really nice. I love my grandfather dearly, but I'm not really a part of the parish—I've been going alone since I could drive, and I've always missed the sense of family that makes communal worship so appealing. Besides," she insisted, wrapping Ryan in a hug, "your aunt really wants Caitlin to start attending church, and since Tommy and Annie won't go, I'd like to help her out."

"Have I ever told you that you're too generous for your own good?" Ryan murmured, holding Jamie close and taking in her calming scent.

"I don't believe you have," she replied, nuzzling her head into Ryan's neck. "Why don't you prepare a list of all of my wonderful attributes, and you can recite them to me when I get back from playing golf." She lifted her head to reveal her impish grin, and Ryan planted soft kisses on every inch that was revealed as Jamie turned her head from side to side to insure full coverage. "We'd better scoot, babe. Your Aunt Maeve doesn't seem like the kind of woman who would appreciate our being late."

"Not when she's got the Hibernians waiting on her," Ryan agreed, referring to the Catholic social club for women of Irish descent. Maeve was the current chairwoman of one of the committees, and her group was sponsoring the bake sale after Mass, leaving Caitlin without a minder until Jamie and Ryan stepped up to offer to watch her.

After a joint shower—which, remarkably, didn't devolve into sex—and a quick breakfast, they stood in front of the closet and tried to decide what to wear. Brendan had dropped in during breakfast and decided to accompany the pair, and he agreed to go fetch the baby from Maeve while they got dressed. Jamie decided to wear a moderately casual yellow linen dress, but Ryan was in a quandary. Brendan had on a long-sleeved light blue oxford cloth shirt and a pair of chinos, and she didn't want to look underdressed in comparison with her companions, but she refused to wear a skirt. She finally decided to wear a pair of slim-fitting slacks in a white cotton duck, with a sleeveless v-neck cardigan in a black cotton knit to top the slacks. Stylish black loafers finished off the surprisingly casual outfit.

Jamie watched her get dressed, eyeing her appreciatively. She thought her partner's attire was far too casual for church, but she was not going to say a word. Ryan looked absolutely luscious, and if she was comfortable in her outfit, it was perfectly all right with Jamie. She went over to a small jewelry box that she had brought from Berkeley and pulled out a string of pearls and placed them around Ryan's neck. As she hooked the clasp, she stood on her tiptoes and placed a kiss on her neck. "Perfect," she said appreciatively as she turned her partner around and looked her up and down. She would have chosen gold accessories for this outfit, but Ryan still wore the sapphire diamonds, and the pearls seemed to work better with the platinum setting. *That's a good idea for her birthday,* Jamie thought. *A platinum necklace in the same design as the settings for the earrings.*

"I truly love the way you look in that dress," Ryan said as she held her lover at arm's length to study her. "The color brings out all of the different highlights in your hair. I don't know how I'm going to be able to think of anything but you today."

"You think you have problems? I get to think of just how little there is between me and your breasts all day. And I didn't get to munch on them yesterday, you little devil."

"Hey! I didn't force you to fall asleep on me ..." Ryan began, but stopped at Jamie's expression of challenge, and smiled when she realized that she had indeed forced her partner into a near-stupor. "Well, okay, maybe I did. I have definitely gotta plan better," she muttered, putting on a mock glower.

They had to borrow Conor's truck in order to take Caitlin and her car seat with them, and the whole endeavor took much longer than either woman would have guessed. Even though they spent a lot of time with Caitlin, they didn't often take her to a place where she would have to keep relatively quiet. This constraint forced them to tote books, toys, stuffed animals, and a baggie full of Cheerios along with the usual diapers, change of clothes, and bottles of breast milk and water.

Caitlin looked quite adorable today, as was her norm. She was wearing a bright yellow dress with an embroidered duck stitched on a little white pique inset on the front that matched the little ducks marching around the cuffs of her white socks. She also had a white pique hat, but Ryan knew it would never rest on her head, given that it was currently being shaken violently by her little pink hand. Tiny black slippers covered her feet, and Ryan also assumed these wouldn't remain in place for long. She recalled how Conor had described her antics as a child in church and thought wryly, *It's payback time*.

The O'Flahertys had been members of St. Philip Parish since Brendan was born. Martin and Fionnuala had actually met at old St. Patrick's near downtown, but when they bought their little house in Noe Valley, they quickly became visible members of the community. All four children had attended the grammar school, and each one had been a standout in some pursuit. They had all participated in the various athletic teams that the school sponsored, and Rory had been a member of the band. Fionnuala had been very involved in the parish, and Martin had kept up his involvement as much as possible after her death. He and Brendan still attended Mass every Sunday, but Conor and Rory had become Christmas and Easter Catholics. Ryan was somewhere in the middle; she had been quite devout as a child, and had been a member of the children's choir and an acolyte until she was in high school. But after she came out as a lesbian and began to study the church's position on homosexuality and the ordination of women, she didn't like what she found. Her cousin Michael's illness had also been an influence in her disenchantment, as she considered it unconscionable to prohibit the use of condoms, even by married couples. Still, even though she was feeling quite alienated, she had been sincere in her wish to spend more time in communal worship, and she was grateful that Jamie was so willing to try to acclimate to the Catholic Mass.

The nine-thirty Mass was designed with families in mind. A large number of children were present for the service and no one seemed to mind all of the screaming babies. Ryan had not been in the church since Christmas, and she had probably not been to the family Mass since she sang in the choir. She was pleased to see that they had made some rather significant changes since she was last there. The piano began to play the opening hymn, and she was delighted to see that the lectors were relatively young children. They were probably in seventh or eighth grade, and they looked adorable processing into the church in front of the priest, with the first young woman holding the Bible over her head for all to see.

A nice breeze was coming in through the door they had been careful to sit by, and everything went well until Mass began. But as soon as people settled in their seats, Caitlin tired of the inactivity. They had only been sitting for fifteen minutes, but she was ready to go, and Brendan's gentle coaxing did nothing to ameliorate her unhappiness. When he was out of ideas, Brendan made eye contact with his sister and gladly passed his little charge off to her.

Ryan held her up high on her chest so she could see over the standing congregation. She knew the opening hymn by heart, and Caitlin was entertained so long as the song went on. She watched Ryan sing with an enthralled look on her sweet face, and when her cousin would pause between verses, Caitlin patted her cheek, possibly trying to get the sound to come back out. But when the song was finished, she had no use for sitting in a pew listening to people read aloud. When it became clear that she was not going to quiet down, Ryan slipped out the exit and took her for a walk around the outside of the church. This went quite well, and she was most entertained during this little interlude. They kept passing back and forth in front of the open doors so that Ryan could have a small semblance of the church experience; she managed to catch about twenty-five percent of the sermon. As the collection plate was passed down the aisles she decided to try sitting again, and they made their way back inside.

When they entered the pew, Jamie lifted the wiggling baby from Ryan's arms and took over for a while. The change of control kept her occupied for a few minutes, but she quickly grew restless again. Jamie was about to take her out again, but when the priest began to recite the Eucharistic Prayer, he invited all of the children to come up into the sanctuary to be a part of the ceremony. Jamie looked at Ryan with a raised eyebrow and Ryan shrugged her shoulders in agreement, hoping that she wouldn't regret her decision. They both stood and joined about fifty others as they gathered around the altar. Many adults had small children in their arms, some much smaller than Caitlin, and a good number of the grade-school-aged children came up alone. The prayer lasted about twelve minutes and the baby was passed back and forth at least once per minute throughout the entire prayer. Wherever she was, she wanted the other. As soon as Ryan had her, she would lean toward Jamie with a pathetic look on her face and hold her little arms out until she became irresistible. Jamie would reach out and take her, but within thirty seconds she would go through the same dramatic act with Ryan as the intended audience. They took her behavior with good humor, realizing that she was just acting her age, and both being thankful that she wasn't wailing.

At the end of the prayer, everyone who could spare one joined hands to sing the Lord's Prayer. Caitlin liked this quite a bit, since she got to watch Ryan sing again. She sat in her arms, facing her, with her little face mere inches from Ryan's. She would occasionally pat her hand over Ryan's mouth, trying to find out how much control she had over the sound. Jamie found the scene truly precious as she watched Caitlin giggle and play with her big cousin.

At the end of the song the priest offered them all the sign of peace and asked them to offer it to the others in the community. The tradition was to either shake hands or hug or kiss your fellow parishioners. Obviously, most people chose to shake hands, but most couples and their children kissed one another. Ryan slid an arm around her partner and gave her a chaste, but heartfelt kiss. She dipped Caitlin down so that she could kiss Jamie, which she did with much more enthusiasm than her older cousin had shown. Caitlin's new trick was to place her chubby little hands on their cheeks and pull them in for a big, wet one. Jamie grasped her and turned her around so Ryan could receive the same bath. They both chuckled as they wiped their faces and shook the hands of the people around them. When they returned to their seats they all kissed Brendan, with varying degrees of moisture attached, then turned to greet the people sitting around them. Thankfully, Jamie was holding the baby when Ryan turned to her left and extended her hand to the woman behind her, for she would have surely dropped the child, such was her shock as she came face to face with Mary Elizabeth Andrews, Sara's mother.

Ryan had not seen her first love's mother since the day Mrs. Andrews had gently told Ryan that Sara no longer wanted to see her. Their final meeting flashed into her mind, and she recalled with startling clarity just how empathetic the older woman had been. Ryan had been a fixture at their house since she was in second grade, and it had been obvious that telling the bereft young woman that she was no longer welcome there was hard for Mrs. Andrews. But Ryan subsequently acknowledged that the woman's first duty was to her daughter, and if Sara demanded that Ryan be turned away, that was obviously what she had to do.

The look of startled surprise on Mrs. Andrews's face slowly changed into a gentle smile, and she pulled Ryan into a hug, whispering, "It's good to see you, Ryan."

"You too, Mrs. Andrews," Ryan said softly as she pulled away. Brendan turned and saw the interchange, and to Ryan's annoyance he turned back toward the altar, refusing to extend his hand to the woman. Ryan gave her an embarrassed shrug and turned around when the priest resumed the service.

Luckily, the rest of the Mass passed quickly and without incident. Caitlin was greatly entertained during Communion, since everyone had to pass by her. Ryan pointed out all of the other babies, and she eyed all of them critically with her little green eyes. Jamie carried her up to Communion, and Caitlin liked it when the priest touched her head and offered her a blessing. For the next few minutes, she somberly placed her hand on Jamie's head just like the priest had done to her.

There were only about ten minutes to go, and Ryan was feeling pretty good. Jamie handed Caitlin off again, and she seemed quite calm. She began to settle in as though she wanted a short nap, but just before she dozed off she tried to pull Ryan's sweater away from her breast. Ryan sat up in shock as she realized how easy it was to push her v-neck sweater down. She tried to remove Caitlin's determined little hands, but without success. Jamie was practically in stitches from trying not to laugh, and Brendan seemed to be having a tough time controlling himself as well. Ryan frantically dug through her bag and found a bottle, but Caitlin would have none of it. Jamie finally took pity and rescued her partner by taking the baby and the bottle and firmly introducing it into her mouth until she quieted down.

Ryan sat back and relaxed as she watched her lover calm the baby so effortlessly. *She just has an instinct for mothering. I don't know where she got it, but it's definitely there.* Her thoughts drifted to Mrs. Andrews, and she wondered if she would linger to speak with them after Mass. *I think she caught the cold shoulder that Brendan so obviously gave her*, Ryan thought with a little annoyance. She loved that her brother cared for her, but she really didn't need for him to fight this battle for her, and she wished he'd just let bygones be bygones. Caitlin was nestled down in Jamie's arms, holding the bottle in her own small hands as she sucked lustily. Her eyes were half-closed, in that twilight state that nursing babies entered, and Jamie looked very serene as she gently rocked her. She looked up and caught Ryan's adoring gaze, and she reached over and grasped her hand, silently sharing the moment.

As the closing song finished, they all breathed a sigh of relief as the congregation began to file out. Caitlin was only half-finished with her bottle, so Brendan offered to go get the truck ready and bring it up alongside the side door when the crowd had thinned. Ryan sat peacefully, watching her partner with a look of pure love on her face. Jamie looked up at her as they once again locked gazes, the emotion that passed between them nearly palpable. She reached out and tenderly touched Ryan's cheek, patting it softly as her thumb brushed across the smooth surface. She looked back down to adjust the bottle and heard a soft voice over her shoulder say, "Hello, Ryan." Mrs. Andrews pointed at the baby and asked, "Is this your niece?"

"No, no it's not," Ryan said, obviously having trouble getting her bearings.

"Oh, I just assumed that this was your brother's wife and child," she said pleasantly.

For some reason that comment knocked Ryan right back into her normal self. "No, Mrs. Andrews," she said as her color came back and her normal self-confidence returned. "I'd like to introduce you to my partner. This is Jamie Evans. Jamie, this is Mrs. Andrews, Sara's mother," she said pointedly.

There was a long moment when Ryan feared that Jamie would repeat her brother's rudeness, but her normal grace returned and she pasted a forced smile onto her face and said, "I'm pleased to meet you."

Now it was Mrs. Andrews's turn to look uncomfortable. "Is this your child, Jamie?" she asked tentatively.

"No," she laughed. "Ryan and I aren't quite ready to start our family yet. This is Ryan's cousin, Caitlin," she said proudly.

"Oh ... I ... see," she said as she fumbled for words. "Do you live in the city, Ryan? I haven't seen you in the neighborhood or at church in so many years I thought ..."

"I lived at home until just a week ago," Ryan said. "We must just not patronize the same stores." She remembered that the Andrewses had always been a step or two higher on the economic ladder than most of the parishioners of St. Philip's, and she reasoned that they might not shop at the same discount stores that the O'Flahertys frequented. "Jamie and I live in Berkeley and spend our weekends here with my family."

"Really?" she asked. "Are you in graduate school there?"

"No," she replied with an easy grin. "It's taken me a bit longer than I had planned to graduate from college. I went to USF for my first two years, then I transferred to Berkeley last year."

"Oh … I thought you were going to Berkeley originally," she said with an unreadable expression on her face.

"I had planned on it, but I wasn't able to keep my grades up in my senior year. I was forced off the athletic teams by the other students once they learned I was gay, so my scholarship offers were rescinded," she said with an even tone, neither her voice nor her eyes revealing the depths of the pain this wrong had caused her.

Mrs. Andrews's face dropped and actually became a little flushed as Ryan recounted her story. "Oh, Ryan," she said as she shook her head, "I'm so sorry that had to happen. You didn't deserve that type of treatment."

A small smile lit up Ryan's face as she said, "I'll concede that it was the most difficult thing I've ever had to go through, except for my mother's death, of course. But if I had to do it over again, I wouldn't change a thing. If I hadn't been so delayed in finishing school, I never would have met Jamie." She turned and looked her directly in the eye, holding her gaze. "She is, by far, the best thing that has ever happened to me. So anything I had to endure to win her heart was well worth it."

Jamie beamed up at her and took her hand as she squeezed it tenderly. "So, what's Sara up to?" Ryan asked as the bottle fell from Caitlin's limp grasp.

"Oh," Mrs. Andrews said, somewhat surprised, "I assumed that you knew she had gone to law school. Her father and I attended her graduation from Stanford just last weekend," she said proudly.

"Small world, isn't it?" Ryan said with a grin to Jamie.

"Pardon?" asked Mrs. Andrews.

"I had no idea that Sara was in law school, much less that she was graduating. I haven't kept up with anyone from high school," she said with another neutral smile.

"Things are going just beautifully for her," she said with more than a hint of pride. "She's accepted an offer from a very prestigious firm, and it looks like she might be getting engaged soon."

"Really?" Ryan asked, a little surprised by this development.

"Yes. Regrettably, she's living with her boyfriend, and her father and I are not very happy about it. But Sara isn't one to be dissuaded once she makes up her mind about something." She laughed gently and smiled at Ryan, patting her hand as she added, "I don't have to tell you what Sara's like, Ryan. You were closer to her than anyone."

"Yes," Ryan said, swallowing the lump in her throat. "I was." The past tense sounded so harsh, even after all these years, and Ryan struggled to stay focused on Mrs. Andrews's part of the conversation.

The older woman saw the hurt in the deep blue eyes and realized that her last remark had been very insensitive. "I'm sorry, Ryan," she said softly. "I'm really and truly sorry that you had to go through that pain. I wish … I just wish I could have done something to make it better."

"It was a tough time, Mrs. Andrews, but as I said, I'm happy with how things turned out."

"Well, I'll be sure to mention that I saw you," she said as she stood to go. "Good luck at Berkeley, Ryan. I'm really happy that things have turned out well for you."

"Thank you," Ryan said politely. "I can't imagine being happier," she said as she gently lifted Caitlin onto her shoulder and extended her free hand to help Jamie up. "Give Sara my regards," she added as they walked toward the side door.

When they had safely buckled Caitlin's limp body into her car seat they both got into the back seat, squeezing in next to the baby for the short ride. They looked at each other and jointly shook their heads, both a little nonplussed by the interaction. "Did you talk to her?" Brendan asked, unable to even speak the name of the woman he felt had betrayed his sister.

"Yes, Bren," Ryan replied, patting his broad shoulder. "We spoke for a few minutes."

"Oh," Brendan replied coldly. "I see her all the time at church, but I always go out of my way to leave by a different door. I'm afraid I couldn't be civil to her, and I don't want to chance it."

Ryan leaned over the bucket seat and kissed him on the cheek. "I really appreciate it that you stick up for me, Brendan, but I can handle this."

He nodded briefly, but added, "You couldn't handle it very well at the time, sis." His blue eyes were clouded with anger, and Ryan realized that it was a losing effort to try to get him to forgive the woman.

"I truly appreciate that I can count on all of my big brothers," she said sincerely, deciding to let it go.

"You know, Jamie," he said, "the O'Flaherty brothers will take care of you, too. Just tell us who you want to get rid of, and they're gone!"

"I could have used you last year to get rid of my roommate," she teased. "But I don't currently have a hit list."

"So, did you give her an earful?" Brendan asked hopefully.

"No, of course not. I owe Sara and her mother an eternal debt of gratitude."

"Well, I don't think you owe them a darn thing," Jamie said. "I find it unconscionable to turn your back on a hurt and confused seventeen-year-old. I don't care what the circumstances were. You figure out a way to stay connected with the child, even if it's difficult. I blame Mrs. Andrews much more than I do Sara. She was old enough to know better."

"Hear, hear!" Brendan said enthusiastically. "My sentiments, exactly."

Ryan smiled at the thought that she hadn't just gained a lover: she now had another member of her protection squad. "The funny part is that Sara went to Stanford for law school. She's in the same class as Jamie's former fiancé."

"Great. More lawyers," he said with a decided lack of enthusiasm.

Jamie had to rush to get over to Olympic for her golf game with her father, but that didn't stop her from peppering Ryan with questions while she changed clothes. "How do you feel about seeing Sara's mom? Was that the first time you've seen her since?"

"Yep," Ryan said. "I stopped going to nine-thirty Mass immediately, since that's when the Andrewses went. I spent the summer in Ireland, so I didn't see her then, either. By the time I got back I had pretty much stopped going to church, so this was the first time I've spoken to her in six years. Gosh, that seems like a long time," she said as she shook her head, remembering the innocent, impressionable young woman she had been at the time.

"Are you at all interested in what Sara's like?" Jamie asked tentatively, wriggling into a pair of close-fitting golf slacks.

Ryan thought about that for a few minutes. "I guess I am," she finally said. "I don't want to see her or anything, but she was an incredibly big part of my life. I would like to see what kind of person she became."

"I understand how you feel," Jamie said softly. "Just because you don't love someone any longer, you still care about them."

Ryan looked at her with compassion. "I know you do, honey. You, more than anyone, know how it feels."

"Do you think Mrs. Andrews watched us after she knew it was you?" Jamie asked.

"I assume she did, why?"

"I was just marveling at how people make reality fit their expectations. You and I were clearly the primary caregivers for Caitlin. I was touching your face in a very loving manner when she came up. She might have even seen Caitlin trying to nurse on you! Yet she assumed that she was my daughter and that Brendan was my husband. That just amazes me!"

"It makes it even weirder since she knows I'm gay," Ryan agreed. "Maybe it makes a little more sense that Sara was so freaked out. Mrs. Andrews might not be the woman I thought she was."

"Maybe," Jamie agreed. "And I still would like to give both of them a pop," she said with green eyes flashing as she slapped her open palm with her closed fist.

"I've got nothing but champions," Ryan teased as she draped her arm around her defender for a gentle good-bye kiss.

Chapter Nine

After Jamie left, Ryan went upstairs to get some lunch started and was surprised to see her father and her aunt enter the house together. "Where've you been, Da? I expected you when I got up this morning."

"The lads were out battling a blaze until four this morning," he said, suppressing a yawn. "I got up and started a big breakfast for them and then stayed to help clean up. Nothing worse than coming on duty to a mess like that to clean." Ryan smiled at him, admiring her father for giving up his time to help the next shift get started smoothly.

"Did you go to Mass?"

"Yes. I was a shade late for nine-thirty, so I went to eleven, and stayed around to offer my sister-in-law a ride home."

"He stayed and helped us clean up is what he did," Maeve scoffed, giving him a mock annoyed look. "You don't have to clean up after every assemblage of people in San Francisco, Martin."

He shrugged his shoulders and reached for the baby who was squirming in Ryan's arms. "I enjoy it," he said simply as he made his way for the kitchen. "What would everyone like for lunch?"

"I'd like to make lunch for you," Ryan insisted, brushing past her father. "You and Aunt Maeve go sit on the porch and I'll cook for a change. Go on," she shooed them out of the kitchen, but Caitlin didn't want to follow. Rather than force the issue, Ryan allowed her to sit on the floor and play with her toys, Duffy agreeing to help her watch the little one.

It was a bit more difficult than she had anticipated, avoiding six feet and one tail as she moved around the large kitchen, but she managed to get a plate of sandwiches and bowls of soup prepared without stepping on any of them. Caitlin's new trick was to grab on to a pant leg to hold herself up, and Ryan patiently let her use her leg as they walked slowly and haltingly into the dining room.

Martin heard the door from the kitchen swing open, and he stood in the dining room and laughed at the sight. The baby was trying to walk between Ryan's long legs, each of her chubby little hands grasping a handful of Ryan's pants. At the rate they were traveling, it would take them ten minutes to get to the table, but Ryan was holding the tray of sandwiches in her hands, and she couldn't rush the baby along.

Duffy was so close behind them that his nose was pressed against the back of Ryan's calf, his big body only halfway through the door by the time Martin got there to assist.

"Do you ever wonder how your mother got a thing done?" he laughed, taking the tray and placing it on the table.

Ryan actually hadn't wondered about that question, but she did now. She imagined what it must have been like to have a six-year-old, a four-year-old, a two-year-old, and an infant all clustered around her while she tried to prepare a meal. "I don't think I'd have the patience to do that," she mused, swooping Caitlin into her arms.

"You do what you have to do," Martin insisted. "If I had to do it over again, I think we might have spaced you all out a little bit more, just for your mother's sake, but when you got older it was nice to have you so close in age."

Ryan mulled that thought over while they all dug in, pausing to consider that if her parents had planned their family, they would likely have run out of time before they had her. "What would the perfect space between kids be?" she asked thoughtfully.

Maeve laughed at the question, reminding her niece, "You've come to the wrong place to get family planning advice, sweetheart. None of us knew a thing about that entire topic! We just took what the good Lord gave us."

Ryan was a little surprised at this, always having assumed that at least her Aunt Maeve had used some sort of birth control. She had only three children, and they were spaced at least three years apart, something that Ryan guessed would be hard to do without birth control. Not wanting to pry, she asked, "But if you were making a recommendation, what would you suggest?"

Maeve's green eyes flickered with mirth as she teased, "Are you asking about anyone in particular, dear?"

"Yes, ma'am," Ryan nodded, her mouth curving into a smirk. "I'm speaking of myself."

"Are you ready to start down that path right now?" Martin's eyes were wide, and he looked like he was controlling an urge to try and talk her out of any such plan.

"No, Da, don't worry," she assured him. "I think we want to wait until we're through with grad school. I'm actually more worried that we won't have time to have all of the kids I want to have."

"Knowing how you feel about children, that wouldn't surprise me in the least," he laughed. "You'd better make sure Jamie's of the same mind, though. It might be tough for her to go from being an only child to having a house full of ruffians."

Ryan adopted an outraged look and demanded, "And just what makes you think my children will be ruffians?"

Both Martin and Maeve laughed at the thought. "Even if you weren't related to the child, you could turn them into a ruffian. It's one of your gifts," her father teased, speaking the absolute truth.

She rolled her eyes and shrugged her broad shoulders, conceding the point, since it was clear that she was well on the way to turning Caitlin into a ruffian. The baby was currently sitting on her lap, playing with some zwieback cookies that were no longer fit for human consumption since Duffy had already had them thrust into his mouth repeatedly. Ryan leaned over and whispered something in her ear, causing the baby to giggle at the tickling sensation. Looking up at her father, Ryan informed him, "Caitlin says she's chosen a rather wild lifestyle all on her own. She assures me that I was not a major influence."

"Uh-huh," he grinned, "just wait until I get my report on your church attendance today, Siobhán. We'll just see which of you was the instigator."

Ryan gave a mental sigh, knowing that her father wasn't kidding about receiving a report. Martin was known to nearly everyone in the parish, and she knew that everyone from Father Pender on down would comment about her rare appearance at Mass. Somewhere in the report, someone would mention seeing her speak to Mary Elizabeth Andrews, so she thought it best to get that little bit of information out of the way immediately. "I uh ... was surprised to find Mrs. Andrews sitting behind us today," she began.

In the blink of an eye Martin's face grew grim and Ryan could see the anger welling up. "Well, aren't you the lucky one?" he snapped. "She avoids the rest of us like we're lepers. I've seen that woman cross the entire church just to avoid leaving by the same door as I do."

Maeve looked at Ryan with a great deal of sadness in her dark green eyes. "Did you speak with her, dear?"

Ryan nodded. "Yes, Jamie and I did. Brendan gave her the cold shoulder though," she admitted.

"Good for him!" Martin insisted. "She deserves no better!"

Ryan gave him a long look and explained, "I don't want to live like that, Da. I'm not willing to hide from people that might upset me. I'm really glad that we spoke." Turning to her aunt she asked, "Did you know Sara just graduated from Stanford law?"

Maeve nodded. "Yes, sweetheart, I did know that. Mary Elizabeth doesn't speak to me personally, but I've heard updates about Sara from some of the other women." Looking at Ryan carefully she asked, "Should I have kept you informed of the things I heard?"

Ryan shook her head briskly. "No. I don't think I was ready before. I think I am now, though." She was absently rubbing Caitlin's unkempt blonde hair, causing the little green eyes to flutter closed. As Caitlin's head dropped, Ryan shifted her small burden and drew her into the crook of her arm to better support her. "This is hard to explain, but being with Jamie has made me more confident about facing people that have hurt me in the past. I'm not sure why that is, but it was really okay to see Mrs. Andrews since I knew Jamie was there." She tilted her dark head and gazed at her aunt. "Do you know what I mean?"

Maeve closed her eyes as a knowing smile crossed her face. "I know exactly what you mean, sweetheart. It's a very nice feeling, isn't it?"

Ryan's beaming grin lit up the room. "It's the best."

It was after one when they finished eating, and Ryan was anxious to do something physical. "I need to get outside and do something," she finally whined.

"You're just like a puppy, darlin'," Martin said affectionately. "You just can't be cooped up too long, or you start chewing on the furniture."

"I thought I could take Caitlin to Golden Gate Park," she suggested. "If I could borrow a truck, I could put her in her jogger and I could Rollerblade for a couple of hours."

"I've got a better idea," Maeve said. "Why don't I drive you, and I can take a leisurely walk while you two speed around."

"That works for me," Ryan said. "I'll run and change."

"Why don't you come with us?" Maeve asked Martin. "I wouldn't mind some company while I'm waiting for the girls to finish their run."

"I've nothing on the schedule," he admitted. "But I need to be home in time to make my baby's favorite meal tonight," he said as he gave his daughter a warm hug. "She's taking off again in the morning, and I want her to remember her old father for another week."

"If I'd known I'd get extra attention, I would have left home years ago," she said with a wink at her grinning aunt.

When Jamie entered the locker room at the club she nearly gasped when she saw Mia sitting patiently in front of her locker. "Took you long enough, James," she chided, jumping up and wrapping her friend in a hug.

"What are you doing here?" Jamie was truly flustered, and Mia enjoyed the atypical bout of inarticulateness that her surprise had caused.

"I decided to come home for the weekend, and my father suggested we get together with you and your dad for a game. I wanted it to be a surprise, so I didn't call you. Surprised?" Her warm brown eyes sparkled as she reveled in her ability to put one over on her friend.

"Totally," Jamie agreed, giving her another generous hug. "I've missed you, Mia. There have been so many times in the past two weeks that I've wanted to share some things with you."

"Is everything okay?" she asked a bit anxiously, still holding Jamie in a loose embrace.

"Everything's perfect." Jamie's smile was very bright, and Mia delighted at seeing the sparkle in the green eyes.

"I've got a seven o'clock flight back to L.A.," Mia said. "How about giving me a ride to the airport so we can dish?"

"You're on, buddy. I've got tons of stuff to tell you."

When the golf match ended, the young women said good-bye to their fathers and retired to the locker room. Very few of the women members used the spa and steam room, so they decided to spend some time relaxing in the deserted area before they had to leave for the airport. It was just three o'clock and they didn't have to leave until five, so they had time to burn.

They were barely settled in the steaming spa when Mia turned to Jamie with a look of rapt interest. "Okay, girlfriend, spill it. I want everything—down to the dirtiest detail."

Jamie laughed at her usual directness and said, "I don't know where to start, Mia. I have never felt like this about anyone." She reached up and pushed her damp hair from her eyes, then took a drink from the lemonade they had carried into the spa area. "I had no idea what it felt like to really love someone."

"That's nice, Jamie. I'm really happy for you," she said mechanically. Then an impish grin crossed her face and she demanded, "Now tell me about the sex!"

"Is that all you ever think about?" she asked with a laugh.

"No, I have lots of things on my fertile mind. But sex is the only thing that interests me enough to get me up at nine on a Sunday to play golf!"

"I'm honored that you agreed to play with us," Jamie offered, acknowledging Mia's uncharacteristic behavior, "but I thought that perhaps you were interested in seeing me just for me."

"You know I'm teasing, James. But I'm dying to know!"

"Okay," Jamie said thoughtfully, deciding that she wanted to share some of her feelings with her old friend. "It's better than I could have imagined, Mia," she sighed. "I mean, I know I loved Jack, and I know that we did make love—but it honestly feels like what Ryan and I do together is a whole different kind of act. She's so loving and caring and patient with me. I've just never felt safer or more protected than when I'm lying in her arms. It's funny," she mused. "We can be lying together so peacefully, feeling all safe and loved, and two seconds later she can get that gleam in her eyes and just drive me insane. She is absolutely irresistible!"

"I'm really happy for you, James," she said with a smirk. "Although I'd love some details, I get the feeling that you're not going to give 'em up today."

Jamie smiled back, acknowledging that she wasn't willing to share the details of her life with Ryan. "It's different when you really love someone, Mia. It's just too intimate to talk about with anyone. Do you understand?"

"I do," she admitted. "You'll notice that I never told you any details about being with Jason—until I knew it was just about over."

"I'm glad you understand," she said fondly. "I don't want you to feel left out."

"No, I'm cool," she said happily, looking very much so. "What's the plan for the rest of the summer—are you just going to hang out and make love?"

Jamie smiled serenely and shook her head a little. "I wish we could. But I think we're both ready to move on with the things we want to accomplish this summer. I'm thinking of telling my parents about us soon."

"Are you nuts?" Mia shrieked, completely surprising Jamie with her outburst.

"N ... n ... no, I don't think I am," she stuttered. "Do you think it's a bad idea?"

"I think it's a very bad idea, James. Why go asking for trouble?"

Jamie shook her head, still puzzled by Mia's comments. "I think I know my parents pretty well, and it's bothering me more to have the secret than it is to consider telling them. Just to get it over with, I might tell them next weekend."

"Boy, that seems fast to me," Mia said. "You do know that they'll flip out, don't you?"

"I know they won't be happy at first, but I think they love me enough to try to work through this with me."

"Uh-huh," she replied again, trying to keep her face devoid of emotion so that she didn't exert undue pressure on her friend.

"Come on," Jamie urged, realizing that Mia was holding back. "Tell me what you're thinking."

Mia smiled at her, glad that Jamie knew her so well, but sorry that she couldn't hide anything from her, even at the risk of hurting her feelings. "I think it's gonna be hard, James. I don't think they'll be nice about it at all, and I'm afraid it's gonna get ugly."

"Do you really?" Jamie was amazed that Mia would assume this about her often emotionally distant parents. "Why?"

"You're their only child, James. If they didn't make you into what they want, they're out of chances. And not to be mean, but your mom is totally into what her friends think of her. She's not gonna want her social set gossiping about you."

Jamie nodded slowly, acknowledging that her mother's clique loved nothing more than a juicy tidbit like this to gnaw on. While that thought was rumbling around in her mind, she remembered that she had promised to pass on some interesting information herself, and now was as good a time as any. "Speaking of parents having a bad reaction … I saw Melissa last weekend."

"M … My Melissa?" Mia squeaked

Jamie nodded slowly, puzzled at that particular moniker. "She's a lesbian, Mia. And she seems pretty happy."

An unreadable expression crossed Mia's face. Jamie thought she detected a note of sadness, but it was gone almost immediately. "So … how is she?" she asked lightly.

"She seems good. She's got a girlfriend, and they live together. I don't know if you knew this, but she's at USF. She's still a cheerleader—Ryan knew her when she was there and playing on the basketball team."

At Mia's raised eyebrow, Jamie assured her, "Not in the biblical sense. They were just in a class together."

"So what was the bad reaction?" Mia asked, looking puzzled.

"Her parents freaked. Cut her off financially for the most part. She seemed pretty cool about it, though. It's hard to tell with her, though, she has that cheerfulness that seems kinda forced sometimes."

Mia nodded, realizing that she was one of the few people who had seen through Melissa's chipper façade. "It'd be hard for her to lose contact with her dad," she said softly. "Her mom is a total whack job, but she cares for her dad." She wasn't sure why, but suddenly she felt like crying. She didn't want to tell Jamie that hearing about Melissa upset her, so she dunked her head into the steaming water and climbed out. "I'm gonna order another drink. You want anything?"

"No, I'm fine," Jamie advised, sensing that Mia was unsettled by the news she'd just shared.

When Mia returned a few minutes later, she carried a large plastic cup of orange juice that assaulted Jamie's nose with the smell of vodka when she set it on the deck of the spa. At Jamie's raised eyebrow, Mia shrugged and said, "I'm not flying the plane, James."

Abandoning their previous topic, she asked, "So, is Ryan moving into the house?"

"Yeah, we're already staying there during the week, then we go to her house for the weekends."

Mia got a contemplative look on her face as she said, "I want you to be honest with me, James. I know this relationship is totally important to you. Do you want me to find someplace else to live this fall so you can be alone?"

"No!" she said firmly. "We both want you to live with us this year. I want you to get to know her better. You're really important to me, Mia, and I want you to be a part of our lives."

"Thanks, Jamie. You're really important to me too. I'm glad you want me to stay," she said as she patted her shoulder. "I was afraid you were going to boot me when you got engaged, but I think things worked out well then. This will just be another little challenge."

"Actually, I have news on that front, too," she admitted, rolling her eyes a little.

"Really? Have you talked to him?"

"I saw him," she said mysteriously.

"Get out! When and why?"

"I went to his graduation."

"Did he invite you?"

"Not specifically. But he called me before the ride and was really sweet. I thought about it and decided that going would let me put our relationship to rest."

"Did it?"

"Yep, but not in the way I was planning. He has a new girlfriend," she said slowly.

"What a jerk! It's only been four months since you broke up and two months since you tried to reconcile!"

"I think he's had her for a while, too. But I can't complain, Mia. I'm already living with Ryan, and I decided I loved her the day after he broke up with me."

"That's no excuse. He should be in mourning for you," she said firmly.

"Well, he's clearly not. He seemed really happy, and I was amazed that it made me completely jealous!"

"Are you serious?" she asked, truly startled.

"Yes. I made a huge fool out of myself. I was crying so hard that he had to hold me just to calm me down. I think it really got to me that his new girlfriend is his law review partner. Do you remember Natalie?"

"That dog! How long do you think they've really been together?" she asked suspiciously.

"That's just what I thought!" Jamie shrieked. "But he convinced me that they didn't start seeing each other until we had broken up. I believe him, even though I think

Natalie might have had her eye on him for a long time. You know how easy men are to manipulate."

"Hey, it's my life's work," she said proudly.

"Anyway, when I saw them together, I totally lost it. I felt like our whole relationship had been a sham, and I just got hysterical. His parents saw me, Natalie saw me, it was totally humiliating, Mia. I hope I never see any of them again."

"You poor baby," she said as she rubbed her arm. "What did you do?"

"I spent the whole day driving around Palo Alto, just letting myself feel the loss for the first time. It was really cathartic, but more painful than I ever would have guessed. I was a wreck when I got back to Ryan's. But she was really supportive and understanding when I told her everything."

"Everything?"

"Yep. And she was really cool about it. She said it made total sense that I was jealous. She said it just showed that I had loved him, and it was really nothing to be ashamed of."

"Boy, she is understanding. Most guys would have killed you if you'd told them that."

"She really is, Mia. I'm telling you, I hit the jackpot with Ms. O'Flaherty."

Mia nodded, sharing a smile with her friend. "I'm totally prejudiced, Jamie, but I think it's the other way around."

At four o'clock Ryan was racing down the street, pushing a laughing baby in her jogger. They had been touring through every mile of the park for nearly two hours after leaving Martin and Maeve near the Hall of Flowers with the promise to meet them back there at four-thirty. "Hey, munchkin, we've got thirty minutes left. Let's go to Stow Lake and watch the boats." As expected, Caitlin agreed wholeheartedly with this plan. She signaled her acceptance by grinning up at her big cousin. Ryan bent over to kiss her forehead as she said, "You are sure easy to please, little one."

When they arrived at the small lake, she removed the baby from the jogger and let her stand for a few minutes while they watched the various paddle, row, and power boats cruise around. After a while she picked her up and sat her on her shoulders, so she could have a better view. She patiently and needlessly pointed out all the points of interest to her, explaining that the small island in the center of the lake was man-made and previously used to disguise the water tanks that served the park. As she was prattling on, something caught her attention. *Is that ...?* she thought to herself. She focused closely and saw that she had indeed seen her father and aunt standing near the Chinese Pavilion, so she decided to wait for them where she was rather than go back to the Hall of Flowers. She bent to get the baby ready to go, but after the few minutes it took to get her set, she saw that they had still not moved on.

She patiently waited, glancing up every few moments, but one glance nearly brought her to her knees. As her mouth dropped in shock, she saw her father lean over and begin to kiss her aunt. This was clearly not a friendly kiss from a favorite brother-in-law. This was the kiss of a man and a woman who were far more than friends. Ryan tried to avert her eyes, but she was mesmerized by the sight. Maeve had wrapped her arms around Martin's neck and was kissing him back with enthusiasm. This was obviously not the first time they had kissed, and her mind reeled when she considered what this meant to the family.

As she stared at them in dumbfounded shock, she forced herself to look at the situation as objectively as possible. When she looked at them with some detachment, she was able to see them as they would appear to a casual observer. Martin was, by any standard, a very handsome man. He was tall, with broad shoulders and a very trim, muscular body. Even though he no longer fought fires, he firmly believed that he had to be physically ready to do so if called upon in an emergency, so he worked out regularly in the small gym the firefighters had rigged up in the station.

His temples were touched with gray but rather than making him look his age, the gray just made him look more distinguished. When Ryan paused to consider it, she had to admit that he had begun to look even better in the last year or so. He had switched barbers and started going where Conor went, and his new cut was more stylish and complimentary to his ruggedly handsome face. He had also started wearing more casual clothes at home and on the weekends. Traditionally he wore an old pair of dark blue uniform pants around the house, but now he could be found in a pressed pair of khakis or some Dockers. His shirts had also undergone a transformation. No longer did he wear a clean white T-shirt at home; now he was just as likely to be seen in a sky blue polo shirt that perfectly matched his eyes, or an oxford cotton shirt, ironed to perfection.

Maeve had changed a bit also in the past year, Ryan observed. She was always a stylish woman, and Ryan had honestly never seen her without a tasteful amount of makeup and an attractive hairstyle. Recently she had put even more care into her appearance. She often wore just a touch of an appealing perfume, and her hair color had lightened up recently, going from her natural auburn to a lighter shade of reddish brown. Her clothes had also softened up a bit, now consisting mostly of sweater sets or shells over tasteful print skirts.

From a distance, they just looked like two mature adults who were falling in love, and Ryan knew that she should welcome this news enthusiastically. But her roiling stomach didn't agree with that sentiment.

Her first problem was what to do with this information. She could let them know that she had seen them and ask them to explain, or she could act as though she had seen nothing. She doubted that she could pull that off without them knowing something was wrong. Her moment of decision was drawing near as she saw them break their embrace and begin to walk back to the shore of the lake. They stopped on the footbridge for one last kiss, and she knew that she either had to disappear for a while to collect herself or just be honest with them. With a heavy sigh she decided to bite the bullet. She was waiting for them when they stepped onto solid ground. They were laughing and paying attention only to each other as they walked along, hand in hand.

"Hi," she said quietly from behind the happy couple.

Martin whirled around, dropping Maeve's hand as his eyes locked on his daughter's. He knew the second he saw her face that she had seen at least some of their intimacies. He cast a quick glance at Maeve, and she gave him a dismayed look and quickly looked away. "I guess we owe you an explanation," he said as he looked straight at his daughter.

"No, Da, you don't *owe* me an explanation, but I would like to know what is going on."

"Did you see us together on the hill?" he asked quietly.

"Yes," she admitted, staring at her feet.

"Then I guess it's pretty obvious what's going on," he said as his face flushed a deep pink.

"That's not what I meant, Da," she said softly. "I know this is private and if you want me to drop it I will, but I don't think I can ignore what I saw. I know this will change how I act around you, and that's why I wanted to tell you that I saw you together."

"Why don't we go have a cup of tea so we can talk about this," Martin suggested. "I think it's time we shed some light on this issue."

They walked to the car in silence. Ryan had brought a pair of running shoes, and she quickly changed into them and tugged on a sweatshirt. Maeve drove to the first coffee shop she spotted, and she and Martin went in to grab a table. Ryan spent a few minutes extracting Caitlin from her car seat before going inside. They were all a little uncomfortable with each other, and they stood in front of the menu board for a moment in silence. "Tea for you both?" she asked, and received two nods in return. She ordered a latté for herself and a milk for the baby, along with the tea. Martin indicated that he would wait for the drinks while Ryan took Caitlin out to a table.

She sat down on the metal bistro-style chair and adjusted Caitlin on her lap. After a few moments, Maeve placed a hand on her arm and asked, "Are you upset with us, honey?"

Ryan closed her eyes for a moment and reflexively rubbed them. Her head was beginning to ache, and she pinched the bridge of her nose firmly to dull the pain. She looked up at her aunt and said, "Of course I'm not upset. It's just a shock, Aunt Maeve. I never suspected anything."

Caitlin was beginning to fuss, and Ryan quickly checked her diaper. Seeing that it was time for a change, she took her into the bathroom. When she came back, she settled into her chair with the baby on her lap. She handed her the biscotti, and the baby happily began to gum the hard cookie.

"Do you want to ask us some questions, or should we just give you the whole story?" Martin asked.

"The whole story would be good," she replied, feeling incapable of forming appropriate questions at the moment.

"Okay," Martin said. "I'll tell you my version of events, and Maeve can correct me if she needs to," he said with a smile at his sister-in-law. "I've been fond of Maeve since the day I met her, Siobhán, which should surprise no one since she's one of the loveliest women around." He shot a shy glance at Maeve, and Ryan had to force herself not to smile at the boyish grin on his face. "She certainly had more than her share of troubles, what with Michael's illness and all of the problems she had with Charlie, but her spirit has never dimmed. She's the same lovely woman I met at church in 1965," he said with another glance at the now blushing woman.

Ryan watched their interactions and had to smile in spite of her mixed feelings. She knew that her father's perceptions of her aunt closely mirrored her own. Maeve was still a lovely woman, and despite the fact that she was three years older than Martin, she had a youthful vitality that belied her age. Her green eyes danced and her mouth curled up into an adorable grin when she smiled, which was often. There was a marked similarity between Maeve and her younger sister, Fionnuala, but Maeve had always been more gregarious and outgoing. She was fortunate that she possessed an optimism that had never really diminished, despite her troubles. And she had, indeed, seen plenty of trouble.

Martin continued with his explanation. "I didn't have a single thought of being with another woman after your mother died, Siobhán. I can honestly say that I had resigned myself to being alone for the rest of my life. But I looked at Maeve in a new light one day not long after Charlie left the house, and I thought, "My God, but she's a beauty." He sat quietly for a moment, laughing a little at his own surprise. "Of course, I didn't tell her or anyone else that I had begun to see her for the lovely woman that she was. But I will admit that the possibility that she might one day return my affections has kept me from seeking out other women."

"I always wondered why you never dated, Da," Ryan said thoughtfully. "I knew that you could have your pick of the single women from church, but you never seemed to even notice them."

"I can honestly say, darlin', that I spent a good six or seven years not even noticing that women existed. When you've had the love of a woman like my Fionnuala it's almost inconceivable that another could compare in your heart. But once I had the hope that Maeve could one day be mine, I had no time to waste on others." He gave her another sidelong glance and gently laid his hand over hers.

Ryan had to smile again as she asked, "So when did you talk about this with each other?"

"When Charlie died I felt that I could finally tell her of my affections, but first I had to let her mourn for the poor man. No matter what he was in his later years, I knew that Maeve had loved him when they were young. So I told her not long after your last birthday, Siobhán."

"And how did you take this news, Aunt Maeve?" Ryan asked with a twinkle in her eyes, now beginning to feel more comfortable with the situation.

She blushed deeply before she responded, "I was more surprised than I had ever been in my life. Of course I had always loved Martin, but I had never thought of him as anything more than a wonderful brother-in-law. I told him that I needed some time to sort out my feelings. But after a week or two I had to admit that there was no finer man to be found, and that I shouldn't let our history prevent the possibility of our finding happiness together."

"I guess I'm just uncomfortable that you felt the need to hide this from us," Ryan said quietly, getting to the crux of her hurt feelings.

"There's a very good reason for that, darlin'," Martin said. "This will obviously take a lot of adjustment for the family, and it didn't make any sense to get everyone upset if it was not working out. So we wanted to spend time together and make sure before we told anyone."

"And quite frankly, I'm afraid to tell my parents," Maeve admitted with another blush. "I really doubt that they'll be happy about this."

Ryan had to laugh at her insecurities, but she reached over to pat her hand. "I guess some things never get any easier, do they?"

"No," she admitted, "I'm still afraid of disappointing my parents, and I'm going to be fifty-seven years old."

"I take it that things have gone well?" Ryan needlessly asked.

The new couple looked at each other fondly. "It's been a blessing for me," Martin said. "A gift that I never expected."

Maeve leaned her head against his shoulder and gazed at Ryan with an open, innocent expression. "I had no idea how being loved could change my life," she said softly. "It took me fifty-six years to feel this, but to win a man like your father, I'd wait twice as long."

Ryan was touched by the honest expression of their love, but she knew that many more issues had to be resolved. "So where do you go from here?"

"We were making plans today to tell the children," Maeve admitted. "After we do that, I'll face my parents. If I have all of the kids on my side, it'll help my confidence."

"Do you think you'll marry?"

"Of course," Martin said immediately. "But that raises more issues, like where will we live?"

Ryan shook her head slowly, knowing that housing was a difficult issue for all but the wealthiest San Franciscans. "What do you think you'll do?"

Martin said, "Well, our house is bigger, but I don't know how Conor and Rory would feel with having Maeve in the house. It'd be a big adjustment for each of them. You know, we've come up with some pretty firm routines around the house, and I worry about changing them. But since Kevin still lives at Maeve's, we'd have the same issue if I moved in there. So it's been a conundrum."

"That's another reason we didn't tell anyone of our relationship. We knew there would be lots of questions, and we just didn't have answers yet," Maeve offered.

"Well, as Jamie and I have discovered, the rest of the issues just fall into place once you make a commitment to one another. I'm sure you'll work all of those details out." She bounced the baby on her lap for a few moments as she began to fuss. "I think Caitlin has been still long enough," she said. "We'd better go."

As Martin held Maeve's chair out for her, Ryan walked around to their side of the table. She handed the baby to Maeve and put her arms around her father. "I'm very happy for you, Da. I want you to have love in your life again, and I couldn't have chosen a better woman for you." He brushed a tear from his eyes as he wrapped his arms around her and squeezed her tight.

"Thank you, Siobhán. That means more to me than you can know."

Ryan sniffed a little as she stood up and took the baby once more. She then handed her to her father and bent over to hug her favorite aunt. "I've always thought of you as a second mother, Aunt Maeve. I'm thrilled for you both."

Maeve was unable to answer in words, but the hug she returned was full of meaning. They hung onto each other for a long time, and when Ryan finally stood up she took the baby again and said to Caitlin, "It looks like you finally get to have a grandfather, sweet pea!"

On the way home Ryan unnecessarily told them that she wouldn't mention a word to the boys, but added that she would like to share the news with Jamie. They were both agreed to that, and a few minutes later Maeve pulled up in front of the house. Ryan got out after kissing Caitlin good-bye, and as she reached up between the seats to kiss her aunt, she said, "Don't rush, Da. I'll start dinner."

Jamie arrived home just as Ryan was coming out of the shower. She took one look at her and immediately asked, "What's wrong?"

Ryan gave her a gentle smile and said, "Nothing really major. I just got some shocking news today."

"What is it, honey?"

"I think Da's getting married."

"Married?" Jamie nearly shouted. "But I thought you said he's never had a date?"

"Apparently he still hasn't," she said enigmatically.

"Did he order a woman from a magazine?" she asked, totally confused.

"No, but it's someone you know."

"Who do I know that isn't married ..." she mused, as she furrowed her brow in concentration. "Mrs. Andrews?"

Ryan had to laugh at that one. "No, she's married."

"But Ryan, I don't know any other single women besides your au—" she started to say, but the words caught in her throat when she saw the confirmation in Ryan's eyes. "Oh, honey," she said, as she went to her and wrapped her arms around her bare waist.

Ryan dropped her head to rest on her lover's shoulder. She closed her eyes and just relished the deep sense of comfort she felt when Jamie held her. "Boy, I needed that," she admitted after a few minutes.

"Do you want to talk about it?"

"Yeah. I'll burst if I don't. They don't want the other kids to know yet. They only told me because I saw them kissing in the park and I confronted them."

"Oh, God, what a terrible way to find out," she said sympathetically, flopping down onto the love seat.

"Yeah," Ryan agreed as she joined her. "But it could have been worse. Caitlin was on my shoulders two minutes earlier. I could have dropped her, my knees were so weak."

"You poor little thing," she soothed. "Tell me how you feel about it."

Ryan smiled at her approach. "I love that you ask me how I feel about it, rather than what I know about it."

"I'll find out the details later. What I care about is you, and how this affects you."

Ryan snuggled next to her and nuzzled her head down into Jamie's neck. They sat right next to one another in silence, until it became clear that Ryan really was having trouble putting her thoughts into words. Jamie scooted down the sofa until she was against the opposite arm, and pulled on her lover until her head was resting in her lap. Ryan tossed her legs up over the other arm and began to relax as Jamie ran her fingers through her dark tresses. After a few minutes of the loving touch, she had relaxed enough to speak.

"I guess what has me the most puzzled is how betrayed I feel," she finally said. "I love my father and I love my aunt, and there's nothing I want more for each of them than that they should find love and be happy. So why does it bother me so much that it's with each other?" she asked plaintively.

"Honey, don't be so hard on yourself. This caught you completely by surprise. If this was a stranger, you'd still be upset because of the suddenness. But it's not a stranger. It's your aunt. And I can only imagine that the image of your father with her is not very comfortable for you. It's probably almost as if he was with his own sister. She's family, honey. It's going to be very odd for all of you for a while."

"That's it!" she agreed. "It's almost like incest!"

Jamie laughed at her characterization as she said, "I'm sure it feels different for them, honey. But you've been related to her since birth. It probably feels like your father is related to her too, but he's not, baby."

"I know that logically, Jamie. But my guts don't know it."

"I can't imagine how this feels for you, honey," she said, continuing to soothe her by stroking her hair.

"I know how much my parents loved each other. Da said today that he didn't know that other women existed for six or seven years after Mama died, but somehow this feels like he's betraying her, too."

"Is that what you called her?" Jamie asked quietly.

"What?"

"Did you call her Mama?"

Ryan's eyes misted over as she nodded. "Either Mama or Mam," she whispered.

"I like that name. Maybe our children will call you that," she said, patting Ryan's cheek gently.

"I'd like that," Ryan's emotion-laden voice murmured.

Jamie kept up the slow stroking of Ryan's head, smiling to herself as the deep blue eyes started to close. Ryan was clearly very relaxed, so Jamie softly asked her a question. "If we had children and you died, would you want me to be alone or find someone else?"

Ryan's eyes popped open and she tilted her head to gaze into Jamie's eyes. "Where …?"

"Just think about it, honey," she insisted. "Tell me how you'd feel."

Ryan spent only a moment thinking about her answer. "I hope you would find someone. You need love in your life, Jamie. You can't survive with just memories."

"What if I fell in love with Conor? Would you want me to marry him?"

After another moment, Ryan's face lit up in a delighted grin. "You should be a psychologist," she said affectionately.

"But you do agree with my obtuse point?"

"Yes. You're right, Jamie. My mother would have been glad that they had each other. She probably would have wondered what took them so long. If it'd be okay with her, it should be okay with me, too."

"I think so, baby. They were both entirely faithful to their spouses while they were married to them. But it's been so long for both of them. Almost seventeen years for your father and eleven years for Maeve. Isn't that long enough to mourn?"

Ryan tossed her legs back over the arm of the love seat and threw her arms around her lover. "Thank you," she whispered. "Thank you."

During dinner, Jamie noticed that Ryan was pretty close to her normal self. Brendan was there and they all chatted about their respective weeks. The boys and Da were extremely interested in Ryan's tryouts, all delighted that she had chosen volleyball for her sport. "I don't think I could have watched your matches if you had decided on soccer," Martin admitted.

"You would have been proud of her, Martin," Jamie said. "We talked about the risks and she immediately decided that she wasn't willing to take the chance, no matter how remote."

"Have you ever seen her play soccer?" he asked with a twinkle in his eyes.

"No, not really. I saw her work out, but that's all."

"You wouldn't think the risk was remote if you had seen her play," he said with a laugh. "My little girl could make sipping tea into a dangerous sport if there was a competition involved."

After dinner they all joined together to clean the kitchen. At around eight Jamie and Ryan went down to their room, but scant minutes later they heard footsteps on the stairs. It was their new habit to leave the door open unless they didn't want to be disturbed, and tonight the door was open. Martin stuck his head in and asked, "Can I speak with you girls for a minute?"

"Sure, Da," Ryan said as she motioned him in. She sat down on the bed and Jamie grabbed the desk chair. He paced around a bit before settling on the love seat.

"I take it that Siobhán told you my news?" he asked Jamie.

"Yes, she did, Martin, and I want to tell you how happy I am for you both. You're two of my favorite people, you know."

"Thank you, dear," he said with a smile. "I hope we do as well as you two have. But I came down to see how you were doing with the news, Siobhán. You didn't seem quite yourself tonight."

Jamie started to stand, saying, "I'll go upstairs so you two can talk."

Almost simultaneously, both father and daughter urged her to stay, with Ryan lifting her arm in a welcoming gesture. "I want you to stay, babe, and Da does too, right?"

"Indeed," he nodded. "Everything that impacts Siobhán has an impact on you too, Jamie."

She smiled at the pair and sat down next to Ryan, snuggling into her side as requested. It still felt a little odd to be physically close in front of Martin, but she knew that the only way to get through her discomfort was to slowly desensitize herself. Accepting Ryan's offers of close contact was a small step in that direction.

She could feel some of the tension leave her partner's body and was glad that she had accepted her invitation to sit next to her. Ryan took in a breath and said, "It's going to take me a while to get used to, Da. Jamie and I talked about it, and I feel a lot better than I did earlier. She pointed out some things that I hadn't thought of, and it cleared up some things for me."

"Is there anything you want to tell me about?"

Ryan looked a little shy about revealing her feelings, but she decided that honesty was the best way to proceed. "Jamie pointed out that it probably feels to me that Maeve and you are already related. When I thought about that I realized that is exactly how I feel. So it feels odd to hear you talk about marrying someone who feels like a blood relative."

He looked down at his folded hands for a long minute. Finally he shook his head and said, "I see your point, darlin'. I've never thought of Maeve as a blood relative, even though I love her like one. But she's always been in your life, and it makes perfect sense that you would feel that way. I imagine the other kids will feel the same."

"I think that's a real possibility," she admitted. "But I don't think it's an insurmountable problem. It's just something that we should acknowledge so we can get over it."

"Anything else troubling you, Siobhán?"

She debated again but once again decided to tell him the truth. Jamie could feel her stiffen, and she had a very good idea what was coming. "Part of me feels that you're being unfaithful to Mama," she said quietly as she stared at the floor.

The look of shock that passed across his face was painful for both women to witness. He began to flush and looked like he wanted to defend himself, but instead he asked, "Why do you feel that way?"

Ryan ran her free hand through her hair and Jamie could feel the muscles in her torso coil even tighter. "In my rational mind, I want you to fall in love again, Da. Loving Jamie has let me see what it was that you lost when Mama died," she said as tears began to roll down her cheeks. "But there's a part of me that doesn't ever want anyone to try and take Mama's place. I know it's selfish and I hate that I feel this way …" she said as she began to sob. Jamie started to wrap her arms around her partner, but before she could blink, Martin beat her to it. He sat down next to his daughter and put his arms around her shaking shoulders.

"There, there, sweetheart," he soothed as he rocked her and patted her back. "It's okay, Siobhán. I feel that way too. No woman could ever take her place in my heart.

And part of the reason I never dated when you were younger was because I didn't want anyone to come in here and try to take your mother's place. But you're all grown now, sweetheart, and to tell you the truth …" He paused for a moment and gathered himself. "I'm very lonely," he said quietly. "When you were all younger, I didn't have time to think about myself, but now, with you all home so seldom …" he trailed off.

"Oh, Da," she said, "I'm sorry I said that. I had no idea that you were lonely."

"You've neither said nor done anything that you should be ashamed of, Siobhán. The only way we'll get through this is if we all promise to be honest about how we feel. I'd rather spend the rest of my life alone than cause any permanent rifts in our family. And the only way to avoid those rifts is to talk about them."

"Okay, I promise I'll talk to you about anything else that comes up. But Jamie helped me with the last issue. She asked me how I would feel about her remarrying if we had children and I died."

A look of absolute panic crossed his face as he gripped her more tightly.

"It's not something I like to think about either, Da, but her question was—would I mind if she fell in love and married Conor?" Martin relaxed his grip and sat back a bit.

"Would you mind?"

"Of course not," she said firmly. "I'd be overjoyed for two reasons. One, I would definitely want Jamie to know love again. And two, I don't know of anyone I would trust to raise my children more than one of my brothers. I was too young to know how Mama and Aunt Maeve got along, but from what you tell me, they were very close."

He sat up slightly, one heavy arm still draped across his daughter's shoulders. A small smile played at his lips as he asked, "Did you know that the biggest reason she came to America was so that she could be with her sister?"

"No, I didn't know that," she admitted. "You don't talk about her life in Ireland very much."

"As you know, your mother was between Maeve and Moira in age—five years younger than Maeve and three older than Moira. But she idolized her older sister from the get-go. They say she was never content from the time Maeve left home until she arrived six years later. It actually has always reminded me of how you and Conor have always gotten on, Siobhán."

"Yeah, it makes more sense that I would have been Rory's pal, but I was a goner for Conor from the day I was born."

"The affection has always gone both ways, darlin'. That boy carried you around the house so much I thought you'd never learn how to walk. And the doctor had us a little worried that it took you so long to talk." He laughed at the memory, giving her a little squeeze. "We finally figured out the problem, and we forbade Conor to give you anything until you asked for it. Within weeks you were babbling away."

"She hasn't stopped, Martin," Jamie laughed, giving her partner a little tickle.

"That's the blessed truth," he agreed. "Even though you picked up words quickly once you started, you had some trouble with the names of the boys. I swear I've never seen a boy with a bigger smile than the day you could finally say Conor's name. He was particularly happy that you didn't even try to pronounce Brendan or Rory, but you could enunciate Conor so clearly, it was just a marvel. I can still hear it now," he smiled.

Ryan tried to sniff away her tears, looking around for a box of tissues. Jamie got up and grabbed a few, bending down to give her a small kiss as she did so. Ryan pulled her down onto her lap and rested Jamie's head against her chest. "It's going to be okay, Da. We'll all be fine after a period of adjustment. I do think we need to give some long thought to your living situation, though. That will be hard for either Conor and Rory or Kevin. I know you couldn't afford to buy another house in the Valley at today's prices, so we'll have to do some negotiating."

"Yes, sweetie, my biggest fear is that one or the other will think they need to move away, and I absolutely do not want that to happen."

"We'll figure out a way, Da. We've faced tougher hurdles as a family."

"I know we have, darlin'. I just want to make sure that you all feel comfortable with this before we move on."

"You know, Da, what Jamie said earlier has made me think about this in a different light. I know how much Mama loved you and I know how much she loved her sister. I can't imagine anything that would make her as happy as knowing that you two were going to care for each other for the rest of your lives. I not only feel comfortable, I support you totally. I'm terribly happy for you, Da," she said, wrapping her arms around him and holding him tightly.

They sat in silence for a few minutes after Martin left. Ryan was sitting backwards on her desk chair, her face failing to hide her still-swirling emotions. Jamie came over to stand behind her and give her a shoulder massage, helping to ease some of the tension she could see radiating from her body. After a few minutes, her dark head started to roll with the rhythmic touch, and Jamie leaned over and whispered, "Let's lie down together, honey. I can give you a better massage that way."

"Okay," she agreed, rarely refusing her partner's offer to rub her back. "Let me brush my teeth first—I know I won't later."

She went into the bath first, and while she stood in the doorway flossing her teeth, Jamie asked a few more questions about the family situation. "I don't think you've ever said much about Maeve and her husband. I know they were separated, but what was the story? I can't imagine anyone being unable to get along with her."

Ryan chuckled at the truth of that statement. "My Uncle Charlie could have picked an argument with a lamppost if he'd had one too many," she admitted, shaking her head at the memory.

"Ooh," Jamie murmured, very sorry to hear that Maeve had been married to a difficult man.

"It wasn't that bad until Michael was diagnosed with AIDS," she recalled. "He drank a lot, but he didn't seem like a mean drunk until then. The fact that they found out Michael was gay at the same time didn't help matters much. As Michael got worse, so did his dad's drinking, until one night about six months before Michael died, Charlie came home drunk and threw Maeve against a wall, nearly fracturing her skull. She spent the night in the hospital and when she came home, Charlie was gone."

Jamie was absolutely appalled. Maeve Driscoll was one of the kindest, gentlest women she had ever met, and it was unthinkable that her own husband would wish to cause her harm. The shock clearly showed on her face and Ryan nodded slowly. "Luckily for him, it was the first time he had ever physically harmed her. I can't think what Da and my uncles would have done to him if he had ever touched her again."

"So what happened?" Jamie looked like she was about to cry, and Ryan regretted answering her original question in so much detail, but she was in too far to drop it now.

"His guilt, and probably his fear, over the incident overwhelmed him. He found a tiny apartment in Bernal Heights and lived apart from his family. They saw him often, but he refused to attend family functions. As his health failed, Maeve tried to convince him to return to the home, but he steadfastly refused, insisting that he had lost the right to live in his own home."

"Well, at least he had the good sense to stay away," Jamie mused.

"I guess," Ryan said slowly. "But I think it was a way to get extra attention too. Poor Aunt Maeve had to drag herself over to his apartment two and three times a day to take care of him during his last years. It would have been far preferable for her to have him back home, but you could never tell Charlie Driscoll a thing."

"When did he die?" Jamie asked, assuming it was long ago.

"Just two years ago," Ryan revealed. "Liver failure."

"Wow." Jamie lay back on the bed, considering the enormous amount of pain Maeve had experienced through the years. "She sure deserves some happiness now," she agreed. "And if her O'Flaherty is anything like mine, she's in for a boatload."

Jamie couldn't stop ruminating about the situation, and a few minutes later she was lying on the bed, staring at the ceiling. "Hey, honey?" she asked absently.

"Yeshhh?" Ryan replied with a mouthful of toothpaste.

"Would it be totally out of the question for me to buy a house over here and let your father and Maeve live in it until we came back?"

Ryan ducked back into the bath and rinsed her mouth. She strolled out of the room with a contemplative look. "I can't imagine that they would agree to that. Even though it's terribly thoughtful of you," she said as she climbed up onto the bed. They were both in their normal bedtime attire of nothing at all, with Jamie resting on top of the comforter, lying on her side with her head supported by her open palm. Ryan imitated her posture as she settled down just inches away. "I know he would want to pay the mortgage if they lived in the house. And there is just no way he could afford that. I'm not sure how much he makes, but I think it's around seventy thousand dollars. Maeve lives on Uncle Charlie's Social Security and his pension. I'm guessing she gets by on about thirty thousand dollars. That's clearly not enough for an eight- or nine-hundred-thousand-dollar home."

"Is that what houses around here cost?" Jamie was astounded at the estimate. She knew that real estate prices were outrageous, but some of the homes in the neighborhood looked like they were less than fifteen hundred square feet.

"That's what a house smaller than this on a marginal street costs. And the prices are going up so fast that it's ridiculous. What we really need is at least one large house with a big living room or a yard for all of our parties. When we all start having kids, it's going to be impossible. And being together is one of the things that keeps us close."

"We've got to put our heads together and help them find a way to be together, Ryan. They've been so supportive of us, we owe them that."

"We will, baby," she agreed.

Jamie lifted her hand and began to play with Ryan's hair, moving up until she was scratching her scalp. "I didn't have a chance to tell you who I played golf with this afternoon," she said.

"Who?" Ryan's lazy, low voice betrayed her desire to get to sleep, and Jamie smiled at her half-closed eyes.

"Mia and her father," she said.

The blue eyes opened fully. "Really? Was she just home for the weekend?"

"Yep. The little devil surprised me. That's her favorite thing to do, you know."

Ryan smiled and asked, "Why do you think everyone in your life tries to tease you?"

"Mmm … maybe because I'm such a sucker?" she posited, a fond smile on her face.

"Just checking," Ryan murmured, rolling onto her back to provide a different surface for the head rub. "I want to make sure you're self-aware."

The pinch she delivered caused Ryan's eyes to pop wide open. "Yow! That was a sharp one!"

"You've heard of the sucker punch? … Well, that was the sucker pinch, and there's plenty more where that came from, Tiger."

"Duly noted," Ryan smiled, rubbing her side dramatically. "Did you have a good time today?"

"Yeah …" Jamie hesitated, still mulling over Mia's advice. "I gave her a ride to the airport, and we caught up on everything that's happened since I saw her in Santa Monica."

Ryan grabbed a pillow and placed it over her face, moaning loudly into the surface. "Does she know absolutely everything about our sex life now?"

Jamie pulled the pillow away from Ryan's face and said with sincerity, "I didn't tell her any details today, babe, and if it bothers you I promise that I never will."

Ryan shook her head and shared a small story. "I got my first computer not long after I came out. AOL was just getting popular, and I found some chat rooms for lesbians. I was on that darned thing every night! That's actually part of the reason my grades were so bad that first semester. I was so taken with everything that was happening to me and the overpowering feelings that came with coming out, I just had to talk to people. It doesn't bother or surprise me that you need to talk about the things that are going on, honey. Have at it."

Jamie took the pillow from Ryan and placed it under her own head. "You know, I think part of the reason I want to tell her things is because I've never really had anything to tell."

"Huh?"

"Mia's always been really frank when she tells me about her life, but I've never had much to tell. I'm kinda proud of myself for finally being able to tell her things that surprise her," she admitted with a slightly embarrassed smile.

"We've just begun to explore each other," Ryan murmured, tracing Jamie's features with the tip of her finger. "You two will be exchanging naughty little stories for years to come."

Jamie laughed at her teasing tone. "I guess that alone is reason enough to keep making love to you." She saucily stuck her tongue out, just barely managing to pull it back into her mouth before it was grabbed by Ryan's lightning quick hands.

"You sounded a little unsure when I asked if you had a good time, babe. Is everything okay?"

"Yeah," she said lazily, stretching languidly as she spoke. "I told her I was going to tell my parents about us, and she really thinks I should wait."

"Uh-huh," Ryan said, trying to keep her voice neutral.

"Come on, Ryan, I know you have an opinion. What do you think I should do?"

"Well," she mused, "neither your grandfather nor Mia seems to think you should do it just yet. They both know your parents and you pretty well. So I'd have to defer to their opinion." Ryan personally thought that it was far too early for Jamie to break the news, but she didn't want to bear the responsibility for encouraging her to wait.

"I just hate to hide, baby!"

"Why don't you do this in a few steps, babe? Tell them I've moved in with you. You've told me yourself that you think they'll like me if they get to know me as your friend first. We could have them over for dinner, or go down to their house a few times this summer. You could spend some time making sure you have a plan and getting feedback from your therapist, and when you're really comfortable you can tell them."

"I guess that would work," she said glumly. "I'm just afraid that Daddy will expect you to start paying rent if I tell him that you're taking Cassie's place as my roommate."

"I want to pay rent," Ryan said in a soft but serious voice. "I talked to Da about it, and he made me see it's best for all of us if we do this aboveboard."

"Honey, you can't afford to pay Cassie's share! If you don't work this year, you'll be broke in no time."

Now Ryan looked uncertain of her decision. "Uhm ... how much did she pay?"

"A thousand a month," Jamie said, rolling her eyes a bit.

"A thou ... thou ... thousand a month?" Ryan's mouth gaped open as she pictured her savings flying from her account. "Did that cover food too?"

Jamie shook her head. "Just rent, baby. With her share of the utilities, Maria Los, and some food, she usually paid about fifteen hundred dollars a month."

"Wow." Ryan stared up at the ceiling, mulling over this unsettling development. "I could handle that, but then I wouldn't have enough to pay for grad school," she admitted. "I've got about thirty thousand dollars total, and fifteen hundred dollars a month would knock that down to twelve thousand dollars by next June." Her sense of humor returned as she suggested, "Could I pay less if I kept my stuff in the garage and we took showers together?"

Jamie patted her cheek and insisted, "I don't want you to pay anything, babe. My father doesn't need your money—you do."

"Cassie paid him? I assumed she would pay you."

"No, she paid him for the rent, and she paid me for the incidentals." She was deep in thought for a few minutes, finally coming up with an idea that seemed like it might work. "How about this? You want to do the grocery shopping and things like that. I'll make a deposit into your account, and you can handle our household expenses. I can make it out to cash so your name isn't even on it. That way you can pay my father every month out of your own account. He won't be the wiser, and it'll look like everything is going along the same way it did when Cassie was here."

Ryan pursed her lips and tried to think of a reason to decline the offer. After a few minutes of contemplation she had to agree that it was the only way to convince Jim she was a roommate without depleting her savings. She wasn't happy with the arrangement, and she knew it was the absolute moral equivalent of a lie, but she nodded her agreement. "Only one problem, sparky," she smirked. "I don't have a checking account."

Jamie's eyes opened wide and she actually had to struggle to contain her shock. She had opened her first checking account the same day she got her driver's license and it amazed her that Ryan could have made it to nearly twenty-four without one. She patted her lover's cheek and promised, "That will change tomorrow, Tiger."

Chapter Ten

"**M**mm, that feels nice," Jamie murmured as Ryan slid back into bed behind her. "Hey!" she said as she shot straight up, "are you home already? It seems like you just left."

Ryan gave her a gentle smile as she checked her watch. "I've been gone for over three hours, sweetness."

"How did it go?" she asked excitedly. "Were the other girls nice to you?"

Ryan's mouth quirked into a grin as she related, "I didn't actually meet everyone. Six in the morning isn't the best time to get to know people. But Coach introduced me and I'm sure I can meet everyone by the end of the week. I ran by myself today but I think I'll try to be a little more social the rest of the week."

"So what did you think of your teammates?"

"They all seemed to be able to run five miles," she said as she gave a little shoulder shrug. "You know how I am when I run, baby. I just focus on my breathing. It's going to be hard for me to pay attention to my teammates, but I think I need to do it just to feel part of the team."

Jamie's mouth turned into a pout as she admitted, "I thought you'd be able to describe everyone and tell me what you thought. I'm disappointed. Did you at least meet Jordan?"

Ryan gave a slightly embarrassed laugh. "I met her all right. Then I spent almost ten miles staring at her back. She's fast!"

"Ooh … faster than you, huh, Tiger?"

"I wasn't prepared," Ryan scoffed. "I was just trying to get comfortable." Jamie loved the fact that Ryan couldn't admit that another athlete could beat her at anything. It was part of the confidence that she found particularly sexy.

Turning the conversation away from any possible weakness she might have, Ryan started to nuzzle her partner's neck. Turning quickly she sneezed violently after her nose was tickled by the flyaway strands of Jamie's hair.

"I need a haircut," Jamie needlessly admitted as she ruffled the long bangs that hung loosely in her eyes.

"It is getting a little long," Ryan agreed as she leaned back in to nuzzle again. "I have to push it out of the way to kiss my favorite place."

"Oh, now that's your favorite place?" she teased with a wide smile as she turned around and slid her arms around her lover's waist. "Last night it was the small of my back. If I'm not mistaken, the back of my knees was the winner on Saturday. Come to think of it, I seem to remember that you were very fond of my earlobes on Friday ..."

Ryan opened her blue eyes very wide as her face broke into a big grin. She shrugged her broad shoulders and said, "I have lots of favorite spots. But the back of your neck is my favorite of all the backs of necks I've ever tasted."

"I think I understand," she said as she hugged her tightly. "I couldn't pick one place on you that I love the most, either. Hey, if I can get an appointment do you want to go with me? I know I said you couldn't cut yours, but out of humanitarian concerns I have reconsidered."

"Really? Why is that?"

"After seeing how hot you got when you were working out for the various teams, I decided that it was inhumane to keep your hair that long. I think you could take off four or five inches and still have it look the same."

"So, is that your biggest concern? You want it to look the same?"

"Partly, but I still think my biggest requirement is that I can grab it and run my fingers through it when we make love. There's nothing I like better than to have you moving over me with that sexy hair tickling my breasts."

"You, my dear, are sounding more like a lesbian every day," she said as she tweaked her nose.

"Nope. I'm still not ready to jump into the pool. I think I'm a Ryanian, or a Ryanaholic, or a Ryanaphile."

"I kinda like Ryanaphile. It's got a nice ring to it."

"I don't believe you answered my question, my sweet," Jamie reminded her as she nuzzled her neck. "Do you want to go if we can get appointments?"

"Sure. I just need to be at work by noon. Can we manage that?"

"I'll do my best," she promised as she crawled out of bed in search of her cell phone.

An hour later they were entering the cozy confines of Giancarlo. Jamie had originally found the shop when she decided to cut her long hair during her freshman year. Giancarlo was the owner and he was a genuine delight. Terribly gay and rather authoritarian, he was also playful, impetuous, and generous to a fault, and Jamie adored him. He was about thirty-five or so, and Ryan immediately noticed his stylish dress. A black silk T-shirt and elegantly cut pleated black pants draped tastefully over his muscular body. He was very attractive, with thick jet black hair that had just a hint of curl to it, brushing his collar in the back. His dark brown eyes were framed by long black eyelashes, and his eyes conveyed every emotion that he felt. When they walked in, he looked up from the head he was cutting and called out, "Cara mia! I've missed you!"

Jamie smiled and waved and took Ryan over to have a seat while they waited. She decided that Ryan should go first in case it took a long time, then went to the receptionist to check on the schedule. "When is Carlo's next appointment?"

"You're his last two until after lunch. It's slow in June with most of the students gone for the summer."

"Great. We might take extra long today."

When he was finished, he waved Jamie over with a flourish. They kissed dramatically on both cheeks and chatted away in Italian for several minutes. Ryan stood openmouthed as she took in this new piece of information about her lover. Jamie noticed her shock and said something to Giancarlo that made him howl. As he was doubling over with laughter, Jamie turned to her lover and just winked. She pushed Ryan down into the chair and continued her conversation in Italian. After a moment, Ryan had had enough. "Hey, don't I even get introduced?"

"Of course, sweetheart," she said as she bent down to kiss Ryan on the cheek. "I was just updating Carlo on my lifestyle change. He's very impressed, aren't you, Carlo?"

"Yes, yes," he said in a nearly incomprehensibly accented voice. "I always knew that Jamie had romance in her soul. I think you help her bring that out, no?"

Ryan blushed furiously as her companions laughed at her embarrassment. Jamie stood behind the chair and spoke in English for Ryan's benefit. "You can't take too much off, Carlo, but she's very active and her head gets terribly hot. What do you suggest?"

He walked around Ryan, deep in thought. He lifted her chin with his fingers and brushed the hair off her forehead, staring intently at her face the entire time. Then he grabbed it into a ponytail and pulled it away from her face and studied her facial structure without interference from her hair, commenting to Jamie in Italian throughout the entire inspection. Occasionally she would agree with some point and would touch Ryan's face or her neck. Sporadic bouts of laughter made Ryan feel that she was the butt of some joke, but she knew that even if the humor might concern her, it wouldn't be malicious.

After Giancarlo made one suggestion, Jamie looked at him in horror. "No, no, no!" she cried. She looked down at Ryan and explained, "He has one client who has hair as long as yours. She hates to be hot, so he shaves her head from just above her ears on down. When she leaves it down it looks perfectly normal. But when she pulls it up in a ponytail, she's nice and cool."

"Hmmm," Ryan said. "That sounds like it might work."

Jamie leaned down and put her face right in front of Ryan's. "No, baby. That's not going to happen."

Giancarlo laughed at this interchange and continued to debate, in Italian, with Jamie, their discussion getting more and more heated. Finally, he stormed off to get a bottle of Levissima while Jamie explained the problem. "He says that your face is too beautiful to hide behind all of this hair. He insists I must allow your chiseled features to receive the acclaim they deserve. He says it's like putting a coat on the Venus de Milo," she said, shaking her head with a laugh.

Ryan surveyed her face in the mirror. "I think he has a point," she mused as she swiveled in her seat.

Jamie shot her a disbelieving glance and was reassured when Ryan broke into a smile. "Can't he just take a few inches off? I could go to Supercuts and be done in three minutes."

Jamie leaned over and whispered, "If you let him hear you say that, we'll be banished!"

Moments later Giancarlo returned. He looked rather depressed as he picked up Ryan's long tresses and lethargically pulled them from her face again. He shook his head sadly as his fingers delicately traced her high cheekbones and her strong jaw. "So sad," he muttered.

Finally, Jamie played her trump card. "Giancarlo, how long is Pietro's hair?" she asked innocently. Pietro was Carlo's much younger, incredibly good-looking partner. He pursed his lips and gave a small shrug as he indicated that his lover's hair was about two inches shorter than Ryan's. "He has incredible bone structure also. Why not cut his hair short?"

Fire glowed in his dark eyes as he whirled around to stare at Jamie. "Never!" he nearly shouted. "His hair is … it is …" he trailed off as he tried to make his point with wild gesticulations of his hands. Immediately his expression softened and he threw his arms around Jamie. "I see! I see! It is for the love that you need the hair. Why didn't you say so, cara mia? For love—I understand!"

By the time Giancarlo was ready to proceed, all of the other stylists had gone to lunch. The front door was locked and they were alone in the small shop. Most salons such as this would never close during the middle of the day, but Giancarlo marched to his own drummer. He needed at least a two-hour lunch to relax and spend time with Pietro. Jamie had learned long ago not to rush Carlo or accept the first appointment after lunch. He could be twenty minutes late, or they might have had a fight—either way, you didn't want him to be angry with scissors in his hand.

After he had washed Ryan's hair with some fabulous-smelling herbal shampoo, he finally began to cut. After fifteen minutes he had barely removed two inches. Now the dark hair just reached the bottoms of her scapulas, but there was little real difference from her previous length. He and Jamie both walked around Ryan slowly, assessing the change. Pursed lips and sharp headshakes indicated that more must come off. Another fifteen minutes saw another two inches fall to the floor. The same process was repeated until they were both satisfied. Ryan was surprised that Jamie had let him take so much off, but she was very pleased with the look. Now her dark tresses fell only an inch or two below her shoulders.

Carlo rubbed some great-smelling product into her hair and pulled out his blow dryer. When he was done, the stylish cut looked absolutely fantastic. Her hair shone brightly due to the conditioner, and it bounced around her shoulders when she walked, which she was forced to do several times so that both of her critics were sure they were satisfied. To Jamie's surprise the normally straight hair had a bit of curl to it at this new length, and it curled under attractively with just the turn of a round brush as it was blown dry. Ryan could still gather it up in a ponytail, and when it was up, it would be off her neck completely.

"Okay, sit back down," he said to Ryan. "Jamie must perform the final test."

He said something to her in Italian and she roared with laughter, but she did as he asked. She climbed up onto Ryan's lap and leaned in for a deep kiss as she slid her fingers through her shorter tresses. She ruffled her fingers through her hair repeatedly as she pulled away and proclaimed, "Magnifico!"

Giancarlo gave them both a courtly bow and a very big smile. "I am inspired by love!"

It was nearly twelve-thirty and very clear that Jamie couldn't get her haircut as well as make it to the golf course, so she opted for the decadent choice. "Carlo, can I buy you lunch?" she asked.

"Si," he replied. "Pietro is at the beach today, working on his tan. I am alone for dinner. Let me cut your hair, then we will be off."

She tossed the keys to Ryan and said, "Go on to work, honey. I'll take a cab back if we finish while you're still at work. If not, I'll page you and you can come get me, okay?"

"Sure," Ryan said as she bent down to kiss her. She turned to Giancarlo and extended her hand, but he wrapped his arms around her in a firm hug and then kissed both of her cheeks. She looked a little shy, but she gingerly returned a kiss to one of his cheeks.

"She is so beautiful and so strong," he said as he ran his hands down her arms. He made another joke in Italian that had Jamie gasping for air. Ryan just waved and walked out the door, hearing their laughter as she started down the street.

"The rich are different than us," she grumbled as she hopped in the car.

Later that night Ryan was getting ready for bed when she commented, "We didn't get anywhere near a bank today, babe."

"I know, hon," Jamie called from her room. "We'll get there sometime this week. The days just get away from us, don't they?"

"Sure do," Ryan agreed. Stepping into the bath, she noticed some of the shampoo and conditioner from that afternoon lying on the counter. "Did you buy this for me?" she asked with a delighted grin as she came out of the bathroom holding one of the bottles aloft.

"Yeah. It made your hair shine so nice and smell so good, I couldn't resist."

"What did today's little escapade set you back?" she asked as she went back into the bathroom.

"Umm, it was more than Supercuts," she said weakly.

"That bad, huh?"

"Well, honey, we took up the space of three clients. I had to tip him really well for that."

"And you had to buy him lunch?"

"No, I wanted to buy him lunch. I really like Carlo and I wanted to tell him more about you. He knows all the best restaurants and I had a fabulous meal. What's wrong with that?"

"Nothing is wrong with it, baby," she said as she sat down on the edge of the bed. "It's just that sometimes I feel really different from you. Do you know what I mean?"

"Not really," she admitted, scooting over to sit close to her partner.

"Like the fact that you can just start speaking Italian without an accent. Were you in Italy so much that you just picked it up?"

Jamie shook her head. "No, I had an Italian tutor when I was little. Mother speaks Italian too, but she didn't learn until she was older and she has an accent. She was determined that I would speak like a native, so she hired a tutor for me when I was about three. I studied until I was in high school. It was kind of neat to be able to take Italian in high school and have some easy A's," she said, remembering her difficult course load in high school.

Ryan nodded her head up and down a few times. "That's exactly what I mean. Your money lets you do things that I couldn't even begin to fathom. Granted, I've been to Europe at least fifteen times, but I stayed with relatives and we had to save all year long just to cover the airfare."

"Honey, I know you didn't grow up with money, but what bothered you today?"

"I don't know," she said as she flopped down on the bed. "It bothered me a little that you could speak Italian and I didn't even know that you could do that. I guess I just felt like you were taking your uncultured servant girl into town to have her hair cut. I couldn't understand a thing you said to each other. You were laughing the whole time, and I assume some of it was at my expense. I didn't even get a vote on how my own hair was to be cut."

"Oh Ryan, I'm so sorry," she said, suddenly seeing the experience through Ryan's eyes. "I never meant to hurt your feelings or make you feel left out. I guess I just got carried away with Carlo." She leaned over so that they were face to face. "I'm truly sorry, honey. That was terribly insensitive of me. Do you hate your new haircut?" she asked as she ran her fingers through the shiny tresses.

"No, I love it. I might not have gone this short, but I'm really glad he did. I worked out after my client and it felt so much better, it was amazing. I haven't had my hair this short since I was little, so I had no idea how much better it would feel."

"So are you more upset about feeling left out?"

"Maybe. I really didn't like that you were speaking a language that I couldn't understand. It just made me feel kind of stupid and coarse."

"I'm truly sorry, Ryan. I should have at least translated for you. That was really rude of me."

"It's okay," she said with a small smile. "I'll get over it."

"No, it's not okay. You don't have to go back there if you don't want to. We can find some other place to keep you trimmed."

Now Ryan felt like she had made too big a deal out of the incident. She tried to back off from her harsh assessment of the day. "No, I really like the way he cut it. But I would like it if you'd speak English."

"I'm not sure that would be an improvement," Jamie mused. "I find him very easy to understand in Italian, but I think he's incomprehensible in English. You might have to translate for me!"

"What the heck were you laughing about the whole time?" she asked, still a little cross at being left in the dark.

"Most of the jokes don't translate well," she admitted. "He makes a lot of plays on words that are very funny in Italian because of the sounds of the words. But the English words don't make the same sound, so there's no joke." She ran her hand along Ryan's taut belly as she recalled one little joke. "Remember when he was talking about how beautiful and strong you were?"

"Yeah," she said, her voice a little higher than normal from the teasing touch playing across her tummy.

"He said something about you being carved out of stone, but having breasts and hips made from goose down. Not at all funny in English, but the words themselves are funny in Italian."

"That really isn't funny," she admitted. Giving in to her insecurity, she asked, "Was he making fun of me at all?"

"No!" Jamie sat up abruptly. "I would never allow that, Ryan! I'm shocked that you would even think that!"

"Well, you were laughing so much, I just felt really left out. I couldn't help but feel self-conscious."

"He was making jokes about your body, but they were all very complimentary. He said he bet I got lost in your big strong arms, and he guessed that a strong woman like you could make love all night long." She began to run her fingers up the firm belly again. "I didn't feel the need to correct him," she said with a sultry laugh. "Then he said if he could have you in bed he might not even miss a penis."

Ryan blushed a little as Jamie kept rubbing her belly. "Maybe it was best that I couldn't understand him," she admitted a little weakly. "I would have been mortified."

"He asked me if I grabbed your hair and rode you like a pony," she whispered into Ryan's still-pink ear.

"What did you say?" she gulped.

"I said, 'Thanks for the suggestion'," she breathed as she slowly turned her over onto her belly and slid across her firm butt until she was straddling her, then laced her fingers through her hair and began to grind against her in a sensual rhythm.

"Maybe he's not such a bad guy," Ryan choked out with her last lucid thought.

Their nighttime frolics had kept Ryan up far too late for her to even think of getting up to run on Tuesday morning. She cracked open one reluctant eye and snapped it shut tightly against the glare of the fully risen sun. As usual, Jamie detected her movement and snuggled up even tighter against her body. "Go 'way," the grumpy blonde growled at the sun, pulling the pale blue sheet over her face.

Ryan's desires matched her partner's perfectly, and she clambered to her feet and crossed the room to pull the window shade down, closing the marine blue curtains just for good measure. "And stay out," she grumbled before falling heavily onto the bed and snaking her long arm out to pull Jamie close. "Are we alone today?" she asked through a massive yawn.

"All day," Jamie murmured as she rolled over to face her partner. She burrowed her head against the junction of Ryan's arm and shoulder until she had created a comfortable pillow for herself, and was asleep before Ryan could express her contentment with that state of affairs.

Jamie was just about to indulge in her morning ritual when Ryan came bounding down the stairs. She was bristling with energy after her nine-hour rest, and she quickly wore out her welcome badgering her partner. "Wanna go to the gym with me?"

"No."

"Bike ride?"

"No."

"Wanna go down to the marina and rent kayaks?"

A much longer pause before the same answer was given. "No ... are you nuts?"

"I feel good!" she proclaimed, stretching her long arms straight out from the shoulders. "It's a beautiful day, I'm well rested, nothing hurts, nothing's broken, I have the most wonderful woman in the world sitting just a few feet from me. How can I not be happy?"

Jamie gave her an aggrieved smile and said, "Could I have just a few minutes to catch up with you, sport? I promise I'll get there if I can have my coffee and eat my toast."

"Sure, love." Ryan leaned over and kissed her grumpy partner on the head. "I'll do better than that. I'll go over to the weight room and work out with some of the people from the team. They get together on Tuesday and Thursday mornings for an informal session."

Jamie offered a guilty smile to her partner. "Am I pushing you away, honey? I promise I'll be chipper soon."

"Not at all," Ryan assured her. "This'll give me a chance to meet some of the guys. You take it easy, and wake up as slowly as you need. Don't give it another thought. I know I can be a little much to take in the morning."

Jamie grasped the hem of her T-shirt and pulled her close. Her hands climbed up the shirt, pulling Ryan toward her with each handhold. "You were a little much to take last night, Tiger," she whispered seductively. "But I'm not complaining. I just have to build up my stamina." A kiss filled with gratitude underscored her words, and she sent Ryan off with a playful swat on the seat. "Go work off some energy, love. I'll be waiting for you with open arms."

"I bet no one else in the weight room will have as much motivation to finish as I do!" And with that, she was off, scampering down the front stairs with glee.

"Hi, babe!" Jamie was in very bright spirits when Ryan came home two hours later. Regrettably, she was already in her golf clothes and had her car keys in her hand. "I talked to Scott and he gave me the name of another woman who's trying out for the golf team. We're gonna go play Tilden this afternoon, but I've gotta go if we're gonna make our tee time."

"That's okay," Ryan said agreeably. She was a little disappointed, but she knew this was important to Jamie so she focused on being supportive. "I know this means a lot to you, so you go play. I should really catch up with my e-mail anyway. I haven't checked it in so long, it's a shame."

"Thanks, babe," Jamie said, standing on her tiptoes for a kiss. "I'll be home as soon as I can, but Tilden takes forever to get around. Don't expect me before six, okay?"

"Fine. Let's just order in since it's not clear when you'll be home."

"It's a deal. Wish me luck."

Ryan watched her trot down the stairs, a slow smile crossing her face as she watched her muscular body move down the front path. *Well, I'm ready*, she thought with a smirk at her rambunctious libido.

She was changing into her work clothes when her pager went off. Checking the number, she failed to recognize it and decided it was one of the many wrong numbers she received. After she finished dressing she went down to the living room to return the call. The area code was from the Peninsula, and she was certain that she didn't know anyone down there, but she dutifully punched in the eleven digits. The phone was answered on the second ring by a woman's soft voice. "Hello?"

"Hi, this is Ryan O'Flaherty. Did you page me?"

There was a slight pause as the voice grew even softer. "Hello, Ryan."

All the blood drained out of Ryan's face and she found herself blindly grasping for a chair to support her rubbery legs. Seconds passed as she tried to collect herself enough to answer. After what seemed like a lifetime, she was finally able to rasp out, "Hello, Sara."

"Is it all right to call you, Ryan?" The mere sound of her melodious soprano voice carried Ryan back to her youth, and she was buffeted by images of her best friend and first love.

"Of course it's all right," Ryan replied, surprised at the strength of her own voice.

"I know I'm six years too late, and I won't blame you if you tell me to go to hell, but I'm calling to apologize."

"Apologize?" Ryan was too stunned to do much more than parrot Sara's statement. She knew she sounded slow-witted, but she couldn't make her mouth behave.

"Yes … I want to apologize. My mother told me a little bit of what you said on Sunday, and I can't let another day pass without owning up to how I wronged you."

"Wronged me," Ryan repeated dully, simultaneously slapping herself in the head for her inability to form a cogent thought.

"Ryan," Sara soothed in the voice that had calmed her fears and bolstered her ego for so many years, "let me come over and talk to you in person."

"In person?" Her eyes grew wide and she actually pulled the phone away from her ear to stare at it for a moment. "You want to come over?"

"If you'll let me," she said. "I deserve to be kicked in the teeth, but if you'll let me, I'd love to apologize in person."

Despite her rapidly beating heart and weak knees, Ryan had to smile at her former friend's self-deprecating comments. "I would never be cruel to you, Sara. I couldn't be," she said softly. "I loved you too much to hurt you."

She heard her former friend draw in a deep breath and thought she could detect her struggling with her composure. "I should have known you'd be too generous to be cruel to me, but it's what I deserve, nonetheless. Mother says you're living in Berkeley now. I can be there in an hour if you'll let me. I promise I won't take much of your time."

Ryan closed her eyes and considered the situation. She had time this afternoon, but how would Jamie feel about having this woman in her home? She decided to follow Jamie's clear instructions and treat the place as though it were her own. If Sara had called her when she was home, she had no doubt that she would have invited her over. Her genuine compassion and overwhelming curiosity took over, and she heard herself answer, "I'm home after three-thirty today. Could you make it then?"

"I'll be there," she said firmly, refusing directions after Ryan told her the address. "I know Berkeley well," leaving unspoken the fact that she had attended school there—without her best friend.

It took several minutes for Ryan to feel confident enough of her body's responses to risk standing. She actually felt too confused to ride her motorcycle, but she was now running late and felt that she had no choice. Luckily, she was able to guide the bike to the gym without incident, and she spent the next three hours struggling with her concentration. She knew that she had not been her usual self, but the clients didn't seem to notice, or perhaps they were just too polite to mention it. Nonetheless, when three o'clock rolled around, she practically ran from the gym to return home.

She got home in time to change, and she shimmied into a clean, faded pair of 501s and a red cotton tank top. The day was warm and she was quite overheated from the stress of worrying about the meeting. As she brushed her teeth, she took one final look in the mirror. "I sure don't look seventeen anymore," she thought wryly, as she walked downstairs to get a cold drink.

She had just finished gulping down a liter of Gatorade when she heard a light knock on the front door. Padding over in her bare feet, she took a deep breath and opened the door. Her mouth dropped in shock when she gazed at the woman on her doorstep. Sara had matured from a rather gangly, but attractive, girl into a truly lovely woman. Even though Ryan would have recognized her anywhere, in a way she looked completely and utterly different, which threw Ryan for a loop.

Her glossy chestnut brown hair skimmed the tops of her shoulders. It was parted on the side and she had a few long bangs that trailed above her chocolate brown eyes. She had grown taller, and now stood five foot eight or five foot nine, but still evidenced a delicate bone structure that carried no more than 125 pounds. Even though she was thin, thinner than Ryan remembered, she looked healthy and fit. As Ryan's eyes trailed down her body, she noticed distinct muscle definition on her bare arms, and saw that she still carried the posture and confident attitude of the athlete that she used to be, and possibly still was.

A sleeveless cotton T-shirt, in a shade of brown that exactly matched her eyes, topped slim-fitting white denim jeans that hugged her long legs, the cut of the jeans accentuating her lithe body as well as her height.

After they stared at each other for a long moment, Ryan rediscovered her manners and moved away from the entryway so that Sara could enter. She stood rather awkwardly, waiting for Ryan to indicate whether or not she should sit, but Ryan was feeling much more like the child Sara had met in peewee soccer than the woman she had become. She fidgeted and shifted from one foot to the other until Sara reached out with her delicate hand and placed it on Ryan's shoulder. "I'm very nervous," she said softly. "It's been so long." That simple statement broke the dam that Ryan had so carefully constructed around the wound that Sara had seared into her soul. Hot tears began to trail down her cheeks, and she began to shake from the emotion she was trying to hold inside.

Sara was swept right along with her, and before she knew it she had wrapped her arms around Ryan's waist and was hanging on for dear life. They held each other through the worst of their tears, until Sara pulled back and asked, in the most winsome voice Ryan had ever heard, "When did you get so tall?" Her hands lifted to brush the wetness from Ryan's cheeks, and the gentleness of her touch caused another bout of tears to fall.

Sara took Ryan by the hand and led her to the love seat, sitting next to her and resuming their hug. Wave after wave of emotion passed through each woman; as soon as one would begin to calm, the other would once again fall apart. Back and forth, each comforted the other until they were both relatively composed. Ryan had pulled a box of tissues onto the love seat during one of her calmer moments, and now they both dried their eyes.

Neither made a move to separate, needing the comfort of the other to journey through their shared pain. Ryan drew in a ragged breath, a solitary tear slipping down her face. She had used the last of the tissues, and as she reached up to wipe the tear away with the back of her hand, Sara captured it with her thumb, brushing gently against Ryan's flushed skin.

They were face to face now, looking deeply into each other's eyes. Neither woman planned what happened next—neither would have believed it if they had been warned—but it seemed like the most natural thing in the world. Another tear fell from

Ryan's eyes, and Sara again captured it, but this time she kissed the tear from Ryan's cheek.

Ryan remained completely still, not sure what was happening, but powerless to stop it. Another gentle, whisper-soft kiss followed the first, then another, and another. Each touch lighter, softer, sweeter than the last, the velvety soft lips blazing an invisible path across Ryan's face. She paused for the barest of milliseconds, hovering just above Ryan's lips, then her head tilted just enough to allow her to reach the deep pink flesh.

Her lips were softer than Ryan remembered, her touch much more gentle than it had been in the re-creation of that moment that had played itself in Ryan's mind night after night for so long. As Sara's lips began to kiss away the years of pain, all conscious thought left Ryan's disoriented brain. All that she knew was that it had all been a mistake—a horrible, horrible mistake. Sara *had* loved her. Sara *had* wanted her. They *did* belong together. A low groan sprang from Ryan's chest as the truth of these statements finally hit her. *It was all a mistake! It'll be all right. We can finally … We? We?*

Ryan yanked her body from Sara's tender embrace and fought to regain her equilibrium. She rose on shaky legs and gasped out, "No! No! I Can't!"

Sara was completely and utterly stunned. She reached out for Ryan, trying to draw her back into her embrace, but the taller woman looked as though she had been hit with a jolt of electricity. "No!" she cried, backing up until she ran into the hall table. "I'm married!" she shouted, loud enough for passersby to hear.

"You're married?" Sara gasped out, feeling more confused than she had ever been in her life.

"Yes, I'm married," Ryan insisted. "And you're engaged!"

"Engaged! Ryan, what's wrong with you?" She was approaching her very slowly, much as one would a frightened animal. "How can I be engaged, I'm a lesbian! For that matter, how can you be married?"

"But your mother …" Ryan began, now feeling overwhelmingly confused herself. "She said …"

"Ryan," Sara soothed. "My mother believes what she wants to believe. She's convinced that my roommate is my boyfriend, and in her fantasy world she's certain that we're going to get married now that we've graduated."

Ryan sank onto the dark oak surface of the sturdy table. "You're a lesbian?" she asked softly.

"Yes. I am," Sara declared for one of the few times in her life.

"Your mother doesn't know?"

"Almost no one knows," she admitted, a slow blush traveling up her cheeks. "My roommate doesn't even know. None of my friends from school know." She looked up at Ryan with deep pain infusing her features. "Only the women I've had sex with know."

Ryan took a deep breath and ran her hands through her hair, surprising herself when she realized how short it was. She slowly massaged her temples, trying to lessen the nearly debilitating throbbing of her head. "I need something to drink before I pass out," she muttered, shuffling into the kitchen on autopilot.

She returned with two bottles of Gatorade and tossed one to Sara, unwilling to come close enough to hand it to her. "Can you explain the married thing?" Sara asked, after taking a healthy swig of her drink.

"It's to a woman, Sara. I haven't changed that much."

Despite the sense of loss she was feeling, Sara gave her a small smile, glad to see that Ryan's sense of humor had grown with her. "Tell me about her," she said, genuine interest reflected in her gaze.

A radiant smile lit Ryan's face, and Sara knew in that instant that the woman who now looked at her had given her heart to another.

"She's ... she's ... everything to me," she said simply, unable to put her feelings into words. "I love her completely, Sara, and I'll do anything and everything to safeguard our relationship." Her tone left little doubt where Ryan thought the threat to her marriage might lie.

"How long have you been together?" she asked, her curiosity getting the better of her pain.

"Technically, I guess I'd have to say a little over two weeks, but we've been exclusive since April."

"Were you with someone before this?" Ryan was far too attractive to be single for long, and Sara assumed she had been snatched up the moment she became available.

"No," Ryan said quietly. "Jamie's the first woman that I've loved since ... you."

"Do you mean to tell me that you've been available for the past six years, and it's only been three months since you've found someone?" Sara asked incredulously.

"Yeah, pretty much," Ryan admitted, startled by the irony of the situation.

As if on cue, a distinctive tread hit the front steps. Ryan took a deep breath and went to the door to intercept her partner. When she opened the door, Jamie was on the top step, and Ryan's eyes widened as she realized what her lover was going to do. She looked up at Ryan with a huge smile and shouted, "Catch me!" as she ran the remaining few feet and jumped into Ryan's arms.

Ryan's lightning quick reactions signaled her arms to grab her lover and hold on tight. But her legs didn't get the same message and she collapsed onto her back, sliding across the floor with Jamie still nestled in her arms. "Are you all right, baby?" Jamie asked with concern, as Ryan stared at her in shock.

Her slowly nodding head was the only answer that she could manage.

"Well, as long as I've got you on the floor, I think I'm going to take you right here," she growled, as she straddled her hips. She dipped her head and began to kiss Ryan with a day's worth of unexpressed passion.

For the second time in an hour, Ryan tried to fend off a woman's attentions. She finally put her hands around Jamie's waist and physically lifted her off of her hips in an amazing display of power. "Honey," she gasped out, "we've got company."

Jamie's face became stark white in the instant it took to register this statement. She slowly turned her head and met Sara's stunned gaze. "Oh, my God," she moaned as Ryan lowered her and she rolled off her hips. She got to her feet and held a hand down for Ryan to grasp. "I am so sorry for that little display," she said, her color returning. She strode over to the sofa and held out her hand, "I'm Jamie Evans."

Sara stood and extended her hand. "Pleased to meet you, Jamie. I'm Sara Andrews."

Jamie dropped her hand as if it were on fire. Her face slowly lost its smile as she turned to look at Ryan, startled to find her lover's lips scrunched up in a guilty-looking grimace. Ryan looked down at the ground for a moment, hoping that Jamie's eyes would leave her, but when she looked back up they were still burning into her with an incandescent intensity. Jamie took in a breath and said in an even voice, "I need something to drink. I'll be right back." As she walked towards the kitchen, over her shoulder she added, "Could you help me, Ryan?"

Ryan now gave Sara a shrug and took off after her lover. When she entered the kitchen, however, Jamie was nowhere to be found. Looking around, she saw that the back door was open. She peeked out the door and saw her partner pacing in a tight circle in the back yard. Before Ryan's foot hit the step Jamie glared up at her and asked in a strained voice, "What is she doing in my house?!"

Ryan bit her tongue to stop herself from coming back with a sharp retort. She walked down the stairs slowly, staring at the ground as she did so. "I thought it was my house too," Ryan said slowly. "She's here because I invited her."

Letting out a deep sigh, Jamie straightened her shoulders and said, "It is your house too, Ryan. I'm just so taken aback that I don't know what I'm saying." She took another deep breath and said, "Let's start again. How did it happen that Sara Andrews is a guest in our home?"

Ryan gave her a small smile and answered as best she could. "Her mother spoke with her sometime after we met in church last Sunday. Sara called me right after you left and asked if she could come over to apologize. I agreed, and she showed up a little while after I got back from the gym."

"Do you want her here?"

Jamie's penetrating gaze was still boring into Ryan, who fervently wished that it would ease off so she could collect her thoughts. "Yes. I do want her here. Are you okay with her being here?"

"If it's okay with you, it's okay with me," she said slowly, with her eyes closed, obviously trying to control her visceral reaction.

"Thank you, honey. I know this is hard for you, but I need for you to trust me on this," she said, holding her arms open for Jamie to fall into.

After she nuzzled against Ryan's chest for a few moments she pulled back and asked, "Is that perfume you're wearing?"

"Uhm … no, I'm not wearing any perfume," she said haltingly.

"Then why do you smell like perfume?" she asked as her eyes began to flicker with anger.

Ryan put her hands on her partner's shoulders and stared into her eyes. "Jamie, I'm asking you to trust me. I've had a really tough day, and I can't take any more emotional scenes. Please just let us get through this afternoon and I'll explain everything."

Jamie let out yet another heavy sigh as she stood to her full height and blinked her eyes slowly. "I have one question, Ryan. Do I have anything to worry about?"

The question was so simple, and Ryan knew in her heart that Jamie never had to worry about her fidelity. But she was certain that her partner would view the events of the afternoon in a very harsh light, and that knowledge caused her to hesitate.

A hesitation that was misinterpreted with disastrous results. A panoply of emotions crossed the smaller woman's face, each one driving a stake into Ryan's heart. "Let's get this over with," she said stoically as she started to walk back into the house.

"No!" Ryan grasped her shoulders and held her still, staring into her eyes as she summoned her confidence. "You have *nothing* to worry about, Jamie." The relief that flooded her partner's features nearly caused Ryan to lose her composure again, but she was truly out of tears. "I love you with all my heart, and I always will."

"I believe you." The confidence in her voice matched the look in her eyes, and Ryan thanked God for blessing her with such an extraordinary woman. Jamie extended her hand and Ryan grasped it as they walked back into the house, together.

Jamie remembered to snag a soda on the way back to the living room, just to give the impression that she really had been seeking a beverage. Sara was sitting right where they had left her, looking terribly uncomfortable. When she caught sight of them, she stood and addressed Jamie. "I know you'd probably rather have just about anyone else in your living room right now, but I just came to try to apologize to Ryan. If you want me to leave, I will."

"No ... no, I'm sorry for the way I reacted, Sara. It was just a shock." She reached out and took Sara's hand again, shaking it firmly. "I'm usually housebroken," she added with an abashed smile.

Ryan sat down on one of the upholstered chairs, and her partner perched right on its arm, hovering over her lover protectively. Ryan looked up at her and gave her an indulgent grin as she placed her hand on Jamie's thigh.

"What did I miss?" Jamie looked from one woman to the other, a bit unhappy to see guilty looks flash between them.

Ryan pointed to the pile of spent tissues on the table and said, "Mostly you missed an emotional meltdown. I think I'm at least a quart low," she added, taking a gulp of her Gatorade.

Now that Jamie looked more carefully at both women she could see that they had been crying. "Do you want me to leave you alone for a while?" she asked. "I know you've got a lot of things to talk about, and I don't want to interfere."

Ryan squeezed her knee and gave her a grateful smile, but she declined her offer. "I want you to stay, honey." She paused a bit and let her insecurities show for a second. "I need you to stay."

Jamie nodded, sliding her arm around Ryan's shoulders as she leaned over. "I'm here for you, Ryan," she said softly, just loud enough for her partner to hear.

"Well ..." Ryan addressed Sara, giving her an encouraging smile. "I think we're both cried out—let's start at the top."

Sara nodded and took in a breath, trying to form her chaotic thoughts into coherent sentences. "I suppose I need to go all the way back," she finally said. "I need to talk about what happened ... that night."

Ryan nodded her encouragement, rubbing Jamie's thigh as she said, "Jamie knows all about this, Sara. We don't have any secrets."

"Okay," she said, letting out a ragged breath. "I was a mess when we woke up the next morning, Ryan, as I'm sure you detected." Ryan gave a short nod, not wanting to interrupt. "A very large part of me wanted to lock the door and spend the rest of my life in your arms." A look of shock crossed Ryan's face and Jamie tightened her hold when she felt her partner tense. "I know I didn't give that impression, but it was true," she said softly. "But I was also so confused. I'd known you since you were seven years old, Ryan," she said plaintively. "I felt closer to you than anyone on earth—much more like a sister than just a friend."

Ryan considered that and had to agree that Sara had been as dear to her as her brothers were.

"I didn't know what it meant to have you touch me that way," she said softly. "Were we still friends? Was I a lesbian? It was just too much for me, and I needed to figure it out before I could face you again. I know, in retrospect, that I should have talked to you about it, but I didn't. I talked to my mother."

"Did you tell her everything?" Ryan asked softly, still remembering the look of pity on Mrs. Andrews's face when she told her that Sara no longer wanted to see her.

"Yes ... yes I did," she murmured, staring at the floor. "I thought she could help me sort things out. It took me a long time to understand that she just made it so much worse."

"What happened, Sara?" Jamie's voice floated past Ryan's ear, filled with so much compassion that Ryan was a bit startled.

"She convinced me that it had been a big mistake," Sara muttered, obviously angry with both herself and her mother. "She said that Ryan had acted really inappropriately with me, and she stressed that I wasn't like that." Thinking that Jamie had probably been taken in by her mother's delusions about a fiancé, she added, "I was, and I am, like that, Jamie."

Jamie nodded slightly, now even more disturbed by the perfume that still lingered on Ryan's body. As she felt her partner tense, it was Ryan's turn to comfort Jamie, squeezing her thigh gently.

"I honestly thought that if I could get away from Ryan, I could get away from these feelings." She dropped her head into her hands and mumbled, "Part of me still believes that."

"Is that why you've never tried to contact me?" Ryan's face was an unreadable mask, but Jamie knew her well enough to know that she was consciously trying to hide her hurt.

Sara nodded, her brown hair barely moving across her shoulders. "I didn't ... I don't ... want to be gay," she sighed.

Jamie gave her a look that was filled with empathy, having been through the same dilemma just a short while before. Sara straightened her shoulders and looked at Ryan once again. "I didn't come here to talk about myself. I want to know about you. Tell me what happened after ... the incident."

Ryan took a breath and decided to tell the unvarnished truth. "I went off the deep end," she admitted. "My father sent me to Ireland for the summer and by the time I got back, I had gotten it clear in my mind that I was a lesbian. But I was so ashamed of myself that I kept it secret from my family. I started to hang out on Castro and I got in with a much older crowd. I started drinking and having sex with a lot of strangers. It was the lowest point of my life," she said, looking up at Sara with sad blue eyes.

Jamie reached out and laid her hand over Ryan's. She slowly closed her fingers and held Ryan's hand in hers in a show of support.

Ryan gave her a slow smile and continued, "My first semester grades came and this was the first tangible sign that Da could use to get through to me. I had a C minus average that term and I thought he would die of shock."

"But Ryan, you were always a straight-A student! School was so easy for you!"

"I didn't do any homework, Sara. I didn't turn in papers or study for tests. Actually a C minus is pretty good considering how little I did. I honestly didn't care if I finished school at all at that point. I just wanted to drink and screw the pain away."

Sara gazed straight into her eyes and said, "I'm so sorry, Ryan. I can't say it enough, even though I know it doesn't change anything."

Ryan smiled gently and continued with her story. "Brendan finally got through to me. I honestly think he saved my life. He sat me down and wouldn't let me leave until I told him what was wrong. He was so supportive and soon afterward I told the other boys and Da and Aunt Maeve. They were all great about it, and I started to get back to my normal self. But none of the coaches that were recruiting me felt confident enough to waste a scholarship on me, especially after I was forced to quit every team. I still don't understand why I didn't make an attempt to get an academic scholarship to Cal or even Stanford, but I just didn't. Da thinks I was punishing myself, but in retrospect I think I was clinically depressed. The thought of going to Cal and not playing on the soccer team was just too painful, so I didn't even try to get a scholarship. I worked full-time for two years and then I enrolled at USF. I transferred to Cal last year, and now I'm on track to graduate this June."

"You worked full-time right out of high school?" she asked incredulously. "What kind of job can you get in San Francisco without a college degree?"

"I went to school to become a personal trainer," she said with a justifiable amount of pride. "I've done well with it, too. I still do it at a gym here in Berkeley."

Sara looked confused for a moment and asked, "Something just registered. Did you say you were forced off your teams? What do you mean by that?"

"Because the girls didn't want me on them anymore after they found out I was gay. I just didn't have the strength to fight anymore, so I quit."

"After all that had happened, why did you tell everyone?" she asked, clearly confused.

"I didn't tell a soul, Sara. You did."

Sara jumped up from her place on the sofa. She stood above Ryan, shaking from head to toe. "Ryan! I did no such thing! I never told anyone at school or any of my friends. I would never betray you like that!"

"Then how did they find out?" she asked, unsure if her friend was telling the truth.

"I swear I didn't tell one other soul, Ryan." Sara was shaking from a combination of shame and rage. "There's only one other person who knew. If you didn't tell, it had to be my mother."

Ryan looked as puzzled as Sara did angry. "But why?" she asked sadly. "Why would she do that to me?"

A cold fury settled on Sara's face and she vowed, "I don't know why, but I'm going to find out." She turned and strode toward the door, surprised when Ryan caught up to her before she got a hand on the doorknob.

"Don't." Ryan's tone was firm and Sara stopped completely, her shoulders sagging as she let the feelings in.

She turned and fell into Ryan's arms again, another round of tears on the way. Ryan shot a helpless glance at Jamie, who gave her an encouraging nod, now feeling somewhat satisfied that Sara's perfume clung to her partner because of Ryan's desire to comfort her.

"I'm sorry," Sara gasped. "I just … I'm just so damned sorry!"

"It's okay, Sara," Ryan soothed, guiding her back to the love seat. Sara dropped down rather gracelessly, wiping her eyes with her hands. Ryan dashed into the kitchen and brought her a fresh box of tissues and a Pepsi. "Are you still a Pepsi fan?" she asked softly, offering the drink.

A fresh round of tears met this small remembrance, and Sara reached out a shaking hand to take the can. After a few long sips she regained her composure and looked at both Ryan and Jamie with a good deal of embarrassment. "I know it must seem like I'm emotionally unstable, but I swear this is an anomaly for me."

"I can vouch for her, Jamie," Ryan said with a fond gaze in her friend's direction. "I've only seen her this way once before."

Sara gave her a puzzled glance and Ryan smiled back at her. "When Fluffy died," she reminded her, referring to Sara's beloved Himalayan cat that had passed away when she was in seventh grade.

A fond smile greeted this memory. "I think this is worse than that, Ryan," she said with a small laugh. "Although Fluffy was pretty special," she added for the record.

A fond, meaningful gaze passed between the two women, and Jamie realized with a stab of regret that these two would always have a bond that she would never be able to share. She fervently wished that it was she who had known the young Ryan, who had watched her mature into a young woman. She felt a sting of anger at Sara for letting the opportunity to love this extraordinary creature slip through her fingers, but she stopped short when she realized that if that had happened, Ryan surely wouldn't have been available to her. In a completely selfless musing she thought, *I would give her up if I could spare her the pain that Sara caused her. If I could turn back time, I swear I'd make Sara face the truth and love Ryan like she deserved to be loved.* But she knew that she couldn't change the past. All that she could do was help her lover get through the pain—and promise that she would never cause her similar sorrow.

"I know you want to confront your mother about all of this, but please don't do it while you're so upset. Give yourself some time to calm down first. Please."

Sara nodded, agreeing with Ryan's advice. "I don't relish the thought of bringing all of this up while I'm supposed to be studying for the bar exam anyway," she said with a shudder. "It's in less than a month!"

There was an uncomfortable silence that stretched on for a few minutes. Looking down at her partner, Jamie could see that Ryan was deep in thought. After a moment the pensive woman looked over at Sara and said, "Something doesn't seem right here."

Sara's brow furrowed and she cocked her head slightly, looking to Ryan to elaborate.

"If your mother intentionally spread the information about me, why would she tell you about seeing me in church? That just doesn't make any sense." One thing Jamie had learned long ago was that Ryan couldn't tolerate situations that didn't seem logical. Knowing Ryan, this lack of logic would bother her nearly as much as the betrayal.

Sara paused as she considered the question. It didn't make any sense, viewed from that perspective, and she had to admit that the inconsistency bothered her. "You're right," she said slowly, twirling a lock of hair around her index finger, in a gesture achingly familiar to Ryan. "When I think about it, though, she didn't tell me voluntarily."

"What do you mean?" Ryan asked.

"Well, I was at her house on Sunday. I chose not to go to Mass with her, and when she came back, she was acting so upset that it was obvious that something momentous had happened. She didn't want to tell me what it was, but she was so upset that she couldn't stop herself."

"What did she say?" Jamie asked, sitting on the edge of the chair.

"She said ..." Sara looked up to the ceiling, trying to remember the exact words. "She said that she'd seen Ryan in church. I must have looked as shocked as she did, because we hadn't really spoken your name since that horrible week."

Ryan didn't have to ask for clarification on which week that was. "Go on," she urged.

"I jumped in and started asking a million questions, but all she said was that you were living in Berkeley and were still in undergrad."

"She didn't tell you any of the details I told her?"

"No. She said that things had been tough for you, but that you seemed fine now."

"Why wouldn't she tell you about Jamie?" Ryan mused. "I would think she would at least mention her."

"I don't know," she muttered, "but I'm going to find out. For both of us."

"Hey," Ryan said, in a no-nonsense tone. "I don't need you to fight this battle for me. I'm perfectly able to go to your house and ask your mom directly. And I plan on doing just that." Her entire demeanor was resolute, and Jamie knew that her partner would get to the bottom of the story, one way or another.

"I know you can take care of yourself. You always could." The look Sara gave her old friend was filled with warmth, recalling the many escapades that Ryan had seamlessly extricated them both from.

"I'll get to the bottom of this, Sara. I'm the one that was harmed—I've got to be the one to figure it out. Besides, you've got your hands full right now. Studying for the bar must be a real grind."

She blew out a breath. "Yeah, it's hard, but once it's over I can relax for a couple of weeks."

"What are you doing after the bar exam?" Jamie asked, trying to keep up her end of the conversation.

"I'm going to work for a firm in the city," she said. "Morris and Foster."

Jamie's mouth dropped as Ryan squeezed her thigh and said, "Jamie has some connections to Morris and Foster."

"Really?" Sara asked. "Do you know someone who works there?"

Jamie was still not able to speak so Ryan continued. "A good friend of hers from Stanford is going there. Do you know Jack Townsend?"

A look of complete understanding crossed Sara's features. "You did say your name was Evans, didn't you?"

"'Fraid so," she admitted with a blush.

"And your father is James Evans, right?"

"Yep," she said with a shrug.

"I guess we all know more about each other than we thought, huh?" she finally said with a chuckle. "Although I wouldn't have guessed the real reason that you and Jack broke up was because you were in love with my Ryan," she said with a laugh. Seeing the fire flare up in Jamie's eyes, she quickly backtracked, "I didn't mean that the way it sounded, Jamie. I just … I … well, there's no excuse for referring to Ryan that way. She could have been mine once, but I blew it, and Ryan's made it clear that I'll never get another chance. I really hope everything works out for you two," she said as she stood to leave.

Ryan came over and gave her a small hug and said, "I really appreciate that you came over, Sara. I mean that."

Sara looked up into her deep blue eyes and returned the hug. "I still can't get over how this all worked out. I hope you can forgive me, and I hope that you realize I never meant to hurt you."

She took Jamie's hand and shook it lightly. "It's good to meet you, Jamie. Take care of Ryan, she's … well, you obviously know how lucky you are." With that, she turned and left through the door that Ryan had opened.

Ryan crossed over to the sofa and threw herself down on it. Jamie followed her, but before she could speak, Ryan made a request. "Can I have a few minutes?" she asked. "I just need a little time to gather my thoughts."

Jamie went to the kitchen without saying another word, taking a bottle from the refrigerator. Walking out into the yard, she sat in the watery sun sipping her beer as she contemplated the events of the day. *What's that prayer I used to like? God gives us this day as a gift. We'll never have another gift just like this one again.* She smirked to herself as she thought, *And to that I say, Amen! Another day like this would kill me!*

About a half hour later Ryan wandered out into the backyard with her own beer in hand. Jamie smiled up at her as she patted the seat of the large wooden bench that sat beneath the arbor of white roses.

Ryan sat down and draped her arm around her partner's shoulders. "Some day, huh?" she asked, taking a long pull on her bottle.

"Let's just say that if we are expecting any more like this, we had better order in some more beer," she warned with a wan smile.

Ryan squeezed her tighter and said, "Are you ready to hear my tale?"

"I'm all ears," she said as she dropped her head to Ryan's chest.

Ryan took in a deep breath, the barrage of thoughts and feelings nearly overwhelming her ability to stay focused. "I've got a lot to tell you, babe," she acknowledged. "The things that happened today cleared a lot of things up for me, and gave me some answers to questions that have haunted me for years." She shook her dark head, reminding herself to get to the most important issue. "I think some things are going to be easier for me now, Jamie," she said thoughtfully.

Unexpectedly, she placed her beer on the ground and slid off the bench, landing on her knees. Her large, strong hands reached out to grasp Jamie's, holding them gently while she looked deeply into her eyes. "Even though I think the events of this afternoon will help heal some wounds for me, I swear that I would have turned Sara away if I had any idea that her visit would hurt you. I'd take back the confusion and the hurt ten times over to avoid seeing this pain in your eyes." Her guilt-filled blue eyes blinked shut, and she struggled to hold her tears inside. "I'd do anything to spare you pain, Jamie, and I despise that I didn't consider that you could be hurt by this. I'm so very sorry." She hung her head in shame, the dark tresses shifting forward to shroud her face.

Reaching out to lift her chin, Jamie leaned over and placed a gentle kiss on Ryan's lips. "You haven't done anything wrong, Ryan."

"But you don't even know what happened …" Ryan began, but Jamie silenced her by placing the tips of her fingers to her lips.

"It doesn't matter what happened, sweetheart. No matter what you did, I know you wouldn't do anything to hurt me—I trust you."

Ryan's head dropped into Jamie's lap and she nuzzled her head against her muscular thighs for a few minutes, soaking up the overpowering feeling of complete love that her partner offered her so willingly.

"Come sit by me and tell me what happened," Jamie said softly.

With a deep sigh, Ryan got to her feet and snuggled back against her lover. "Okay," she began, obviously still trying to sort her thoughts out. "When Sara came to the door, she broke down in tears nearly the second I opened it. Something about those tears broke something in me, and I swear we cried together for what seemed like forever. I was so drained that I finally sat down on the couch and we held each other until we could get control of ourselves again."

Jamie looked up with a big smile and let out a sigh of relief. "That makes perfect sense. I know you don't have it in you to be unkind to anyone. I should have known that you had a perfectly innocent explanation for why you smelled of her perfume."

Ryan wished that she could leave it at that, but she couldn't. "That's not all that happened," she admitted. "I don't want to tell you this because I know it'll hurt you, but I can't lie to you."

She sat up straight on the bench and faced Ryan directly. "Tell me," she said softly.

"After we calmed down, she … she leaned over and kissed me," Ryan said softly. "And I let her."

Jamie looked at her with wide, unblinking eyes. She concentrated on keeping her breathing even as she asked the only question that mattered, "Why?"

Ryan closed her eyes and let her mind focus on the question. After a long pause, she finally answered. "I honestly felt like I was seventeen years old," she admitted. "I've never had a flashback like that in my life. I felt like we were in Sara's room and I was making love to her. But this time she wasn't reticent about it. She wanted me as much as I wanted her. When she kissed me, I swear I could feel some of the pain and the betrayal just flow from my body. I have no other way to explain it, Jamie. It was a deeply healing moment for me. I just despise that I've caused you pain because of it."

"Did you want her to make love to you today?" she asked in a wavering voice.

"No, baby, no!" Ryan's head was shaking forcefully. "I wanted her to make love to me six years ago. When it dawned on me that this was 1999 and you were my spouse, I pushed her away immediately. I told her that I was married to you, Jamie. I told her that I could never do anything to hurt you, and she immediately backed off. It was over as soon as I told her that, honey. I just wish that I'd had the presence of mind to tell her sooner."

A very heavy sigh left Jamie's lungs, and she struggled to focus on how obviously contrite Ryan was. "I wish you had, too, Ryan. I … I'm having a hard time getting my mind around this. It's gonna take me a little while."

"I know this sounds crazy, but I was in some sort of fugue. I never thought I'd say this, but I felt like I had temporary amnesia for a minute. I was truly out of my mind."

Jamie reflected on her partner's statement. It made sense, in a way, even though it was terribly hurtful. Nonetheless, it was understandable that Ryan would be confused and thrown off her stride by Sara's unexpected visit. But something was eating at her, and she couldn't resist asking, "Ryan, I have to ask you this, and I want you to be honest with me. I want you to search your soul before you answer, so please consider this carefully. If you were not with me now, would you have made love to Sara today?"

The speed with which Ryan replied took Jamie by complete surprise. "I don't have to look very far for that answer. I would have made love with Sara today if I were not committed to you." She saw the stunned look on her lover's face and added, "But that's not the important question. The important question is: who would I choose if both of you existed in my mind?"

She could see that Jamie was holding her breath, so she answered quickly, "I don't have to look very far for that answer either, honey. I choose you. I choose you for today, and tomorrow, and for all of the days of my life. I love you, Jamie. I always will love you and I want nothing more than to wake up next to you until I never wake up again."

Jamie's lower lip began to quiver as she fought for control, "But if that's true, why would you have made love with her today?"

"Because I loved her," she said simply. "She was the only other woman I had ever loved—and I would have jumped at the chance to be with her if I didn't have you. She meant more to me than anyone ever had." Ryan gathered her partner into her arms and gave her an emotion-filled hug. "That's all in the past now, Jamie. What I felt for Sara was love—I admit that freely. But that feeling, as powerful as it was, is nothing compared to what I feel for you. Only you can reach that hidden part of my soul that I show to no one else." Ryan dropped from the bench and knelt in front of her partner. "I love only you, Jamie. You're the last woman in my life," she whispered fervently as she laid her head in Jamie's lap. "I'm so very, very sorry that I've hurt you," she whispered, her voice ragged and thin. "I'd do anything to take back what happened today."

Jamie ran her fingers through the ebony tresses as they both shed a few more tears, neither able to change the events of the past hours, no matter how they wished they could. After a long while she pulled Ryan to her feet as she stood up on shaky legs. It was nearly nine o'clock, but for once in her life Ryan was not hungry. Jamie looked up at her and asked, "Can we go to bed?"

"There's no place I'd rather be," she agreed.

They crawled into bed together, after hastily stripping off their clothes. Ryan held her partner in her strong arms, rocking her slowly as she ran her fingers through her hair. She rocked her until she felt her begin to drift off, murmuring the whole while, "Only you, Jamie. I love only you."

Chapter Eleven

As Ryan's eyes blinked open on Wednesday morning, she shivered a bit at the chill that pervaded the room. It was early, she reasoned, as the sky was just lightening to show a touch of blue at the base of the indigo darkness. She turned over and lay on her back, wriggling around quietly to stretch it out. Her right hand reached out automatically to make sure the sheet was covering Jamie, knowing that the chill would disturb her partner if she was not properly protected. To her surprise, a soft voice said, "Hi."

Turning quickly, Ryan felt a stab of pain hit her as she focused on her lover. Bloodshot green eyes blinked at her, tiny smudges of violet creating faint half-moons under the sleep-deprived orbs. A wave of guilt washed over Ryan as she realized that while she had slept peacefully and well, her partner had obviously been awake for some time, if not the entire night. The guilt and compassion she felt showed clearly on her face, and Jamie grasped the hand that moved to caress her. She placed a kiss on the fingers and whispered, "I'm okay, honey. I just had a hard time staying asleep."

Ryan gathered her in her arms, unable to say anything to assuage the pain that she had caused. She held Jamie tenderly, running her hand through her hair while she stroked her bare back. They lay together, Jamie's warm breath flowing over Ryan's chest, for a long while, neither speaking a word. At five-fifteen Ryan's watch alarm began to beep, and she placed a gentle kiss on Jamie's head and released her hold. She stumbled into the bath and took a quick shower, knowing that she had to get something into her stomach before she could go on her run.

To her shock, when she emerged from her room, Jamie was sitting on the bed, tying her running shoes.

"Are you going with me?"

Jamie gave Ryan a look that indicated her displeasure at her partner's obvious amazement. "I *have* run before, Ryan," she said briskly, tugging on a tan cotton Cal baseball cap.

"I didn't mean to imply that you couldn't run with me if you wanted to, Jamie," she said softly, settling the cap squarely on her partner's head. "I just didn't think this was how you liked to spend your mornings. That's all, honey. Really."

Jamie grasped one of the hands that now rested on her shoulders and brushed the knuckles with a light kiss. "I'm a little grouchy, babe. I'm just feeling a little sensitive."

"I'm glad you're going with me," Ryan said honestly. "I'd like to have you close today." Ryan dropped to her knees in front of her partner so that she could look directly into her eyes. "I'm gonna skip my run today, honey. It's obvious you had a very tough night. Why don't we get back into bed and cuddle for a few hours." Her expression was one of complete empathy, and Jamie felt some of the chill in the room start to melt.

She ran a hand through Ryan's dark hair, working out a few tangles that brisk drying had caused. "I appreciate the offer, but we're up now so we may as well go. I think it'd help my golf game to increase the stamina of my legs," she replied, getting to her original reason for participating in the run. "I know I'll have more determination to stick with it if I'm with the real jocks."

"You are a real jock, stud muffin," Ryan insisted, leaning in and ducking the bill of the cap for a small kiss.

They arrived at the designated meeting area at six sharp. Coach Placer and his assistants were already there, ticking off names on a clipboard. Ryan had been told that the runs were optional, but she had a feeling that the main option was whether or not she wanted to play during the season. The fact that the coach took attendance cemented that idea.

The other team members were slowly straggling over, most of them very bleary-eyed. Jamie walked up to the coaching staff and reintroduced herself, greeting all three with poise. Coach Placer invited her to join the group whenever she chose, welcoming her to run at the back of the pack with him if the team members were too fast for her at first.

At 6:05 he decided that the latecomers would just have to catch up on their own. He marked off everyone in attendance and told them to get going, smiling to himself as the ragtag team members stumbled away in groups of two or three. About twelve women were present, and Ryan recognized a few of them from Monday's run and Tuesday's workout.

As they started off she said to Jamie, "What pace do you feel most comfortable with?"

"Evolutionary," she mumbled.

Ryan patted her gently on the back and said, "Okay, I can do that one."

They proceeded at Jamie's preferred pace for a short while, but Ryan was not running like she normally did. Her gait was heavier, and Jamie could hear her foot strike, an anomaly for the normally light-footed runner. "How do you normally start?" Jamie asked.

"I like to do a very quick first mile to clear my head and find my pace. But this works, too," she insisted.

Jamie rolled her eyes and said, "I don't need you to hang back here, honey. I'll get a workout at this pace, but you won't. Now go on—shoo!"

"You sure you don't mind if I take off?" It was clear that she wanted to go, but equally obvious that she wanted to stay and be supportive of Jamie's efforts.

"Not at all. Just don't leave without me."

The wounded look that flitted across Ryan's face made Jamie wish she could yank her last comment right back. She shook her head and tried to soothe the hurt away. "I meant that as a tease, honey. Things just aren't coming out right today."

Ryan nodded, adding a weak smile. "I know it's hard today, Jamie. Let me go blow some energy out and I'll be back in a few." She leaned over and gave her a little kiss. When Jamie looked up in surprise she said, "Might as well get them used to it right away." She shot her a grin and took off, gliding down the street in her inimitable style.

Now that's better, she mused as she watched Ryan quickly become a blur in the distance. "Pardon?" she asked, snapping her attention back into focus.

The woman who was speaking to her was tall, and blonde, and drop-dead gorgeous. There was something familiar about her, and Jamie narrowed her eyes in contemplation, trying to recall if they had been in classes together. She looked a little like an L.A. surfer, tons of bronzed skin showing against the bright yellow running shorts and sky blue singlet that barely covered her body. The sleekly muscled body made a strong statement that she was an athlete, but the vaguely Nordic features and cool blue eyes gave the impression that they belonged to a high-fashion model. "I said that I didn't think we'd met before," the woman said in a voice that was higher pitched than Jamie would have chosen for such an imposing figure. "I'm Jordan Ericsson."

"Nice to meet you, Jordan, I'm Jamie Evans. We spoke on the phone the other day."

"So we did," she said with the beginnings of a smile warming up her frosty countenance. "It's good to meet you in person, Jamie," she said in a friendly, welcoming tone. They ran along for a few hundred yards, Jamie struggling a bit to keep up with the long, smooth stride of the leggy blonde.

Jordan cast a glance or two at Jamie's heaving chest and finally asked, "Do you run often?"

"No," she admitted with a small laugh. "I'm trying to use you all to motivate me to run. It's not my natural state."

"I see," said Jordan, casting a smirk at the panting woman. "Did you *want* to run alone, or did Ryan abandon you?"

That particular choice of words didn't go down well after the events of the previous night, but Jamie did her best to hide the pained look that tried to surface. "She's far too quick for me to keep up with," she explained, thinking that phrase applied to many areas. "It didn't seem fair to ask her to hang out back here."

"She did seem pretty quick," Jordan agreed. "But I think the view back here is much more pleasant." Her expression was still very cool, and Jamie was puzzled as she tried to reconcile the flirtatious comment with the impenetrable mask of her face.

Rather than even try to engage in the repartee, she quickly changed the subject. "Is this your first year on the team?"

Jordan gave her a quick glance as she tried to determine if Jamie was kidding. "Uhm ... no. I'm a senior. This is my fourth year on the team."

"I didn't mean to imply that you looked immature or anything, Jordan," she said with a smile.

Jordan's features softened, and she laughed a little at the comment. "No offense taken, Jamie. I'm used to most of the new people knowing who I am. I thought that Ryan might have mentioned me."

"No," she had to admit. "I don't think Ryan knows a lot about volleyball, to tell you the truth. She's more into soccer."

Jordan slowed down, staring at Jamie with a puzzled expression. "What do you mean, she doesn't know much about volleyball? I heard she kicked butt in her tryout—and I know one of the girls she beat out from a camp I went to earlier this year. She can play!"

"I didn't say that Ryan couldn't play," she said with an impish grin. "I meant that she has been away from the sport for quite a few years."

Jordan's face resumed its tranquil, unreadable expression. She ran in silence for a few minutes, obviously trying to put the pieces of the puzzle together. "Is she from California?"

"Yes."

"Where from?"

"San Francisco," she supplied, adding, "She went to high school at Sacred Heart Academy."

Jordan shook her head. "Never heard of it. You say she's been away from the sport—where's she been?"

"Long story," Jamie huffed, having a devil of a time speaking while she ran. "She played for one year at USF. I think that was her freshman year—she's a senior now."

"That's it!" Jordan proclaimed, her face breaking into a sunny grin that almost seemed incongruous. "I knew I'd seen her before. We played USF when I was a freshman. We got our butts kicked, as a matter of fact. I think Ryan was responsible for the major part of that butt kicking, too." She grew quiet, running along for several minutes. Finally, she turned and said, "I need to pick up the pace a bit, Jamie. Nice talking to you." Before Jamie could open her mouth, the lanky woman kicked her body into a gear that Jamie didn't possess and took off effortlessly, gliding along past her fellow teammates.

Jamie gave a little wave to her back as she settled down to a more comfortable pace. She was tiring, but all in all she felt pretty good about her performance so far. She was much more comfortable than she had been on the few runs she had taken with Jack, and she assumed that the long hours on her bike had paid off in both leg strength and cardiovascular fitness.

After about three miles Ryan appeared in the distance. She was chatting with one of the other women, and it was clear that she was running much more slowly than was typical for her. Jamie put on as big a burst of speed as she had in her and caught up with them. "Hey, speedy," Ryan smiled.

"I'm dying," she gasped.

"Do you want to walk for a while?"

"No, I'm going to tough it out. But you don't have to go as slow as I do. I know you must be itching."

Ryan laughed and shook her head. "I'm fine, Jamie. I'm going to do a big workout at the gym today, so I don't need to leave all of my energy out here."

"That reminds me, I've got to get my butt back into the gym. I'm going to lose all of my hard-won muscle."

"You've got a ways to go before that happens," Ryan said with an admiring glance. "We do need to tailor your program to focus on your golf game, though. Why don't you skip playing today and come with me?"

Jamie knew that the request was as much for her benefit as Ryan's, and she appreciated that her partner was trying to look out for her. "Okay, but will I get in the way?"

"Of course not. My twelve o'clock is a really nice woman. I'm sure she wouldn't mind if I worked you both out at the same time. We can go a little early and I'll show you the exercises I want you to do, then I can just keep an eye on you."

"I'd like that, Ryan," she admitted. "I'm feeling a little shaky today."

"I am too, babe," Ryan agreed. "I think you might feel a little less shaky if you got some more sleep. Why don't we go home and take a long nap?"

She looked up at Ryan with a shy smile. "Would you do that for me?" She knew that as a general rule, Ryan hated to sleep in, and going back to bed at seven o'clock was even more out of character.

"Without question." Her expression was soft and gentle, the look in her eyes one of utter devotion.

Jamie nodded her acquiescence. "I appreciate that."

"It's gonna take a few days before we get over this." She cast a long look at her partner and assured her in a voice filled with confidence, "But we *will* get over this."

By one o'clock Jamie was toast, but she found that she still had a need to stay close to her partner. Ryan did her best to devote as much attention to her as possible, and she decided to dedicate some time to getting in a good, long stretch to keep her muscles loose. Every few minutes Ryan would appear and help her get into a certain position, or gently move her body a few degrees in one direction or another, and Jamie spent a minute thinking about how odd it felt to experience those familiar hands touching her in such a public setting.

She recalled the first time she had worked out under Ryan's tutelage, and how delicious it felt to have the cool, sure hands move her body like a poseable doll. She watched her lover move her client around the gym, observing the slight reserve that masked the open attitude she revealed at home. Considering the image she presented to the public, Jamie acknowledged that there was an inner fire mixed with a startling vulnerability that Ryan kept very well hidden from almost everyone. She was absolutely certain that none of Ryan's clients, few of her friends, and even fewer of her lovers had ever seen the inner Ryan, no matter how much of her body they might have been exposed to.

Lost in these thoughts, she realized with startling clarity why she felt threatened by Sara. It wasn't just that Ryan had allowed herself to be kissed. Jamie really did understand how that had happened, and she had to agree that it was sometimes surprisingly easy for your emotions to carry your body away. No, the kiss was not the issue. She knew that one kiss would never have a serious, lasting, negative impact on what she and Ryan had built together.

It was not the physical intimacy that Ryan had shared. Rather, it was the emotional intimacy that these women had experienced—an intimacy that, in some ways, she and Ryan would never share. The Ryan she knew would always have a hard, protective shell over some part of her soul. Jamie was actually glad that she had it because it served to protect her fragile psyche. But Sara knew Ryan before that shell had been so carefully erected. She knew the young Ryan who was just coming to grips with the recent death of her mother; she shared the experience of Michael's illness and death. She had, in essence, been a member of Ryan's family during those tumultuous years, and Jamie recognized that there were feelings shared between the two that she could never hope to understand or experience.

This, to her, was the threat. This woman, who was such an important part of Ryan's life, had risen from the dead. Ryan had resigned herself to the fact that Sara was lost to her, but here she was, seemingly being forgiven for her betrayal. Jamie's mind reeled at the thought that Ryan would want to welcome her back into her life. She had no idea what such a development would portend, but she didn't feel able to prevent Ryan from pursuing it. She knew her partner had a very difficult time when she felt she was being dictated to, and Jamie had early on resolved never to do so. Her mind scrambled around the issue—trying to come up with a way to allow Ryan her autonomy, while preventing Sara from invading their nascent relationship.

She was unsure how long she had been mulling the issue over when a warm presence at her side indicated that Ryan's workday was complete. She looked into quizzical blue eyes, and smiled at the open gaze that greeted her. "You finished, babe?"

"Yeah. Uhm … do you want to go home, or do you like snoozing on this mat?"

Jamie snapped back into the realization that she was lying prone on the thin mat, and that she had likely been in just this position for quite a while. A slight flush climbed her cheeks as she offered a thin cover for her actions. "I didn't follow my morning routine today."

Ryan recognized the excuse for what it was, but gamely played along. "We don't run tomorrow, love, so you can relax and let the day approach more gently."

"It's a deal," she agreed, getting to her knees and then her feet with the assistance of Ryan's extended hand.

"Home?" Ryan asked, cocking her head slightly.

"Definitely." Jamie desperately needed a warm shower and a long nap before dinner, and she thought there was a good chance that she could convince her partner to join her for both.

A long, hot shower was the first order of business. When the water was at the correct temperature they entered the enclosure and stood rather awkwardly for a few moments. Ryan poured some shower gel into her hands and held them up in front of her partner. "Wash your back?" she asked with just a touch of hesitation in her voice.

The smaller woman leaned forward and kissed the taut skin that stretched against Ryan's breastbone. "You don't need permission, love. That would be nice."

She turned to face the water and soon Jamie felt the stress in her body begin to melt away under Ryan's firm touch. The large, smooth hands glided over her skin on a layer of lavender-scented bubbles as Ryan massaged each weary muscle.

The gentle rubbing continued until Jamie feared her legs would give way. She leaned back against Ryan, letting her partner's solid form hold her upright. Now the touch became even gentler and lighter as it moved to the front of her body. Ryan's pace never wavered, her hands moving the entire time. They caressed every inch of skin until Jamie's entire body tingled with desire. She slowly turned in her lover's embrace and slipped her arms around her neck, the soap allowing their bodies to slide against each other sensually. A soft moan escaped her lips as Ryan bent to cover her mouth with a wet kiss. Within seconds they were wrapped around each other in a fervid embrace, their bodies grinding against each other as their shared passion grew. The thrumming water had rinsed them clean and Ryan reached blindly for the control, shutting it off roughly while supporting much of Jamie's weight. She shook her head sharply, tossing her bangs back as she did so. Without wasting the time to dry off, she bent and lifted Jamie into her arms, smiling down at her partner as she laced her hands behind Ryan's neck. "Careful, love," Jamie whispered as the powerful legs stepped over the short lip of the shower stall.

"I'll always be careful with you," Ryan murmured. "You're the most precious thing in my life."

The heartfelt words, coupled with the earnest look in Ryan's eyes, caused Jamie's heart to soar, and she pushed every worry—every niggling doubt—from her mind and took Ryan at her word. She offered her body to the woman who possessed her soul, knowing in her heart that both would be guarded with the most tender care.

Their lovemaking was the epitome of gentleness this warm summer afternoon. They explored each other's bodies with a slow thoroughness that seemed brand-new, yet terribly familiar to both of them. They caressed each other simultaneously, never ceasing their attentions, until both were gasping for release.

Ryan's body covered Jamie's, her weight nearly squeezing the breath from the smaller woman. No matter what efforts Ryan made to slide off, Jamie resisted, holding her tight—desperately needing to feel the solid mass of flesh and bone press into her. Arms and legs wrapped tightly around Ryan, holding her with surprising strength until she looked deep into Jamie's eyes and whispered, "Don't worry. I'll stay right here for as long as you need me."

Sea green eyes fluttered closed, afraid to let Ryan see the consuming need that she felt for her. "I'll always need you, Ryan. Always."

Ryan's dark hair trailed across her throat as she nuzzled her face into Jamie's neck. "I'll always be here for you, Jamie. I promise you." Her words were clearly enunciated despite her position, the sound humming against Jamie's skin. The sincerity in her voice, and the simple yet fervent vow reached the wounded part of Jamie's soul, and she welcomed Ryan back into the place she had been shielding. Her eyes opened wide as Ryan's head lifted, their eyes locking in an ardent gaze that never faltered as their lovemaking continued long into the afternoon.

Jamie had been trailing her fingers through Ryan's hair for a while when Ryan finally woke. Her head was resting heavily upon Jamie's hip, but the smaller woman had no desire to evict her. It felt so comforting to have the normally hyper-alert woman lie upon her body in such unguarded vulnerability that she was certain she would never tire of it. Soft eyelashes tickled Jamie's belly, and she knew her partner was coming into full consciousness. "Did you have a nice nap, sweetheart?"

"God, yes," she moaned, stretching languidly. "I can't think of anywhere I'd rather be, I can't think of anyone I'd rather be with, I can't think of a time I've been more physically sated or emotionally fulfilled." She rolled over onto her back and looked up at Jamie. "How about you?"

"I didn't sleep much," she admitted. "I don't get many opportunities to hold you like this while you sleep. It was too irresistible to pass up. I do agree with all of your sentiments, though." She smiled down at her lover, her mist green eyes twinkling in the late afternoon light.

"I can't believe how easily you put me to sleep," Ryan mused. "I cuddle up against that perfect little body, and it's lights out!"

Looking down at Ryan, Jamie cocked her head slightly and asked, "You've never told me what you like about my body. Will you tell me now?"

Ryan was a little surprised at the question and, deciding to attack head-on, she replied, "I could spend all day singing the praises of your body. But I *am* curious as to why the question came up."

"Uhm … I don't know. I was just thinking about the women I know you've been attracted to. None of them look like me, so I was wondering what it was about me that you liked."

"None of them looked like you because no one else is as beautiful as you are," Ryan said sincerely. "The moment I saw you, I knew I had a new favorite type."

"Sure you did, honey," she said as she patted Ryan's cheek. "That's why the woman you tried to make your girlfriend looked just like Sara."

Ryan sat up in surprise at this comment. She had never thought about it that way, but Sara and Tracy could have been sisters. Actually, from the back, it would have been hard to tell them apart. When she thought about it for a moment, she realized that one of her "types" had always been a tall, lean brunette with delicate features.

While Jamie was many wonderful things, she was neither tall, nor lean, nor brunette. Her delightful features were certainly not coarse, and Ryan loved them just as they were, but she had to admit that Jamie didn't have the ethereal delicateness that she often was drawn to.

"I'm happy to talk about this, but I'd like to know what's going on in your head first," she said, refusing to back off without knowing what was on Jamie's mind.

"I think it's obvious that I'm feeling a little insecure, honey," she admitted. "I can't get over how gorgeous Sara is, and when I think about it, Tracy was just as pretty. I know you think I'm attractive, but I also know that I'm nowhere near as pretty as they are."

Ryan pursed her lips and shook her head so roughly that her bangs flew around her forehead. "That's your opinion, Jamie, but it's not mine," she said firmly. "I might not be able to convince you of how attractive I find you, but I refuse to have you tell me who is and who is not pretty. Beauty is entirely subjective, and to my very experienced and rather hypercritical eyes, you are the most beautiful woman I've ever met."

"Thank you, Ryan," she said rather indulgently as a pink flush graced her cheeks. "But you have to admit that they both fit your type more than I do."

Ryan took a breath to frame her answer carefully. "That's true. If I had to choose my mate from a photograph, I'd probably choose someone who was tall and thin and had dark hair and fair skin. That is my usual type." A quirky smile curled her mouth and she tilted her head a little as she asked, "Would you be insulted if I used a dog analogy to clarify my point?"

"Ahh, no, I guess not," she said warily, uncertain if she was about to be insulted.

"Okay, we didn't have a dog when I was young, and in retrospect it was a wise thing because we would have driven the poor thing insane! But ever since I was little, I wanted a basset hound. I don't know why that particular dog appealed to me so much, but I was absolutely wild about them. If I was running around and saw one on the street, or at the park, the owner had better have had some free time, because I was down on my knees petting that dog until they dragged it away!"

Jamie laughed gently at her partner's description of her younger self. "When did your opinion change?" she asked.

"It hasn't," she said firmly. "If I had to pick a dog based on their descriptions in a book, or just from a picture, I would still pick a basset hound. Now, imagine a basset and then compare it to my Duffy Boy," she said in challenge.

Jamie thought about this for a minute and decided that, except for brown eyes, there was no more similarity between those two breeds than there was between her and Ryan. They were the same species, but that's about the only thing they had in common. "Well, if that's true, why did you pick Duffy?"

"I didn't," she explained patiently. "Duffy picked me!"

Jamie smiled at her sweetly, acknowledging Ryan's often stated claim that Jamie had picked her. "But you love Duffy for lots more than his looks," she reminded her. "It's not that big of a deal that he's not what you really want your dog to look like."

"Exactly my point, although you're entirely wrong about one major element. Duffy *is* what I want my dog to look like. I didn't take him because I was settling for less,

Jamie. I think Duff is the most beautiful dog I've ever seen. I absolutely love his coat and his big brown eyes and his big, sturdy body. He's just perfect! In fact, I'd have to say that he is the dog I would choose over all others—I just didn't always know it!"

"I think I'm beginning to understand your analogy," Jamie said with a smirk. "Sara and Tracy are basset hounds and I'm a big poodle/lab mix."

"Exactly! You're my sweet puppy, and I would choose you over a thousand basset hounds!"

"But won't your tail always wag when you see a really hot-looking basset hound walking down the street?" she asked, rather tentatively.

"Well, yeah, probably," Ryan said thoughtfully. "I am just a dog, you know," she added with a smile. "But you're the only one I want to hump." She spread her legs and climbed on top of her lover's thigh, simulating a dog in heat for several enthusiastic thrusts.

"Okay, okay," Jamie gasped through her giggles. "I get your point, but I'm just afraid that I'll be a little jealous every time we see one of those basset hounds."

"Well, this probably won't ease your mind, but of all of the women I dated in the last few years, the woman you saw me with at the bookstore turned me on more than any of them. And she couldn't be farther from my type if she tried."

Jamie considered this information and thought for a moment. The extremely dark-complexioned African American woman was rather short, had very wide hips, didn't look very athletic, and her head was nearly shaved. "Is that really true? What was so compelling about her?"

"I don't know. It was just chemistry, I guess. But I was wet and ready ten minutes after saying hello every time we went out. We just clicked, Jamie, and it didn't matter that she didn't possess one item from my usual list. Robin was tremendously attractive to me, and that's all that mattered." Ryan rolled her eyes, finding the explanation for her reactions elusive. "It's a waste of time to worry about one type of woman that I might be attracted to. I can find something attractive in almost every woman, and I can be terribly turned on by a wide variety of looks. Attraction and arousal are very, very complex, Jamie. All I know is that you are more than your outward appearance. You are the sum of all of your fantastic qualities. There is a glow that just radiates from you, and it pulls me right in. I can't explain it, because I don't understand it. But something about you calls to me like the sirens of ancient mythology." Ryan leaned in and wrapped her arms around her partner, whispering into her ear, "I honestly find you irresistible."

"I want to believe you, Ryan," she murmured, trying to accept her partner's assurances.

Ryan sat up and wrapped an arm around her partner, drawing her tight against her chest. "Let me say it this way. I freely admit that I used to treat women like they were photographs. I admit that I used to just want to be with them for the packaging. I didn't spend nearly enough time getting to know most of the women I was with, and sometimes when I met someone who had a better package, I was more than willing to go after her."

Jamie nodded, the flyaway strands of her hair tickling Ryan's chest. Ryan ran her hands over the silky wisps, brushing them tenderly into place. "That's not how it is with you, Jamie," she insisted. "I got to know you, and I grew to love you. You're so much more than a body to me. I love your body, but I also love your soul. You are everything to me, baby. It hurts me when you don't believe that."

"I normally do believe it," Jamie said quietly. "I just got thrown off track by Sara showing up. I know you loved her too, Ryan. She wasn't just a body to you."

Ryan took a breath, nodding her head as she acknowledged the truth of the statement. "That's true. I did love her. I'm sure that part of me always will. The seventeen-year-old Ryan still loves the eighteen-year-old Sara. But that's not who either of us is any longer, Jamie. It's impossible to go back and try to reclaim something from so long ago. We'd both have to be willing to throw those old images away and try to start over. It'd be like dating a stranger in a way. So the question becomes, do I want to look at every woman that comes along and decide if she might be just a touch better than what I've already chosen?"

Jamie just looked up at her partner, still having a difficult time of it, desperately wanting to be reassured.

"That's not what I want, babe," she said emphatically. "And as far as I am concerned, there is no one better than you. I have pledged my fidelity to you, Jamie. I want us to spend the rest of our lives trying to love each other better, day by day."

Jamie nestled her head up against her lover's chest and closed her eyes as she breathed in her reassuring scent. "You're right, babe," she murmured. "I want that too, but it's gonna take me a while to get over my insecurities about this."

"If the situation was reversed, I'd feel the same. What happened with Sara scared me. I promise I'll try to never again be in a situation that has the possibility of being that dangerous."

Jamie gave her a firm squeeze, grateful that Ryan had not been defensive about her fears. "Thank you for acknowledging that it scared you. It really shook me, baby, and I don't want to have to go through anything like that again."

"I guarantee that Sara was the only woman who ever had that kind of pull for me. I never cared enough for anyone else for them to even make me turn my head." She leaned over and placed a few kisses on Jamie's mouth. "I believe you asked me a question a while ago, and I'm ready to answer it now," she said with a grin.

"What's that?"

"I want to show you what I like about your body," she murmured, giving Jamie a look that suggested the little show-and-tell was going to be a very pleasurable experience.

Jamie flopped down onto the bed in a completely submissive pose. "Have at it!"

Ryan moved around until she was sitting cross-legged on the bed. She rubbed her hands together and licked her lips in an exaggerated bout of lasciviousness as she gazed at the expanse of golden-toned skin. "I guess I'll start with the wrapper," she said with waggling eyebrows. "I absolutely love your skin. I'm quite sure I've never known a woman that had such beautiful skin." She ran her hands slowly over her torso and down her legs. "I can't even begin to describe the color. It's not pink and it's not quite cream," she mused, staring intently. "I guess the closest color would be a soft peach. Where your skin is exposed, like here on your arms, it nearly glows. It honestly looks like spun gold in some light. I never tire of just looking at your skin and trying to describe it to myself."

"I never knew you felt that way," Jamie said shyly, blushing fiercely under the scrutiny.

"That's because I've been extremely remiss in telling you how I feel about you," she said. "But I intend to remedy that oversight from this day forward. Now let's start at the top. I've decided that I don't want you to grow your hair long. Even though wrapping my hands in it in a fit of passion does sound appealing, I just love the way it frames your face when it's short. It serves as a beautiful gilt frame for your lovely face." She ruffled her fingers through the short, blonde tresses and elaborated. "When I was little, there was a copy of a painting by Botticelli in our church. I don't know the name of the piece, but there were these gorgeous cherubs surrounding the Virgin Mary, who was holding Jesus. They had the most beautiful golden hair," she said, shaking her head at the memory. "I used to sit there and stare at them through the whole Mass." She lovingly ran her fingers through the golden tresses again. "Yesterday morning, when I came out of the shower, I took a quick glance to make sure you weren't up yet. The sun was just beginning to hit the bed, and it was glinting off your hair. I was immediately struck with the memory of those lovely angels," she said with a small smile. "So, you see, I haven't always been partial to brunettes."

Jamie sat up and wrapped her lover in her arms. "That was so sweet," she whispered tenderly. "I'll always remember that, Ryan," she said as she began to kiss her.

After several minutes of slowly building passion, Ryan pulled away and protested, "I've only gotten to your hair! I've got at least thirty-five more things I want to tell you about."

"Later," she breathed, desire beginning to suffuse her body once again. "We've got our whole lives to get through the list."

Thursday dawned foggy and cool, and Ryan shivered mightily as she slipped out of bed. It was just five-fifteen when she checked her watch, and she reconsidered her morning run for just a moment. Her routine won out, though, and she decided to do a shorter-than-normal loop just to get the cobwebs out.

They had gone to bed early the night before. Actually, they had ordered Chinese food, and when it was delivered they ate it in bed, essentially not leaving the confines of the cozy king-sized space after three-thirty the previous afternoon. *I have never spent so much time in bed*, Ryan mused as she smoothed a pair of Lycra tights over her legs. *Not that I'm complaining, of course.* She felt pretty good, all things considered. Jamie seemed to have gotten past the worst of her anxiety, and the anger Ryan had expected had never materialized. Ryan was confident that they were back on track, even though she realized that they would feel the aftereffects for a long while. *I learned my lesson through all of this*, she thought with a shiver. *I will never—ever—let an ex-lover in the house with me alone. If I see Sara again, I'm gonna have her come to the house in the Noe Valley on a weekend with the entire family present!*

She spent the first mile of her run saying her morning prayers, but her mind kept drifting to her old friend. She was unsure if she even wanted to see her again, given the pain that her visit had caused Jamie. But there were so many questions that Ryan had not had time to ask that she really wished they could talk again. *Better to have a bucketful of questions than cause Jamie another sleepless night*, she decided. *At least I know the answer to the most important question. Sara did break my heart—there's no denying that. But she didn't betray me. That's been the worst part of the whole incident for me to reconcile. Now that I know she didn't tell the people at school, I think I can put it away and just forget about her role.* A determined look crossed her face as she vowed, *But neither Mrs. Andrews nor Coach Ratzinger is getting off that easy. Those two have got some serious explaining to do.*

By six o'clock she had whipped out a quick three miles and was back in the kitchen, looking for nourishment. Not wanting to spend the time cooking a hot meal, she had a bowl of mixed cereal, one of her small quirks. She liked several brands of cold cereal, but she didn't like any one of them well enough to make an entire meal out of. When she was young, her father bought industrial-sized boxes of cereal, often containing three different brands shrink-wrapped together. Since being a picky eater was never an option, she usually mixed them all together, a habit she continued, to Jamie's amusement. Today she had Cheerios, Frosted Flakes, and Kix with a sliced banana and milk.

Partially satisfied, she decided to take a shower in Mia's bathroom to avoid waking Jamie, who was obviously trying to set some sort of record for lying in a horizontal position. Grabbing her shower supplies, she let the warm water rejuvenate her. She spent a few minutes brushing her teeth while the water beat down on her back, smiling a little when she considered how much her habit amused her partner. Ryan just didn't see the point of showering, then brushing your teeth, since there was a good chance of getting toothpaste all over your chin. Doing both at the same time just seemed more efficient. Even though Jamie teased her about it, she honestly thought that she liked it, since she often licked her chest and stomach, trying to find a small hint of Crest on her body.

Ryan was debating going back to bed but realized that she was still hungry, so she went downstairs and ate a beautiful, ripe peach while she waited for some bread to toast. When it was ready, she spread it with some wild fruit preserves that Jamie had purchased. *Ohh, this is mighty tasty,* she thought appreciatively. *I know another few places that I'd like to spread this on,* she added with a chuckle.

When she was fully fed, Ryan figured she might as well help Jamie set her record, so she went back upstairs and slid back into bed, barely causing a ripple in the sheets. Moments after her arms slid around Jamie she felt the first stirrings of wakefulness. As was her usual habit, Jamie made some cute little noises while she slowly stretched and opened her eyes. A delighted grin crossed her face when she realized that Ryan was still in bed. "Hey, it's almost light out. What gives?"

"Can't I choose to stay in bed once in a while?" she asked with a sweet smile.

"Sure you can, but you never do," she teased. "So, what gives?"

"You know too many of my tricks already," she said with narrowed eyes. "I can't get away with anything."

"Try to remember that the next time an ex-lover shows up at our front door," she said with a smile, but Ryan knew there was still some hurt behind the jest.

"I'll never even give my address to another ex-lover," she said sincerely. "They can go to Noe and let Da take over. They'll never get past the front door with him on guard."

Jamie patted her partner's cheek, pleased that her pointed comment had not dampened her mood, but gratified that Ryan didn't just brush it off. "So, for the third time, why aren't you running? You aren't sick, are you?"

"Nope. I did go running, I'll have you know. I was just about to start dinner, but you looked so cute and cuddly I just had to come back to bed."

"Very funny, Tiger. It's not even seven o'clock, you goof."

"You've got me there," Ryan agreed, glad that the sparkle was back in her partner's eyes. "I want to go work out with the team, but they've decided to start meeting at ten o'clock. They're apparently not early birds," she said with a mock aggrieved look.

"So if we're not going running, what should we do for the next three hours?" Jamie asked, wiggling her eyebrows.

Ryan had actually been planning on catching up on her e-mail and newsgroups, but the unspoken invitation to stay in bed was not the sort of thing she was wont to refuse, particularly now, with Jamie still showing signs of uneasiness about Sara. "I was thinking of doing something horizontal," she replied softly, with a seductive gaze. She slid closer and placed several soft kisses on and around Jamie's mouth.

"Ohh, you've already showered. And I think," she said as she licked all around Ryan's mouth, "that you've had breakfast."

"You are very perceptive," she replied with a grin. "Guess what I ate?"

Her partner set about tasting and licking every inch of her mouth and lips. After a few minutes of this thorough survey she dropped back onto the bed with her breathing slightly quickened. "I'm sure you had orange juice. And I got a real hint of fruit, like raspberry. So you must have had jam, 'cause that's the only thing we have with raspberry in it." She closed her eyes, deep in thought. "I tasted some kind of cereal, but I could never tell which kind with you," she teased. "So let's call that Ryan's Jumble. I couldn't taste it, but I know you put a banana on your cereal 'cause you always do." She sat up with a confident look in her eye. "How'd I do?"

"You've missed your calling, sweetie. You should have been a detective."

As she trailed her fingers seductively over Ryan's chest she asked, "If I take a quick shower, will you allow me to investigate the rest of your luscious body?"

"Absolutely," she said happily. "But it's okay with me if you wait until after we've finished the investigation. You'll need one then anyway if I have my way," she whispered.

"Nope," Jamie insisted, hopping out of bed before Ryan's quick hands could grab on to her. "If I get to play with a nice clean body, so do you. Fair's fair, Buffy." As she scampered into the bath she decided, "I think I'll even brush my teeth in the shower today. We can play 'Find the Crest' all morning."

Ryan shot her a dazzling white grin, confident that tooth decay would be a thing of the past if everyone got to play that game on a daily basis.

Ryan was going to go straight to work after her weight-lifting session, so Jamie had the house to herself for the first time since they'd been back in town. A substantial pile of unopened mail had been building up, so she decided to tackle that little project and then go to the driving range to work on her middle irons for a couple of hours.

It was nearly noon when the ringing phone snapped her out of her absorption. "Hello," she said rather absently as she reviewed a statement from her trust fund.

"Jamie, it's Cassie."

In less time than it took to snap her gaping mouth closed, Jamie's defenses went up and she was spoiling for a fight. "And ..." she said curtly, surprised at the coldness she heard in her own voice.

Strangely, Cassie didn't rise to the bait. "And," she replied quietly, "I wanted to know if it'd be all right if I came over to the house for a few minutes."

"Why on earth would you want to do that?" Cassie's gentle tone was making her wonder about her motivations for calling, but Jamie had no desire to hide her wrath.

"Um ... two reasons." Her voice was much quieter than normal, and there was almost a frail quality to it. "One, I left some things in the floor safe in the library, and I'd like to retrieve them."

"I can get them and send them to you," Jamie snapped.

"Well, um ... you could, but you'd have to have a locksmith come," she reminded her. "I was the only one to use it, and I have the only key."

"I can afford to have a locksmith come, Cassie. It's well worth the expense to avoid seeing you again. I'd rather blow the house up than have you enter the door again." She had never—ever—spoken to someone in such harsh terms, and it took her a second to understand that she wouldn't have been so angry at Cassie's actions if they were only meant to hurt her. But she had been cruel to Ryan, and Jamie couldn't tolerate that, under any circumstances.

Cassie sighed deeply and continued her request, in an even quieter voice. "I deserve that, Jamie. I really do. I'm not going to even try to defend myself. There is no justification for what I did. I treated you horribly, and I just want you to know that I'm sorry, and if there was any way to make it up to you, I would." She said this entire statement in a rush, the words tumbling out so quickly that she nearly stumbled over them. She sucked in another audible breath and said, "I'm sorry I bothered you, Jamie. I'll send you the key so you don't have to see me."

"Wait!" Jamie said, loud enough for Cassie to hear as she hung up. "Wait." Quieter this time, but firm and decisive. "I'm sorry for being so rude, Cassie. I ... I ... well, you do deserve a good kick in the pants, but it's not my nature to be cruel. It doesn't feel right, and I'm sorry I came across that way."

"It's okay, Jamie," she said quickly. "I don't blame you in the least."

"You said you had two reasons you wanted to come over. What's the second?"

"I want to apologize, Jamie. I've … uhm … I've had some time to think about things over the last few weeks, and I'm … uhm … I just have a different perspective … on life."

Jamie had known Cassie since they were in kindergarten. They were never best friends, but they had spent a lot of time together, both because of school and their mothers' friendship. In the sixteen years she had known her, she had never heard Cassie genuinely apologize for anything. A part of her wanted to just have her send the key back, but another part of her was curious about what had caused this apparent introspection. "What's going on, Cassie?" she finally asked. "You don't seem like yourself at all."

"I can't explain it on the phone, Jamie. I'll write to you if you are interested. It's just … too personal to do on the phone. I kinda thought … well, never mind what I thought. I'll send you the key, Jamie. Thanks."

"Cassie, hold on a minute," Jamie insisted. "Tell me what's going on."

There was a pregnant pause as the woman on the other end decided how much to reveal. "Some things happened to me in New York that have really confused me, Jamie. I don't know why I thought you'd be willing, but I had this notion that maybe I could talk about it with you." She let out a heavy sigh and said, "I don't have any friends in New York, and … I just … I just thought you might be willing to help me through this."

"What about Chris?" Jamie asked, referring to Cassie's boyfriend.

An even bigger sigh was her reply. "That's why I'm here," she admitted. "Chris and I broke up. I came back this week to tell him. It just wasn't fair to lead him on." She sounded nearly desolate, and Jamie felt a surprising amount of empathy for her former friend. There was something so fragile about her—a quality that Jamie had never seen before. Before she knew it, the words were coming out of her mouth: "I have a little time before I need to go out. Can you come over right now?"

"Yes!" Cassie jumped at the chance, and Jamie felt confident that she had done the right thing. She didn't want to see the woman who had caused her so much pain, but she couldn't convince herself to be as cruel as Cassie herself had been. "I'm in Berkeley right now, Jamie. I'll be there in ten minutes."

Jamie ran around the house, removing every visible sign of Ryan's presence. There wasn't much, actually, Ryan being perpetually neat, but she didn't want to reveal any details of their living situation to Cassie. She certainly was not ashamed of Ryan, but she didn't trust Cassie any further than she could throw her, and she didn't want her to have any grist—whether or not she was in the mood to use the mill.

A few minutes later, Jamie answered the light knock at the door. Cassie looked about the same physically, long blonde hair parted down the middle, frosty blue eyes revealing little of her internal feelings. Cassie was a good six inches taller than Jamie, but today she gave the impression of a much smaller and frailer woman. She seemed almost meek—a term Jamie would never have thought to use for the normally brash woman.

They didn't hug one another—both knew those days were over—but Cassie stood patiently on the front porch, not making any overtures toward entering until Jamie stepped back and said, "Come on in, Cassie."

She did so, standing uncertainly in the entryway, waiting for a signal. As they made their way into the living room Jamie spied a pair of Ryan's shoes on the floor by the heavy table near the stairs. She managed to silently kick them out of sight, thanking the heavens that Cassie had been in front of her.

Cassie sat gingerly on the edge of the love seat, while Jamie chose one of the upholstered chairs. "Thank you for this, Jamie," she said quietly, refusing to meet Jamie's eyes.

"Tell me what's going on, Cassie," she urged.

The taller woman looked over at her and hesitated before beginning her tale. "It's been an interesting few weeks in New York," she ventured, fidgeting nervously on the chair. "Most of the people I work with at Time-Life are East Coasters, and they're just so different from us. They're ... I don't know ... more artsy or something."

Jamie smiled at this comment, knowing that there were plenty of arty people at Cal—Cassie just didn't hang around with them.

"One of the women that I work with goes to Smith," she explained. "She's a New Yorker, and her parents own a gorgeous apartment in the Dakota." Cassie tilted her head, silently asking if Jamie knew the building near Central Park.

"That's where John Lennon lived, wasn't it?"

"Yes," Cassie confirmed, a little surprised that a Left Coaster had heard of it. "Anyway, Zoey's parents are retired, and they spend most of their time out on the island."

Jamie rolled her eyes slightly, already tired of Cassie's attempts to sound like a New Yorker. "Yes ..." she led, hoping to get to the point.

"So ... she offered to let me stay with her this summer."

Jamie furrowed her brow, thinking that she recalled some other arrangements. "Didn't you agree to share a sublet with another intern?"

Cassie nodded perfunctorily. "Yes, I did, but staying with Zoey was going to be free," she said, as though that explained why it was all right to pull out on well-established plans at the last minute. "It's really expensive in New York, and I didn't want to spend my whole allowance on rent."

Jamie shook her head in consternation, thinking, *Same old Cassie.*

To her surprise, Cassie once again grew pensive, a rather uncommon occurrence for the woman. "I thought this would be a nice, easy way to save a few thousand dollars," she said, nearing tears. "But it's ... it's ... confusing me so badly I don't know what to do."

Jamie was sure that at some previous time in her life, Cassie had been moved to tears, but not in her presence. A few drops tumbled out of her eyes, not a torrent by any means, but a clearer sign of her humanity than Jamie had ever witnessed. "Tell me what's happened," Jamie said, leaning forward on the love seat.

Cassie sighed, letting out a breath as she shook her head sharply, the long, golden tresses falling neatly against her shoulders. "Zoey is … she's … I can't even begin to describe her, Jamie. I've never met anyone like her."

Jamie's brows knit closer together as she tried to guess where this path was leading. "Go on," she urged.

Cassie's face broke into a gentle smile as she continued, "She's so interesting, and bright. She can talk for hours about music or art …"

"She sounds like an interesting person," Jamie interrupted, "but what does that have to do with your problem?"

Cassie rested back against the chair, tilting her head until she stared at the ceiling. She let out the breath she held and revealed, "I think I'm falling in love with her."

Jamie nearly laughed in her former friend's face, but the fragile, wounded look on Cassie's face brought her compassion to the forefront. "Have you … told her this?"

Cassie shook her head so sharply that her hair flew around her head. "No. I haven't said a thing. I don't know what she'd do, or if she'd even be interested." Looking at Jamie with a plaintive look she asked, "What should I do, Jamie?"

There were many avenues that Jamie could take. With anyone else in the world, she would have revealed her own struggles with the issue and reassured her that she should try to find out the truth about her own feelings first. But Cassie had never proved to be a very trustworthy person, and she honestly didn't think she could risk it. Instead she said, "As you know, I took the class on 'The Lesbian Experience'."

Cassie nodded, looking a little embarrassed. Jamie hoped her embarrassment was over her role in torturing Jamie about the class, but she could never be sure with Cassie.

"I still have the reading list that gives resources on some books that might help you sort out your feelings. Would you like it?"

Cassie nodded, looking a little unsatisfied, but somewhat grateful. "That would be nice."

Taking pity on her, Jamie said, "I do know one thing, Cassie. Some of the best people I know are lesbians. There is no shame in it, if that is who you turn out to be. I'm sure it'd be hard for you, but being yourself is really the only option."

She nodded again, her eyes blinking closed as she tried to hide her tears. Jamie got up to go to her room, patting Cassie on the shoulder as she passed.

"I'll go get my jewelry from the safe while you find the list," she said quietly.

It took a few minutes for Jamie to find the reading list, but she pulled it from a binder just as she heard Cassie ascending the stairs. She looked around her room and saw the unmade bed, sheet and blanket thrown into a pile on the floor, two pillows neatly stacked atop one another next to the bed, used in an effort to provide a better angle and some cushioning for some of their morning activities, an open jar of raspberry jam on the bedside table, a damp washcloth stained with the deep red color of the jam, and the unmistakable aroma of sex—plenty of sex—from the very recent past. She practically ran for the door, jumping across the threshold just as Cassie hit the landing, and drawing the door closed after herself.

Cassie looked a little surprised by her actions, but merely said, "I think I left a few things in my old room. Can I take a look?"

"Uhm …" Jamie scrambled for a valid reason to keep Cassie from going into the room. Ryan's unmistakable mark was everywhere—from the family photos atop the dresser to her clothes hung neatly in the closet. "There's nothing left in there, Cassie. I had Maria Los clean the room thoroughly."

Cassie's hand was on the knob, and Jamie considered grabbing her and propelling her down the stairs, but she knew she had to behave like a rational human, at least until she got rid of her former housemate.

"Maria Los was never very thorough, Jamie. I'd like to take a look around." She paused for a moment, tilting her head slightly. "Unless there is some reason you don't want me to, that is."

"No, of course not," she said smoothly as she put one hand on Cassie's shoulder and the other on the opposite arm. "I've been through the room with my normal thoroughness, though, so I know there's nothing in there of yours. I'm having the room wallpapered, so it's completely empty now." She guided the somewhat surprised woman down the stairs, preferring to allow Cassie to have suspicions about her rather than facts.

When they returned to the living room, Jamie said, "I really hate to have to rush you, Cassie, but I've got some things I have to do this afternoon."

"No problem," she said, looking rather crestfallen. Jamie felt another stirring of guilt over treating her former friend so brusquely but, try as she might, she couldn't summon the empathy that she needed to treat her in a more compassionate way.

Extending the reading list she said, "Why don't you e-mail me after you've looked at a few of these titles. I'm sure this is a hard time for you, and I'll try to help you out in any way that I can."

"Thank you, Jamie," she said softly, a few more tears leaking out of her eyes. "You've been much kinder to me than I deserve."

She opened the door, still sniffing away her tears. Just as she stepped out onto the porch, a deliveryman came bounding up the stairs carrying a lovely bouquet of golden roses and sprigs of lavender. "Mrs. Ryan O'Flaherty?" he asked, looking from one woman to the other.

Her weeks of scheming were immediately fulfilled, causing a wide, satisfied grin to cross her face. "That's your woman," Cassie said triumphantly, pointing at a stunned Jamie. The deliveryman handed the arrangement to Jamie and ran back down the stairs accompanied by Cassie's haunting laugh. "For a minute there I thought you'd finally gotten a brain, Jamie." Her glee was so great that she had difficulty forming words through her laughter. She snatched one of the roses from the bouquet and practically skipped down the stairs, adding, "When I tell you I'm gonna kick your ass, you can take it to the bank!"

Ryan came bounding up the stairs at three-thirty, her helmet in one hand, the mail in the other. "Jamie?" she called, looking up the staircase as she juggled her burdens, puzzled that the Boxster was still in the driveway.

"I'm here, Ryan." A very small voice came from the upholstered chair to Ryan's right.

One look at her partner's face caused Ryan to drop everything with a loud clatter, and she dashed across the floor, covering the few feet that separated them in the blink of an eye. "What's wrong? What happened?" She dropped to her knees as her hands frantically roamed across her partner's face and body, looking for something to explain the desolate look on her face.

"Cassie happened," she mumbled, leaning forward until her head rested on Ryan's shoulder.

"Cassie …?" This made no sense at all, but Ryan held her questions, trying to provide the calming presence that her partner obviously needed.

"I got your flowers," she mumbled, nudging her head in the direction of the table. "Cassie was here when the delivery guy showed up."

It took a second, but the realization dawned on Ryan with a sickening thud right to her gut. She sank back onto her heels, gazing up at Jamie with a mixture of befuddlement and contrition. "Oh, sweetheart, I am so, so sorry." Her eyes closed slowly, and she shook her head at her romantic gesture gone awry.

Jamie looked into her eyes as Ryan opened them, and she asked in a small voice, "You're not mad at me?"

Ryan's body snapped to attention as she got to her knees. "Mad at you? Why on earth would I be mad at you?"

"Because I invited her in," she moaned, still enormously angry with herself for letting the traitor into the house.

"I'm sure you had a good reason to let her in, honey. Don't give that another thought. We just have to decide what to do next." Ryan's face held nothing but sympathy, making Jamie feel even worse.

"Mia said you wouldn't be mad," she mumbled, unable to face her magnanimous lover.

Ryan got to her feet and extended a hand to her partner, pulling her from her chair and settling her onto the love seat. She wrapped her arms tightly around her and said, "Come on now, don't tell me that Mia knows me better than you do."

Jamie shook her head, acknowledging that was not generally the case. "No, but … I was mad at you for letting Sara come over. This was the same thing."

Ryan laughed gently, smoothing Jamie's hair off her forehead as she placed a soft kiss there. "No, it's not, baby. Unless you've omitted a very important part of your past, you were never in love with Cassie. My sin wasn't that I let an old friend come to apologize. It was that I let someone that I cared for a great deal come over when I was alone. There was a risk of temptation there that I should have recognized."

Jamie sat up a little and rolled her eyes. "Not only haven't I loved Cassie, I've often not even liked her," she agreed. "But one thing this incident did is let me see how easy it was for you to allow Sara to come over. It's very tempting to have someone who hurt you try to make amends."

Ryan's eyes closed briefly, and she hugged her partner tight. "Thank you for saying that," she whispered. "I was tempted, but I never will be again." They sat in silence for a few moments, letting the events of the day run through their minds. "I'm just a little miffed about one thing, though," Ryan admitted. "Why didn't you page me?"

Jamie shrugged, knowing that she didn't have a good reason. "I was embarrassed," she admitted. "I felt like it was all my fault."

"Jamie," Ryan soothed. "Having this come out doesn't hurt me. Everybody in my life knows about us." She paused for a moment, recalling that her statement was not technically true, then decided to rectify that oversight that very day.

"I know, honey," she agreed. "Mia knocked some sense into me. She also agrees that Cassie and her mother are probably on their way to my mother's house even as we speak."

Ryan sat up in shock, finally grasping the complexity of the situation. "What should we do?"

"Relax, hon, I handled it."

Ryan cocked her head, waiting for the explanation.

"I called Marta and found out that Mother isn't due home from Italy until Saturday afternoon. Marta agreed to hold any messages from Laura Martin until I came down there."

"How did you explain that little request?" Ryan wondered.

"It wasn't fun, but I've never asked Marta to bail me out of trouble before. I guess she figured I was due. I just said that I needed to talk to my mother before Mrs. Martin got to her, and Marta promised she would help me out."

"No questions?"

"Nope. She's not the type to pry."

Ryan nodded, figuring that attribute could go a long way to insuring longevity as a domestic. "So ... we'll go down on Saturday and tell them?"

Jamie gave her partner an immensely grateful look—terribly pleased that Ryan assumed they would do the deed together. "I appreciate that you want to go with me, honey, but I think it'd go better if I talked to them alone. I thought I could play golf with Daddy in the morning, and then go down to Hillsborough with him afterwards to tell Mother."

Ryan settled back into the love seat, pulling Jamie close. She nodded her head slowly, knowing that Jamie's plan was wise, but wishing she could bear some of the burden for her. With a start, she realized that another vital member of Jamie's support team was not available either. "Bummer of a time to have your therapist on vacation, babe."

Jamie nodded, adding a wry chuckle. "Thankfully, my grandfather is in town. He's coming over for dinner."

"Mmm, a therapist that makes house calls. Now that's a good thing."

When Rev. Evans arrived they all spent a few minutes discussing the events of the afternoon. By prior agreement, Ryan left them to continue the discussion alone. She went to Jamie's room and booted up her computer, mulling over the task she had assigned to herself.

I didn't think it'd take me this long to come out to my grandparents, she thought. *I'm not even sure why I've delayed it so long.* She mulled the issue over in her mind, finally acknowledging that it had been easier to leave it unsaid.

John and Brigid Ryan were in their eighties, and neither was very worldly. They lived in a very small town—a village, really—in County Mayo on the northwest tip of Ireland. Their village consisted of a Catholic church, a four-room National School, a "necessaries" store that doubled as a post office and bank, a pub, a take-away fish and chips shop, and one small store that seemed to change hands every time Ryan visited. It had been everything from a florist shop to a music/video store, but the town just couldn't support the ventures.

John Ryan had been a fisherman, working on various vessels in the commercial fleet that plied the cold sea that abutted their village. He had retired when Ryan was quite small, but his profession soon became his only hobby. Most days he could be found on one of the small streams and rivers that blanketed the region, fishing for whatever was running during that particular season.

Brigid Casey Ryan was clearly a force to be reckoned with in the Ryan family. She had an opinion on nearly every topic, and she was more than willing to share it with you, whether you wished to hear it or not. Her headstrong, rather closed-minded outlook had been the deciding factor in keeping Ryan from being honest with them about her sexual orientation, but she decided that if Jamie could do it, she could do it.

An hour and a half later her screen remained blank. When Jamie went to call her for dinner she was lying on the bed, hands laced behind her head, with a very contemplative look on her face. "Honey?" Jamie said, causing Ryan to start.

She shook her head and gazed at her partner. "Whoa … I was really out of it there." Getting to her feet she approached her partner and rested her hands on her shoulders. "Everything okay, honey?"

A small nod accompanied by a gentle smile was all the reassurance that Ryan needed. "Yeah … I feel pretty good. Poppa has really calmed me down."

Ryan wrapped her in a hug and murmured into her hair, "I'm so glad to hear that. And I'm so glad you have him in your life."

"Me too," Jamie agreed. "We thought we'd grill some salmon steaks outside. Will you perform your usual grill duties?"

"My pleasure. Nothing I like better than showing off for my girl."

Jamie gave her a playful swat to the seat. "No wonder you're in such a good mood all of the time, Buffy!"

Rev. Evans left early, at about eight o'clock. Jamie insisted on cleaning up alone, since Ryan had done all the cooking, so Ryan decided to make another attempt at writing her letter.

Jamie came up to find her sitting at a blank computer screen, a faraway look in her eyes. "What's up, babe?" she asked, standing behind Ryan and giving her scalp a little scratch.

"I've decided that I need to finally write that letter to my grandparents. I want them to know all about you," she said with a smile as she turned her head to meet Jamie's eyes.

"That's sweet," she said, leaning over to kiss Ryan's cheek. "Looks like you're having a little trouble getting started."

"Yeah, I am. I write to them about once a month but I never really tell them anything personal. I've mentioned you before but not to an extent that would let them know what you mean to me," she admitted.

"Are you sure you're ready to do this?" Jamie asked gently, letting her hands drop to Ryan's shoulders to continue the rub.

"Yeah. Absolutely," Ryan said firmly. "I'm angry at myself for waiting this long."

"What do you want them to know?" she asked as she grasped Ryan by the shoulders and turned her around in her swivel chair.

"Hmm, I guess I want them to know that I've fallen in love and that I'm going to spend my life with you. I want them to know that I'm permanently committed to you, and that you make me happier than I had any expectation of being. And I want them to consider you to be my spousal equivalent."

Trailing her fingers through Ryan's dark hair, she shared some of the advice her grandfather had just given her. "That's asking a lot," she mused when she considered Ryan's list. "I don't think you can ask for them to consider me your spouse, honey. I think all you can do is treat me like your spouse and hope they do the same."

Ryan leaned back in her chair and considered this for a moment. "I see your point. I can hope they are open-minded, but I can't really demand that of them."

"Exactly," Jamie said as she kissed her partner on the top of her head. "You know, I don't really know how you feel about your grandparents. How do you get along?" She sat down on the bed and kicked off her shoes, placing her feet onto Ryan's lap on the off chance that her partner wanted to rub them for her.

Ryan smiled at her none-too-subtle move and acceded to the implied request. "Well, let's say that the distance is not entirely unwelcome," she admitted. "If you didn't see his chest moving you would think my grandfather was stuffed. He doesn't get the opportunity to speak his mind very often when my grandmother's around, and he obviously stopped trying long before I was born. We used to go fishing together in some of the little streams around the county and I really grew quite fond of him. He's a very sweet man—I'm certain my mother and my aunts got their kindness and gentleness from him."

"He sounds nice," Jamie agreed, guessing that some of her partner's gentle nature might have come down through the Ryan line, too.

"Now my grandmother is an interesting creature. She's very headstrong and opinionated, and most people just give in to her. So in a way, she's tough to be around for long. But she also cares for people very deeply, and she's very generous with her time and her abilities. She has a really good heart, but sometimes it's more pleasant to appreciate her from a distance."

"How about you? Do you stand up to her?"

Ryan nodded contemplatively. "I'd say that of all of the grandchildren she and I have the stormiest history. She always used to say that I was just like Aunt Maeve. To her that was an insult, of course, but to me, it was quite a compliment."

"She and your aunt don't get along?"

"They were like oil and water, to be honest. As soon as Maeve was old enough, she lit out for America with a friend, and never went back."

"I got the impression that your father wasn't a big fan, either," Jamie observed.

"I don't think I had any idea that was true when I was young. But over the years he's let a few things slip that make me agree with you. Aunt Maeve has told me that my grandmother was very unhappy when my mother left home, and her displeasure increased greatly when she fell in love and decided to stay. I think my grandmother thought she had married beneath her station, which is funny because she and my grandfather are as poor as church mice. I know she thinks that Mama got ill because she lived in the States. She seems to believe that the U.S.A. is one big carcinogen," she said with a smile.

"So how do you think they'll react to your news?"

"Only one thing I'm sure of. Whatever her reaction, it'll be unequivocal!"

Jamie lay down to finish looking over her bills for the month as Ryan stared at her computer. After a long while her fingers began to fly over the keys, barely pausing until she was finished with her draft. "What do you think?" she asked, handing the printout to her partner.

The letter read:

Dear Mamó and Daideó,

Jamie paused, turning to Ryan with a questioning look. "How do you pronounce the names you call them, honey?"

"Oh," Ryan laughed, coming to stand next to her partner. "What did I use?"

Jamie handed the letter back and Ryan took a glance and nodded. "Those are kinda like Granny and Grandpa. They are pronounced MA-moe and DA-doe."

"That's cute," she smiled, trying out the names on her own uneducated tongue.

"I've got a million of 'em," Ryan laughed. "I'll teach you as much as you want to know."

"Cool," Jamie grinned. "I've always wanted to be quadrilingual." She patted Ryan's back and said, "Let me get back to business here, my wild Irish rose." Holding the letter up to the light, she started to read:

I have some news to share with you about a very important part of my life.

I'm sure you've noticed that I've never brought up the subject of my love life with either of you. There have been two reasons for that omission. Primarily I've not had anyone special enough to talk about; but secondarily I've been reticent to talk about my love life because I thought you might disapprove, and I didn't want to upset you unnecessarily.

I've known since I was seventeen that I was only attracted to other women. I know that homosexuality is a difficult subject for many people and I can only assume that this might be hard for you to accept. I want to make it clear that I'm certain this is the life that I was born to live. I know that the church has a dim view of gay behavior, but I feel strongly that God created me exactly as I am. I feel that I have a right to express my love in a physical way, so long as I do so in a loving fashion. I hope that you can accept my lesbianism, either immediately or over time. I want you to know that I am not only happy with my life, but I truly look at my sexual orientation as a gift from God.

My news is that I've recently been given another gift from God. I've fallen in love with the most wonderful woman it has been my privilege to know. Her name is Jamie Evans and she is a classmate of mine from university.

As you can see from the enclosed picture, she is a truly beautiful woman. But when you meet her, I hope you are able to see that her true beauty lies in her soul. She is kind and loving and generous and very giving, and I can honestly say that she makes me happier than I had any hope of being. I am honored that she has chosen to spend her life with me, and I want to spend the rest of my life making her as happy as she has made me.

I hope that you are able to share in my joy at having found my life-mate. No matter how you feel about it, please know that I love you both and will continue to do so even if you are not able to give me your blessing.

The picture that I enclose is from this year's AIDS Ride. Jamie did the ride with me this year and it was a very special blessing to be able to start our life together participating in such a moving experience. Even though she did not have the opportunity to know Michael, Jamie understands how much he meant to me, and it was wonderful to have someone that I could share my feelings with for the first time during the ride. It made the experience much more meaningful, but also much more emotional for me. As always, I made a stop at the small mission church named for his patron. It might just be wishful thinking but I swear I can feel his spirit every time I pray there.

Please let me hear from you when you have time to reflect on this news. I love you both and I hope you can be happy for my newfound joy.

Love always,

Siobhán

Jamie looked up with tears in her eyes as she whispered, "This is so beautiful, Ryan. It makes me think of your birthday when you told me about Sara. I remember thinking, 'How can she be so open with her feelings?' It just amazed me that you could be that loving and connected and yet never have a woman that you were connected to enough to love. It just seemed like an emotional oxymoron to me."

Ryan smiled down at her as she patted her cheek. "I wasn't that emotionally open to everyone, honey. I was just able to open myself up to you very early on in our relationship. I still don't know if I was falling in love or if I just felt comfortable with you as a friend. But I guarantee that most people didn't see that side of me."

"I'm eternally grateful that I get to see it," Jamie whispered, then stood and wrapped her lover in her arms.

"Being vulnerable is the best and the worst part of being with you," Ryan said softly. "It still scares me a little bit but I'm very happy that you get to see deep into my soul. It's an intimacy that I've not had before but I'm grateful that I have it with you."

"We're both doing something pretty scary here, partner," she said, looking up into those clear blue eyes. "All we've talked about all day is all of the problems that we might have to work through. Why don't we lie down together and remind ourselves of one of the wonderful benefits of loving each other."

Ryan linked her arms loosely behind Jamie's neck, slowly bending to place a gentle kiss on her lips. "And you always say I have the good ideas."

Chapter Twelve

As they stood on the eighteenth tee, waiting for the group ahead of them to clear the landing area, Jim Evans looked at his only child with obvious pride. When Jamie had told him the previous weekend of her plans to try out for the golf team, he was so excited she thought he might hyperventilate. Only her embarrassed pleas had kept him from boasting about her during the entire round that they had played with the Christophers. Now that they were alone, however, he kept up a running commentary about his plans to aid her future development. "You like working with Chip down at the beach, don't you?"

"Yes, he helped me a lot," she admitted, acknowledging that her game had improved significantly under his tutelage.

"Why don't you spend your weekends down there? There is nothing to hold you in Berkeley. Actually, why not stay down there until school starts?" he suggested, the excitement showing in his voice. "You could hire Chip to work with you full-time. I'm sure the club would be happy to let him—"

"Daddy," she interrupted. "I don't want to spend my summer in Pebble Beach."

"Why not, honey? There's nothing holding you in Berkeley, is there?" He looked puzzled by her refusal to accept his eminently logical suggestion.

"Just my life," she replied, a flicker of irritation showing on her face.

"What?" he asked, now even more puzzled.

"I live in Berkeley, Daddy. I have things I do, people I see. I don't want to give that up."

"Well, of course you do, Jamie," he agreed with a small laugh. "I don't think you live in an isolation tank. But you need to make some sacrifices to achieve a goal like this."

The determination in her eyes grew brighter as she insisted, "I know that, Daddy. I'm very willing to make sacrifices, but leaving my home is not one of them. I'm sure I can find someone in the San Francisco area who can help me out also."

"Oh, well, I didn't know you felt that way," he said, the confusion continuing to grow on his face. He wasn't used to Jamie having such firm convictions, but he shrugged it off and got back on track quickly. "Mark Griffin, here at Olympic, is very good. After the round, let's have him take a look at your swing and see if he'd like to work with you. What's your schedule like during the week?"

"I've decided to start running again, so I'll do that on Monday, Wednesday, and Friday. I lift weights on Tuesday, Thursday, and Saturday. I've played or practiced nearly every day since I set this goal, so my afternoons have been dedicated to golf. I guess afternoons would be the best time to work with Mark, if it works out."

"Great," he said, a broad smile now covering his face. "Maybe we should find someone to make sure your weight program is up to snuff."

Jamie's eyes narrowed as she approached her ball. Unleashing some of her frustrations, she sent the innocent little white orb on a screaming flight right down the center of the fairway. "I have someone, Daddy," she informed him firmly.

"Oh," he said, nodding at the memory. "Is your friend … Ryan … still working with you?"

"Yes, she is," she said simply, not wishing to elaborate at this point.

"I'm sure she's a great friend, honey, but are you sure she's competent? Anybody can call themselves a trainer, you know."

Swallowing her ire, she affixed a smile and said, "I'm certain that she's competent. We work beautifully together, and I have no plans to switch."

She noticed the confused look he shot her way as he addressed his tee shot, but offered no further comment.

Walking back to the cart he said, "I don't remember you being very interested in running. When did you start?"

"I've been running with the volleyball team. Ryan just made the team as a scholarship player, and I thought it'd be a good motivator to keep me moving. I don't want to look like a wimp in front of those real athletes!" She was still miffed about his attempts to direct her life, but she had to admit that he was only exercising his right of eminent domain, as he had since she was born. She knew that he wouldn't stop without a good deal of work on her part, and she knew that the path wouldn't be terribly smooth.

"That's pretty impressive," he said. "She must be quite an athlete."

"She had her pick of soccer, volleyball, or field hockey." Her obvious pride was impossible to hide, and she made no real attempt to do so. "She's really unbelievable."

"Well, she certainly has the body of an athlete," he said appreciatively, a smile crossing his face that rankled Jamie to the core. She was about to snap off a sharp comment when he saved her by asking, "Did she play before?"

She shook her head to clear it, reminding herself that telling her father to keep his eyes off Ryan's body was not the best way to start the conversation she knew they had to have. "Not at Cal. She's a transfer from USF. She didn't play last year because you have to sit out a year when you transfer. Plus, she worked so much she couldn't possibly have managed a sport."

"What changed for her?" His question was innocent, almost offhanded, but Jamie knew the answer would be revealed soon enough.

"Uhm, her financial situation got a lot better this year," she said.

"That's good. I got so much out of playing sports, I can imagine how happy that made her. It's nice when a lack of money doesn't stop someone from using their talents."

The pro that Jim wanted to speak to was busy giving a lesson, so Jim left a message for him to call Jamie when he was free. "Now I want you to try to make time to work with Mark," he instructed. "I'm sure the competition will be fierce for those spots."

"I know, Daddy," she said fondly. "Thanks for caring so much."

"I care a great deal, cupcake," he said, sliding his arm around her shoulders. "You make me very proud, honey," he said as he turned to face her and lock eyes. "I hear some of the other guys talking about their kids, and how much trouble they cause them, and I thank God that I have you."

She wrapped her arms around his waist and gave him a squeeze. "Thanks, Daddy. I'm glad I have you, too." *I just hope you still feel that way later today.*

After they had showered and changed, they met in the lobby and decided to have lunch. As friends and colleagues passed by, Jim went out of his way to introduce Jamie and brag about her attempt to make the golf team at Cal. "Daddy, you've told everyone except the busboy," she finally said.

"I'm just really excited about this, Jamie. I never thought you wanted to go farther with your golf game, and it just makes me happy to boast about you."

When they had finished their lunch he remarked, "I guess I'll see you next week?"

"Do you have plans for the rest of the day?" she asked, a part of her hoping that he did.

"Not really. I've got an appointment at four to see an Oldsmobile 442 that I'm thinking about buying, but that's it. Why?"

"I think I'll come down and wait for Mother to come home. She should be there about then, shouldn't she?"

"She'd like that, honey, and so would I." Giving her another fond smile he said, "Things like this are exactly what I mean when I say how proud I am of you, Jamie. Most kids your age would have no idea when their mother was due home from a trip. It's really nice how much you care."

She smiled back, not having any intention of telling him that Marta was the one he should be proud of.

It was nearly one-thirty when they arrived at the massive French provincial home. As she pulled into the long drive Jamie found herself staring at the huge edifice in a critical way for the first time in her life. The house was lovely, she had to admit, set as it was into the densely wooded site in a way that protected it from the stares of casual passersby. Not that there were many of those in Hillsborough, of course. By ordinance there were no sidewalks or streetlamps allowed, so not many braved the narrow, curving streets on foot.

It was not the look of the house that bothered Jamie today, though. It was the size. She shook her head and marveled at the fact that she had grown up in a home that could have accommodated all of the O'Flahertys, cousins included. *One small family should not waste resources like this*, she mused as she left the car in the drive and walked up to the front door.

She had not been home since her failed attempt at reconciliation with Jack, so she looked around the place for a while admiring the latest furnishings that her mother had purchased. Realizing that the time for delay was past, she steeled her nerves and turned to her father saying, "I need to talk to you about something important, Daddy."

"Sure, cupcake, what is it?" He gave her an interested look as he sat down on one of the large sofas in the living room and patted the seat to indicate that she should join him.

It took her a moment to gather her courage, but now that she had broached the subject it was obviously too late to turn back. "I've changed a lot in the last year, Daddy. Or maybe I've just found my true self. Whatever it is, I'm not the same person that I was a year ago."

He smiled at this statement and silently acknowledged the truth of it as he gave her an encouraging smile. Jim had noticed quite a few changes in his daughter in the last year, and he was very happy with most of them. She seemed more confident and more determined, and she was definitely more athletic. In fact, the only change that he was unhappy with was her recent tendency to disagree with him about certain issues. Jamie had always been an eminently compliant child, and he had to admit that her previously acquiescent style was more to his liking. Nonetheless, he knew that he had very little to complain about, and he counted himself among the lucky few who had no major problems with their children.

She gazed at him with a determined look in her eyes and continued with her comments. "I've gotten stronger, both physically and emotionally, in the last year. I've learned a tremendous amount about myself. I'm really happy with the changes I've made, and I want to share them with you."

He sat up a little straighter when she uttered her last sentence. "Sure, honey. I'm always interested in your life. You can tell me anything."

She smiled at him and continued. "One of the things that I really struggled with this year was my breakup with Jack. It was really difficult for me, and I actually started to see a therapist to try to work out my feelings."

He looked a bit shocked and said, "Jamie, why didn't you tell us this was so hard for you? We could have talked to you about it. I mean … you just seemed to take it in stride."

"Daddy, we were engaged," she said patiently, amazed that he would assume she wouldn't feel the aftereffects of a broken engagement. "Of course it was a big deal."

"I just wish I had known," he said as he pursed his lips and shook his head.

She patted his leg fondly, smiling at him in a reassuring way. "It's okay, Daddy. This was something I had to work out on my own. I don't think anyone could have done much to make it better."

He gave her a smile laced with regret over his inability to help her get over this pain. "So did this therapy help?"

"Yes, it helped a lot, actually. I learned that one of the biggest problems in our relationship was me," she said simply.

"You? That's ridiculous, Jamie. I'm sure you would have been a wonderful wife." His incredulity was nearly as great as his outrage, and he was about to launch into a spirited defense of his daughter when she interrupted.

"No, Daddy, the problem *was* mostly mine. I learned in therapy that I wasn't able to give myself completely to Jack. We had a lot of problems, Daddy, and I believe that most of them were because I withheld my true self. He didn't really know me, because I didn't know myself. But over the past four months I've come to know myself much better, and I've learned to accept and even embrace some parts of myself that I had been trying to hide for a long time. What I'm saying is that I'm learning to love myself completely for the first time in my adult life. I really feel good about that, and I want you to understand it and support me, if possible."

He was fidgeting nervously as he sat on the sofa. He knew his daughter was going to unleash some sort of bombshell by the tension she displayed, but he honestly had no idea what the news could be. "This sounds really positive and helpful, Jamie, but you're being a little abstruse."

"I probably am," she admitted with a nervous laugh. Several deep breaths later, she gazed at him and got out the most important part of her message. "The bottom line is that once I came to know myself better, I was able to open up to others a lot more. And the wonderful thing is that I fell in love. For the first time, and hopefully the last, I am truly, deeply in love."

His face lit up in a delighted smile, relieved beyond measure that Jamie had such good news to share. "That's great, honey. Just great! When do we get to meet the lucky fellow? Or have I already met him?" he asked with a twinkle in his eye.

Jamie instantly realized where this path was leading. "You have met, but it's not what you think," she warned, her eyes growing wide.

"Oh?" Now the confusion was back onto his face. "I thought it might be Ryan's brother. They sure are a fine-looking pair of siblings."

"No, Daddy. It's not her brother. It's Ryan. I've fallen in love with Ryan."

He opened his mouth at least three separate times trying to speak, but, for one of the few times in his life, no words would come. Giving her a completely helpless look he finally uttered, "Are you sure?"

"Yes, Daddy, I'm very sure. I've never been more certain of anything in my life." Now that the words were out, Jamie was, amazingly, the soul of composure. She looked much older than her twenty-one years, and Jim was suddenly struck with the thought that his little girl was truly no longer a child.

"D ... d ... does *she* know?" he stuttered.

"Yes, she knows," she said softly. "She feels the same for me."

"Have you ... have you ... been ... together?" This last word was practically wrung from his mouth, and he looked a little ill as he articulated it.

She blushed deeply and debated with herself for just an instant. The details of their relationship were really not something she wished to share, but this was such a big issue, she decided to tell all. "Yes, Daddy, we have."

"And you're still certain?" he asked, rather perplexed that his daughter could be with a woman in that way and still think she was in love.

"That's what made me certain," she admitted despite her embarrassment. "I felt like I was finally home."

"But honey," he said as his mind started to wake up, "Young women like you don't just wake up one day and decide that they're ... that they're ... lesbians."

"My realization didn't come in one day," she assured him, putting aside the issue of whether she was, in fact, a lesbian or not. "When I look back on it now, I've had clues for years. It was never right for me with men. I didn't connect with them, emotionally or sexually," she admitted.

Now he began to flush as he asked, "I know this is a private matter, Jamie, but how many men have you really been with?"

She didn't like this line of questioning, but since she had started it, she felt that she had to finish it. "That is private, but I want to help you to understand this, so I'll answer. I was only with Jack, Daddy. And I didn't sleep with him until last summer."

His hands dropped to the cushion as his mouth fell open. "I just ... I just assumed that some of the boys in high school had convinced ..."

"No, no one convinced me of anything. Not then and not now."

The confident, determined look that covered her face spoke volumes about her resolve, and he felt just a flash of respect for her well-thought-out position. But his protective, parental voice quickly reasserted itself. "But why did you wait so long? I thought girls were having sex in grammar school now. Did something happen to you when you were younger?" he asked, grasping at straws.

"No! Of course not! No one ever touched me. I waited because I wasn't interested. I wasn't really interested with Jack either, but I knew I couldn't make him hold out forever. I'm amazed he waited for two years," she admitted with a sardonic shake of her head.

He dropped his head into his hands and sat very still for a long while. He finally lifted his head and asked, "And you are ... interested ... in that way ... with Ryan?"

She slowly nodded her head as she closed her eyes momentarily. "Very," she replied. "Completely."

His body had nearly been in shock, and now that the reality of the situation started to hit, he felt the familiar clenching in his stomach and worried briefly that he was going to be sick. His hands were clasped loosely together, hanging between his spread knees, and his drooping head mirrored them. "I just don't know what to say, Jamie. This is the very last thing I ever expected from you." He looked up at her with a mixture of fear and sadness. "I'm really at a loss."

She had never seen such a lost, haunted look on her father's face, and it suddenly hit her how difficult it was for him to hear this news. Not that she thought being gay was a bad thing, of course. But she had a sudden insight into her grandfather's warning that the worst thing for her parents would be the realization that their plans for her wouldn't come to fruition. Her voice grew gentle, and she reached out to lightly grasp his linked hands. "Did you understand what I said at the beginning of this conversation? This makes me very happy."

He looked up at her and gazed deeply into her eyes for a moment. He saw the determined, confident expression that covered her face, but it just made no sense to him. "How can it?" The question lay at her feet like an unexploded grenade. She fought the urge to lob it back at him with a smart remark, focusing instead on the gap that she had to try to bridge.

Maintaining his gaze, she spoke the simple truth that filled her soul. "It's true because being with her has allowed me to be the best 'me' that I have ever been. She completes me." A soft, bemused laugh escaped her lips and she explained, "I used to think people were speaking a foreign language when they spoke of the kind of love I feel for her. I never thought it was possible to feel like this about another person, Daddy, but now that I know, I swear that I will never give it up. I will never give her up."

Her sincerity affected him deeply, and he let her words rumble around in his mind for a moment. His gaze lingered on the earnest, self-possessed young woman who looked back at him, thinking how much she reminded him of himself at her age. He opened his arms and bit back a tear as she collapsed into his embrace. Placing several light kisses upon the top of her head, he patted her back lovingly, giving her a final squeeze as he said, "I need some time to think about this, Jamie. This is an awful lot for me to get my mind around."

"That's okay," she murmured, sitting up once again. She ran a hand through her hair and he smiled when he realized that gesture was identical to one he had seen Catherine use hundreds of times. "I tried to hide the truth from myself for years. It's okay if it takes you a while to be comfortable with it."

He shook his head a little more forcefully. "I don't think I'll ever be comfortable with this, honey. But I'll try to understand."

"That's all that I ask of you," she said, meaning every word.

A glance at the clock on the mantel alerted him to his appointment and he excused himself as he stood. "I need to call the fellow who was going to show me that car to tell him I can't make it."

He had only traveled a couple of feet when she said, "Why don't you go ahead and go. I'd like to talk to Mother alone, if you don't mind."

His eyes opened very wide as he commented, "I don't know that this is a very good way to be welcomed home, Jamie. Couldn't you wait a bit?"

She shook her head firmly. "I'd really prefer to do it today. I don't think it's fair to Mother to hide this from her any longer."

Sighing heavily, he offered a small smile to his determined daughter. "As you wish, Jamie. Tell your mother I'll be home for dinner." He started for the front door, pausing briefly as he entered the foyer. He looked as though he were about to offer some bit of advice. Instead, he gave her a somber look and said, "Good luck."

As soon as he walked out the door, Jamie pulled her cell phone from her belt and paged Ryan. In moments, the call was returned, her partner sounding rather breathless. "Hi, sweetheart," Jamie said softly.

"Are you okay?" Ryan asked simultaneously.

"Sure … of course, baby. I spoke with Daddy, and it went better than I thought it would."

She could hear the relieved breath that whistled through the receiver. "God, that's good news."

"Yeah. It wasn't a cause for celebration or anything—but he didn't go ballistic."

"I'm very, very happy to hear that, honey," Ryan murmured, her voice breaking up a little because of the poor connection.

"Mother should be home soon, babe. I'll call you after round two."

"You take care of yourself, Jamie." Ryan's voice was serious, and Jamie could just picture her earnest face.

"I will, love. I'll call you when I can."

"I love you, Jamie," Ryan soothed. "No matter how it goes today, you will always be loved—by me and your O'Flaherty family."

A calming, warm sense of relief washed over her, and she could actually feel some of the tension leave her body. Her voice dropped an octave, and she softly replied, "That means everything to me, Ryan. Absolutely everything."

"Marta?" Jamie called as she walked into the kitchen in search of the Evans family cook.

Jamie had been so focused on starting the conversation with her father that she hadn't taken the time to seek out her old friend when they first arrived at the house. She had always considered Marta a member of the family, but she knew that Marta didn't exactly share that feeling. It wasn't that Marta didn't care for the members of the Evans family, she did—quite a lot, in fact. Rather, it was that she had never mistaken the pleasant, friendly way that Jim and Catherine treated her for anything other than well-mannered people being good employers.

Jamie, however, was another matter. She felt a deep bond with her—a bond that had begun even before her birth, when Marta would make special meals to encourage Catherine to eat a balanced diet during her pregnancy.

Nonetheless, Marta would never come into the living areas to welcome Jamie home. She would remain in the kitchen, or in her large, well-appointed room, waiting for the familiar light knock that always brought a smile to her face.

Failing to find the cook in the kitchen, Jamie poked her head out the back door, pleased to find Marta sitting under an umbrella, enjoying a tall glass of lemonade. As Jamie drew closer she smiled when she spied another glass, waiting just for her. "Madrina," she said affectionately as she bent to kiss Marta's cheek.

"Mi hija," Marta replied with a wide smile, in her standard fashion. For as long as Jamie could remember, she and Marta had referred to each other as "Godmother" and

"My daughter." The term was not of a proprietary nature. Marta never considered that it was her place to act as Jamie's mother. It was more a sign of the deep affection that the two had always had for each other.

"I'm sorry I didn't come to find you earlier," Jamie said, as Marta poured the lemonade for her. "I needed to speak to my father for a few minutes."

"It's quite all right, Jamie," Marta said, her grin crinkling the corners of her eyes. "I am always happy to see you, whether I am the first or the last to be greeted."

There was no sting in her words—she was merely expressing the reality of their situation. She had always attempted to show Jamie that there was a dividing line between her, an employee, and Jim and Catherine. It was a hard lesson for the child to learn, especially because she spent more time with Elizabeth and Marta than she did with her parents. But Marta knew that unemployment was just around the corner for the person who tried to breach that invisible, but impenetrable, barrier.

"Are you preparing a special meal for Mother's homecoming?" It was an old joke between the pair. Catherine ate slightly less than Caitlin, and twenty-two years of trying had still not revealed the secret to getting the elder Evans woman to clean her plate.

"I believe I have finally given up that quest," Marta replied with a small smile. "But if you will be here for dinner, I will pull out all of the stops."

"I hadn't planned on it, Marta," she said, sparing a glance at her watch, "but it might be a good idea, after all. I need to speak with Mother, and it wouldn't be polite to run out as soon as I'm finished."

Marta gave her young friend a long, interested look. She wouldn't intrude by asking Jamie the nature of her business this afternoon, but she was more than willing to lend an ear if it was needed.

Jamie understood the slight gesture perfectly, having grown very proficient at reading the older woman's body language, but she didn't feel comfortable sharing her news with Marta before she spoke to her mother. She also didn't relish the thought of coming out to three people in one day. As much as she cared for Marta, she was not at all sure how the older woman would react. Marta was a staunch Catholic, and she took a very active role as a volunteer at her church. Jamie didn't know a lot about Catholic dogma, but she was certain that the church didn't approve of homosexual pairings. She assumed that even if Marta disapproved of her relationship with Ryan, she wouldn't say so, but she still didn't want to take the risk.

Marta cocked her head slightly, her features stilling as she listened intently. "Your mother is home," she said softly.

Jamie visibly tensed, a reaction not lost on the older woman. "It will be fine, Jamie. Your mother loves you."

Getting to her feet, Jamie leaned over once again and placed a grateful kiss on Marta's cheek, smiling to herself as she detected her calming, lilac scent. "I know, Marta. This is just going to be a tough day for all of us. Thanks for caring."

"I do care, mi hija. Never forget that."

By the time Jamie entered the foyer, the limo driver had made three trips to unload the seven massive suitcases that Catherine had taken to Italy. "Jamie," she said with a delighted smile when her daughter appeared. "What a lovely surprise!"

"Hi Mother," she said, matching her smile. They exchanged light kisses on both cheeks, somehow managing to keep the majority of their bodies from touching. "I thought I'd come down to welcome you home."

Catherine did a quick double take at that bit of news, truly surprised to see her daughter—and even more so to be the reason for her visit. The driver had finished, and he lingered at the door, waiting for his payment. Catherine gave him a very generous tip, thanking him for his help in unloading all her bags.

She turned back to Jamie as she closed the door and asked, "Is your father home?"

"No. We played golf this morning, but he had an appointment to see someone about a car. He said to tell you that he'd be home for dinner."

"That's nice, dear," she said, giving Jamie another pleased smile. She looked in the gilt-framed mirror in the foyer and fussed with her hair for a moment. "Oh my, I'm afraid I look as exhausted as I feel."

"You probably want to take a nap before dinner," Jamie realized. "I can come down another time to see you."

"No, no, don't be silly. It's not even five o'clock. I think I'll have a little something for dinner and turn in early. I've got to get my clock back on West Coast time."

"Are you certain?" Jamie suddenly felt very selfish for springing this news on her mother when she was obviously tired. Italy was nine hours ahead of San Francisco, and she knew that her mother had a hard time sleeping on planes. But she was in too deep to turn back now, and she was certain that Laura Martin wouldn't hold her tongue for long.

As if on cue, the telephone rang and Catherine walked into the living room to pick it up. "Hello, Laura," she said graciously after her friend had identified herself.

Her fear becoming fact so suddenly, Jamie nearly fainted dead away. She found her way into the living room, and fell gracelessly onto one of the enormous couches in the massive room. Her stomach clenched violently, and for one fleeting moment she considered jumping up to wrest the phone from her mother's hands, but she decided to allow the inevitable to occur.

"No, I didn't get your message, Laura. To be honest, I just walked into the house. I was very pleased to find my lovely daughter waiting for me." She turned to give Jamie a fond smile, and was startled to see her daughter's face resembling that of someone being led to execution.

"Pardon?" she said, focusing her attention back on her friend. "What did you say, Laura?" Catherine paused, then looked at Jamie. "No, she's alone. ... why do you ask?"

Jamie leaned over abruptly, dropping her head into her hands. Catherine could see how upset she was, and it was obvious that Jamie already knew what Laura was trying to convey.

Moments later, all of the color drained from Catherine's face. She blindly felt for and grasped an elegant little carved writing chair and lowered her body into it. "No, I didn't know that Jamie referred to herself that way," she said in a weak voice. Jamie felt like impaling herself on the fireplace tools when she heard the tone in her mother's voice. It was the most emotion she had ever heard from the woman, and she realized how tremendously hard it must be for her to hear this news from outside the family.

To her amazement, her mother's cool resurfaced almost before she registered its loss. "I'm sure that was a little joke, Laura. Jamie is not Mrs. Ryan O'Flaherty. I can assure you of that." Catherine turned to lock her gaze onto her daughter's—and saw the guilt reflected in the moss green eyes.

"Of course we know of Ryan, Laura," she said blithely, her face an expressionless mask. "It's just not possible for women to marry in California. Don't you have any gay friends, dear?"

Jamie's brow furrowed as she tried to get her mind around her mother's words. It suddenly became obvious that Laura Martin was not going to get the satisfaction that she wished from this interchange. It was all Jamie could do not to shout, "Go Mother!"

"Yes, of course, we know of their relationship. Jamie just hasn't been ready to share it with the world at large yet." Her large, warm brown eyes softened as she saw the gratitude that emanated from her daughter. "That does, of course, beg the question of why you thought it your place to bring this to my attention, Laura. You obviously thought this was news to me."

A stonily determined look had now replaced the warmth in her eyes, and Catherine looked away from her daughter, staring out the windows of the living room as she said, "Jamie has never given us one moment of trouble, Laura. She is the most wonderful child I could hope to be blessed with, and her sexual orientation doesn't change that in the least. This is an intensely private issue for Jamie, and I should think that you would respect her privacy."

Catherine smirked, going in for the kill. "No, we are truly not concerned about her. I'm intensely proud of my daughter, and I'm happy to say that she's generous, kind, and thoughtful to a fault. She's never hurt anyone intentionally, Laura, and those traits are far more important than who she sleeps with."

As her expression reverted to one of warmth, she turned and shared a small smile with her daughter. "Oh, I'm *sure* that was your intention, Laura," she murmured with obviously false sincerity. "Of course I'm gratified that you are so concerned about her. I'll relay your good wishes. Yes, of course I'll be at the board meeting on Monday. I'll see you then."

After Catherine replaced the receiver onto the cradle, she sat absolutely still for a few minutes. She got to her feet and turned to a still-shaken Jamie and said, "I have just one question, dear. Will you join me for a drink?"

A long silence passed between them as they sat in the same chairs Jamie and Marta had occupied earlier. The robotic pool cleaner was making quick work of the few leaves that had the temerity to spoil the pristine aqua waters of the large, deep pool, and Jamie spent a few minutes watching it, glad to have something to occupy her mind.

Marta had prepared a large tray that held decanters of vodka, gin, scotch, sweet and plain soda, vermouth, and Campari. Jamie decided on Campari and soda, and Catherine echoed her choice, mentally extending the feeling of Italy when she took a sip.

"I had a Campari every afternoon at around this time during my trip," she said softly, a wistful look in her eyes.

"I bet part of you wishes you were still there," Jamie offered, deciding to break the ice.

Her mother turned and looked at her closely for a minute, then said, "Not in the least, dear. It was a lovely surprise to see you when I walked in—I haven't changed my mind."

Jamie was a bit nonplussed by the tone in her mother's voice. For the first time in her life, her mother sounded ... tired. There was some quality of resignation—almost of defeat—but the words themselves were gentle, welcoming.

"Are you ... all right with this?" she asked, unsure of how to approach the topic.

"All right?" she said slowly, trying to decide what her reaction should be. "I don't think that term would convey my feelings, no."

"What would, Mother?"

Catherine took another sip of her drink and set the glass on the table. "That's difficult to say, Jamie. I would suppose that I could best sum up my feelings by saying that I'm far from surprised—and I'm deeply wounded."

"Wounded?" she asked in puzzlement, thinking that was an odd choice of words.

"Yes, I'm wounded. I tried to get you to be honest with me when I came to your house. It was clear to me then that something was going on, since I found Cassie's original story too believable to be dismissed. I truly wish that you had told me then. It hurts to know that you lied to me, especially since I made it clear how important it was to me that you tell me the truth." The look on her face was still calm and her voice was cool and even. But Jamie could see a deep hurt reflected in those velvety eyes, and she knew that she was responsible for it.

She hung her head, unable to face her mother. She had never knowingly lied to her before that incident, and it still bothered her despite Ryan's and her grandfather's reassurance that she was just protecting herself. "I'm sorry, Mother, I really am. But I couldn't tell you then because I was in the midst of figuring it out for myself."

Catherine tilted her head to stare at her daughter for a moment. "Tell me more," she said softly.

The sun was obscured by a very large bank of clouds, and Jamie began to shiver, both from the cold and from her trepidation about revealing the intimate details of the journey of her sexual awakening.

"Let's go inside," Catherine suggested. "You look chilled."

"Okay," Jamie agreed, glad for the break. She carried the tray into the house, deciding to take it into the living room for the inevitable refills.

Once they were settled, she began to speak. "I've had some notion that something was amiss in the way I felt about men for a very long time."

Her mother tilted her head in question, but didn't comment.

"I didn't tell you this, but last fall I took a class called 'The Lesbian Experience.' Jack and I had been engaged three months at the time, but I was so unsatisfied." She glanced at her mother's concerned face and added, "Physically as well as emotionally."

Catherine nodded, encouraging Jamie to continue. She leaned over and refilled her glass, this time adding vodka to the mix.

"I met Ryan on the first day of class, and what started out as a friendship grew to be more and more. The day after Jack broke up with me, I realized that I was in love with her." Even though this was a hard thing to discuss, Jamie couldn't help but smile when she said these words. Her mother caught the look and reflected it, her smile erasing years from her face.

"That was a very, very hard time for me. I was so devastated by all of my conflicting emotions that I decided to get into therapy. My therapist and I worked on this issue nonstop through April, and it was only then that I revealed my feelings to Ryan. We decided to take things slowly—very slowly—so that I could get used to the way I felt. We waited until just three weeks ago to be together … physically."

Catherine performed the simple math and recognized that her daughter had used the house in Pebble Beach as more than just a vacation getaway. She knew it was small-minded, but part of her was angry with Jamie for using their family retreat as a place to tryst. She tried to dismiss the thought, but her mind was assailed by images of her daughter in another woman's arms.

Jamie didn't notice her look of consternation, and she continued, "I was unwilling to tell anyone until I was absolutely sure that this was right for me, Mother. When you asked me if I was involved with Ryan, I just couldn't be honest with you."

"Well, technically, you could have been," Catherine corrected, "but you obviously didn't feel that I would be supportive. I must bear the responsibility for that." Her eyes were dark, and she suddenly looked older than her years. "I have a question about all of this, Jamie. I know you're justifiably angry with her, but I should tell you that Cassie told Laura about your attempts to get back with Jack. And Laura had to tell me, just to …" She stopped and took a breath. "How does Jack fit into this equation?"

Jamie stood and walked around the elegantly decorated room for a few minutes. She picked up various items and examined them as she considered the question. A picture of the three of them caught her eye and she held it so that her mother could see it. "I was afraid," she said quietly. "I was afraid that I couldn't have this if I admitted who I really was."

Catherine got up and stood next to her daughter. She placed a gentle hand on her shoulder and asked, "I don't understand, Jamie. What were you afraid of?"

Jamie blew out a breath and said, "It's so much easier to be straight, Mother! I was ready to jump into a relationship with Ryan, but I pulled back at the last minute. I thought I'd be willing to have a relationship with a man even if it wasn't what I really wanted, because it'd be so much easier!"

"But you couldn't do it?" she asked carefully.

"No, I couldn't. When Jack made love to me I could only see Ryan's face, and once I acknowledged that, I just couldn't go on with the charade."

"I'm sorry, Jamie," Catherine said softly. "And I'm sorry this has been so hard for you."

"But it's not now!" she said with genuine enthusiasm. "Once I made the decision it's been so freeing! I'm amazed at how marvelous I really feel, Mother. I swear I've never felt this wonderful in my whole life!"

"I'm happy for that," Catherine said with a small smile as she walked back to the sofa. "I just … I just wish that you felt that you could work out your issues *with* us, rather than just inform us of them."

Jamie had a very strong suspicion that her mother's wish was rather fanciful, so she asked, "Is that really what you want? Would you really want me to tell you I was attracted to Ryan if it was just a passing interest?"

Catherine considered this scenario for a moment, pursing her lips as she tried to determine how she felt. "I'm not sure, Jamie. There is a part of me that would like to help you figure things out, but I will admit that it might be difficult for me to help you struggle through your sexual feelings. I suppose that talking to a professional was the best choice."

"I just didn't think that people who loved me could be objective about this," Jamie said, trying to convince her mother that she wasn't trying to shut her out.

"Even though I admit that I'm not objective, I would hope that I could listen to you without trying to influence you too strongly. I would really love it if you would at least try to talk to me before you make any major life choices, Jamie."

"Maybe I will be able to in the future. I'd be happy to try to be more open with you about things in my life, if you'd really like me to."

"I would, dear. As I told you at your home, I wish that we were closer. I feel like you're slipping away from us, honey, and it scares me." Tears began to slide down Catherine's patrician features, and Jamie stared at her for a moment, paralyzed with indecision. She had never seen her mother cry, and she was confused as to how she should react. Going with her feelings, she moved closer and put her arms around her mother and held her. Catherine was tense at first, but she soon loosened up and gratefully returned the hug. She clung to her daughter tightly, her head on her shoulder, just letting the tears come.

After a long while, she sat up and looked for a tissue. Jamie got up and brought the box over to her, watching as Catherine took a few, wiped her eyes, blew her nose, then looked up at Jamie and said with a small smile, "That felt strangely good."

"I've cried more this past year than I did all of my previous years put together," she conceded. "And you're right, it does feel strangely good."

Catherine placed her hand on her daughter's cheek and trailed her fingers down her face in a loving way. "Why have you cried so much?" she asked softly.

Jamie considered the question for just a moment. "Partly because of my breakup with Jack," she said, "but mostly because I *feel* so much with Ryan. Everything is more vivid, Mother. When I'm sad, I'm really sad. When I'm upset, I'm terrifically upset. Yet, I'm happier than I've ever been," she insisted. "No matter what the emotion is, it's indescribably intense!"

"It sounds like opera," she said, smiling.

Jamie had to laugh at this characterization, but she also had to admit that it was accurate. "I guess you're right. Everything is brighter and louder and more emotion-filled."

"That's because you're really in love," Catherine said. "That's what every opera is about."

Jamie leaned against her mother and let her wrap her arms around her. "You understand," she said as her tears began to flow. "You really understand."

"I've been in love myself," she whispered into her ear.

They sat that way for a long time, holding each other for the first time in years. The feeling was strange for Catherine, who felt rather exposed emotionally. But she fought with herself to stay connected to her daughter, and after a few minutes she actually felt some portion of her emotional self-protection diminish as she opened her heart to her only child. Jamie finally sat up and drained the rest of her drink. Her mother did the same and mixed two more. Jamie laughed wryly and observed, "We'll be drunk when Daddy gets home."

Catherine gave her a surprisingly rakish grin and laughed. "He can get drunk on his own time. This is for women only."

Hearing her mother's usually hidden sense of humor surface gave Jamie much more confidence. Somewhere deep in her soul she had the calming thought that everything would eventually be all right with her mother—perhaps even better than things had been before.

After they sat for a few more minutes, she asked, "Don't you have any questions for me?"

"Thousands," Catherine laughed softly, shaking her head a bit. "But I'll let your father run through his list first. You did tell him earlier, didn't you?"

"Yes. I wanted to tell you separately so that you could each have your own reaction."

With a slight tilt of her head, Catherine asked, "Did it go all right?"

Jamie's brow furrowed a bit and she considered the question for just a minute. "Yes, I suppose it did. Daddy started to act like I was on the witness stand," she observed. "But he calmed down and seemed okay by the time he left."

A sardonic smile crossed Catherine's face. "He's a man and he's a lawyer. That's a tough combination when you're talking about feelings."

"I suppose," Jamie agreed. "You don't have to let him ask all the questions, though, Mother. I'd be happy to tell you anything that you want to know."

"I do have questions, Jamie, but none that can't wait. I'd like to finally meet the woman who has captured my daughter's heart, but other than that, there's no rush."

"Are you really okay with the fact that I'm with a woman? I thought it'd be harder for you."

Catherine gave that a moment's thought. Shaking her head softly she admitted, "I wouldn't say that I'm 'okay' with it, no. It's not what I would choose for you, dear, but I'm coming to realize that my vote doesn't carry much weight any longer."

Jamie started to interrupt, but her mother placed a hand on her arm and continued. "You're an adult now. What little influence I had on forming your personality and character is in the past now. You need to follow your own heart."

Tears slid down Jamie's cheeks and she struggled with her emotions. She was so overwhelmingly grateful for this simple acknowledgment that she wanted to throw her arms around her mother and hug her. But even though they had done that just moments before, she felt reluctant to do it again. She honestly thought that they had pushed their boundaries far enough for one day, so she merely patted her mother's hand. "Thank you, Mother," she whispered. "I can't tell you how good that makes me feel. It's okay with me that you don't embrace this part of me immediately. It's just nice that you aren't put off by it."

"I have so many gay friends and acquaintances that homosexuality really doesn't have much of a negative connotation for me anymore," Catherine admitted. "The gay men that I know seem just as happy about their sexual orientation as I do about mine. This is a tough world, Jamie. If you can find someone to help you hold the darkness at bay, you have my blessing."

Unable to contain her natural exuberance for another minute, Jamie grasped her mother's hand and squeezed it gently. "That's such a perfect way to put it, Mother. That's just what it's like with Ryan! I feel safe! I feel like things can't hurt me when we're together. Does that make any sense?"

"Perfect," she agreed, sharing a smile with her beaming daughter.

Just then the front door opened and Jim strode through the door. He was every inch the confident, high-powered attorney now, and Jamie immediately recognized that this meant nothing but trouble. "I've figured out what was wrong with this whole thing," he stated.

"What's that, dear?" Catherine asked absently as she drained her drink. Jamie was shocked beyond words that neither of her parents even bothered to greet the other. They had been apart for three weeks now, but they acted as though Jim had just stepped out to get the mail. She was also nonplussed to see that her mother's usual cool demeanor had descended like a shroud, and wondered if it was only her father's return that had caused it.

"I'm talking to my daughter as though she were to be married. She's talking about everlasting love, and commitment, and I haven't really even spoken to this person. You would never do that with a man, Jamie. You're trying to get the sanction of our approval, but you don't even have the gumption to bring this woman here to face us. How are we supposed to react?"

"This is more about me than it is about Ryan," she said defensively.

"So tell me," he said as he went for the kill, "if you were not in love with Ryan, would you be actively searching for another woman? Are you a lesbian?"

I hate it when you're right, Poppa. "I'm not comfortable answering that question," she said shakily.

He sensed her weakness and continued his line of questioning. "Jamie, this is a major change in your life and your identity. It's important for us to know the ramifications of this. Are you a lesbian, or just in love with Ryan?"

She swallowed hard and answered, "I can only say that I'm in love with Ryan."

"Then how can you say this isn't about her?" he crowed. "This is primarily about her!"

"I disagree, Daddy, but I can see that you don't want to give in on that point. So let's say that it is; what do you want to do about it?"

"I want her to come down here and answer my questions. I want to know who this woman is, Jamie. I can't give you my approval until I've spent time with her."

Jamie knew that bringing Ryan down here would be like throwing a lamb into a den of wolves, so she tried to talk her way out of it. "I'm sure that Ryan would like to come down to spend some time with you, but I think we should work out some of our issues first."

"Jamie," he said firmly, "I have only one issue at this point. I want to sit down with Ryan and get to know her a little bit. If you're unwilling to have her come today, have her come tomorrow, or even to my office on Monday."

None of those options sounded much better, and she reasoned that Ryan would probably rather get it over with. "I'll call her and see if she can come down," she said as she rose to go to her room for a little privacy.

Ryan answered the page in less than three minutes. "Hi, baby," Jamie said rather lethargically.

"Are you okay?" the anxious voice responded, her panting indicating that she was a bit winded.

"Yeah, it's been hard with my father, but incredibly easy with mother. You were right again—it's never what you think it's going to be."

"So are you coming home?"

Jamie had a hard time hearing her over the din. "Where are you?"

"I'm playing basketball with Conor and Brendan and Kevin and Donal and Niall. We've been playing three-on-three for hours. We're killing 'em," she laughed as Jamie heard the ball bouncing nearly inside the phone. "They miss you," she said with another laugh, pushing Conor away from the pay phone she was using.

"I miss them too," she said wistfully, wishing that she could be there to see their game. *I don't really want to do this to her, but it'll have to happen sooner or later.* Jamie took a deep breath, then tentatively made her request. "I know this is asking a lot," she rushed the rest of the sentence before she lost her nerve, "but would you be willing to come down here? My father wants to talk to you."

Damn, what's going on down there? "Sure, I can come right away."

No hesitation or questions, just love and support. No wonder I love this woman! "Ryan," she said softly, "it won't be fun. He'll cross-examine you, and I promise he'll have you so mixed up you won't know if you're coming or going."

"If you want me to come, I'm there," she said firmly, tossing the basketball to her brother when he tried to distract her by lobbing it at her.

"Okay," Jamie said as she breathed a sigh of relief. "Can you take down directions?"

"I'll just look it up on Mapquest. I've got their address from when I sent them a thank-you note after Pebble Beach. I'll be there as quick as I can."

Before Ryan could disconnect, Jamie spoke again. "Uhm, Ryan?"

"Yes, honey?"

"Don't take this the wrong way, but take a shower first, okay?"

She laughed long and hard at that. "I'd take a shower before I took out the trash given how I look right now! And I'll dress like a girl. Don't worry, babe, I won't embarrass you."

Damn. "That's not what I meant, honey. I just know that you get focused, and I could see you grabbing Conor's keys and taking off before you had a chance to think. I could never be embarrassed by you, Ryan."

"Okay, baby, I love you." Jamie could hear a chorus of deep male voices parroting her "I love you" in the background. "Knock it off, boys," Ryan shouted. "I'll be there as soon as I can," she said, adding another soft, "I love you."

Forty minutes later, Ryan and Brendan were cruising down the freeway in Brendan's black Dodge Dakota. He had offered Ryan the use of the truck, but when he learned that Jamie had driven herself he decided to drop her off, ostensibly so that she could ride home with Jamie, but she suspected that he wanted to have a little talk on the way.

"I'd be happy to stay down on the Peninsula if you'd feel better to have me close by," he offered.

Ryan found the gesture terribly touching, even though she insisted that there was nothing to worry about. "He's not a shotgun-wielding lunatic," she teased. "He's a big-time lawyer."

"That's the worst kind," Brendan said. "He's used to getting what he wants, and if he wants to split you up, he won't play fair."

"Jeez, Bren, he doesn't have the power to do that, even if he wants to. Jamie just said he had some questions for me."

"Yeah, like what country would you like to be deported to?"

She blew out a breath, trying to remind herself that Brendan harbored a deep distrust of corporate lawyers. "Let's say you're right," she conceded. "How can you help if he tries to do that?"

"I might just have to show some O'Flaherty muscle," he said, a fierce glower darkening his eyes. Brendan rarely made a physical threat against anyone, and Ryan knew that he was genuinely worried to do so now.

"I appreciate your offer, Bren, but I don't think we can strong-arm him into accepting us. I didn't get the impression that he was being unreasonable, just that he was giving her a hard time. I'm sure it'll be okay in the end. They've had a very good relationship up 'til now, and I can't imagine this would make him forget that. I think he really loves her."

"You don't get to be managing partner of a firm like that by giving in, Ryan. I think you should be prepared for him to really put pressure on you," Brendan cautioned.

"I'm as prepared as I can be," she said, anxiously tapping her foot against the dashboard. "Do I look okay?" she asked as she turned in her seat to face her brother.

A big smile lit up Brendan's face. "I don't think you've ever asked that before in your life," he said affectionately. "Actually, I don't think I've ever seen you this nervous before. This really means a lot to you, doesn't it?"

"Jamie wants to build a better relationship with her parents. It means a lot to me to be supportive of that."

"Well, I think you look lovely. Did you do something different to your hair?"

"Uhm, yeah," she said with a tone that implied it should be obvious. "Didn't you notice?"

"Uhm, did you change the color?"

She laughed wryly and shook her head. "Keep guessing, pal."

"Hmm … it looks like you did something to make it curly or something," he suggested, scrunching up his eyes to get a better look.

"Excellent powers of observation," she said exasperatedly. "I got almost nine inches cut off!"

"Well, how was I supposed to know that?" Brendan asked helplessly. "You never get a haircut, how could I know to even guess that?"

"Uhm … if you looked at me once in a while, you wouldn't have to guess."

"Aw, Ryan, you know we don't look at you like you're a girl," he explained patiently.

"Well, that makes me feel a lot better," she responded facetiously. "I'm going down to meet my girlfriend's parents and try to convince them that I'm not some big predatory dyke, and my own family doesn't think I'm a girl!"

"That's not what I meant and you know it. We just think of you as our sister, not like a real woman."

"Oh, that's much better," she said through her thin smile.

"I've never really been down here," Ryan admitted as they entered the Village of Hillsborough. "I've been to Palo Alto a couple of times for games, but other than riding my bike down El Camino Real one time, I don't think I've even been past Hillsborough."

"Why would you have a need to be? People like us cater to people like this," he said derisively. "We can work on these houses, and teach their kids, and guard their neighborhoods, but we wouldn't be invited in for dinner. Like right now, for example. Even if they see me drop you off, I guarantee they don't ask me in. But if her parents dropped Jamie off at our house, Da would be hurt if they didn't come in and let him fix them a little something."

"You may be right," Ryan said. "But I have to say that Mr. Evans has been very generous with me so far. He knows Jamie took me to Pebble Beach, and he was happy that she takes me to play golf at the club. He seems very gracious."

"And how many times have they invited you to their home for dinner?" he asked, knowing the answer. "By the time you'd mentioned Jamie's name twice, Da was begging you to have her over."

"You're right, Brendan, but they don't have the kind of traditions that we do. Jamie says that she has never tasted a thing that her mother made. She didn't even make her cocoa when she was sick!"

"No cocoa!" he shouted in outrage.

"Nope. She had a nanny and a cook who took care of her. When she skinned her knee, the nanny put a Band-Aid on it. And she was a real piece of work. She told Jamie that sick children should not be coddled, so she didn't even make a fuss over her when she was ill."

"She sure doesn't seem as screwed up as she should be," Brendan marveled. "How did that happen?"

"She does have a marvelous grandfather whom she really cares for. He's a great guy. He's an Episcopal priest over on Nob Hill. I want to have him over for dinner some Sunday. I know Da would love him."

"I guess it's true that even one loving person can change a child's life for the better," Brendan said. He considered his own statement for a moment. "Gosh, what will that make Caitlin?" he mused. "She's got at least twenty loving people in her life!"

"I don't know how Caitlin will turn out, but I know she'll never doubt that she was loved," Ryan said thoughtfully. "Just like I haven't," she added as she turned to smile at her brother.

The Evans home was bigger and more imposing than any Ryan had ever seen, making even the Pebble Beach house pale in comparison. It was a French provincial style, and even though it was mostly shielded from the street, they could easily see the tops of the turrets before they drove onto the property. As they pulled into the circular drive they got a much better feeling for the grand scale of the place, and both siblings turned silent. Brendan finally spoke. "There must be thirty rooms in that place."

Ryan shook her head. "I just have this image of a tiny little Jamie, all alone in that huge place with no one to play with."

"That's right," he said. "She's an only child, isn't she?"

"Yeah," Ryan said, "just her and the old English nanny rambling around that place."

As Ryan put her hand on the door, she looked a little nervous. Brendan patted her leg and reminded her, "Now, do you promise to call home before you leave here?"

"Yes, I promise," she replied with a smile. "I appreciate your concern, Bren, and I know Jamie will too."

As she got out of the truck, she went to his window to kiss and hug her protective oldest brother. "Thanks again, Bren. This means a lot to me."

As he watched her climb the front stairs, Brendan mused. *I don't think Ryan has any idea what she's gotten herself into with this guy. He's got a well-deserved reputation as a lethal trial attorney. People I've talked to say he's ruthless when he really wants something. I'm sure he won't hesitate to do whatever he thinks he has to do to get what he wants—or in this case—what he doesn't want.*

Chapter Thirteen

J amie heard the bell ring at 7:05. She shot down the stairs, calling out, "I'll get it!" as she ran. She flung the door open and quickly stepped outside as she closed the door behind her. She was puzzled to see Brendan's truck pulling away, but her attention quickly reverted to her lover. She threw her arms around her neck, pulled her down for an emotion-filled kiss, and hung on to her tightly, squeezing her until Ryan's back started to ache. She finally let her go and backed up a step to survey her. "You look really nice, honey." Ryan had donned a pair of slim-cut white chinos with a side zipper, a banded collar, long-sleeved white cotton blouse, very crisply ironed, and her sleeveless black v-neck cardigan, neatly buttoned. She looked absolutely perfect for the setting—not too dressy and not too casual. Jamie marveled at her ability to always look appropriate for the occasion. *She must just have an innate sense of style. I know that no one taught her these things.*

"Are you really all right?" Ryan asked with concern, running her hand through Jamie's hair.

"Yeah, I'm fine now," she said as she leaned in for another hug. "I guess we'd better go in. Are you ready?"

"Yes, I am," Ryan replied. "But I want you to remember something. Your parents don't have any real power over you anymore. And there's nothing they can do to me. Their approval only means anything to me because it's important to you. So if this doesn't go well, we'll just regroup and try again later, okay?" she asked as she leaned over a bit to stare directly into Jamie's eyes.

"You're right, honey," she said with a small smile. "I'm just worried because I want them to love you too."

"That's not going to happen right away, baby. I'm kind of an acquired taste, like blood sausage," she said with a wink, referring to one of her grandfather's favorite cold cuts.

"I'm so glad you're here," she said as she rested her head on Ryan's shoulder. "I feel like myself again when you're with me."

"Let's go in, honey. They're probably getting anxious."

"I don't want to hurry. That's a strategy I learned from my father. Keep them waiting. It shows you have the power," she said with an eyebrow wiggle as she turned to open the door.

Ryan didn't really have the opportunity to notice the gorgeous foyer they walked through, because as soon as they were halfway through it, Jim was upon them. He stuck his hand out and said, "Thanks for coming, Ryan. I appreciate your responsiveness."

"You're welcome," she said with a smile. She felt uncomfortable calling him "Jim" given the circumstances, but she didn't want to revert to "Mr. Evans" since she knew that Jamie was right that she shouldn't relinquish any advantage she had, so she decided to avoid calling him anything, if possible.

He escorted her into the living room, and Catherine rose as they entered. She gave Ryan a dazzling smile and strode over, extending her hand. "Catherine Evans," she announced confidently. "It is a delight to finally meet you, Ryan."

Ryan gave her a dazzler in return as she said, "The pleasure is mine, Mrs. Evans."

"I would feel more comfortable if you called me Catherine, dear," she said, still holding Ryan's hand. As she was being led over to the sofa, Ryan took a moment to assess the woman who pulled her along. Catherine looked almost nothing like her beautiful daughter, but she was mighty beautiful nonetheless. She was at least two inches shorter than Jamie, but she looked much smaller, probably because her bone structure was so delicate. She actually looked like a strong wind could blow her away, and Ryan offered up a silent prayer of thanks that Jamie had inherited a much sturdier build. *I'd be worried about crushing her when we made love if Jamie was that tiny.*

Catherine indicated that Ryan should sit beside her, giving her a chance to study her face for a moment. To Ryan's surprise, she noted that Catherine honestly didn't share one feature with her daughter. Her nose was smaller and her lips were thinner than Jamie's pouty ones. Her eyes were a warm dark brown rather than Jamie's misty green. Catherine's cheekbones were stronger than her daughter's and her forehead a bit wider, giving her a look very demonstrative of her English heritage.

Ryan had to admit that Catherine was truly lovely, despite her outward fragility. Her skin was flawless, much like Jamie's, but the coloring was very fair and it looked like she spent very little time in the sun. It was hard to tell if her hair color was natural, but it looked so perfectly matched to her skin tone that Ryan assumed she was a real blonde. Her hair was longer than Jamie's, and cut in a style that Ryan wouldn't have chosen for her. She was a very youthful-looking woman, but her mid-length cut didn't emphasize her youthfulness. Rather, it was the style Ryan saw so often on the photos of wealthy society matrons in the *Examiner*. *She could look thirty with the right haircut.*

Catherine looked at her with a friendly but reserved smile and asked solicitously, "What can I get you to drink? Jamie and I are having Campari and soda, but I can get you anything you want."

Ryan's playful side considered asking for a Guinness Stout, but she didn't think the attempt at humor would play well with this audience. "That would be fine," she said, hoping that she liked Campari, whatever that was. While Catherine fixed the drink, Ryan shot a quick glance at her partner. *I'm glad I'm driving home,* she thought. *I wondered what I tasted on her lips. I guess that explains why she looked a little dazed.*

"Have you had dinner, Ryan? We've waited for you."

"No, I haven't," she admitted, hoping her stomach didn't start to growl.

"Superb," Catherine said with real pleasure, then got up and strode toward what Ryan guessed was the kitchen. As she walked, Ryan took a moment to gaze at Catherine's elegant clothing. The buttercream yellow slacks and short, square-cut jacket looked a bit like suede, but Ryan reasoned that there was no animal that had a hide as soft and supple-looking as this, so she assumed the fabric was Ultrasuede. The unbuttoned jacket was collarless, and an even paler yellow silk shell peeked out. The entire ensemble was so perfectly tailored to Catherine's slim body that Ryan assumed it had been custom-made. *Gee, I wonder if she changed into that when she got home ... I can just imagine what that little number would look like if I wore it during a flight from Italy. You would be able to name the entire menu just from looking at my clothes!* she thought, as she considered how easy it was to spill food and drink on your clothing during a bumpy transatlantic flight.

Catherine emerged a moment later and announced that dinner would be ready in half an hour. "Do you have any dietary restrictions or preferences, Ryan?"

I'm sure you mean, besides Jamie, she thought, a small smile curving her lips. "No, ma'am," she said.

"Excellent. I'm certain that Jamie told you why Jim wanted you to join us. He has some concerns that he wants you to address. But I want us all to have a nice meal and get to know one another first. Is that all right with you?"

"Yes, ma'am," she said with a smile. "That would be lovely."

"Tell us a little bit about yourself, Ryan. Are you from the Bay Area?"

"Yes, my family lives in Noe Valley," she began, but Catherine's puzzled glance made her elaborate. "That's a neighborhood that's also called Eureka Valley. It's between the Castro and Twin Peaks."

"I don't believe I've had the pleasure of visiting the area," she replied, gracing Ryan with an interested smile.

"There's not much there unless you're visiting someone. It's just a small residential neighborhood. No historical significance."

"I'm sure it's lovely," Catherine said. "Do you still live with your family?"

"Yes, ma'am. Although Jamie and I have been staying at her house in Berkeley during the week, as I'm sure you know."

Catherine had not known this since neither Jim nor Jamie had shared the information with her, but her unflappable gaze didn't reveal this to Ryan. "I see," she said. "Who is at home with you?"

"My father and two of my brothers. I have another brother who lives in an apartment nearby."

"What about your mother?"

"She died when I was seven," Ryan replied neutrally, not one shred of vulnerability showing.

"Oh dear! That's so young to lose your mother. Who raised you?"

Ryan looked a bit perplexed as she replied, "My father did."

"Without help?" Catherine couldn't imagine a man being able to raise four children without significant help.

"My brothers are all older than I am. Brendan was thirteen when my mother died, so he and the other boys helped a lot. I also have four aunts and several older cousins who were always available to help. But mostly it was my father."

"That's a terrific responsibility for a man to take on. Was he able to be at home a lot?"

"He's a firefighter, so he worked two days and was off three. Until I was ten or so, one of my aunts would stay with us on the nights he was gone. But after that, the boys were in charge."

"Didn't that leave you unsupervised a lot, especially during summer breaks?" Even though Catherine herself hadn't spent a large amount of time with her daughter while she was growing up, an adult had been in the immediate vicinity at all times. She couldn't imagine leaving four children alone much of the time, but she reasoned that some people had few options due to circumstances just like these.

"Yes, I suppose it did. But my oldest brother was very responsible at a very early age. I suppose he had to be responsible since my mother was sick on and off from the time I was three. He kept good track of me during the school year. And during the summers I went to live with my maternal grandparents."

"Where do they live?" she asked.

"In Ireland," Ryan replied. "Both of my parents are immigrants."

"How fascinating," Catherine enthused, making it sound like a very exotic state of being. In fact, she found the young woman who so effortlessly responded to her questions to be very charming indeed.

Jamie piped in. "Ryan was actually born in Ireland, also."

"Really, dear?" Catherine asked, cocking her head in question.

"Yes, my mother had to visit her mother because of an illness when she was pregnant with me. It got too near her due date, so she had to stay. We left when I was about two weeks old. So I have dual citizenship."

Hmm, Jim thought to himself, *I guess I can't have her deported. I wonder if her father is legal.* "How did your father gain citizenship?" he asked cordially, trying for a neutral tone of voice.

Ryan resisted the impulse to smile, recalling Brendan's comment about deportation, knowing Jamie's dad was headed down a dead-end trail. "He and his brothers were actually born here, but their parents couldn't make a go of it and they returned shortly after World War II." If Jim was disappointed, it was not evident from his carefully schooled, polite expression.

"Have you many relatives in Ireland?" Catherine asked.

"Yes, besides my grandparents, my mother's younger sister and her husband have four children. And then I have cousins too plentiful to count," she said with a laugh.

"She has fourteen cousins who live in Noe Valley, too," Jamie added.

"Fifteen, Jamie," she corrected. "You forgot the most important one."

"How could I forget her?" she laughed. "Ryan has fourteen cousins, all gorgeous men, and a precious little one-year-old named Caitlin."

"How nice," Catherine said. "She must be terribly spoiled."

"About as bad as I was," Ryan admitted. "I'm the only girl in my generation in America."

Just then an attractive older woman emerged from the same direction that Catherine had previously traveled. "Dinner is ready," she announced in a clipped Spanish accent.

"Thank you, Marta. We'll be in momentarily."

"Would you like to freshen up before dinner, Ryan?" Catherine asked.

"Yes, thank you, I would."

"Jamie, dear, show Ryan the powder room, will you?"

Jamie stood and waited for Ryan to rise. In a pointed move she took her hand and led her to a small but elegantly appointed powder room, far from the dining room. She walked into the tiny room and gestured for Ryan to follow. She had to squeeze a little, but was just able to close the door. "How do you know I don't have to go?" Ryan teased, referring to Jamie's penchant for privacy.

"You can hold it until I leave," she said with a smile. "I just needed another kiss before dinner." She slid her arms around Ryan's neck and pulled her head down. Several kisses followed and Ryan felt a familiar flush building up.

"Baby, that's about all I can take," she whispered. "I'm at my peak of sexual receptivity."

"Really? Why's that?"

"I'm due to get my period. Right beforehand, I'm hotter than a firecracker."

"So that's why you've been so needy," she said with a grin. "You were actually grinding against me in your sleep the other night. I almost woke you, but I decided to let you have your erotic dreams."

Ryan flushed a little at this news. "Why didn't you tell me that?"

"I forgot about it. I was half-asleep myself. It was actually the day we got our hair cut. You were holding my hips and rubbing yourself against my butt in the most sensual way; I really almost woke you up and had you."

"That must have been the residuals from your pony ride. I wanted to go for a ride too," she whispered into her ear.

"Let's get through this evening and we can ride all night," she promised with another kiss.

Ryan turned and washed her hands. She grabbed the doorknob and they both nearly tumbled out. "Your house is beyond spectacular," she observed. "Should I ask for a tour?"

"Maybe next time. Mother could easily spend all day extolling all of her treasures."

Hand in hand, they walked into the ornate dining room. The table was made for sixteen and they looked a little lost, clustered at one end. Ryan wondered why they didn't have a more casual setup for family dinners, but she decided that they certainly didn't consider her family, and perhaps they never would.

The food and the wine were so incredibly good that Ryan had a hard time staying focused on the conversation. Jamie spared a few teasing glances her way, acknowledging the look of absolute pleasure on Ryan's lovely face. Ryan noticed that Jamie accepted a half glass of wine, but didn't take more than a token sip. Ryan had more than usual, finishing off two good-sized glasses of the extraordinary merlot that they enjoyed. To her amazement, Marta brought out another bottle of the wine when they were no more than halfway through dinner, and the Evanses made quick work of it also.

The meal was so sumptuous that she wanted to compliment someone, but she knew that no one at the table had anything to do with the preparation so she didn't quite know what to say. She considered her options, but decided that, "You sure do know how to hire a cook," was probably not the correct avenue, so she said nothing.

During the meal, they spoke of Ryan's athletic career, and then Jim told Catherine all about Jamie's desire to try out for the golf team. As Ryan watched him relate the tale, she had to smile at his rampant enthusiasm. It occurred to her that Jim was awfully invested in Jamie's plans, and she hoped that her partner was being honest with herself when she said she was playing as much for herself as for her father.

Ryan was eyeing the last bit of coconut cake that remained on Jamie's plate when Jim stood up and indicated that Ryan should join him for their discussion. Jamie stood also, but he shook his head firmly. "I want to speak to Ryan alone," he said in a tone that normally wouldn't allow for dissent. To her own surprise, she found herself staring directly into her father's eyes, saying, "I don't see the need for you to speak to Ryan alone, Daddy. She's not interviewing for the position, you know." There was a touch of humor in her voice as well as a pleasant smile on her face, but Ryan knew that both were a thin cover for her determination.

Jim stopped and stared at his daughter for a full minute. As the managing partner for a very large law firm, he was familiar with unblinking obedience to his requests, and he found that he didn't appreciate this sign of disrespect from his own daughter. "I thought we had covered this, Jamie," he said evenly. "I wanted Ryan to come down here to answer some questions …. What part of that request did you not understand?"

Ryan could see that this little contretemps could easily get out of hand. She hated to show a lack of support for her partner, but she was perfectly comfortable answering Jim's questions, and she let him know that. "It's really all right, Jamie," she assured her. "I don't mind speaking to your father alone."

Jamie shot her a grateful look, glad to be spared the fight that she feared would ensue if she held her ground. "Okay, honey," she said softly, squeezing Ryan's hand as she left.

Jim led her back through the living room and down a long hall until they reached a wood-paneled library. It was a very imposing room, and as he walked around the place he seemed very much in control. "I'm having a brandy. Will you join me?"

Ryan had never had brandy in her life, but she wasn't going to admit that. She knew that the power imbalance between them was massive, and she wanted to appear as cool as she could manage. "That would be nice," she agreed, figuring, if nothing else, that her first taste of brandy would be the good stuff.

He handed her a snifter, then sat behind the huge, ornately carved desk. His chair was a deep burgundy leather, enormous in scale. He rocked back and placed his feet on the desk and gazed at Ryan with an inscrutable look on his face. The only chair available for her was directly across from the massive piece, and to her amusement she noticed that it was just a hair too small for most adults. It was leather also, but straight-backed, and it required her to fidget quite a bit to attempt to get comfortable. *Isn't this subtle?* she thought. *I wonder if the KGB helped with the design?*

He reached behind his desk and took a massive cigar from a humidor. *Don't laugh!* she chided herself, forcing the jokes about Monica Lewinsky and the president from her mind. He fussed with the cigar for a few minutes, and when he had it lit, leaned back again and narrowed his eyes as the smoke wafted into them. "You don't mind if I'm direct, do you?"

"I'd prefer it."

"Good," he said as he rocked back and forth, sucking on his phallic symbol. "You seem like a fine young woman, Ryan."

For a blue-collar, working-class, immigrant lesbian, that is, she added for him. She responded civilly to the statement, deliberately taking it at face value. "Thank you, sir," she said as she waited for the "but".

"I believe that you love my daughter, and I'm certain that she believes that she loves you."

Here it comes, she thought. *Three … two … one ….*

"But … I'm absolutely convinced that she does not belong in this type of relationship."

No, you would have much preferred that she marry Jack, even if she would have been miserable in the end. Ryan resisted her impulse to deliver a scathing retort and struggled, but maintained her composure. "What type of relationship would you prefer that she be in, sir?" she asked politely.

"I believe that you know what point I'm trying to make. I do not believe that my daughter is a lesbian."

Knowing that Jamie did not style herself as a lesbian, Ryan couldn't dispute his statement, but she was willing to let Jamie be in charge of that discussion. "Don't you think she's in a better position to judge that, sir?"

"No, I don't!" he said with his voice beginning to rise. "She's in a very fragile state, Ryan, and I mean no disrespect, but I believe you've taken advantage of that."

He's implying that I seduced her when Jack broke up with her. That sonofabitch. Ryan took a deep breath, controlling the anger that roiled within her. *This is Jamie's father. He's important to her. I can do this … for Jamie.* Completely under control, she finally responded. "Why would I be offended by that characterization?"

"I'm not implying that you've done so intentionally. I can imagine that your feelings for her are genuine, but I think you've put ideas into her head that do not belong there!"

"I mean no disrespect, sir, but that is not true. I would never try to influence anyone who had just gone through an upsetting breakup. Jamie was very, very thorough and careful every step of the way. This is not a whim for her. And I assure you she made up her own mind. I certainly haven't had much luck in changing her mind when she's determined about something. Have you?"

"No," he reluctantly admitted. "I haven't. But my point remains, Ryan. Do you mind if I ask you some personal questions?"

"I'm happy to answer anything about my life. But I'm uncomfortable talking about our relationship out of Jamie's presence."

"Fine," he said. "My questions are about you."

I was afraid of that, Ryan thought, having a good idea of the direction his questions would take.

"I don't think I've ever seen you so nervous," Catherine remarked, slightly puzzled by her daughter's restlessness.

Jamie had stacked, scattered, stacked, and scattered again the coasters that sat upon the coffee table in front of the sofa, and she looked like she was about to repeat the cycle but stopped on hearing her mother's comment. "I just don't like it, Mother." She ran a hand through her hair, partly to stop herself from playing with the coasters, now that her little compulsion had been noticed. "She doesn't have to answer to Daddy for anything that's happened."

"I know, dear," Catherine soothed, placing her hand upon her daughter's back. She added a few gentle pats, surprised at the sturdy muscularity that she encountered. "He forgets sometimes that there is a difference between home and the office. I wouldn't worry so, Jamie. Ryan seems very able to handle herself."

"She is." Jamie dropped her head, letting out a heavy sigh. "She's just … sensitive, Mother." Turning to face Catherine she added, "I don't want him to hurt her feelings."

"There is always that possibility," Catherine agreed. "He can be a little overbearing." Now a small frown caused a few faint lines to appear in Catherine's forehead. "If you want me to, I'll go poke my head in to see how things are going."

Jamie considered the offer for a moment, shaking her head briefly to refuse it. "I don't think that will help. Once Daddy decides he wants to know something, I don't think either of us can stop him."

"Are you worried about anything in particular, dear?"

Hmm … her sexual past, the disparity in our finances, our plans to have me support her …. She decided not to share her specific concerns with her mother, irrationally worrying that giving them voice might make them come true. "Not really," she said. "I just know that Daddy has the ability to make people feel small and insignificant, and it'd really upset me to have him do that to Ryan."

Catherine gave her another pat on the back, adding, "I can see how significant she is to you, Jamie. That's what's important."

The Evans women shared a warm smile, with Jamie offering up a silent prayer of thanks that her mother was being so understanding.

Jim took several deep puffs on his cigar, nearly blinding Ryan, but she refused to give in to her urge to cough. "I take it that you consider yourself a lesbian?"

"Yes, sir."

"How old were you when you had this realization?"

"At some level I've always known. But I was certain when I was seventeen."

"Have you had much experience with men?"

"Only with living with them," she smiled. "But no, I've never had a sexual relationship with a man."

"Have you dated a lot of women?"

Ryan spent a moment looking at her shoes. She was certainly not going to reveal the extensive numbers of women she had slept with, but she decided that she needed to be truthful. "Yes, sir. I have."

"And have you ever dated a woman who was roughly in my daughter's situation? Someone who had previously considered themselves heterosexual but nonetheless was attracted to you?"

"Yes, sir." Ryan could see the paint beginning to surround her as he edged her closer to the corner.

"And did those women stay in the lesbian community to your knowledge?"

"No, sir, they did not," she replied as she drank the last of her brandy. He rose from his chair and poured another two inches for her, stopping to replenish his own snifter with a prodigious amount of the amber liquid.

"Why do you suppose that happened?" he continued with his back turned as he replaced the bottle.

"I don't believe they were lesbians, sir. I think they were just experimenting."

"Precisely!" he said triumphantly. "That's exactly what I think Jamie is doing."

"I beg to disagree, sir. I got a different feeling from Jamie from the beginning. I never thought she was just playing, and that's why I was reluctant to move forward with her."

He considered her statement as he sank back into his chair, the leather squeaking in the otherwise silent room. "How many seemingly heterosexual women have you dated, Ryan?"

She looked down at the floor again. She knew this was a surefire loser argument, but she felt that she had to answer. "About ten or so."

"Ten?" he replied with a look of amazement. "You did say ten, didn't you?"

"Yes, sir. I said about ten."

"You did understand my question, didn't you?" He tilted his head and furrowed his sandy blonde eyebrows together. "I didn't ask how many women you had been with in total. Just the ones that you thought were heterosexual."

Oooh, Jamie, only for you ... "I understood your question," Ryan said, giving him a steely gaze.

He shook his head and stared at her for a few long minutes, finally blinking his eyes slowly. "All right," he finally said. "You claim the number is about ten. So it could even be more?"

"Yes, sir. Or fewer," she added, for the record. She thought to herself, *If I get confused I can always have the court reporter read my last statement back to me.*

"And not one of these women remained involved in a lesbian lifestyle?"

"No, sir. To my knowledge, not one did."

"But you're confident that out of all the straight women you've dated, my daughter is the only true lesbian."

She fidgeted in her seat, wishing that she didn't feel the need to be completely honest. "I didn't say that, sir."

"Pardon?" He blinked slowly, thinking that she was giving in awfully quickly.

"I didn't say that Jamie was a lesbian. I do know that she's in love with me, and I'm confident that we're permanently partnered, but I think it's premature to affix that label to her."

He sat back in his chair and took several more deep puffs. He looked very satisfied with himself as he said, "Well, that's an interesting admission, Ryan. Very interesting indeed." He rocked a few times, smiling at her the entire time, finally adding, "I shall defer to your expert opinion on that."

His smirk gave Ryan her first tinge of regret for having slept with so many women. But she realized that if she had only one such woman, he would have used that to say she didn't have enough experience, so she let the point slide.

"Time will tell, Ryan. Time will tell."

As Jamie handed her mother a just-mixed drink, Catherine held onto her extended hand for a moment. She didn't say a word—instead, she pointedly glanced at the third finger of her daughter's left hand, then lifted a perfectly curved eyebrow in question.

Jamie didn't need to look at her hand to understand the silent inquiry, but she did, nonetheless. It gave her a great deal of pleasure to look at the ring Ryan had given her, and she found that she did so several times a day. "It was Ryan's mother's wedding band," she said softly, deciding to let her mother ask for further details if she wished them.

A look of pain crossed Catherine's face, and she found that her voice cracked a bit as she asked, "Did you have some sort of ceremony?" She held her breath, hoping that her only child had not seen fit to exclude her parents from such a meaningful event in her life.

Jamie gave her a gentle smile, squeezing her mother's hand as she sat back down beside her. "Not technically. We sat by the sea down in Pebble Beach and pledged our love to each other, but it was very impromptu. We would like to have a formal ceremony someday, but we decided that we'd wait until everyone we love was able to celebrate with us." She gave her mother a slow, sweet smile, adding another squeeze of her hand. "I wouldn't dream of having a ceremony without you and Daddy and Poppa being there."

In a very unexpected move, Catherine took her daughter's hand and lifted it to her lips, placing a gentle kiss there. For once in her life she decided to allow the feelings to come without concern, the tears sliding down her face with abandon. "I'm so happy that you decided to wait for us," she whispered on a ragged breath.

Jamie's composure fractured at this display, and once again she sobbed in tandem with her mother. "We'll wait, Mother. We'll wait for you. I promise."

Jim rocked slowly in his massive chair, nodding to himself as Ryan sipped her brandy. "Jamie tells me that you're on scholarship this year," he said conversationally.

"Yes, I am. I was lucky enough to make the varsity volleyball team, and they had a scholarship to award."

"You won't be able to keep your job while you compete, will you, Ryan?" he asked in the same conversational tone.

DANGER! DANGER! DANGER! All of the alarms went off in her head, but she had to answer. "No, I was planning on quitting at the end of the summer."

"What will you do to pay for entertainment or to keep up your car? Will your father be able to support you?"

"No, sir. He won't."

"Well then?" he asked in a silky tone.

Ryan just barely kept herself from wincing, the raw subject of money and the lack of it being the only discord she and Jamie had experienced thus far. "Jamie was going to pay for our living expenses during the school year."

"So you were going to live at my house and have my daughter support you?" he said slowly, as if he was trying to let the information sink in.

"Well, actually, I was going to offer to pay Cassie's part of the rent since I'm taking her place in the house. I thought Jamie was going to mention that to you." She knew that this was stretching the truth quite a bit, but since it had been their intention to do so, it didn't feel like a complete lie.

With what she thought was a glimmer of respect in his tone, he commented, "I think that would be best. It would set my mind at ease to know that you were paying your own way, Ryan."

She nodded briefly, regretfully acknowledging that she would be unable to allow Jamie to pay the rent for her, as they had agreed. "What are your plans after graduation?"

"I'm in the process of applying to graduate school." *Although if I have to pay rent and expenses this year, I'll have to live on bread and water.*

"Really? In what field?"

"I'm applying to Ph.D. programs in chemistry, biology, and math as well as medical school."

"Very impressive," he said with a smile. "I trust that your grades are good?"

"Yes, sir. They're excellent." That last sentence got out without conscious thought and she reminded herself, *The worst thing you can do is brag or taunt him. Stick to the facts, damn it!!*

"Are you planning on receiving a scholarship for these programs?"

"Possibly. I'm certainly going to try for one."

"And if you are not awarded a scholarship, what will you do?"

If the choice had been hers, she would have turned and run from this line of questioning. But the choice was most definitely not hers. Taking in a breath, she looked him straight in the eye and replied, "The programs are all very different. I'd probably have to pay tuition only in medical school."

"Yes," he nodded. "Then how would you pay tuition in medical school?"

Jamie has offered to lend me the money for tuition, books, and fees."

"Did you say, 'lend'?"

"Yes, sir."

"Then why not take out a student loan? I'm sure you would qualify."

"I'm not comfortable weighing myself down with that much debt," she said, but wished that she could pull it back in immediately. *Stupid! Stupid! Stupid!* she screamed to herself.

"If you borrow that money from Jamie, isn't that still debt?" he asked pleasantly.

"Yes, sir."

"But I assume you would have a more generous repayment plan with my daughter," he said with the same pleasant smile.

I didn't know that "repayment plan" was a euphemism for stealing! Ryan shouted to herself. Aloud she answered, "Yes, sir. Jamie doesn't want to put a due date on the note."

Switching gears for the fifth time he asked, "What kind of car do you drive, Ryan?"

"I don't have a car."

"No car? Have you ever had one?"

"No, sir."

"As much as you love them, that must be difficult."

"Not really. I love cars, but I can appreciate them from afar."

"Umm-hmm," he said with that same deadly pleasant smile. "Would I know anyone in your family, Ryan, from a club or organization?" he asked in that same pleasant, conversational tone. He seemed interested, but Ryan knew this was code for "Are you anybody?"

Deciding to play his game, she answered, "My father is in the Knights of Columbus," naming a Catholic fraternal organization. "Are you a member?"

"No, I'm afraid not," he said with a thin smile.

"We belong to the YMCA," she added helpfully.

He gave her a slightly puzzled glance, trying to figure out if she was just incredibly naïve or was trying to be obnoxious. But the big blue eyes that gazed back at him seemed completely innocent, so he let it go. Deciding that their chat had set the proper tone for their future interactions, he stood and said, "Well, I think I know you a bit better, Ryan. I appreciate your honesty. You really do seem like a fine young woman, and I hope that your future plans work out."

As long as they don't include Jamie, she thought. She started to stand also, but he came around to the front of the desk and stood in front of her, making her feel not only small, but young. She looked up at him, seriously wondering if he had been trained in his intimidation tactics, or if they came naturally.

"Ryan," he said softly, sitting down on the corner of the desk. "I don't want to see you hurt. I know that Jamie cares for you a great deal, but I'm convinced that she's confused that caring with love. I urge you, for your own protection, to take things slowly and see what happens."

She nodded, showing that she had heard him. She was not going to dispute his opinion, since it was just his opinion. Deciding not to express her own thoughts, she offered a smile and he seemed to accept that as a reply. He stood and backed away from the desk, giving her room to move. She stood and paused for a moment, trying to get her sea legs after the uncharacteristically large amount of alcohol she had consumed. *Oh, Jamie … please be sober, or we're gonna have to stay over, and I don't want to be introduced to the servant's quarters tonight!*

"There's one thing I really need to apologize to you for, Mother," Jamie said after they had both composed themselves again.

"What's that, dear?"

"I'm so sorry that this is going to be all over the gossip mill down here. I know it was hard to hear this from Mrs. Martin, and I'm very sorry that it happened this way." She was genuinely sorry that the revelation had come from her mother's closest friend, and her feelings showed clearly on her face.

A gentle laugh floated up from Catherine's chest, and Jamie shot her a very puzzled look. "Oh, dear, that's sweet of you to be concerned, but don't give it another thought."

"But Mrs. Martin …"

"Jamie, Laura and I have been close since you and Cassie were in grammar school. Do you really think that in all of that time I have not gotten a very clear impression of exactly who she is?"

"But …"

"Dear, Laura and I share a number of things … but she lives to gossip about others. She's done it to me and to every other person we know. You are certainly not going to be immune from her wagging tongue."

"I don't care about me, Mother, it's you and your relationship with her that I'm concerned about."

Catherine let out another small laugh and patted Jamie's knee. "If this is the worst thing she ever has to say about our family I'll be eternally grateful," she said. "We have friends whose children have died from drug overdoses, who've spent time in alcohol and drug rehabilitation centers, who've gone through sizeable fortunes by the time they're twenty-five years old. Having a daughter whose only detour from the usual path is to enter a loving relationship with another woman is a very, very small variation, dear. Don't give it another thought."

Jamie was stunned at her mother's reaction. She was certain that the views of her friends would have been very important to her. With a shake of her head she realized that there were parts of her mother that had been very well hidden—and that she would have to work at to be able to access. "This is … surprising … yes … surprising," she managed to get out.

"The bottom line is this, Jamie. My social circle loves to hear a juicy bit of gossip. You will be the hot topic for a while, but as soon as a hotter topic arises—and believe me, it will—you and I will revert back to our usual anonymity."

"I just thought …" she said weakly, "that you might be treated differently by your friends …"

Another laugh startled her and Jamie gaped at her mother's blithe response. "Have you really not experienced the almost total acceptance that our money buys?" Catherine's head was cocked slightly, and a very amused grin covered her face. "No one on the Peninsula can afford to be on my bad side, Jamie. I'm on the board of nearly every important charity in the Bay Area. If any of these women want a dime— and believe me, they want far more than that—they know not to shun me."

Jamie nodded slowly, understanding that their wealth put them in a strange social position, but honestly never having thought about the automatic acceptance that it carried. The thought that most struck her, though, was the detachment that her mother exhibited toward the people Jamie thought were close friends to her. *If she feels that way about Laura Martin, who is she close to?*

She was startled from her musings by the sound of footsteps coming along the long hallway. Grasping her mother's hand quickly, she gave it a squeeze for luck and took a deep breath, waiting to see the look on her partner's face. When Ryan and her father entered the room, Jamie hopped to her feet, sliding an arm around Ryan's waist, pleased to find her calm and collected. She asked quietly, "Are you all right, honey?"

Ryan smiled down at her and gave her a small wink to show that she had emerged unscathed. "I think we'll be off now, Catherine," Ryan said, extending her hand. Catherine returned her shake and got to her feet, looking surprisingly steady.

"Are you sober enough to drive?" Jim demanded, noticing that Ryan looked a little loose-limbed.

"I'm driving us both, Daddy," Jamie informed him. "Ryan's brother dropped her off."

"Are you completely sober, Jamie?" he asked, stooping a little to look into her clear green eyes.

"Yes, I am. I had a couple of drinks before dinner, but that's been hours. I'm sober now."

"As long as you're sure, honey. You know you can stay the night if you want." Jamie was touched by the offer, knowing that it would be hard for him to have her and Ryan sleeping together in his house.

"I'm fine, Daddy. I appreciate your concern, but I'm fine." She stood on her tiptoes to kiss him good-bye, and then gave her mother their standard kiss. Ryan shook both of their hands, and they escaped into the night without further incident.

Jim Evans stepped away from the front door and surveyed his domain, drawing comfort and reassurance from being surrounded by the evidence of the obvious rightness of his world. His wife was sitting on the couch, collapsed into its cushioned comfort, obviously tired from the events of the evening and from her trip. He crossed to her and placed a perfunctory kiss upon her drawn cheek. "I just realized that I didn't even welcome you home." The semi-apology was extended readily, from years of practice. "This thing really caught me totally by surprise. I hardly know if I'm coming or going," he admitted, running a hand through his stylishly cut hair.

Catherine could plainly see the fatigue on his face; the fine lines that years of excessive sun exposure had etched were carved more deeply than normal. "That's all right, Jim," she said easily. She was as skilled at accepting his excuses as he was at offering them. Her rigid self-control had been tenuously re-established, and any softening that she had shared with Jamie didn't extend to her husband. "We did have a rather disruptive day."

He walked over to the well-stocked bar that rested on a beautifully crafted bird's-eye maple cart. "Brandy?" he asked, holding the bottle aloft.

It isn't only "sleep" that knits up the raveled sleeve of care. "I'd kill for one," she replied, adding a gentle laugh at her exaggeration.

They sat beside one another on the sofa, quietly reflecting on the events of the day—together, yet separate. Letting out a ragged sigh, Catherine allowed a few tears to roll down her cheeks, only slightly irritated with herself for showing her feelings so openly. Unexpectedly, Jim scooted closer and wrapped his muscular arm around her shoulders, feeling a little surprised at how small she felt when she cuddled up against him. She hesitated just a moment, unaccustomed to receiving comfort from him, then rested her head on his shoulder, draping her other arm around his waist. After a few minutes, she felt more composed, and murmured, "I just wish it weren't true."

He was running his hand up and down her arm reassuringly, and when she expressed this wish, with its tacit acceptance of Jamie's revelation, he stopped and grasped the painfully thin appendage, giving it a gentle squeeze. "It's not, Cat." He rarely used this pet name anymore, and she gave a start when she realized she had not heard it in years.

He reacted to her gasp, assuming that she disputed his words, rather than his rare use of the diminutive. "She's just going through a phase." His confidence was so complete that for a moment she doubted her own observations.

"But, Jim ..."

"No buts, Catherine." Now his voice was firm, resolute. "No one knows Jamie better than you and me. We would have seen some sign of this before now. Ryan seems like a fine young woman—a good person to have as a friend—and I can see how Jamie would have relied on her to get through a tough time."

"But ..."

"She's not a lesbian, Catherine. Even Ryan admitted as much to me."

"She did?" Now she was truly confused. She had not had the opportunity to speak with Ryan alone, but none of this made sense, and the alcohol she had consumed didn't make figuring it out any easier.

"Ryan is a lesbian—that much is clear. I think Jamie just has a bad case of hero worship, to tell you the truth. I think we need to just let this play itself out for a while."

Ah, ignore it and the problem will go away. Well, that is an approach that has worked for him in the past. "Play itself out? I don't think that is going to happen, Jim." She was certain that the determination she had seen in her daughter's eyes was genuine, and the love they reflected when she spoke of Ryan could not be denied.

"I know my daughter, Catherine. This is a crush that will resolve itself. We just need to be patient with Jamie until she comes to her senses. Trust me."

Trust. Such a simple word for such an important thing. She could tell that Jamie and Ryan shared it. With a weary sigh she dropped her head again, relaxing into her husband's embrace. *I might not know Jamie as well as you think you do*, she thought, *but I know her well enough to know that she's irrevocably in love with Ryan. We may as well get used to the idea, Jim, because that young woman is here to stay.*

"So, what do you think, Tiger?" The question was deliberately open-ended, but Jamie was anxious to hear Ryan's assessment if she chose to share it. Jamie had dropped the top of the Boxster, hoping the brisk wind would keep her alert as well as help to sober Ryan up. Her partner wasn't really drunk, but she was tipsier than Jamie had ever seen her. They were cruising along 101, the traffic quite light on this Saturday night.

"I thought the Irish were the drinkers," Ryan said slowly, with a rather hazy gaze. "Your parents sure don't like to see the bottom of a glass."

Jamie nodded, knowing that Ryan was not trying to be unkind, but her words still stung a bit. Both of her parents, but particularly her mother, had an enormous capacity for alcohol, and she had often wondered if she should make a comment to either of them about their drinking.

"Other than the profusion of alcohol, what did you think?" Jamie repeated, hinting at her interest in the content of Ryan's conversation with her father.

Ryan tilted her head up to stare at the murky gray/black sky. There were no stars visible, not an uncommon occurrence in the Bay Area. "I think," she drawled, "that we've got our work cut out with your dad. He seems to be pretty focused on the lesbian label."

"Yeah, he focused on that pretty heavily," Jamie agreed. "Not a good sign."

"It's funny," Ryan mused. "If he had a friend that even looked at another man in the locker room, I bet your dad would think the guy was gay. But you tell him that you're having sex with me and totally loving it, and all he can focus on is whether or not you admit to being a lesbian. It's just incongruous."

Jamie shook her head, her lips beginning to purse as she did. "I tried to get him to see that the title doesn't matter, but he doesn't seem to want to listen to my reasoning." She took in a deep breath and held the wheel with her left hand while the right rubbed up and down Ryan's leg. "What matters is that I love you. I think I'd love you just as much if you were a man," she said thoughtfully. "But we'll never have to find that out, because you're a woman. You're a wonderful, gorgeous, fabulous woman, and I'm madly in love with you!"

Ryan gave her a dazzler of a smile, her blue eyes sparkling as the oncoming traffic reflected off of them. "I couldn't agree more," she said, running her hand in a similar manner up Jamie's thigh. "It's gonna be hard for them to accept that you've chosen to spend your life with me, but we need to remember that no matter what they think, we're a part of each other now—for better or worse."

"I have a sneaking suspicion that we're gonna have more better than worse," Jamie smiled, then a glimmer of concern passed across her face. "Do you want to tell me what he said when you were alone?"

"No, not really," Ryan decided. She didn't want Jamie to be angry with her father, and she didn't think anything had transpired that merited discussion. "It was nothing that we didn't expect, love. He said some things that might upset you a little bit on my behalf, but he was just being your dad." She recognized that Jim was just flexing his lawyerly muscle with his interrogation, and she felt that she had done as well for herself as could be expected.

Jamie spared a glance in her direction that indicated she needed some more detail from her partner. "He didn't hurt your feelings, or upset you, did he, honey?"

Ryan gazed back at her partner lovingly. It made her heart swell to know that Jamie was more concerned about her than about herself, and she had to admit that her own desire to shield her partner from Jim's inferences sprang from the same wish. "Nah," she said lightly. "He just asked a bunch of questions about me and my plans for the future."

"What else?" Jamie asked, fixing Ryan with a look that warned her to reveal what she was hiding.

"Look, Jamie," she said calmly, not surprised that her light tone didn't fool her lover. "He's a big-time attorney. What he does for a living is try to make people feel uncomfortable under questioning. He did that with me, but it wasn't really a big deal. The bottom line is that he thinks you'll eventually break up with me when you discover this isn't right for you."

Jamie would really have preferred to hear what her father had to say so that she could be fully prepared for any future encounters, but she trusted her partner's judgment and respected Ryan's decision not to disclose the particulars. She chose to let the subject drop and responded lightly, "Well, if that's what he's waiting for, everything will be just fine, because we both know that's never going to happen. I love you and I always will." Ryan favored her with a full-wattage smile, then closed her eyes and rested her head back against the seat.

As they drew nearer to the city, the traffic became increasingly heavy until they were finally at a complete standstill due to some sort of problem ahead. This allowed Jamie to do what she had been wanting to almost since they had left the house—reach across the car and grab Ryan by the shoulders, pulling her close and planting a very hot kiss on her brandy-flavored lips. Her voice was low when she released her partner, smiling slightly at the stunned look on her face. "You've ruined me for anyone else, Tiger. I could wander the face of the earth looking, and never find anyone who could even come close to making me feel the way you make me feel."

Blinking her eyes slowly, Ryan reached up and touched her lips, the tingle still fresh. "Wow!" Her natural arousal at Jamie's touch surged to the fore, and her lips weren't the only part of her body that felt the tingle from even that brief contact. Another slow blink and she said, "You uhm … wanna take me home and do that again when we're dressed more appropriately?"

Jamie spared a glance at Ryan's outfit and gave her a seductive smile. "You look perfectly fine to me. What would you rather be wearing?"

A waggling eyebrow punctuated the reply. "Just this," she offered, sharing a luminescent smile with her partner.

A light flush suffused Jamie's cheeks as she assessed what she was being offered. "Why, Ms. O'Flaherty," Jamie drawled, "I do believe you are propositioning me."

Only every day of your life, Ryan thought, but kept her response light in turn. "I do believe you are absolutely correct, Ms. Evans. It's been far too long since I've experienced your munificent charms."

Jamie patted her partner's leg, smiling at her hyperbole. "I guess two days is cruel and unusual punishment for your throbbing libido, isn't it, Tiger?"

Ryan captured the errant hand, considering, for a fleeting moment, the advisability of directing it to where Jamie could judge the truth in that statement for herself. Instead, she cocked her head, seemingly considering the comment for a minute longer. "That would be a good porn name, don't you think? Throbbing Libido …"

Well aware of the beating pulse in the thigh resting beneath her palm, Jamie was distracted for an instant, then pulled her attention away from the rising heat and back to the question. "Porn name?" Jamie quirked a grin at the odd direction the conversation was taking.

"Yeah." Ryan shot her a lopsided smile and admitted, "Ally and I used to come up with porn star names for each other. It was a … competition."

"And what was your favorite, hot stuff?" Jamie's hand flexed on Ryan's leg, fingers splayed.

"Not telling." Ryan's head shook slowly, indicating her refusal. "Porn names are in the eye of the beholder. You have to come up with your own."

"I'll try to think of a few when I have you in your costume," Jamie agreed, giving her partner a smirk, and with a final squeeze she reclaimed her hand and placed it firmly back on the wheel.

"Oooh, I like that costume," Ryan agreed, having a pretty good idea which one Jamie was referring to.

They rode along in silence for a few minutes, mulling over the events of the night so far, while a certainty of the more pleasurable events that were still to come teased at the edges of their thoughts.

"I thought your dad's comments about you eventually leaving me would upset you," Ryan mused as she gazed thoughtfully at her partner, "but you seem really happy."

A brilliant smile lit up Jamie's face as she turned and admitted the truth of Ryan's observation. "I expected them to flip out, to be honest. Obviously, it would have been nice if they had shouted for joy, but their reactions were really pretty tame compared to what I had envisioned. One thing Anna told me is that coming out usually is a multistep process. She cautioned me not to expect too much, and I really tried not to."

Ryan smiled at her fondly, acknowledging Jamie's gloom-and-doom predictions of the previous days.

"Starting from where we left it tonight is a pretty darned good place, don't you think, honey?"

Ryan considered the events of the evening. No voices had been raised, no tearful pleas to return to the heterosexual fold, no threats, no intimidation. Okay, some intimidation, but only toward her. All in all, she had to agree that it had been very civilized and calm. "I think it went quite well," she agreed. "I think you handled yourself beautifully, babe, and that was the winning element."

Jamie shot her a grateful glance and insisted, "I was very proud of you, too, honey. You were so polite and well spoken—you didn't let any of their questions or comments get to you ... you were just a pleasure to watch all evening."

"I felt surprisingly at ease with your parents," Ryan agreed. "I had some catastrophic thoughts too, but mostly concerning how they might treat you after you told them. I would have had trouble dealing with it if they had done anything to hurt you. It is nice to know those fears were unjustified."

Jamie nodded, her mouth curling into a slow smile as she recalled, "It went better for you than it did for Jack."

"Really? With all of the things he had going for him? How so?"

Jamie shivered as she remembered the excessively long time the poor man had been held hostage in her father's office. "I never did find out all of the details, but Daddy had Jack in that office for the better part of an afternoon! When he came out, he looked like he'd been through the Star Chamber!"

Ryan laughed at what she assumed was an exaggeration. "It didn't feel like the Spanish Inquisition to me, babe. But he did try to make it clear that he knew who you were ... and that I didn't."

Jamie jutted her chin out a bit in a defiant gesture. "I know who I am, Ryan. I am the same person I was this morning when Daddy was telling me how proud he is of me. I'm the same person I was when Mother showed how terribly happy she was that I came down to welcome her home. Nothing about me has changed—and nothing has to change for them if they don't let it. They have a wonderful new daughter-in-law who I know they will love once they get to know her. Other than that, everything is the same."

Everything is the same for you, love, but their image of you has forever changed. "You seem ... I don't know ..." Ryan gazed thoughtfully at her partner, trying to put a name to the emotions she was seeing. There was relief, yes, but also, "You seem ... almost giddy."

Jamie laughed and nodded enthusiastically. "I feel giddy! I was prepared for the worst and it didn't happen. I really feel that we'll eventually build a relationship with them, Ryan. Even if it's no more than what we had today, that will be okay. They were polite to you and pretty much normal with me. That's more than I hoped for, and it's such a relief that I want to shout with joy!"

Ryan grasped her thigh, giving it a little squeeze. "I'm really happy for you, babe. I've known a lot of people who didn't have such a pleasant experience. I think we've got a lot to be thankful for."

"I let them see me more fully today, Ryan. Now they can start to know me as I am."

Her confident expression was absolutely beautiful to Ryan's appreciative eyes, and she realized that she had unconsciously begun to hum a song that fit the occasion perfectly. With an impish smile she offered, "Jamie, a couple of weeks ago I showed you the secret handshake." Twinkling green eyes gazed at Ryan, causing her breathing to catch for a moment as she felt herself drawn in by their seductive charms. She shook her head to clear it and continued, "Would you like to learn the theme song?"

"There's a theme song, is there?" She smiled broadly at her partner, continually seduced by her charming, playful manner.

"Oh, yes." Ryan was nodding seriously, calling to mind the earnest young girl that Jamie had seen in pictures and had a very clear mental picture of. "Every group needs a theme song."

"Is this a lesbian theme song?" Her tone was light, teasing, and Ryan took it as such.

"No ... it's definitely not for lesbians alone. Although I have a song for that too," she admitted, continuing her unbroken string of being able to come up with a song for every occasion. "I'd say this song is for anyone who has come to terms with who they are—and is happy with her discovery." Leaning over in the seat, Ryan kissed her partner on the cheek, and whispered in her ear, "Someone like you." Sitting back in her own seat, she was gazing at Jamie with an absolutely delighted smile, and the smaller woman was terribly pleased that Ryan was with her to share in her self-discovery, in oh-so-many more ways than one.

"Let's hear it, babe. It sounds like perfect music for a traffic jam." They had finally begun to crawl through the worst of it, and both could now see that there were a number of flashing lights up ahead, indicating a serious accident of some sort.

"Okay," Ryan agreed happily. She cleared her throat and started off slowly, almost speaking the words. She intoned the first verse dramatically, capturing Jamie's rapt attention:

I am what I am, I am my own special creation
So come take a look, give me the hook
Or the ovation.
It's my world and I want to have a little pride in
My world and it's not a place I have to hide in
Life's not worth a damn
'Til you can say I am what I am!

Once the first verse was out of the way, Ryan started to move her body in the seat, her shoulders and hips starting to twitch in accompaniment to the song obviously playing in her head. Her eyes fluttered closed and Jamie could see her lungs fill with air. She knew the next verse would be sung—and she had a feeling it would be sung at full voice. Her prediction came true as Ryan tossed her head back and belted out the next verse.

The last line of the song burst forth from her body with unrestrained joy. In that moment Jamie realized exactly why she loved the marvelous woman at her side. It was because that line was the essence of Ryan—and she hoped that, someday, those words would define her as well. Ryan was essentially … completely … herself. She put herself out there for the world to see, and if they didn't like her, that was their problem, not hers. She had plenty of friends, and plenty of family members who loved her unconditionally; she didn't need to curry the favor of the unfortunate few who didn't appreciate her "Ryan-ness."

They reached the scene of the accident and realized why traffic had been so horrible. A truck had lost a load of baled hay onto the roadway, and Caltrans workers, firemen, and California Highway Patrol officers were scattered across the road, trying to clear the lanes. Only one lane in their direction was open, and as they crawled along Ryan started the last verse. With the open top, her head nearly stuck out the top of the small car. Every person they passed stopped and stared at her, most smiling at the exuberant display.

By the end of the song, they had passed the congestion and were cruising along at a good clip. The slow traffic had allowed Jamie to pay close attention, and by the time they reached the Bay Bridge she felt confident enough with the words to reprise the last few lines.

The brisk breeze whipped their hair around their heads, adding to the exhilaration of the song. Jamie had to pay attention to her driving, but Ryan was dancing rather wildly in her seat, the beat she heard in her head providing all the accompaniment that they needed. Her arms were stretched out above her head, thrusting into the air as their voices joined together to sing,

It's one life and there's no return and no deposit
One life so it's time to open up your closet
Life's not worth a damn, 'til you can shout out I AM WHAT I AM!!!

As the final notes were carried away on the wind, Jamie captured Ryan's left hand and brought it to her lips, bestowing an almost reverent kiss on her palm. Ryan subsided into her seat, reveling in the sensation of that intimate caress. Rather than releasing her grasp, Jamie drew Ryan's hand to her chest and pressed it over her rapidly beating heart. She smiled as a sidelong glance at her love took in the raised eyebrow that presaged a question. Ryan didn't disappoint.

"So," she asked with a smile, "you like the theme song?"

Jamie nodded. "I did, love, but that's not all."

Her hand still clasped over Jamie's breast, Ryan gave the slightest of squeezes. "So then, what was this for?"

Jamie sent her a quick gaze so filled with love that Ryan felt like she'd taken an elbow to the solar plexus. The short look was all she could spare, since she had to focus on her driving as they passed from one section of the bridge to the next. Even though her body was fully engaged in the act of driving, her mind had been composing the thoughts that she now shared with her spouse. "For loving me enough to give me the space and the support I needed to discover for myself more of who I am and what I'm about. For loving me so much that you'd risk losing me to Jack, if it would make me happy. For subjecting yourself to my parents, just because you knew it was important to me. For making me a part of your family … and your life." Her hand softly pressed Ryan's where it rested against her chest, and she shared another love-filled look with her partner. "For being my heart."

Ryan absorbed the loving warmth of Jamie's words, then took the hand that covered hers and brought it to her lips for a kiss of its own. Mirroring Jamie's gesture, she settled it over her heart, clasping it firmly while she gathered her own thoughts. "I know that you think you've learned from me, but I've learned so much from you. You've helped me to be able to give up control, to feel safe even when I'm most vulnerable. From you, my heart has learned the truth about love and the wonder of what a relationship can be. I know that my heart is safe with you, Jamie, and I hope you know that your heart is safe with me." She gently relinquished the hand that she held, knowing that its rightful position, for now, was on the steering wheel, but also knowing that she would find other, more interesting occupations for it later. Leaning over, she delivered an almost chaste kiss to the wind-chilled cheek, then settled back in her seat and closed her eyes again, anxious to get home.

Despite money disagreements, the differences in their upbringing, past hurts, and former lovers, their deep, abiding love for one another would always keep them together. And, as long as they were together, wherever they were would be home.

Jamie glanced over at Ryan's beautiful profile and a happy smile played around her lips. It wouldn't be much longer now. They were speeding across the bridge, their home city spread out beneath them in the distance, twinkling lights, like beacons, welcoming them home once again.

The End